RIO DIABLO AND THE PROUD GUN

Two Full Length Western Novels

GORDON D. SHIRREFFS

WOLFPACK
PUBLISHING
— EST 2012 —

Rio Diablo and The Proud Gun
Paperback Edition
© Copyright 2022 (As Revised) Gordon D. Shirreffs

Wolfpack Publishing
5130 S. Fort Apache Rd. 215-380
Las Vegas, NV 89148

wolfpackpublishing.com

Paperback ISBN 978-1-63977-427-2
eBook ISBN 978-1-63977-426-5

RIO DIABLO AND THE PROUD GUN

RIO DIABLO

CHAPTER ONE

The distant figures of the mounted man and his horse on the timbered slope were dwarfed by the towering immensity of the mountain backdrop: The madly rushing Rio Diablo forced its way through almost solid rock; tier after tier of natural terraces reached upward like gigantic steps to end at last in a sheer wall of salmon-colored rock that tilted back and formed Mount Diablo, eleven thousand feet high. The eastern slopes of the Diablo Mountains flowed downward into New Mexico Territory—a chaotic, virtually unexplored and perhaps impassable mountain wilderness.

A lean man sat with his broad back against a tip-tilted rock high on the slopes. From there the road seemed little more than a twin-rutted track, coming from nowhere, leading into nothing. Vic Jamison worked his cigar from one side of his mouth to the other as he focused his binoculars on the lone horseman so far below his eyrie. The fine German lenses, the best made by Vollmer of Jena, picked out the features of the big man riding the blocky clay bank. A great nose was outthrust from a seamed face the color of aged mahogany. A thick dragoon mustache, salted and peppered with age, sagged down on both sides of the wide mouth.

"Bass Burnett," Vic murmured.

Even as Vic watched the Arizona Ranger riding slowly along the track, Bass Burnett suddenly turned his head to look back over his left shoulder. Vic lined up the glasses on a motte of silver spruces two hundred yards behind Bass. The intermittent wind swayed the trees. The bright late afternoon sun filtered between the trees to form golden-lighted glades amidst the dark greenery of the spruces. Something flashed so quickly Vic wasn't even sure he saw it. A red-tailed hawk soaring low from the upper slopes suddenly veered aside from the motte and flew rapidly away.

Vic lowered his glasses. Bass was being tailed. The standard operating procedure of the Arizona Rangers was to work under cover until time of arrest. But Bass's recent report to Arizona Ranger Captain Burton Mossman had requested immediate relief from duty in the Rio Diablo country because he felt he was no longer working undetected and could be of no further use in that wild, wooly region of rustling and unsolved murders of honest ranchers and lawmen. There had been seven slayings in the past twelve months. Three of them had been lawmen—a deputy sheriff and two Arizona Rangers. Bass had been sent in as a last resort when conditions had warranted one of the key men of the small ranger force. Bass was long on experience and service as well as on *age*. He was in his mid-fifties, slightly crippled from an old gun wound, aided and abetted at times by rheumatism, product of too many long trails in rain and snow and too many nights of sleeping on hard ground in bitter weather. Now, after only three months in the Diablos Bass wanted *out*. It had been the first time in his twenty years as a lawman—stock detective, deputy sheriff and Arizona

Ranger—that Bass Burnett had wanted to quit a case as yet unsolved.

There was almost a static and dreamlike quality about the terrain except for the slowly moving figure of the horseman. Yet there was also a hidden warning that came to Vic Jamison. It was a sort of sixth sense that was an advantage to a manhunter and yet, at the same time, a sort of a curse as well, for a man with such a sense could never be completely at rest at any time in the dangerous and exacting profession which he followed.

Captain Mossman had read between the lines of Bass Burnett's badly scrawled letter at the secret meeting Mossman had had with Vic Jamison in Nogales just ten days past. "It's just not like Bass to quit on an assignment, Vic. He's never, to my knowledge, ever quit on a trail during his twenty years of wearing the star. It's more than the fact that he thinks he has been detected. He says he's not feeling well and thinks that he should be replaced."

"He's fifty-five years old, Burt," Vic had reminded Mossman.

Mossman had shaken his head. "It's *not* his age. The man seems *afraid*. I believe that for the first time in his life he *is* afraid. Have you ever known him to be afraid?"

"No, which is more than I can ever say for myself."

Mossman had nodded. "And myself as well."

"I can't believe that he *is* afraid. Still, he does feel that he has been detected and that he's of no further use on that assignment whether he's afraid or not."

"Which is exactly why I've asked you to rejoin the Rangers, at least until we can clean up the Rio Diablo country."

"*We?*" Vic had half smiled.

"Damn it, Vic. You know what I mean!"

"Exactly."

They had eyed each other like two wrestlers trying for a telling hold or two professional card sharps trying to deduce whether the other one was bluffing.

"I put in two rough years with you once, Burt. I've no desire to stick my tender ass in the line of a .44/.40 slug or to feel a Mex rustler's knife in the middle of my back some dark night. *Not* for one hundred dollars a month."

Mossman had smiled wryly. "The manhunting profession must be really paying off for you, Vic, although it's not any less dangerous than being a Ranger, as you say, for one hundred dollars a month." Burton C. Mossman was a leader of hard men. There wasn't much he didn't know about the singular business of hunting that most dangerous game of all —*man*. He also *knew* men with a knowledge equal to that of his knowledge of manhunting. He had slanted his gray eyes at Vic Jamison knowing full well that he knew this man as well, or perhaps better than any others who had been under his command. "The deputy sheriff who was killed up in the Diablo country was Mack MacIntyre," he had continued. He knew damned well that Mack and Vic had once ridden stirrup to stirrup in the same cavalry troop. "Bunkie" was the word the yellowlegs used to describe such a man. A man who ate with another, slept with him, got drunk with him, whored along with him and would die for him if the need ever arose. "Cal Hayden, who you will well remember, and one of our best, was beaten to death by someone up there in the Rio Diablo country." Cal Hayden had been an older man, quiet and unassuming, liked by all and with a wife and three kids in Globe.

It had been a quiet night, that night in Globe. It was very quiet in the room where Vic and Mossman had conferred over a bottle of Vic's favorite and fiery Tezopaco brandy.

"Sam Nelson went into the canyon of the Upper Rio

Diablo and was never seen again," Mossman had added inexorably.

Vic had lighted a long nine to give himself time to think. He had studied Mossman over the flare of the match and through the drifting cigar smoke. "That's your ace card, isn't it, Burt?" Vic had asked quietly. Mossman had known full well what Sam Nelson had always meant to Don.

"You'll go then, Vic?"

The question was simple enough—it was the deadly facts behind it that had made the answer most difficult. No lawman had ever tamed the Rio Diablo country. The army had given up ten years past. To the north were the rawhide tough Mormon cattlemen who had settled the Little Colorado River country. To the south were the little Mexican *poblados* inhabited by tough *pistoleros* who made a lucrative business of horse thieving and cattle rustling. Between the Mormons and the Mexicans was a hard core of ranchers dominated by the hardcase Scalp Knife

outfit, mostly Texans who had left the state rather hurriedly when the Texas Rangers had begun to study them with great thoughtfulness. To add more explosive force to the deadly simmering brew in the Rio Diablo country there were the White Mountain Apaches, considered to be at peace, as long as no one interfered too much with their illicit *tiswin* brewing and their historical way of life—snapping up a stray beef or two and stealing horses, which was an absolute fetish with them. Moreover, there were still "bronco" Apaches in the virtually unknown mountains (at least to the white men) along the high-altitude border between Arizona and New Mexico territories. They were the real "rimrock" 'Paches, those who had never been tamed—the *Netdahe,* or Wild Ones. There were perhaps only a handful of them, but one, or a handful, was bad medicine indeed for any lone white man if he rode a good horse, had a fine hat and carried good weapons.

"A hell's broth," Burton Mossman had added quietly. It was almost as though he had read Vic's mind. He was good at it. There was none better. "You know that country, Vic?"

"By hearsay mostly. I can't say I've liked what I've heard."

"I'll swear you in now and issue you your commission."

"I haven't made up my mind as yet, Burt."

Mossman had leaned back in his chair and had sipped at his brandy, all the while probing into Vic Jamison with those gray eyes of his. "There are John Doe warrants for murders committed in the Rio Diablo country. The total reward money is about fifteen thousand dollars offered by the county, the territories of New Mexico and Arizona, the governor of Arizona himself and Colonel Clayton Mostyn no less, owner of the Scalp Knife and about as much other property as he can get his hands on—mines, a sawmill, real estate, town businesses in Tonto Springs, the metropolis of the Rio Diablo country, et cetera, et cetera, et cetera.... In short, the man who goes in there alone and cleans up that country can have sole claim to the combined rewards."

"You didn't tell me that before, Burt."

"I thought I'd surprise you with it."

Vic had relighted his cigar. "You're all heart, Burt. The sum total of that reward money indicates why such good men went into that damned country and died for it. MacIntyre, Hayden and Nelson all left wives and kids to struggle for survival without the hundred dollars per month so generously allowed such men by the noble Territory of Arizona. They *needed* that reward money."

"Exactly," Mossman had agreed dryly.

Burton Mossman knew men and he knew Vic Jamison.

"I don't need the money, Burt."

Mossman had blown a neat smoke ring.

"I've got a lead on one of the most fabulous lost mines in the history of Mexico—the Lost Tayopa."

The gray eyes had slanted at Vic. "That so?"

"It's a sure thing, Burt."

Then it had become very quiet again.

"You are to meet Bass Burnett at Stray Horse Canyon in five to eight days. Listen to what he has to say. If you don't want to go on turn your commission over to him and no hard feelings."

Vic had slowly raised his right hand as he had stood up. "God help me for a sentimental fool," he had murmured with a rolling of the hard gray eyes upward.

The sun was slanting slowly to the west by the time Bass Burnett rounded a rock spur and passed from Vic's sight. Stray Horse Canyon was five miles to the southeast behind a saddle-backed ridge. It would be dusk by the time Vic reached the canyon. He studied the motte again. Nothing showed there and nothing moved within the trees. It was now thick with shadows. Vic cased his glasses and worked his way through a jumble of huge boulders, keeping out of sight of anyone who might possibly be on the lower ground. He trotted easily down the long slope and then scaled the ridge to reach his bayo coyote dun. As he rode down the southern slopes of the ridge the dusk came silently over the vast land and the wind began to blow strongly down the canyons and the slopes to the lower ground.

There was a *tinaja* in Stray Horse Canyon. It was usually filled with good water during the frequent summer thunderstorms. There was a long-abandoned and deteriorating fieldstone building near the *tinaja* once used as an outpost by the army during the troubles with the White Mountain Apaches. As Vic led his dun down the last slope to reach the bottom of the canyon, he heard the faint whinnying of a horse carried on the dusk wind from somewhere near the *tinaja*. Vic clamped a big hand over the nose of his dun to keep him from returning the greeting. He ground-reined the dun downwind and eased his Winchester '73 from its saddle sheath. It was a country where no man walked unannounced into the presence of others *particularly* after darkness.

A light grew softly in the old fieldstone jacal down near the *tinaja*. The open doorway and the two small windows were limned in the soft yellowish light. In a little while, sparks soared up from the chimney of the shack and a sudden spouting of flame eerily lighted the towering canyon wall behind the building. Bass Burnett must be feeling pretty sure of himself contrary to what Burton Mossman had said about him: "I believe that for the first time in his life he *is* afraid."

Vic catfooted through the darkness. Now and again, he would turn and look to the west toward the dim mouth of the canyon. He faded into the thick brush at the side of the road and then moved silently like a hunting cat up the lower part of a talus slope beyond which was the jacal. The odor of brewing coffee came to Vic, and he suddenly remembered he had not eaten all that long day.

Bass Burnett squatted by the smoke-blackened beehive fireplace in one corner of the shack waiting patiently for the wood to burn down into a thick bed of embers so that he might cook his food. Smoke from a thick gun barrel of a cigar wreathed about his tired face. His big, mottled hands were clasped tightly together between his heavy thighs. Fifty-five years of life was a heavy burden for a still active lawman. Suddenly he raised his head and reached for his rifle.

"Stay right where you are, Bass. It's Vic Jamison," the soft dry voice came through one of the rear windows. "Don't talk. Don't give any too obvious sign of recognition. Just listen. Nod very slightly for yes. Twice for no. *Comprende?*"

Bass nodded almost imperceptibly.

"You think you were being followed?"

One nod.

"By who?"

Bass shrugged and held out his big hands, palms upwards.

"How long? One day? Two? More?"

Bass extended two fingers behind his back.

"Why?"

Bass turned his head a little and looked directly toward the window. The look on his face answered Vic's question.

"I'm going back down the canyon, Bass. As long as you aim to cook make a double ration. You can feed me through a rear window. I'll donate a bottle of Sonoran brandy for my part."

Bass forced a tired grin.

Vic was gone as silently as he had arrived.

Bass unfolded the legs of his spider and placed it over the glowing bed of embers. He filled the pan with thick sliced bacon. He shifted the coffee pot to one side and opened a bag of biscuits. Now and again, he would raise his gray head to listen, but he heard nothing but the night wind scrabbling gently through the canyon. It was what he expected to hear. He knew Vic Jamison could move silently through the roughest country like a puff of wind-driven smoke. Some said Vic Jamison could out-Apache an Apache. He had proven that quite a few times. It was the acid test of survival in that country.

Vic stood in the brush with his lean hawk's-face turned toward the canyon entrance. If anyone had been following Bass—and both Bass and Vic were now sure of that fact—they would likely come through the canyon entrance in the thick darkness rather than over the ridge as Vic had done. Few men, other than Apaches, could have come down that rough slope as silently as Vic Jamison.

The night was graveyard-quiet except for the dry murmuring of the wind in the sere brush. Overhead the first of the ice-chip stars had begun to stipple the dark blue blanket of the sky. Nothing moved.

Vic went back to the dun and shifted him. He filled his hat at the *tinaja* and watered the horse. He then picketed him in a side canyon where there was some scant grazing and then catfooted back to the rear of the jacal.

"All quiet along the Potomac, Bass," Vic announced.

Vic was handed a tin plate full of biscuits soaked in bacon fat and tastefully draped with thick strips of bacon still stippled with short bristles. This was followed by a steaming mug of Arbuckle's best. Vic rested plate and cup on the windowsill. The fire had died down to a thick bed of ashes through which now and then a secretive red eye peeped and then as quickly closed itself. The wind whispered unintelligibly through the open doorway and fanned the ashes so that tiny dancing flames appeared to spread an eerie bluish light over the embers.

"Surprised to see me here, Bass?" Vic asked around a mouthful of hot biscuit.

"No," Bass replied.

"How so?"

"Easy enough. Mossman wrote that you'd be here."

"When he wrote he didn't know that I had agreed to re-up."

Bass laughed softly. "Yes, he did."

"I don't have to stick with it. That's part of the deal."

Bass shook his head. "Then take my advice and get to hell out of it. Pronto! I've never seen anything like it. Three good ranches have been rustled and hurrahed out of business. Another one will go any day now—the Star Cross. I worked there for a while, undercover of course. That leaves only one good-sized one beside the Scalp Knife—Jemson's Slash Bar J, as tough a bunch of boots in one family as I've ever seen, but no tougher than the Scalp Knife *corrida,* and a helluva lot smaller."

"They both been rustled too?"

Bass nodded. "Which makes the tangle worse."

"They could be rustling their own stock to make themselves look good."

Bass turned. "You think I haven't figured *that* out?" His voice cracked a little. "But try to catch them at it!"

"What about the Mormons?"

Bass shrugged. "They've been quiet a few years since Burt Mossman went up there and did a little plain talking to their bishop up around Snowflake way." He grinned. "The first rustlers Mossman caught up that way *were* Mormons, although not in good standing with their church, according to the bishop. Mossman said he'd get the district attorney to draw a straight Mormon jury, so they couldn't claim any Gentile was prejudiced if he served on a jury. That way, it would prove whether or not the Mormons would stand against their fallen brethren as a matter of good faith. They did and the rustlers were convicted.

"That didn't stop the wholesale rustling in the Rio Diablo country though—in fact, it got worse. Vic, this damned county is run by rustlers and mankillers. There hasn't been a conviction in five years, outside of those few 'fallen' Mormons and they were smalltime at that! Cattle stealing and wholesale murder to cover it up are the biggest industry in the whole damned country!"

"What about the Mexicans?"

Bass nodded. "They live mostly by rustling and horse stealing. But they can't account for the hundreds of head of cattle that have been rustled."

"The Apaches?"

Bass shook his head. "They steal a few beeves for food and some horses because that's born and bred in their systems. Any Indian I ever knew looked at horse thieving as an art, not as a crime, sort of a testing of their ability as warriors. A good thief rates higher in their book than a brave warrior. But why am I telling *you* that, of all people!"

"But you must have some suspicions, Bass."

Bass looked away. "Cigar?" he offered.

Vic accepted a long nine and lighted up as Bass touched off a fresh cigar for himself. His faded blue eyes looked at Vic over the flare of a Farmer Boy match. "I've told you all I know, Vic." There was a hint of desperate defiance in his voice.

"But you worked that area for three months!"

Bass looked at the tip of his cigar as though he had never seen one before. "I haven't been feeling well, Vic. I've been thinking of resigning for some time. Got my eye on a small ranch in the San Simon country. My old lady is tired of having me away from home so much. I'm tired myself! Twenty years of law enforcement has taken all the fire out of me. All I've got to show for it are a few bullet holes and knife scars, a gimp leg and the hell of rheumatism in the winter."

"Why don't you tell me all you really know then? What difference will it make now?" Vic challenged.

"What makes you think I know something else?" Bass demanded angrily.

"Because you're too good a lawman to have spent three months in the Rio Diablo country not to have some clues, ideas or at least some deductions about the rustlings and the killings."

Bass passed a brown mottled hand across his tired eyes. His lined face was shadowed in the dimness of the room.

"You're well on your way out of the case," Vic persisted. "Resign and get that little ranch in the San Simon country, but for God's sake if you know anything at all that can help me, tell me now!"

Bass stirred up the fire. "They've got a long arm, Vic," he said over his shoulder. "If they suspect me in the least of knowing anything at all they'll never let me live long enough to tell what I *do* know."

"You're still a Ranger," Vic reminded him.

Bass withdrew his commission from the pocket sewn inside his shirt. "I'm afraid, Vic," he admitted shamefacedly. The faint firelight reflected from the cold sweat on his seamed face. "I don't want to live the rest of my life with the fear of assassination hanging constantly over me." The fire flared up in the draft from the doorway and the dancing flames made his large shadow a grotesque humped caricature on the wall behind him.

Vic threw down his cigar. "Wait!" he called out.

Bass quickly ripped his commission in two and threw it into the fire. "For God's sake, Jamison! If you value your life stay out of the Rio Diablo country!"

A horse whinnied sharply near the *tinaja*.

The commission flared up. Bass stepped back with a tired smile on his face. "There! It's done at last!"

The crashing report of the rifle slam-banged itself back and forth between the narrow canyon walls. Bass Burnett staggered sideways as the slug whipped through the open doorway and sent him crashing sideways to the floor just below the window near which Vic stood.

Vic started to round the side of the jacal and then stopped short. He slowly lowered his rifle. The smell of powder smoke drifted to him on the night wind. A white man usually runs to the sound of a shooting; an Apache does not. There was much of the Apache in Vic Jamison. Besides, Bass Burnett was dead. Vic was sure of it the way Bass had been head-struck and the way he had fallen. A brain-shot man makes no outcry. Besides, it wouldn't do for Vic to be seen by the man who had evidently trailed Bass Burnett to Stray Horse

Canyon to kill him at last. That is, if Vic was to pick up his mission in the Rio Diablo country that had been suddenly and surely bequeathed to him by a man who had been his friend.

Boots thudded on the slope across the canyon. Detritus rattled down the slope like hard rain on a tin roof. Shale clashed loudly. Boots thudded on the hard-packed road.

Vic flattened himself back to the rear wall of the jacal. He looked over his right shoulder into the dimness of the one room of the shack. The room was in darkness now with only the faint glowing of the ash-covered embers to light the interior of the beehive fireplace and cast a faint semi-circle of reflected firelight onto the packed earthen floor. Nothing moved except the night wind and the tiny flickering flames.

A foot grated by the doorway.

The blood-covered face of Bass Burnett was faintly lighted by the fire. The faded blue eyes were fixed unseeingly on the flickering embers.

The killer stepped softly within the room. He walked to Bass Burnett, trailing his heavy rifle. He was a square hewn block-shouldered man whose face was shadowed under his hat brim. He hooked a boot toe under Bass and threw the lawman over onto his back with outflung arms. The man knelt beside the body and began to search swiftly through the clothing. He'd never find Bass's Ranger commission.

It could be so easy. The killer was within ten feet of Vic. He'd never know what had hit him.

"Christ's blood!" the man snapped in border Spanish. He stood up with the wallet in his hands. He stripped the bills from it and threw the wallet into the fireplace.

Killing or capturing the assassin would do Vic no good in his mission. Whoever the killer was he'd likely return to whoever had sent him to report that the mouth of Bass

Burnett was shut forever: *"Los muertos no hablan." The dead do not talk....*

Yet he might not know that Bass had been an Arizona Ranger and surely not that his replacement, one Vic Jamison, was already in the Rio Diablo country and standing in the outside darkness not ten feet from the murderer of Bass Burnett.

Just as the flames flared up around the wallet, the killer abruptly left the jacal. His boots grated on the road. In a little while hoofbeats rang like cracked bells on the road, heading west toward the mouth of the canyon.

In the darkness before the dawn Vic placed the blanket-shrouded body of Bass Burnett in a cleft up on the talus slope. He covered the body with slabs and chunks of the talus. Vic padded down the slope and hid the dead man's saddle, weapons and other gear in another cleft and covered them up, saving only the food, cartridges and tobacco for future use by himself. He turned the clay bank loose with a rifle slap across the rump to speed him on his way.

Staghorn lightning suddenly flickered across the dark sky and faint thunder rumbled its drums in the deep, impenetrable canyons of the diablo Mountains.

Vic filled his canteens at the *tinaja*. In the faint illumination of the constantly flickering lightning, he catfooted across the rutted road and up the slope to about where the murderer might have fired his killing shot through the open doorway of the jacal at the dimly lighted figure of Bass Burnett. He stepped from rock to rock, scanning the decomposed granite during the intermittent flashes of lightning. He found footprints in a shallow patch of loose soil. He waited for the next lightning flash. The light reflected dully from a long brass cylinder.

Vic lighted a match and cupped the flame in a big hand. The mouth of the cartridge case was blackened from the powder discharge. Stamped on the rim of the base were the letters U.M.C. and the numerals .50-.95. He remembered all too well the large hole that had been blasted into the side of Bass Burnett's head. It had been a Union Metallic Cartridge Company Express cartridge, one with a hole drilled into the tip of the bullet for the insertion of a .22 caliber blank cartridge, which would cause it to explode on contact and form a ghastly wound. No other man that he had ever known, with one exception, neither the best or the worst of them had ever used Express cartridges on anything but big game animals, and few enough of them on animals, as a matter of fact. Vic placed the empty cartridge case in a shirt pocket. It was a rare and unusual cartridge for that part of the country.

He led the dun up rather than down the canyon toward the Rio Diablo country. He didn't want to forecast his coming. Not yet anyway. He planned to come the long way around from the New Mexico side of the border between the two territories. That was the way the owlhooters and long riders came from New Mexico a jump, a spit and a holler ahead of Territory peace officers.

CHAPTER TWO

The distant low rumbling sound echoed through the many tangled canyons of the Diablos. Slanting veils of smoky-looking, icy-cold rain drove against Vic Jamison's slickered back and against the nervous dun. The Upper Rio Diablo was rising swiftly here, not too far from its unknown source somewhere in a narrow slot of a canyon that trended to the northeast. The river forced between sheer banks of rock and raced through the natural channel like a millstream, frothing and dashing wildly against its banks. Vic had not been able to find a way to cross the rushing waters. Dusk was already creeping in beyond the slanted sheets of rain. Lightning slammed and crashed high up against the razor-sharp tip of Mount Diablo and thunder rolled and tumbled down the slopes in vast explosions that stunned the eardrums. The trees across the river thrashed and swayed in the redoubled icy beating of the wind-driven rain.

Vic suddenly raised his head. From far upstream came yet another dreaded rumbling sound that did not mutter off and die away as the thunder always did. It came from somewhere up the narrow, tangled canyon that channeled the Upper Rio

Diablo in its mad race down to the low country off to the west. Vic swung up into his saddle. The river was in flash flood, and he had only minutes to get to hell out of that death trap of a canyon. He spurred the nervous dun alongside the roaring torrent. The dun whinnied shrilly as it lost its footing and went down sideways. Vic kicked his right foot free from the stirrup and rolled from the saddle. The rain slashed down in icy fury as the dun hung partway over the riverbank, struggling to get up on its feet.

Vic freed his reata from the horn string. "Take it easy," he pleaded with the horse. He dragged at the reins as he started up the steep water-streaming slope beyond the riverbank. Thunder crashed and echoed in the gorge. The dun whinnied pitifully as it slid closer to the edge. Vic cocked a loop and cast it. The loop went right over where the dun's head had been a fraction of a second after it had fallen into the river.

The rumbling sound increased. Vic cast a quick glance up the gorge. There was something there that looked like a grayish black wall built across the gorge and it was moving downstream at tremendous speed. Vic set himself at the slippery slope, clawing at the treacherous surface for hand and footholds while icy fear seemed to lash at his wet back. The roaring increased. It was the rumbling, grinding, thudding cacophony of rocks, tree trunks and other debris being scoured along the bottom of the Rio Diablo by the flash flood. Vic clawed with bloody, broken-nailed hands at the sharp-edged rocks. The flood caught at his boots and swept around his knees and then rose icily up about his thighs. With a last desperate effort, he heaved himself up onto a ledge, inches above the roaring flood.

A piercing cry rose upstream, heard by Vic even above the roaring dissonance of the flood and the strident crackling of the incessant lightning. Vic stood up. The flood was frothed with spume, brush, tree trunks and dead and drowning animals. A dark and rounded object swirled into view. It was a human head and even as Vic stared at it the mouth of it opened to square itself for another hoarse screaming.

Vic swiftly formed his loop and cast it from the left side of his body. "Throw up your arms!" he yelled. The hoolihan loop made its one prescribed revolution and settled neatly over the upthrust arms of the man who still had the presence of mind to ride the loop further down the upper arms just a fraction of a second before the wet reata tightened about the chest. Vic dropped to a knee and braced himself, dallying the reata about a rock just as the shock of the weight of the body driven by the racing flood took up the slack with a jerk that squirted the water from the wet strands of the reata. The man swung sideways toward a jagged rock face. Vic teetered out along the ledge and then dropped belly-flat to catch the man about the neck. The man's body swung upward from the force of the current and Vic rolled over to cleanly lift the man from the river. Just as he did so a huge log butt with thick medusa-like roots packed with wet earth came driven down the torrent like a battering ram, to pass directly over the place where the man had been in the water an instant before.

"Come on!" yelled Vic. He dragged the man to his feet and clawed his way up the steep slope above the ledge. The water was already lapping over the ledge. Vic freed the dally tie and started up the slope, again dragging on the reata and cursing savagely in time to each muddy boot planted on the slope. Vic reached a higher ledge which was protected by a rock overhang. He looked down the slope. "Gawddammit!" he roared. "You've got to make a *little* effort on your own, mister!" He hauled in on the reata as though landing a giant fish. The wet head appeared at the edge of the ledge and the mouth opened. "I'm adoin' my gawddamnedest, mister!" she gasped.

Vic stared at her as he reached down from the ledge to

place big hands under her arms. He felt the fullness of her breasts through her wet clothing as he dragged her body across his to place her on the ledge. Her great dusky brown eyes looked into his hard gray eyes. "Will it rise any higher, mister...?" she asked.

Vic loosened the reata from about her body. "Purcell," he lied. "Vic Purcell. I think the river has crested." He grinned. "At least I *hope* it has. We can't climb any higher on this slope."

"You saved my life. It's a good thing you had that reata ready."

"It was really for my dun."

"Where is he?"

He looked down the flooded gorge and shook his head. "He never made it, ma'am."

"I know how it is," she agreed sympathetically. "My mare went right out from under me up the canyon and I never saw her again."

"You know this country?" he suggested.

"Yes. I live just southwest of here. The Star Cross."

"And yet you rode into this canyon in such a rain?"

"So did you," she countered.

He squatted beside her and felt within his slicker for the makings. "I had good reason." He held up a sack of Ridgewood. "All right to smoke in your presence, ma'am?" he asked while a faint grin marked his scarred face.

"I'm Deborah Cross. Yes, if the first cigarette is for me, Vic Purcell."

Her fair skin was lightly tanned with a dusting of freckles across the nose and cheekbones. Her mouth was a little too large to be considered beautiful, but the lips seemed full and soft, and downright interesting to Vic.

"Your daddy know you smoke with strangers?" he asked as he placed the quirly between those inviting lips.

She smiled around the cigarette. "I sometimes smoke with my Daddy," she admitted.

He thumb-snapped a lucifer into flame and held it to the tip of her cigarette while looking deep into those dusky brown eyes of hers. "They say it's the first sure step on the Road to Ruin," he suggested. "Whoever 'they' are."

"I'll risk it," she countered while drawing in the good smoke. "Does my name mean anything to you?" she added. It was as though she expected some reaction from him but if she had she was disappointed, for no expression crossed his face.

He ran his tongue along the edge of a cigarette paper and rolled it together. He lighted the quirly.

"You're on Star Cross range," she added pointedly.

Vic blew a smoke ring. "Do tell," he said politely.

"It means nothing to you?"

He shrugged. "Should it?"

"You must be a stranger in this country."

He nodded with mock solemnity. "Just a wayfaring stranger, ma'am, whose lonely tracks are swiftly washed out by the rain, covered by the drifting snow or erased by the moaning winds. Here today and gone tomorrow, leaving no trace of my passing except a string of cold and lonely camp-fires, cigarette butts and empty liquor bottles from the Panhandle west to the mighty Colorado."

"You sound like a poet." She grinned.

"I have the bad habit, for a working man, of reading books."

"You came from New Mexico?"

He looked quickly at her. "How did you know that?"

"No man comes through the Diablos from the east unless he is coming from New Mexico, and there are very few of them at that." She blew a smoke ring. "And *they* are usually on the run."

He looked down toward the racing flood. "I just figured it was the shortest way. I didn't know what I was getting into. I'll never pull a damned fool stunt like *that* again."

"There are much safer ways to the north and to the south."

"I should have figured that."

"You must have been in a godawful hurry," she suggested slyly.

He flipped his cigarette butt into the river and began to shape another smoke.

She would not press him further. The only lone riders usually in the Diablo Mountains were rimrock Apaches, riders from the Star Cross, and none of them were left anymore, or from the mighty Scalp Knife spread. Outside of them, there were the usual owlhooters running into Arizona to escape New Mexico lawmen or running into New Mexico to escape Arizona lawmen.

Vic looked up at the streaming sky. "If we don't get a move on, we'll sit here all night," he observed. "But how can we cross the river?"

"There's a natural bridge north of here," she replied.

He stood up and helped her to her feet, and as he did so he looked again into those deep pools of her eyes, and something turned slowly and inexorably over inside of him. This was no ordinary young ranch woman. He led the way along the slope above the rushing river. They crossed the Diablo on the natural bridge with the muddy, frothing waters roaring just beneath the arch of the bridge. They passed into the dubious shelter of the firs, pines and spruces that thickly carpeted the long gentle slopes of the mountainside. The trees thrashed in the rising wind and showered Vic and Deborah with icy water. "We'll probably have to stay on our feet all night," he said. He stripped off his slicker and put it over her head and shoulders.

"There's a line shack just beyond that ridge," she chattered.

"How far to your ranch house?"

"More than ten miles."

They slogged up the ridge and then down the western side of it, splashing through pools of icy water toward a mountain meadow far down the tree-mantled slopes stippled here and there with great outcroppings of tilted rock formations, with a greenish gray cast from the lichens and growths which somehow managed to survive on the rocky surfaces.

He put an arm about her and drew her close to himself in an effort to shelter her from the rain and wind. She looked up into his face and smiled.

The meadow was softly veiled by the slanting rain. A rain-darkened line shack stood within the shelter of the trees not far from a small stream that had overflowed its banks. No friendly light showed through the cracked and dirty windows nor did a twist of rain-beaten smoke rise from the rusted chimney pipe. The dusk light was gone when Vic pulled out the stick that held the door hasp and pushed open the warped door. He thumb-snapped a match into light. "Well," he quietly observed, "it ain't the La Fonda Hotel but it will do for the night." He lighted a crack-cylindered Argand lamp that swung in a rusted wall bracket.

Deborah sat down on the single bunk and watched him swiftly shave a firestick, light it and thrust it under the dry kindling in the fireplace. In a little while, a merry, spark-shooting crackling arose from the fire and the resinous odor of the burning wood filled the cabin.

"Get over here and dry out," he suggested. He placed a chair in front of the fire. "All my gear and grub went along with the dun," he added, "but I'd offer you a drink if you weren't such a lady."

"I'll take it," she said quickly.

He grinned. "I know—you sometimes drink with your daddy." He took the Mexican silver flask from his inside jacket pocket and snapped open the hinged stopper. "Tezopaco is the drink for heroes," he said as he offered her the flask.

She drank quickly of the powerful brandy. Her eyes watered a little and her breath caught in her throat. "Good God!" she gasped. Vic grinned as he took the flask from her hand. "Takes a while to get used to," he warned her.

She wiped her eyes. "I thought you said you came from New Mexico."

"I did." He drank deeply and wiped his mouth, eyeing her as he did so. "Why do you ask?"

"That's a Mexican flask."

"I've had it for years. They're not uncommon in New Mexico."

She shook her head. "No, but that brandy is strictly Sonoran style, isn't it?"

She was smart. Vic had filled the flask in Mexican Nogales before he had crossed the border on his way to meet Mossman. He had a penchant for strong Tezopaco. He looked at a wall cabinet. "Might be some food in there," he suggested.

"There should be. I know there's coffee at least. There always *used* to be."

"This your land?" he asked.

"Not exactly," she replied.

The tone of her voice kept him from pressing the question. The words of Bass Burnett came back into his mind: *"I've never seen anything like it up there. Three good ranches have been rustled and frightened out of business. Another one will go any day. That leaves only one left beside the Scalp Knife, the Jemson's Slash Bar J-as tough a bunch of boots in one family as I've ever seen, but no tougher than the Scalp Knife and a helluva lot smaller."* He had not mentioned the Star Cross.

Vic opened the cabinet and made a quick inventory. "Not bad," he observed. "Beans— naturally—embalmed beef, peaches, tomatoes, rice, salt, flour, sugar, pickles and Arbuckle's best coffee. You want it a la carte or on the dinner?"

"On the dinner," she replied. "It's cheaper that way."

"It's a pleasure to take you to dinner, ma'am," he said.

"Times are hard everywhere," she countered.

He nodded. "Is that why you were out riding range in this kind of weather?"

She studied him for a moment. "I was looking for strays."

She went no further. Vic had a feeling she didn't want to talk about it. He placed a can under a drip. "The fall will soon be here. I figured on being in California about now."

"What's to stop you?"

"Little things. A horse, saddle, food and a little *dinero.*"

"There's work here," she suggested.

He picked up the water bucket. "Here?" he asked.

"It's possible. But you might not like it."

"One place is like another."

She shook her head. "Not around here anymore."

He opened the door and dashed to the stream to fill the bucket and then dashed back again to the shack. He slammed the door shut. "This is going to keep on all night." He found a deep iron skillet. "You want to build the meal?" he added.

She smiled winningly. "You have such a lovely start."

He placed rice and water in a pan and placed it on the embers to steam. He cubed embalmed beef into a mixture of canned tomatoes and flour and then started the coffee. He placed the coffee pot at the rear of the fireplace. When the rice was steamed, he poured it into the mixture of beef, tomatoes and flour. He judiciously added seasoning and a trickle of pickle juice for piquancy and then placed the covered skillet in the center of the embers. "Best get out of those wet clothes," he suggested. "I've got to get more wood and water.

There are some army blankets on the cot. You can use them to cover up." He left the shack, refilled the water bucket and then walked into the lean-to out of the slanting rain. He thumb-snapped a match to light the interior. Wood was piled to the ceiling at the rear of the lean-to. There were several bales of hay and straw to one side. He fished his Arizona Ranger commission out of the slit in the lining of his left boot. He had wrapped it in oilskin before hiding it there and it was still dry and clear. He rewrapped it in the oilskin and temporarily hid it in the space between the ceiling and the shanty wall. He carried the wood and water into the shack.

She stood by the fire, draped in one of the old gray army blankets belted about her slim waist with a length of rope. Her long, dark hair hung about her heat-flushed face and over her shoulders, glistening in the firelight and the lamplight. Once again something stirred deep within Vic, bringing back memories of another such woman of years past. He shook off the emotion. Deborah was at least ten years younger than he was and a woman in figure, though not perhaps yet in mind, but still she had some maturity about her.

Vic placed the firewood beside the fireplace. "It'll be a wet night," he prophesied. "This unusual weather?"

"Not at this time of the year. Usually the cattle are driven down to lower ground before long, to avoid the winter weather. It gets snowed in around here. Well, it's one thing we won't have to bother about much now."

"The weather?"

She turned to look at him. "No, driving the cattle down."

"Why?"

She shrugged. "Several reasons. We've very few cattle left. We may lose the ranch before long. And, in any case, we can't get local men to work for us."

"You can't pay them?"

She shook her head. "Around here you either work for the

Scalp Knife or you don't work at all, unless you're downright foolish."

"Why?"

She shrugged again. "The Scalp Knife pays better."

"There's more to it than that," he suggested.

She eyed him. "Men are afraid to work for us and some of the other ranchers, all except the Jemsons of the Slash Bar J. They're all related, one way or another, a real mountain clan, and they're the only ones around here the Scalp Knife can't frighten or swindle out of business. Not yet anyway."

"A great set of neighbors," he observed dryly.

"It wasn't always that way. We held our own in these mountains until Clay Mostyn took over the Scalp Knife three years ago. Have you ever heard of him?"

Vic shook his head. Lie upon lie, he thought, but possibly to a good end.

"Ambition is his name. A hard-driving, merciless, ruthless sonofabitch!"

Vic raised his eyebrows. "Such language!"

"It fits him! I can't think of any other word that describes him so accurately!"

Vic grinned. He waved a casual hand. "Pass," he said.

"He came into these mountains and bought out the Scalp Knife and turned it into a small kingdom and he plans to make it an empire. There's no end to his ambition. He virtually owns Tonto Springs. He wants money and more money, but even above that he wants political power."

Vic shrugged. "The two seem to go together." He took the skillet from the embers and placed it on a piece of flat wood on the table. He took the steaming coffee pot from the embers and refueled the fire.

Vic doled out two tin plates and graniteware cups. "Set," he invited.

"Is there anything I can do?" she asked.

"You're a little late in asking, but you can say grace."

He was actually shocked to see her sit down and clasp her hands, then to bend her dark head. He sat down and bowed his head. He was still mentally fumbling with a long unaccustomed silent grace when he looked up to see her smiling at him. "Fooled you, didn't I?" she asked.

He smiled. "You're almighty good at it," he said.

"Daddy taught me," she added.

Vic doled out the steaming food. "Seems like your daddy is a man of many parts."

She leaned forward and inhaled the succulent aroma of the food. "Wonderful! What do you call it?"

Vic shrugged. "Glurp," he replied laconically.

"An old family recipe, perhaps?"

"It might be a couple of generations from now because I just made it up as I went along."

The two of them emptied the skillet. Vic shoved back his plate and sighed. "Eat well tonight and forget about tomorrow. We'll have the beans for breakfast."

"Can't we walk out of here tonight?"

He cocked an eye at the ceiling. "Listen," he suggested. The rain drummed steadily on the roof and the water dripped into the pan. Another leak had started. Vic placed the skillet under it. "The streams will be bankful and running like mill-races. Step into one of them in the dark and you'll never come up." He glanced sideways at her. "I can sleep in the lean-to. Leaks less than the shack anyway."

She sipped at her coffee. "Are you an Arizona man?"

He shook his head. "Colorado," he replied. It was really New Mexico, at least *originally*.

"But you've been in Arizona before?"

"Years past, passing through, so to speak."

"Going to California?"

He nodded. "Fort Yuma, on the California side of the Colorado. That's as far west as I've ever gotten."

"You were in the army?"

He began to shape a cigarette. "For one hitch. I like variety in my life." He had actually served at Fort Bowie, Arizona Territory.

"And now you're a wanderer?"

He grinned. "The word today is 'saddle tramp'. It seems more fitting than 'wanderer'." He leaned across the table and placed the cigarette between those lovely full lips. He was beginning to like the action more and more. He lighted the cigarette. "Funny thing, though, once I get beyond that mountain that's always just ahead of me, I seem always to see another mountain with the same lure."

"And the next one, and the next one, and so on and so on..."

He shaped a quirly for himself.

"But you're a skilled hand, aren't you?"

"How would you know?"

"I'm living proof," she replied soberly. "The way you used that blessed reata of yours and that hoolihan loop proves that you are skilled."

"In casting a loop?" He smiled.

She shook her head. "Not only that. Your actions and everything else you do shows through all the time. You're a professional."

"I was a horse wrangler," he admitted. "I was in the cavalry chasing Chiricahuas. Spent a lot of time with horses and jugheads before, during and after my hitch."

"Then got tired and moved on. Where?"

"Spent time as a government scout against the 'Paches. The Chiricahuas mostly, the *worst,* or *best* of the lot, depending on whether you are a white man or an Apache.

They were tamed, temporarily...I moved on. East and north this time. To Colorado."

"Ranching?"

"Muleskinner, teamster and then hostler for a stagecoach line. The railroad came in and the stagecoaches went out. There wasn't exactly a demand for hostlers or wranglers for Standard locomotives." He shrugged. "So, I drifted south and west again." He blew a smoke ring. Lie upon lie, he thought.

"What happens when you reach California?"

"*Quién sabe?*"

"There's the Pacific Ocean out there."

"I've heard of it. I hear they have cowpokes in Hawaii."

"And sheepherders in Australia," she countered.

"I'm surprised to hear such language from you, and you a cattleman's daughter!"

She studied him. "I can't believe you're just a saddle tramp."

"Why?"

"There's a purpose about you. I can't say what it really is, but it shows through you."

He grinned. "When you find out what it is, let me know."

"What would you really like to do?"

He studied his cigarette. "Raise horses I guess." He wasn't lying now.

"What stopped you?"

He looked up at her. "Time passes and dreams fade."

"You sound like you've been defeated."

He couldn't help himself this time. "I've *never* been defeated," he said firmly. He stood up and picked up his slicker, hat and reata.

She had been startled at the look in his gray eyes when she suggested he might have been defeated. She took a blanket from the cot and handed it to him.

"Will one be enough? I will have the fire."

"There's plenty of straw and hay in there. Will you be all right?"

"Just fine."

He unbuckled his gun belt and draped it over a wooden peg on the wall beside the cot. "I will be up early to start down the mountain and get horses."

"What makes you think I might need the pistol?"

He shrugged. "I seem to *feel* you might."

"But you might need it."

He grinned and held up the reata. "I have this."

"Be careful. There's been so much horse thieving in the Rio Diablo country that it's almost an unwritten rule that the thief gets hanged by his own reata while seated on the horse he stole."

"That the rule on the Star Cross too?"

She looked away. "It's been done," she admitted. "But years ago."

He shrugged. "I'll take my chances," he said. "Good night."

She nodded. She smiled. "You're one damned good *cocinero,* if no one's ever told you before."

He waved a hand. "Glurp is the only recipe I know." He closed the door behind himself. He cut the bindings on some of the straw bales and spread them on the floor. He retrieved his commission and replaced it in his boot. He hung an old tarp across the open end of the lean-to and then lay down on the thick bed of straw, drawing the blanket over himself. He slanted his hat across his eyes and lay there for a long time listening to the drumming of the rain on the lean-to roof and the patter dripping from the eaves.

Now and then he could hear her moving about within the shack. The near memory of those dusky brown eyes and the soft full lips came to make him uneasy. He remembered very well the firm pressure of her breasts against his body as he had hauled her up the slope to the ledge to save her life. She owed him something in return. He attempted to thrust the thought from his mind. His last contact with a woman had been one of the *mariposas* in Magdalena. *Chihuahua!* She had been a real buster!

"Star Cross," he said aloud. That had been one of the first spreads to operate in the Rio Diablo country some time before the Civil War when the Apaches still haunted that country. Old man Eb Cross had been a younger man then, a Mexican War veteran who had given the Apaches as good as they had handed out and better at that. He had *stayed.* It had taken a lot of staying. Fighting rimrock Apaches, Mormon rustlers from the Little Colorado country, Mexican cattle and horse thieves from around the Blue River country, and local rustlers trying to set themselves up into business at the expense of the Star Cross and the other legitimate spreads in the Rio Diablo country. Eb Cross was likely the girl's grandfather. Vic shifted on his straw bed and a mouse squeaked from within it. "Take it easy," said Vic, "There's room enough for both of us."

Something stirred in his mind. She had said the Star Cross had few cattle left and that they might lose the ranch before long. She had also suggested that there was work on the ranch, but that few men wanted to work for the ranch because of the fear of the Scalp Knife. There wasn't much likelihood of him working for the Star Cross as Bass Burnett had done, because that would place him squarely in the enemy's camp as far as the Scalp Knife was concerned and he'd likely never learn a thing about rustlers and murders in the Rio Diablo that way. He might even earn a .50/.95 Express bullet in the side of his head as Bass Burnett had done. The law and order record was not good. Two Rangers and a deputy sheriff had been the count until Bass Burnett had been dry-gulched in Stray Horse Canyon. Vic Jamison held himself partly to blame for that. He should have known of the presence of the killer. The very fact that the killer had managed to get into position for a killing shot despite the presence of Vic indicated the type of outlaw he was up against.

Vic rolled onto his side. "I had it made in Sonora this last trip down there," he mused softly. "Good money, Tezopaco brandy and the best *mariposas* in old Magdalena..."

The rain hammered down and the cold wind soughed eerily through the dripping trees. Vic Jamison was a long way from the fleshpots of old Magdalena.

CHAPTER THREE

Vic awoke shivering in the dawn chill. The rain had stopped. He pulled on his stiff boots and picked up his reata. He pushed aside the damp tarp to look into a drifting wooly mist. It was shortly after dawn light. The shack was quiet, and no smoke arose from the chimney. Vic fortified himself with a good stiff jolt of Tezopaco from his flask and then rolled a smoke. He lighted up and then crossed the meadow to a rusted wire fence that lay flat on the wet ground, wires and posts alike. No one had been riding fence for quite some time on the Star Cross, he figured.

The mist began to drift off as the dawn wind crept up the long timbered slopes. A horse whinnied somewhere within the timber. Vic coiled his reata in his left hand. He swung to approach the horse from downwind. The wind had begun to sweep tenuous corridors in the drifting opaqueness of the mist. A saddleless horse drifted into view knee-deep in mist. It was a fine-boned sorrel mare with a white blaze on her forehead. Vic moved like a hunting cat. He stepped behind a tree just as the mare raised her head and looked in his direction. The wind blew harder, dissipating the mist.

The mare began to graze, moving slowly toward Vic. He cocked his loop for action. She stopped fifty feet from him, now and then raising her pretty head to look about herself. Vic picked up a broken piece of branch and hurled it high overhead to land beyond the mare. She reared a little and then ran toward Vic. When she was twenty feet from him, he stepped out into her full view. He slipped the reata loop vertically on her right side and then jumped to his right. She was startled and threw herself to her right to land her forefeet into the falling loop. Vic flipped the loop up high to place it neatly about her forelegs before he tightened the loop. She crashed sideways in her excitement. Vic walked down the reata to her, keeping up the tension on it. "Hoh, hoh, hoh, hoh," he husked. She did not try to get up but looked up at him with soulful brown eyes. "You're a man-killer, sis," he said with a grin.

He cut enough from the end of the reata to form a hackamore and then put it on her so swiftly and expertly that she did not resist. He loosened the loop from about her forearms and then gripped the hackamore. "Come on, sweetheart," he urged her. "You aim to lie there all day in the wet, eh?" She struggled to her feet and then rubbed her nose hard against his shoulder, pushing him back a little. He laughed as he coiled his reata.

"Well, by God, he's got his rope on her, sure enough," the hard voice said from behind Vic.

Vic whirled instinctively, dropping his right hand to his thigh. The girl had his Colt. He heard the crisp and unmistakable metallic sounding of a lever action being worked and he looked into as hard a pair of green eyes as he had ever seen in his life—like chips of bottle glass. Beyond the man he saw two horsemen walking their mounts through the tatters of mist.

"You got a hideout gun, mister, you just drop it on the ground."

Vic slowly raised his hands to shoulder level. He shook his head, but his stingy gun was hidden under his left sleeve cuff in a small spring-type half-breed holster.

Green Eyes was square-faced, square-jawed and immensely square-shouldered. He had virtually no neck and the hands that held his Winchester pointed just above Vic's belt buckle were big, looking like chunks of native granite. "That was as neat a sneak catch as I've ever seen," he admitted. "Who are you?"

"Purcell," Vic replied. "Vic Purcell."

"Where was you aimin' to take the mare?"

"The line shack over in the meadow."

"Why?"

Vic glanced toward the two horsemen. Jesus God, he thought, these three hardcases think *I'm a horse thief!*

"I asked you a question," Green Eyes reminded Vic.

Vic cleared his throat. "Lost my own cayuse in the Diablo. Flash flood. I was walking out when I saw the mare."

"That wasn't too bright," one of the horsemen suggested.

"The mare wasn't for me. There's a girl at the line shack. It was for her." It sounded damned stupid even to Vic.

Green Eyes grinned loosely. "Well, do tell! Listen to that, Sid and Jack! Goddamned if he ain't got a gal in the upper meadow!"

"Wet weather for lollygaggin' with a filly, Cass," one of the horsemen opined. "Fella could get the rheumatiz."

Vic looked up at him. "It's Deborah Cross from the Star Cross," he explained.

"Matt Cross will love that," Sid said.

"She lost her mare in the same flash flood that I lost my dun," Vic explained, feeling damned foolish as he did so. "We got down to the line shack last night and stayed there. I came out this morning to find a horse."

"Jesus!" Cass exploded. "That's a booger if I ever heard one! Should I tell you what we do to horse thieves in the Rio Diablo country?"

"Be careful," Deborah had warned Vic. *"There's been so much horse thieving in the Rio Diablo country that it's almost an unwritten rule that the thief gets hanged by his own reata while seated on the horse he stole."*

"And he brought his own rope," Sid said cheerfully.

"Wait," Vic said quietly. "You've no right to sit as jury, judge and executioner on me."

"Listen to *him!"* Cass jeered. "Sounds like he reads books."

"Nothing wrong with that," Sid put in. "You ought'a try it sometime, Cass."

"Maybe he's better at readin' books than he is at horsethievin'," Jack suggested.

Cass shoved the rifle muzzle hard against Vic's lean gut. "Me, I hate horse thieves with a passion."

"I've told you the truth," Vic insisted. He was getting concerned now. *They meant it!*

"We can always take him to the line shack," Sid suggested. "Maybe she could clear him at that. *If* she's there at all."

Cass shook his head. He raised his rifle and tipped Vic's Stetson back with the muzzle of it. He shoved the hat up and back so that it fell off. "Pick it up and put it back on, Purcell," Cass ordered. "I wouldn't want you should catch cold while we're handin' out justice here."

Vic reached down for the hat. Cass shoved him. Vic fell sideways and braced himself with one hand. A boot slammed down hard on his wrist, crushing the hand into the soft wet ground.

Vic looked up into those icy green eyes. "What the hell is the matter with you?" he demanded.

The rifle muzzle was placed against Vic's chest. "Now you just start talkin', Purcell and by God, you'd better tell the truth this time!" Cass viciously pressed down the boot on top of Vic's hand before he withdrew his foot.

Sid hooked a leg around his pommel. "Maybe he is telling the truth, Cass. I still think we ought to take him to the line shack."

Cass grinned. "Mebbe. Come to think of it what would that old sonofabitch Matt Cross do to this saddle tramp if he found out he'd been whorin' with his daughter in a line shack?"

Vic knocked the rifle barrel aside and uncoiled from the ground, rising straight up, his right arm tipped with a balled fist that caught Cass right under the jaw and snapped his big mouth shut so hard his teeth powdered. A ramrod left sank into the beefy belly just above the gun belt buckle and a right cross to his block of a jaw seemed to near loosen his head on his short neck. He fell sideways on one knee but came up almost instantly to meet a crisp left to the jaw and a piledriver right that thudded just over his heart. He fell backward, half stunned, and as he did so Vic plucked his Colt from its holster and tossed it to one side. Vic stepped back between Cass and his Winchester. Cass lay flat on his broad back staring up unbelievingly at Vic.

"Christamighty," Sid said in awe. "We sure got a real fist-fighter on our hands for once." His handsome face broke into a pleasing grin.

"You mean ol' Cass has, don't you?" Jack asked dryly.

There was no chance of Vic making it with his double-barreled stingy gun. The derringer only had two rounds and the two horsemen had both rifles and pistols and they looked like they knew how to use them. Vic would be dead by the time he got off the second round.

Cass got slowly to his feet and shook his block of a head.

"You hit hard when a man ain't ready. You ain't licked Cass Page yet, not by a damned long shot, *Mister* Purcell. I'm the big he-coon in the Rio Diablo country, mister." He looked slowly at Sid. "You think this is funny, Decker?"

Sid Decker wasn't afraid of Cass Page; *not* when he had his guns easy to hand and Cass was unarmed.

"You got to admit he turned the tables on you, Cass."

"What about you. Sorley?" Cass asked.

Jack Sorley shrugged. "It ain't funny to me at all. Now let's get this horse thief straightened out. We been ridin' all night in the damned rain. I want to get back to the Scalp Knife and get some dry clothes, grub and sleep."

"I won't take long. I got to teach this saddle-bum a lesson."

"It's your deal," Vic offered. "Just keep your two friends out of it." His guts formed a tight and icy ball. Cass was right —Vic *had* hit him hard when he wasn't ready. The big man looked like a fighting machine bereft of fear or any other emotion.

Cass grinned but there was no mirth in his green eyes. "I won't need 'em," he said softly, *"but you* might, before I get through with you."

"This is loco," Jack Sorley put in.

"Let them go to it," Decker said. "Cass is always so damned certain he can lick any man in the Territory I'd like to see him get his comeuppance for once."

"I think he can, but I got to admit I don't like the way he goes about it. Remember that older fella Cass beat to death?"

"Shut up!" Cass snapped.

"Hayson was his name," Jack persisted.

"Hayden. Cal Hayden," Sid corrected.

Cass glared at them. "I said shut up!"

Sid spat to one side. "Whyn't you go and take your licking like a little man?" he asked sweetly.

Cal Hayden—the name meant much to Vic Jamison. A quiet older man with a slow and easy smile who had tried to support a wife and three kids on his meager Ranger's pay because he thought it was his duty.

"He had his chance," Cass insisted.

"He was fifteen years older and forty pounds lighter than you," Sid reminded him.

To die under one blow is nothing; to be beaten slowly to death is a horrible thing and without the swift mercy of the bullet or the knife. Vic moved back a little from the animal in human form who stood there with his head bent forward, glaring at Vic from under shaggy brows almost like a Neanderthal man. To be beaten to death by a man like Cass Page would have been too much for even Jesus to bear.

Cass plunged in. His left drove into Vic's lean gut with the impact of a hydraulic ram. Vic's head involuntarily snapped forward to meet a bruising right uppercut that reversed the forward snap of his head so hard that for a fraction of a second, he thought his neck had been broken. He staggered back and caught two belly blows and a right cross that sent him flying sideways into the muck. Cass rushed in for a booting, but Vic still had sufficient reaction sense left to grip the oncoming foot and then force himself to stand up quickly enough to dump Cass flat on his ass in the mud.

Vic staggered back as Cass literally seemed to bounce up onto his feet. Vic crossed his forearms in front of himself to take the painful impact of the sledgehammer blows, expecting at any moment to feel the snap of a broken bone. His back struck a tree, and he threw himself sideways to evade a fist that smacked solidly into the tree. Cass grunted in savage pain. A looping right caught him on his big hairy left ear and sent him crashing into the next tree. A left hit him before he could recover and a right sent him down on his broad butt.

Vic stepped back, breathing harshly. He wiped the blood from his mouth and chin and tried to get Cass into focus as one man instead of two.

"For Christ's sake!" Sid yelled. "Give him the boot, you damned idiot! *Don't let him get up!*"

Cass was up on his feet and running at Vic like a charging grizzly bear and looking twice as mean. "I'll remember that, Decker!" he flung back over a shoulder.

Cass lowered his bullet head at the last instant to take two punches against his hard skull that stung Vic's fists. Cass butted Vic in the chest and Vic went down with Cass atop him, working his powerful talonlike hands up Vic's bloody, sweating face to get at his eyes with broken black fingernails. A hard knee came up into the big man's meaty privates and he gasped in agony as Vic threw him off. Vic rolled sideways and up onto his feet to launch a foot out so that the boot heel bounced off Cass' blocky jaw. Another boot heel hit the Scalp Knife man on his low forehead. He crawled away from the punishment waggling his head from side to side and grunting like a hog.

"Time," Vic said. He danced about, feinting and blocking, ducking and dodging, and all the while shooting out phantom blows.

"Look at that crazy sonofabitch," Sorley whispered in awe.

"He's sure got Cass' number," Decker admitted. He grinned. He *liked* that.

Cass got up and charged in again, all brawn and no technique, and the fury of his attack drove Vic ever backward. He *had* to stay on his feet. To go down was to be maimed for life or perhaps to die a bloody senseless hulk as Cal Hayden had. But Cass was tiring. The steam was out of his blows as he drove them at the lean, taunting face of the man who always moved a fraction of a second before the bloody abraded fists made contact. Cass finally dropped his arms. His eyes were wide in his head and his breathing was harshly erratic. A right hook smacked his jaw. A left jab glanced from his forehead. Another left drove the last of his wind out of him and a right cross hit him so hard on the jaw that spray and blood flew outward from his battered face. He was game; no doubt about that. He was game, or senseless. He charged right into an old-fashioned one-two that sent him crashing onto his back. He lay there staring unbelievingly up at Vic and he could not get up.

Vic wiped the blood from his knuckles. He looked sideways at the two horsemen. "Well?" he asked.

"You licked the big sonofabitch all right," Decker admitted. "I never expected to see this day. But, in *my* book, mister, you're still a horse thief."

"Look out, Purcell!" Jack Sorley yelled.

Vic whirled. Cass stood there with his muddy Winchester gripped in his great bloody paws and the look of killing on his battered face.

"Stay right where you are, *Mister* Page," Deborah ordered from out of the drifting mist behind him. She cocked Vic's Colt. "Drop that rifle!" She looked at the two horsemen. "Don't interfere. I know how to use a six-gun."

Decker laughed. "You sure as hell do, Miss Cross!"

"This just ain't Cass Page's day," Jack Sorley opined. "First he gets licked by a saddle tramp and then a lady gets the drop on him."

"Maybe Purcell was telling the truth all the time," Sid suggested.

Cass made his move before he dropped his rifle. Vic slipped sideways and down-gripped the rifle but Cass violently tore it loose and accidently rammed the muzzle up against the left side of his face. The blade front sight ripped into his left eye. He grunted in savage pain. He dropped the rifle and staggered backward, while clasping his big hands over his bloody left eye. "Jesus! Oh, Jesus!" he yelled hoarsely.

"He can't hear you, you sonofabitch," Vic said. He picked up the rifle and quickly turned while levering a fresh round into the chamber.

Both Scalp Knife men were staring in horror at Cass Page.

Vic saw for the first time that the mare he had roped was branded with a Star Cross—a five-pointed star with a Saint Andrew's Cross within it. "This is Star Cross range, isn't it?" he asked quietly.

"Sure is," Jack Sorley admitted. "For the time being, that is."

"That's a Star Cross mare I roped?"

"Sure is," Sid Decker replied.

"Then get to hell off this range and take that one-eyed bastard with you!"

"It ain't quite that easy," Decker said. "Maybe Miss Cross didn't fill you in on some of the details. *I* can. Most of the Star Cross and what little stock is left on it are under litigation. The court sort of turned much of it over to Colonel Clayton Mostyn, our boss, to take care of it until the matter is settled legally. Matt Cross is a constant drunk and incapable of handling himself or the ranch. He hasn't one hand working for him now. If, within the next month, he pays off his debts to Colonel Mostyn, which isn't likely, Cross can regain full possession. Meanwhile *someone* has to take care of it."

"Like Colonel Mostyn?"

Decker nodded. "You've got the idea. So, *Mister* Purcell, you are standing on the very ground that might well be Scalp Knife territory within a matter of weeks, and if I was you, I'd get to hell off of it and keep moving until you reach some part of the Territory where they never heard of the Scalp Knife."

"Which ain't very likely," Jack Sorley added. "So dust up a storm for parts unknown, Purcell. Say, ah, Mexico?"

Vic looked at Cass Page. He stood with his head resting on his saddle while slowly beating a fist on the pommel. "You'd better take care of your friend there," Vic suggested. He picked up the hackamore of the mare and dropped the rifle into the muck. He led the mare to Deborah and together the two of them walked back through the mist toward the distant line shack.

"That took guts," Vic said to Deborah when they were out of earshot of the Scalp Knife men.

"You're bragging," she accused.

He grinned. "I meant you."

"You've made a terrible enemy," she warned him. "Cass Page will never forget that he took a beating from you and in front of his friends too."

He shrugged. "They didn't seem *that* friendly with him."

"He's a loner; a killer. He'll do anything he can to get at you again."

"I may be around for a little while."

She looked up into his bruised and bloodied face. "I hope not, for your sake anyway."

He felt inside his jacket for the makings and shaped a cigarette. He placed it between her lips and lighted it. He shaped another cigarette for himself and lighted it. He blew a smoke ring and idly watched it drift into the mist. "I sure have a way of getting right into the thick of things," he mused, almost as though to himself.

She looked sideways at him. She was positive now that this man was no saddle tramp, no ordinary man.

CHAPTER FOUR

"The star CROSS," Deborah said quietly. There was sadness in her voice and yet there was a tinge of pride in it as well.

A long slope extended from where the two of them stood to a winding stream which threaded its way through a mountain meadow land, lined by wind-swayed trees fresh and green from the downpour of the day and night before. The morning sun slanted down from the clear and cloudless sky to touch the wavelets of the swiftly rushing stream with silvery glintings. A house constructed of large logs stood on higher ground beyond the stream with the outbuildings grouped behind it. The sun reflected from the rain-washed windows. A lazy thread of pale blue-gray smoke arose from the huge field-rock chimney to be wafted off by the fresh wind. A lone steer bawled from a pasture and a horse whinnied a greeting to Deborah's mare from a peeled-pole corral. The morning wind made soft sighing music among the pines, firs and spruces that extended on all sides from the ranch house clearing, shaking loose crystal-clear sparklets of rainwater from the dark green finery of the trees.

"Beautiful," Vic murmured. It was almost as though he were seeing a dream place come true at last.

She shrugged. "It's about all we have left now and we're likely to lose this too. We can hardly make a living out of some ranch buildings, a handful of steers and horses and a few rods of timberland."

"Isn't there anything your father can do about it?"

"Wait until you meet my father, Vic," she replied quietly.

Vic led the mare to the stream and swung easily up behind Deborah in order to cross it. Once, halfway across, she turned her head a little and looked up into the scarred face of the man who sat behind her with his hard body pressing against hers.

Vic dismounted to open the picket gate that led into the fenced yard in front of the house. As he did so he thought he caught a furtive movement behind the curtains of one of the windows. Vic tethered the mare to the fence.

She paused at the foot of the porch steps. "You heard Sid Decker say that my father is a constant drunk and incapable of handling the ranch. Well, he was right." She studied him for a moment before she continued on up the steps to the porch.

Vic followed her into the large living room of the house. It was dominated by a massive field-rock fireplace. Old rifles and later models hung on the walls amid a profusion of bridles, fancy spurs and bits, coiled reatas, quirts, hides and pelts of various animals and colorful Navajo blankets. In the center of the upper part of the fireplace was a pair of crossed Apache lances with a painted rawhide shield hung at the intersection of the weapons.

"This place is like a museum," Vic said.

She nodded. "That's just about what it is now. Wait here. I'll get my father."

It must have been her father who had peered between

the window curtains. Vic could hear low murmuring voices in the hallway that led past the bedrooms to the rear of the house. Deborah reappeared steadying a gray-haired man by his left arm. His right sleeve was tied in a knot and swung loosely at his side, for he had no right arm. "This is Vic Purcell, Father," Deborah said. "Vic, this is my father, Matthew Cross."

Vic awkwardly shook Matt's strong left hand. Matt raised his bloodshot eyes to look at Vic. "I'm a little clumsy today, Purcell," he said thickly, "having only one wing and a left one at that." The sour, fruity odor of liquor and vomit came on his breath.

Deborah helped her father to a chair. He sat down heavily. "Thought something had happened to my little girl, Purcell. Thanks for what you did. Deborah, you go make some Arbuckle's like a good girl." He reached under the seat cushion and withdrew a bottle. "Half empty," he said regretfully.

"Or half full," Vic suggested, "depending on how you look at it."

"I'm not an optimist, if that's what you mean. My daughter thinks I drink too much."

"Fine girl, Cross."

"Too damned good for an old drunk like me, eh, Purcell?"

Vic fixed the older man with his hard gray eyes. "I didn't say that, Cross."

Matt Cross looked away from those eyes. Years back he would have given Vic Jamison or any other man measure for measure and eyeball to eyeball, but that had been long ago; *too* long ago. "Well, she just told me you saved her life," he mumbled.

"She did the same for me."

Matt unstoppered the bottle. "Glasses are in the kitchen. I don't want to get them. I don't want her to think I'm drinking too much today." He handed the bottle to Vic. "This is rye."

Vic took the bottle. "I'm a Tezopaco brandy man myself." He drank a little. His eyes watered and he lost a little of his breath. "Jesus!" he exploded.

Cross smiled. "Rough stuff. Best I can afford these days. But Tezopaco is spic stuff." He eyed Vic slantways. "You ain't part *spic* by any chance?"

"No, but I've spent a lot of time down there."

"I thought so." Cross drank deeply and never turned a hair. His voice was hoarser when he spoke again. "I've told Debbie time and time again to stay out of those damned canyons east of here. She won't find any of our strays in there—if they are strays. The Upper Rio Diablo keeps whatever goes into it." He eyed Vic. "What happened to your face?"

"You mean the old scar?"

Cross shook his head.

"I ran it into a pair of fists owned by a man named Cass Page."

Matt stared incredulously at Vic. "Cass Page? *Jeeeesusss!*"

"You should see Cass Page."

"You whupped Cass Page?" There was utter disbelief in Matt's tone.

"Yes and no. It was whip him or get whipped and maybe get maimed to boot. Besides, he had two of his *compañeros* with him—Jack Sorley and Sid Decker. I was lucky enough to get the drop on them, with Deborah's help of course, and ran them off your range."

Matt Cross quickly handed Vic the bottle. "You faced down Cass Page, Sid Decker *and* Jack Sorley?"

Vic drank from the bottle, looked slantways at the older man, wiped a slow hand across his mouth and then nodded.

"Then you'd better bust the wind getting to hell out of the

Rio Diablo country. Don't even take time to stop long enough to take a crap! Get to hell out of here! *Now!*"

Vic shrugged. "I haven't got a horse and gear. Lost it all when my dun went down the Rio Diablo."

"Then take a horse and gear from me! I haven't got much but what I do have is yours. I can't give you any money though. Now, *git!*"

Vic drank again. "I move along when I'm ready to move, Matt."

Matt slowly tapped the empty sleeve at his right side. "You see this, Vic? There was a time when I thought *I* was the big he-coon of the Rio Diablo country. *No* man could take me on with gun, fist or boot. I was just as big a damned fool as you are now, and I played my hand a mite too far."

"Gracias," Vic murmured.

"Por nada," Matt responded. He hiccupped. "It was Cass Page that cost me that arm a year ago. By God, I was lucky to get away with just that. I was damned fool enough to try to run him and Decker off my land. I drew on him and Decker put a .44/.40 slug through my elbow joint. Goddamned bullet near cut my arm in half! Cass Page roped my arm and dragged me along behind his horse. My goddamned arm come loose at the elbow! Page rode off dragging that poor bloody thing that had been part of me for over fifty years! The two of them were laughing all the time!" The pain and fear of the horrifying incident came crowding back on Matt Cross. He drank again. "I made it back here with a tourniquet about my arm and stuck the stump in a barrel of flour to staunch the bleeding. Deborah was gone at the time. I got me a bottle and drank it dry and then passed out. God alone knows why I didn't bleed to death. They found me three days later. Gangrene had started. I was lucky enough as it was that they caught it in time to save my life..." His voice died away. He closed his eyes and quickly turned his head to one side.

Vic shaped a cigarette and lighted it. "I can see now why you punish yourself with the booze. But isn't it about time you drove that cork back into the bottle and left it there? You can't beat the bottle, Matt. Ever..."

"You sound like a goddamned circuit preacher! It was me that lost the arm, wasn't it?" Matt demanded.

"The loss of an arm never stopped a lot of good men."

"It's too late for me."

"It's never too late, as they say. Whoever *they* are."

"For Christ's sake! Who are you? A Pollyanna? A rooftop evangelist? All sweetness and light and undying faith in the future? Dammit, Purcell! I can't fight these rustlers and killers alone. Clayton Mostyn wants to build his own little kingdom here in the Rio Diablo country and he's just about made it. What can *I* do? I haven't any stock left to speak of. I haven't got a *corrida* of gunfighters to back me up. Mostyn has the sheriff on his payroll. Sheriff Lem Baggott jumps when Clayton Mostyn snaps his fingers."

"Can't you fight this out in court?"

"I have no evidence to prove who is doing the rustling. It could be the Mormons from up north, or the greasers from down south, or maybe it's the 'Paches, or maybe Jemson and his Slash Bar J clan. No one has ever caught any rustlers as long as Mostyn has been taking over the Rio Diablo country one way or the other. Besides, I wouldn't put it past Mostyn to rig the courts the way he has rigged just about everything else around the valley."

"Then get a change of venue to another county."

Cross looked quickly at Vic. "I've thought of that, but I haven't got the funds for an extended battle in court."

"Can you borrow it on your property?"

"If I could, I'd *have* to win, or lose everything anyway. Besides, I've signed options on the land to pay off some of my debts. I borrowed anywhere and everywhere. Mostyn went behind my back and bought up all the options and even paid my I.O.U.s on unpaid debts."

Deborah came into the living room. "You might as well tell Vic the rest of it, Dad," she suggested quietly.

Matt shrugged. "Might as well. I got into a big poker game in Tonto Springs one night. I always did fancy myself as a poker sharp. I lost steadily that night. I put up much of my northern range for collateral and lost it. I had been drinking heavily that night. It wasn't until a week later I found out that the man who had beaten me was on Mostyn's payroll. He was a professional gambler imported from Tucson by Mostyn."

"Wasn't there any way you could have called Mostyn on that?" Vic asked. He knew better than to ask that.

"How? I had no proof, and even if I had there was nothing to prevent the man from selling his winnings, other than cash of course, to someone else. What could I have done?"

"Breakfast is ready," Deborah said.

Vic stood up and helped Matt to his feet. The older man jerked away from Vic. "I can make it on my own," he said angrily. He staggered into the hallway and through it to his bedroom. They heard him crashing heavily on the bed. Deborah closed the door behind him. She led the way into the kitchen.

"He's like that days on end," she said back over her shoulder. "You see how it is now? He's been broken. No one in this country can fight against Clayton Mostyn and his Scalp Knife outfit and win. It's a hopeless situation. They sat down at the table. Vic leaned forward. "Is there any chance of your saving part of the Star Cross until you can prove some of the accusations against Mostyn? Once he gets full possession likely nothing will ever move him if I know the type."

She shrugged as she filled the coffee cups. "Mostyn might just leave us a little something. Enough to get by on perhaps. He doesn't really want to wipe us out completely. It's a cute little trick of his. After all, the Crosses were once big people in the Rio Diablo country." She smiled wryly. *"And* after all, Clayton Mostyn will need constituents."

"For what, may I ask?"

"Clayton Mostyn doesn't intend to sit out the rest of his life in the Rio Diablo country. He has his eyes on the territorial capital. In order to get elected to the territorial legislature he'll need votes. After that? Perhaps the governorship, and even Washington."

"He must be quite a man."

"I think he has a Napoleonic complex."

"More likely Attila the Hun." Vic grinned at his own poor joke.

She launched her attack. "Dad needs a ramrod, Vic. A man he can trust. He'd be all right if he had someone who would work along with him. A man who is not afraid of Mostyn and his *corrida* of hard-cases."

He looked steadily at her. "A gunfighter you mean?"

She flushed a little and looked down at her plate. "In a way," she admitted.

"Like me?"

She looked up at him. Her meaning was plain enough in her expression.

Vic looked into those sloe-brown eyes and almost drowned his will and purpose within them, so deep and inviting were they.

"Will you?" she asked. She was confident of success in the way she looked at him.

Vic shook his head. He shoved back his plate and felt for the makings. "No, Deborah. It's not my fight. I'm a drifter, a wanderer, a saddle tramp if you will but *not* a hired gun. I want no part of any range war."

"Particularly one with the odds so top heavy," she suggested.

He shrugged. "I've fought too many losing battles in my life," he admitted.

"Maybe you should work for Mostyn then. He seems always to win." There was a touch of dry sarcasm in her tone. She could be scrappy at times Vic thought.

He held the cigarette out toward her. She shook her head. He lighted it for himself.

"It's California then?" she asked.

"*Quién sabe?* I can at least start out that way."

She stood up. "Take a horse, saddle and any gear you need. You can have a rifle if you want one. And food. We owe you that much at least."

He stood up. "You owe me nothing. I'll pay for them when I can."

They eyed each other.

"I suppose you'd want to know what was in it for you if you took my offer," she said. There was a slight teasing tone to her voice.

He shook his head. "Not really, although it might be interesting to hear your answer. What can you possibly offer a man for compensation if he was to take a job on a rundown ranch in hock, with only a few head of stock, a one-armed drunken owner and a lonely young woman as boss? Facing up to a *corrida* of cold-blooded killers who'd likely kill him on sight for what he did this morning?"

"Are you suggesting anything?" she asked angrily.

He walked to the rear door and then turned to look at her. "If I want a woman, ma'am," he said quietly, "I don't have to take a job with a guarantee that I'd probably be dead or maimed as soon as Cass Page gets his eye patched up."

Her face tightened and went white. "Damn you!" she snapped.

"I just thought I'd clear the smoke a little."

Vic closed the door behind himself. He roped a chunky

clay bank and saddled him with a good, well-used Frazier saddle. He led the clay bank around to the front of the house and tethered beside the mare. He walked up onto the porch and tapped on the door. It swung open at his touch. Deborah was seated in a large chair by the fireplace, shaping a cigarette. She did not look at him.

"Rifle," he said.

She waved a hand.

He selected a Winchester '73 .44/.40 and filled the magazine with cartridges from his belt loops. He turned and looked at her. "I'm sorry," he said.

"I deserved it."

"But you didn't mean it."

She looked up at him. The answer was plain enough—she *had* meant it. That was the hurt, to have been turned down on such a broad proposition to a total stranger that he serve her own ends.

Vic Jamison rode down the long timbered slopes toward the valley road. Once he turned in the saddle and looked back up the slopes. Someone was watching him. He couldn't see anyone. He knew someone was up there.

He reached the junction with the valley road and turned to the right toward Tonto Springs. There would have been no way he could have worked for the Star Cross and still accomplish his mission. The sun passed behind a bank of drifting clouds and a sudden chill seemed to come over the valley of the Rio Diablo and Vic Jamison. Rain began to fall in long slanting silvery veils. He touched up the clay bank with his spurs.

CHAPTER FIVE

Tonto Springs sprawled down a low slope of the foothills of the Diablos, with the north-south road widening out on both sides to form the main street of the town, gridded by the east-west streets. The road from the south crested a low ridge and afforded a fine panoramic view of the town and the valley, as well as the foothills sloping back and upward to the east, forming the approaches to the mountains. A light bluish haze of smoke issuing from the tall stack of a sawmill on the east side of the town hung over Tonto Springs. The rain had stopped.

Vic dismounted from the clay bank and shaped a quirly. He sat down on a rock and lighted the cigarette and then felt within his jacket for his flask. There was one solid drink of Tezopaco still in it. He needed time to think. Events had happened so fast since he had reached the Rio Diablo country that he had been almost crystallized into a situation not of his own making or choosing. Fate had forced him into a seeming alliance with the Crosses and a confrontation with three of the hardcase Scalp Knife *corrida* and also into the bloody defeat of Cass Page at the hands of a stranger to the

Rio Diablo country. It was not exactly an auspicious start for a man who was supposed to work undercover.

Four good lawmen had preceded Vic into the Rio Diablo country. Three of them had been murdered and the fourth, Sam Nelson, had gone into the tangled canyons of the Upper Rio Diablo and had never been seen again.

Vic sipped half of his Tezopaco. He stood now in the doorway of his future in the Rio Diablo area. He could still go back; there was yet time. He scanned the recently rain-washed and sleepy-looking valley spread out at his feet and then looked beyond the hazed foothills to the towering monolith of Mount Diablo. He could see some of the tangled canyons veining the great rockbound slopes of the mountains. Afternoon clouds dotted the bright blue sky, drifting westward, their fleet shadows moving ahead of them on the wet hills and the great valley floor. Somewhere up there, according to Burton Mossman, Sam Nelson had vanished. Vic half-closed his eyes and saw in his memory the seamed face like old saddle leather and the kindly brown eyes of Sam Nelson, the man who had probably meant more to him at one time in his life than any other man he had known.

Vic took off his battered Stetson and let the early afternoon breeze play through his sweat-damp reddish hair. Mack MacIntyre had been Vic's bunkie in the cavalry and had ridden in the same four in B Troop for a full enlistment. Mack had had the guts to wear a deputy sheriff's star openly in the Rio Diablo country and he had paid the price of his reckless-ness for it. Cal Hayden, a man who had no known enemies, except perhaps the man who had murdered him with his fists, had hired out with the Tumbling K, one of the Rio Diablo country ranches that had been swallowed up by the voracious Scalp Knife. Sam Nelson had played the part of a prospector, a part he knew well enough, for he had prospected throughout Arizona Territory in his younger days. Either someone had gotten wise to him, or he had met a common enough fate in the Diablos—that of just plain *missing*. Bass Burnett had drifted about the valley for a time, working for one or another of the local spreads until he had made the mistake of going to work for the doomed Star Cross. Bass Burnett had learned something of importance while working there. It had been obvious to Vic, but Bass had also grown a cancerous deadly fear of someone or something. Bass had had a knowledge of something that had been important enough for him to have been trailed all the way from the Valley of the Rio Diablo to Stray Horse Canyon and then to be dry-gulched there.

"The Scalp Knife," Vic said aloud.

It would be the bold and obvious course, a colossal bluff and a casting down of the gauntlet to the fate responsible for the deaths of three good lawmen and the possible death of another, for Vic to ask for work at the Scalp Knife. One thing bothered Vic—if the Scalp Knife *was* behind the wholesale rustling then in all probability, they were responsible for at least some of the killings in the Rio Diablo country. If that were so, then how much could they know about the lawmen they had possibly killed? Mack MacIntyre had worn his deputy sheriff's badge openly and had died with it pinned to his vest, but Cal Hayden, Sam Nelson and Bass Burnett had worked undercover. How had that been found out? Vic remembered all too well how Bass Burnett's killer had risked entering the jacal, not really knowing whether or not Bass had been alone, to search through his clothing. If it had been Bass Burnett's Arizona Ranger commission the killer had been looking for then he might have suspected or *known* that he was a Ranger. The ashes of Bass Burnett's commission had been in the fireplace embers just a few feet from the body and the man searching it.

Vic took out the .50/.95 cartridge case he had found in

Stray Horse Canyon, where the killer had fired at Bass. Somewhere in the valley of the Rio Diablo there rode a man with a Winchester rifle specially chambered for that unusual cartridge. A man who did not scruple to use an explosive bullet on a human being. A deadly marksman. A killer. If Vic could find that one man and get his big hands on him, he might be able to wring from him the information necessary to break up the rustling and, most important of all, the killings.

"The Scalp Knife," Vic repeated.

He emptied the flask. The sun was slanting to the west. He sat there for quite a while—*na-tse-kes,* as the Chiricahui would say, or turning one thought over and over in his mind to the exclusion of all others. To ride into Tonto Springs and ask for work at the Scalp Knife might be tantamount to his own death sentence.

A logging rig piled high with timber groaned along the rain-wet road ahead of Vic as he reached the outskirts of Tonto Springs. Buckboards and hip shot horses lined the hitching rails on both sides of the wide dirt street. The damp boardwalks were thronged with people, including children and poke-bonneted women. Vic suddenly realized that it was late Saturday afternoon.

There were several two-storied buildings in town, one of them very new while another showed the effects of the hard winters of the Rio Diablo Valley. The older building dominated one corner of the two main intersecting streets of the town and was marked as the Tonto Springs House. The newer building was across the street from the Tonto Springs House and the late afternoon sun picked out the gold black-edged lettering on one of the rain-cleansed upper windows—C. Mostyn Enterprises. The lower floor was occupied by the Springs Saloon; Vic swung down from the clay bank in front of the hotel and looked down the main east-west street. The sun shone on the sign painted in large white letters on the tall red smokestack of the busy sawmill—Mostyn Lumber Company. Vic shrugged. "Figures," he said to himself.

"I see you didn't take our advice," Sid Decker said from just behind Vic. "I figured you'd be busting up a storm on the way to Mexico by now."

Vic turned slowly. Decker smiled with a great showing of even white teeth beneath the Mexican dandy mustache he affected. "You're either a little soft in the head or you've got a helluva lot of guts," Decker added. "I know you've got guts, so that must be the answer."

"You're very bright," Vic said dryly. He felt for the makings.

Decker leaned against a post. He eyed the Star Cross brand on the clay bank. "Or maybe you've decided to stay at the Star Cross," he suggested. There was subtle insinuation in his tone.

Vic shaped a cigarette. He thumb-snapped a lucifer into flame and cupped it about the tip of the quirly. As he lighted the cigarette he slewed his eyes sideways in both directions to see if Decker was backed by anyone—Cass Page in particular.

"I'm alone, Purcell." Sid Decker grinned. "That is—right *here*. There are a few other Scalp Knifers here and there in town."

"That figures. Is Tonto Springs Knife territory?"

Decker nodded. "Sort of."

"By rule of terror?" Vic asked politely.

Decker shrugged. "Not really. Clay Mostyn has a big payroll around here, one way or another. Most of the people in town work for Mostyn Enterprises."

"He doesn't seem satisfied with taking over the valley. Well, money talks, as they say. I'd like to get some of that talking money in my Levi's."

"Easy enough. Ride for the Scalp Knife."

It was *too* easy. Vic leaned back against his horse. "I figured I might not be welcome after tangling with you three Scalp Knife men out there on the Star Cross range."

"No hard feelings. Happens all the time. We've had quite a few recruits from other ranches who finally saw the light and joined us."

"What about those that didn't?"

Decker looked at his fingernails. "They got the message." He looked up at Vic with his hard and clear light gray eyes. "Now, what about you?"

"You doing the hiring?"

"Not exactly. I'm a sort of *segundo* to Buck Fresno. Buck Fresno does the hiring. He's the ramrod. A hard man, but fair enough."

"Bueno! Then I'll go see him."

Decker nodded. "Look, I owe you a drink. Come on over to the Springs and I'll set you up."

"You don't owe me anything."

Sid Decker looked up and down the street. "It did my old heart good to see you whup Page," he admitted in a low voice.

"You've got a great loyalty to the Scalp Knife."

"But not to that bigmouthed sonofabitch."

"How is he, by the way?"

"Mostyn sent him into Holbrook to see a doctor about that eye being saved."

"Was it that bad?"

Decker nodded. "And he blames you for it, Purcell."

"He rammed that gun muzzle into his own eye."

"Are you sure you didn't help with a little shove?"

Vic shrugged. "I couldn't think fast enough at the moment or I would have," he admitted ruefully.

"Well, he won't be back for a few days, maybe more. If he had been in town this afternoon, I would have advised you to get the hell out of here and the Rio Diablo Valley altogether. He won't ever forget what happened though."

"Maybe I'd better forget about joining up with the Scalp Knife."

"I figure you don't scare easy."

"I can't. Not in my line of work."

"Such as?"

Vic placed a hand on the butt of his Colt and then flicked his fingers across the butt of the scabbarded Winchester hanging from his saddle. "It's just that a man can hardly do his best work when he's worrying about a fellow rider getting behind him on a dark night."

"Like Cass Page?"

"You catch on quick, Decker."

"Buck Fresno has been fed up with Cass Page for months. He disobeys orders. He's careless. He gets into trouble on the range and in town. He's dangerous to the Scalp Knife."

"And to everyone else it seems. Maybe it's sort of a Scalp Knife trademark."

The hard gray eyes studied Vic for a moment and then Decker flashed that winning grin of his. "I get it! But you're wrong. Mostyn stands for law and order around here, Purcell. It's really his way."

His law and order, Vic thought. "I'll take that drink," he suggested, to change the tender subject. "Where do I find Fresno?"

"I'll show you where he is."

They crossed the street together toward the Springs. Vic glanced into a window of the saloon and saw the reflection of a man stepping out of a doorway close by to where Sid Decker and Vic had been conversing. He was looking directly toward Vic. Vic turned a little and the man stepped hastily into a doorway. The man was Jack Sorley.

"Your crowd ever work as loners, Sid?" Vic asked. Sid looked quickly at Vic. "Why do you ask?"

Vic shrugged. "Just curious. Do they?"

"You mean riding fence and such like?"

"Not exactly."

Sid eyed Vic closely. "Just what *do* you mean?"

Vic shrugged. "Your friend Sorley is just across the street. He's been watching us, *or me...*"

"So? It's Saturday afternoon. Quite a few Scalp Knife men in town."

"Then who's out on the range?"

"There are riders out there. Mostyn keeps a big *corrida*. He needs it. He owns or will own most of the Rio Diablo Valley. There are only two ranches holding out—the Slash Bar J and the Star Cross. One of these days he'll have them too. Take my advice, Purcell. You've heard of hitching your wagon to a star? Well, you just hitch your little red wagon to Clayton Mostyn Enterprises and see how far you can ride in it. There's a future with him. He's going places."

"Suits me," Vic agreed amiably. "I'm easy to get along with."

"One thing. Once you ride with the Scalp Knife you don't quit it. You might get fired, *but you don't quit. Comprende?*"

Decker's meaning was plain enough. Vic nodded.

Decker pushed through the batwings of the springs. He turned as he entered the saloon. "Another thing. Don't ever cross Buck Fresno. Play along with him. He's almighty touchy about his job."

Vic eyed him sideways. "Why? Someone else got their eyes on it?" he asked innocently.

Decker studied Vic. "Sometimes I think you could almost be a little smarter than you look."

Vic grinned. "My mother always thought so."

"Yeh? But what did your *father* think?"

"That's another story. Let's get that drink."

Sid led the way past the men lined up at the long bar and then rested an elbow at the very end of it.

"What's yours?" he asked Vic. About half of the men lined along the bar had greeted Sid by name. Scalp Knifers, thought Vic Jamison.

"Rye will do," Vic replied, "unless they got Tezopaco."

"They feed that stuff to the rattlesnakes around here to get rid of them, friend," the bartender put in.

"It's good for snakebite too," Vic added.

A poker game was going on at a rear table with a kibitzer seated in a chair, its back tilted against the wall. Two more men, an older man accompanied by a much younger one, sat at a table just beyond the end of the bar. The younger one was a soft-looking giant gone to fat. The older one raised his head and looked steadily at Vic with a pair of glacial blue eyes, in startling contrast to the seamed leather of his face. His beak of a nose jutted out over a thick graying mustache. There was a facial resemblance between the two men that ended with the eyes, for while the eyes of the older man were almost an ice blue and adamantine hard, those of the younger man were rather a vacuous blue as though something mental was missing behind them.

Sid filled the glasses. He raised his glass. "*Salud,*" he toasted Vic.

Vic responded: "*Salud y pesetas.*"

"I don't like spic talk," the kid at the table said.

"Neither do I," the older man agreed.

Sid turned a little. "Purcell," he said, "meet Buck Fresno."

Vic smiled. "Which one?" he jibed.

There was no responding smile on the faces of the two men at the table. The kid tried to fix Vic with the same basilisk stare the older man affected so well but he managed to fail miserably. It was all Vic could do to keep from smiling again.

"We got a comedian here," the kid said.

Buck Fresno waved a hand to cut the kid off.

"Purcell wants to ride with the Scalp Knife," Decker explained to Buck Fresno.

"Is he man enough?" the kid sneered.

Again, the kid was cut off by an imperious wave of the hand.

Sid refilled the glasses. "Maybe you missed the name, Kid. It's Vic Purcell. He's the one who whipped Cass Page."

It grew very quiet in the saloon as Sid Decker's voice carried to the other men. The poker game had stopped. Vic had the uneasy feeling that every man in the place was looking at him. "Quite a few Scalp Knife men in town," Sid Decker had told Vic. Vic had a tense feeling that most of them were in the Springs right now.

Vic smiled a little weakly. "The fight was fair and square, Fresno," he explained.

Fresno nodded. "I know all about it. But it seems to me that I heard *you* started it."

The Kid was sizing Vic up and down, taking in the trail-worn clothing, the amiable smile, the soft-spoken voice and the plain walnut grips of the Colt holstered at Vic's side.

Vic shrugged. "Well, Fresno, if you were on a strange range, on foot, with a freshly roped horse at the other end of your hackamore wearing a brand that wasn't yours, and all of a sudden three hardcases came out of the mist and said they planned a little rope justice right then and there, would you have just stood there waiting to die?"

No one smiled or laughed. It wasn't quite time for that. The time came when a slow and somewhat frosty smile creased Fresno's leathery face. "By God, Purcell! I see your point." The only man in the place who wasn't smiling was the one called Kid. Likely he hadn't got the joke.

Fresno lighted a cigar. "Well, you sure as hell had your share of guts to stand up to Cass Page in a bare-knuckler, no-holds-barred free-for-all. Ain't many men around here would do that."

The Kid spat to one side, tough-like.

"I had an idea of what would happen to me if he beat me," Vic said.

Fresno studied Vic over the flare of the match. "Yeh. Where you from?" he suddenly shot out.

"Come from New Mexico."

"New Mexican?"

Vic shook his head. "Not originally. Colorado. Yampa River country."

"Who'd you work for there?"

"Running K."

Fresno looked at the man in the chair leaned back against the wall. "Bert?" he asked.

Bert nodded. "It's there all right."

Fresno eyed Vic. "Who owns that spread?"

"Marty Martin," Vic replied.

Fresno looked at Bert. Bert shook his head. Fresno looked back at Vic. "Well?"

Vic held out his big hands, palms upwards. He shrugged.

"Marty Martin died last year," Bert added. "Place being run by his son Willy." He grinned at his little joke.

It wasn't funny at all to Vic Jamison. "That must have been after I left for New Mexico," he explained.

"What were you doing up in the Diablos?"

"Passing through, Fresno. Just passing through."

"That's a sure sign you either don't know that country or you were in a helluva hurry to leave New Mexico."

Vic casually refilled his glass and that of Sid Decker. "I don't know. I figured it was the shortest way."

"Straight uphill," Sid put in.

Fresno stood up. "Wait here, Purcell." He opened the rear door of the saloon and then closed it after himself. They heard his heavy footfall on the stairway leading up to the rear of the second floor.

"Gone to the boss," Sid said.

"Mostyn?"

"Who else?"

"He's upstairs?"

"He holds court on Saturday afternoons."

"He the judge too?"

Decker grinned. "No, but you'll probably see what I mean."

The Kid still sat at the table intently watching Vic with his baby blues.

"Who's Big Eyes?" Vic asked as he tilted his head toward the Kid.

Sid casually spat into the spittoon. "Gene Kelso. Fresno's nephew. Product of Fresno's only sister Grace, and Jim Kelso, a Mormon rancher up in the Little Colorado country."

"You talkin' about me?" Gene demanded.

Sid glanced at him. "Why should we be?" he asked.

"I don't like it!"

Decker shrugged.

"Whyn't you come right out with what you think, Decker?"

Sid grinned. "I don't want to embarrass you, sonny."

"Why, goddamn you!" The Kid got to his big flat feet. He tried to ape Buck Fresno's icy stare-down look, but it didn't quite come off.

Sid leaned back against the bar and rested his elbows on it. "Better wait until Uncle Bucky gets back here, Kid, before you try making any moves of your own," he suggested.

"I don't need him!"

One of the men down the bar laughed. Most of the others watching the little byplay had sly grins on their faces.

"One of these days, Decker, you fancy sonofabitch, I'll..." the Kid's voice died away as he slowly realized the enormity of what he was doing.

It was very quiet.

Sid Decker straightened up. "You'll what?" he asked softly.

The vacant blue eyes of the Kid darted back and forth but there was no one to encourage him or back him up.

Fresno opened the rear door. "Purcell!" he called out.

Vic emptied his glass, wiped his mouth, tipped his hat to the onlookers and walked to the rear door past the flustered Kid.

"What the hell is the matter with you now, Gene?" Fresno asked the Kid.

The Kid looked back and forth. "Decker," he said. "Decker, he..." His weak voice trailed off. "Nothin'," he added. "Not now, anyway..."

For a few seconds Fresno's icy blue eyes studied Decker but the man did not look away. "Come on, Purcell," Fresno said at last. He closed the door behind himself. "Up the stairs," he said.

Vic opened a door on the second floor and walked into an upper hallway lined with office doors.

"Wait a minute," Fresno said. "What was going on between Gene and Sid?"

Vic turned. "I don't know. Something private, I guess.

Fresno studied Vic. "The Kid is all right, Purcell. A little rough about the edges and a little wet behind the ears but he'll do all right. You understand?"

Vic didn't understand but he nodded anyway. He remem-

bered Sid Decker's remarks about "playing along with Buck
Fresno" and "He's almighty touchy about his job". He remembered too what Decker had said about tying his little red
wagon to Mostyn's Enterprises to see how far he could ride in
it. Vic hoped it wouldn't be a hearse instead.

Fresno tapped on a glass-paneled door at the end of the
hall. It was lettered in gold—Clayton Mostyn. President and
General Manager. Mostyn Enterprises. It looked quite new.
"Watch your manners, Purcell," Fresno warned.

"Come in," the voice called out from within the office.

Fresno opened the door and let Vic in ahead of himself. A
man stood near a wide front window which afforded a
magnificent panoramic view of the distant Diablo Mountains
and the sharp horned peak of Mount Diablo. A large-scale
ordnance map of the Rio Diablo Valley and its environs hung
on the wall beside the window. Various blocks of the valley
were marked off in differently colored crayon. To one side
was a large table upon which some artist in plaster and paint
had recreated in miniature topographical form the little
isolated world of the Rio Diablo country and the great mountains to the east of it. Vic had never before quite realized how
isolated and small the area really was compared to the rest of
Arizona Territory.

"Colonel Mostyn, this is the man I told you about, sir.
Name of Purcell. Vic Purcell," Buck Fresno announced. He
took off his Stetson.

Clayton Mostyn slowly turned. He was a rather handsome
man of good size gone a little to soft flesh about the middle.
He had a thick head of wavy dark hair shot with streaks of
gray like a badger's pelt. He affected an Imperial type of
mustache and beard, very neatly trimmed. There was almost
an imperious air about the man. An affected style, Vic
thought. He was almost like the pre-Civil War type of
Southern Gentleman planter image, or perhaps a genteel

gambler on one of the prebellum Mississippi River packets. There was also a vague and disturbing resemblance to something else—a picture of Napoleon III of France, the charlatan emperor which Vic had seen some years past while down in Mexico, about the time of the Franco-Prussian War. There was something else Vic noticed—as Mostyn had turned, his tweed coat had swung open a little to show the pearl-handled butt of a hideout gun, held next to the left armpit in a half-breed holster.

The dark eyes studied Vic. "Precisely what happened between you and my man Cass Page, Purcell?" Mostyn asked.

"I'd make a guess that you already know all the details, Colonel Mostyn," Vic replied. He ignored the hard and horrified look Buck Fresno shot his way.

Mostyn nodded. "I do, but from the viewpoint of Cass Page himself. I am a fair man, Purcell. Please explain your version of the affair, if you will."

"I was on Star Cross range. I had roped a Star Cross mare for the use of Miss Deborah Cross. Three of your riders came up and Page threw down on me. I think they figured on saddle horn justice. Page made a nasty remark about Miss Cross. A slur that no gentleman would stand for, sir." Here Vic was playing up to the image of the Southern Gentleman aspect of Clayton Mostyn. "I hit the sonofabitch. He figured on beating me to a pulp. He didn't..."

"And you maimed him?"

Vic shook his head. "The man accidently injured his own eye."

"Then it is possible that you committed assault and battery on a Scalp Knife rider on what is virtually Scalp Knife range." Mostyn's dark and unblinking eyes fixed themselves on Vic's gray eyes, in a possible attempt to make him uncomfortable and to look away from the commanding presence of the great man himself.

"Am I on trial here, sir?" Vic asked quietly.

"Shut your mouth, Purcell!" Fresno snapped angrily.

Mostyn waved an imperious hand. "No, you are not on trial here, Purcell. But you did attack him first?"

"After he threw down on me, knocked off my hat, tromped on my hand when I attempted to pick it up and then insulted Miss Cross." Vic gave Mostyn measure for measure with the hard-fixed stare. "I might add that I don't think you do yourself and the image of the Scalp Knife and Mostyn Enterprises any great good by having such men as Cass Page riding for you."

The shot struck home. Mostyn looked out of the window and over the intervening roofs toward the distant heights of the looming Diablos. Napoleon contemplating his crossing of the Alps in imitation of Hannibal, thought Vic.

There was a long pause.

"You're right there, Mister Purcell," Mostyn admitted quietly. "I *have* tried to create an image with the Scalp Knife. In time I want the people of this valley to look upon the Scalp Knife riders and myself as friends, protectors, benefactors, if you will. Do you understand?" He did not wait for Vic to answer his question. "I see in you a man of intelligence, possibly self-educated, and probably of some good breeding." Here the mechanical smile, done only with the lower facial muscles.

His munificence would only last until he got control of the valley of the Rio Diablo, Vic thought.

"I must admit, however," Mostyn continued, "that sometimes our methods must seem tactless and even forceful, but it is a means to an end that will benefit all the people of this great valley."

It was now very quiet in the large office. It was almost a hushed quiet, as though one were in a church or mortuary, Vic thought. The man evidently thought of himself as an empire builder whose methods, once proven successful to establish his purpose, would be forgotten in view of the results—results which would do Clayton Mostyn the greatest good.

"Were you offered a job on the Star Cross?" the colonel asked suddenly.

"Yes, I was, sir."

"And you refused?"

"I did."

"Why?" Mostyn mused. "Fine ranch. Fine looking woman with some breeding and education. Good stock there." He smiled again, a fixed, mechanical smile done with the facial muscles but not with the eyes, as though someone had activated a drawstring on a puppet to work the features. "It might have led into a future for you, Purcell," he added.

Vic shrugged. "Odds are that she'll never inherit the Star Cross, Colonel Mostyn. I make a practice of playing with the winners and not the losers. That's why I am here."

"Good. But you must understand that I require implicit loyalty. However, there is still the question of the assault on one of my retainers."

He sounds like a medieval lord now, Vic thought.

"I have the reports of two witnesses, of course, Purcell."

"Jack Sorley and Sid Decker—Scalp Knife men."

Mostyn fixed Vic with that staring look of his.

"Neither one of them seemed to want me to fight Page, sir. Sorley said something about a man who had been killed by Page with his fists. An older, smaller man. I..."

"Did he name the man?" Mostyn shot out.

"Yes. Harson or Hayden, something like that."

Mostyn sat down at his desk and toyed with a letter opener shaped like a saber. "I require implicit loyalty as I have told you. Buck Fresno will take you on then. On probation, of course..." Again the unfeeling and mechanical smile.

"Our rules are difficult. Our requirements are sometimes dangerous. To build an empire requires devotion, courage, enterprise and above all—loyalty! *Loyalty!* That is the key word for all employees of the Scalp Knife and of Clayton Mostyn Enterprises. Why, you may well ask?" He smiled again. "We have plans," he added softly. He turned a little to look at his particolored map. He stood up, crossed his arms in a thoughtful pose, with head bent a little. He half turned away from Vic to look sideways out of the wide window.

Vic looked uncertainly at Buck Fresno after a few minutes. Fresno placed a finger on his lips and then jerked his head toward the door. Vic glanced again at Mostyn. The man's head was bent, and he had cupped his bearded chin in the hollow of his right hand while supporting the elbow of the right arm in the hollow of his left hand. It was as though he were in deep thought far beyond mortal ken.

By *we,* he meant *himself,* Vic thought. He must think of himself as a sort of Napoleon—Napoleon IV that would be. "The Napoleon of the Rio Diablo Valley." By God, he might just be right at that!

Vic followed Fresno from the office. Buck Fresno softly closed the door behind them. He walked toward the rear stairwell. He descended the stairs and waited for Vic at the bottom of them.

"Well?" Vic asked.

"You're hired—on probation, of course."

"Just like that!"

"Just like that!" Fresno imitated Vic. "One thing the colonel didn't mention. Once you ride with the Scalp Knife you don't quit it. You might get fired, *but you don't quit it! Comprende?*

Those had been the meaningful words of Sid Decker before he and Vic had walked into the Springs and into the employ of Clayton Mostyn Enterprises.

"Any questions?" Buck asked.

"One. Was Mostyn an actor before he became an empire builder?"

"What the hell are you talking about?"

Vic smiled. "I just wondered. Where did he get the 'colonel' handle?"

"He was in the war."

"Cavalry, infantry or artillery? North or South?"

Buck eyed Vic closely, as though trying to detect any sarcasm. "Infantry," he replied. "Yankee."

"A war hero, no doubt? Perhaps a 'boy colonel'?"

Fresno shook his head. "Kansas militia. Actually he was a sutler. The 'colonel' was honorary, that was after he became an Indian Agent."

Vic raised his eyebrows. "Under the Grant administration?"

"Yes? Why do you ask?"

Vic shrugged. "Just curious." Corruption had been the name of the Indian Bureau agents during Grant's adminis-tration.

"You got any money?" Buck demanded.

"A little—damned little," Vic admitted.

Fresno took out his wallet and doled out ten ten-dollar bills to Vic. "Go get yourself rigged out in some decent-looking clothing."

"Gracias," Vic murmured.

The ramrod waggled a hand. "That comes out of your salary."

"My rifle, saddle and horse are Star Cross."

"We can outfit you with anything you need."

"When do I start work?"

"Monday morning, day after tomorrow, unless, of course, you might be needed before then."

"I'll have to return the Star Cross property."

There was an amused look in the foreman's eyes. "Why? It will all belong to the Scalp Knife soon enough."

They walked together into the saloon. Gene still sat at the rear table. Sid Decker had left but there were still a number of other Scalp Knife riders in the saloon.

"Where's Sid?" Buck asked Gene.

"Out whorin', I guess. He said he was goin' over to Belle Lestair's place for the evenin'." Gene eyed Vic. "You get taken on, Purcell?"

Vic nodded. "I passed the acid test, Kid."

"Am I free now?" Vic asked Buck.

Fresno nodded. "Just show up Monday morning. Sober!"

"What about the Star Cross stuff?"

"Take it back if that's what you want to do. Waste of time."

The foreman downed his whiskey. He wiped his mouth with a shirt cuff and looked slantways up at Vic. "By the way, if you do any drinking in Tonto Springs, you do it in here."

"Mostyn's place?" Vic asked with a faint smile.

"It's where we Scalp Knifers do our drinking, Purcell. You'll do the same."

"Safety in numbers, eh?" Vic leaned back against the bar and held up one finger to the bartender. "Might as well get started," Vic suggested with an amiable grin.

Gene reached for the rye bottle on the table, but his uncle gripped his wrist. "You've had enough for today, Gene," he said firmly. "Now, get moving."

"Along the Upper Diablo? They had a cloudburst up there and then a flash flood. Maybe I can't get through."

Fresno looked at Vic. "How's the water up there?"

"It was high, but it should be down about now. Watch out for slides on the upper slopes."

"That all, Uncle Buck?" the Kid asked.

"No! You stay away from the Slash Bar J range! I've told

you that before and you never listen to me! You got that clear this time? You don't put one gawddamned foot on that man's range! You hear me good?"

"It's shorter that way. Besides, I ain't afraid of them!"

"Well, you ought'a be! Now get moving! The boys working along the Upper Diablo will soon be short of grub."

Gene glanced at the bottle and left the saloon.

Vic downed a drink. "Nice, pleasant young fella, Buck," he observed.

Buck was too far along in his drinking to catch the subtle tone of irony in Vic's voice. "He's my favorite sister's only child. Nice kid, as you say, but only in some ways. Sometimes he can be as stupid as a gawddamned chicken in the road. I can't call him a stupid bastard because my sister was legally married to that stiff-necked Mormon Ben Kelso up in the Little Colorado River country."

Vic paid for his drink. "I'll need a horse, saddle and rifle, Buck," he said over his shoulder.

"You can get them out at the ranch Monday."

"Not if I aim to take the Star Cross stuff back. I don't like the idea of walking back here. Besides, I like to ride my own horse and saddle and use my own rifle."

"Fussy, eh?"

"I am when my life might depend upon them."

"All right! All right! Get them here in town then. Just charge them to the Scalp Knife."

"I know, it'll come out of my wages."

Buck Fresno watched Vic leave the saloon. Len Garrett, a Scalp Knife rider and one of *the segundos* to Buck, sat down at the foreman's table. "You want Jack Sorley to tail him, Buck?" he asked.

Buck nodded. "Actually he's only going to the Star Cross."

"With a good horse, a rifle and a saddle which will actually be Scalp Knife property?"

Buck bit off the end of a cigar. "You always did think small, Lennie, that's why you ain't full foreman like me."

Len shrugged. "He's hardcase though, or I miss my guess."

"He's independent too. He'll bear watching. Talked right back to Mostyn as though he was an equal."

"And Mostyn took it?"

"He did." Buck lighted the cigar.

"Why?" Len asked curiously.

"How the hell should I know!" the foreman snapped around the cigar. "Now get to hell out'a here and let me do some drinkin' in peace and quiet!"

Len walked to the bar. "Fresno seems as sore as a bear with a bee-bit behind, Baldy," he observed to the bartender.

Baldy nodded. He placed bottle and glass in front of Len. "He's worried about holdin' on to his job. He knows Sid Decker is after it," he said in a low voice.

Len laughed. "Decker? Not a chance!"

"Would you say the same about this new man— this man who calls himself Vic Purcell?"

Len glanced over his shoulder at the brooding Fresno. "I never thought of that."

"Every man like Purcell is a threat to Fresno's job. Men like Fresno and Purcell are cut from the same bolt of cloth except that this Purcell has gotten some education and is a helluva lot more intelligent than Fresno. Fresno is gettin' old and he's drinkin' too much. It's a tough job to handle men like Cass Page, Jack Sorley, Sid Decker and yourself, Len. You got to keep an eye on them and keep one jump ahead of them all the time. Let me tell you, he'll keep a close eye on this new man—Purcell."

Len studied the bartender. "How the hell do you know so much about men, Baldy?"

"I been a bartender for twenty years, ain't I?"

Lenn Garrett didn't have a rebuttal for *that* one.

CHAPTER SIX

The sun was up high and slanting its rays down through the treetops to dapple the meadowlands as Vic Jamison topped a rise and rode down a long and gentle slope toward the Star Cross ranch buildings. He led the chestnut he had charged to the Scalp Knife and wore the new clothing he had bought with the money given him by Buck Fresno. The Star Cross was about as ideal a setup as Vic had ever seen for his long-deferred dream of raising top-grade horses. There was everything on the Star Cross a man could want for his purpose—a year-round supply of grazing and good running water; game in the forests and trout in the streams; clear, winey air that made a man's head swim with the tonic of it. Vic looked up the long, forested slopes to the foothills and then the timberline and thence to the towering facades of rimrock that were the Diablos, and he felt good deep within himself.

He turned a little to glance quickly backward as he forded the stream. He was being tailed. He dismounted from the Star Cross clay bank and tethered both horses to the fence about the house. As he did so he caught a furtive movement in a *bosque* just beyond the stream.

Vic rapped on the kitchen door. Deborah opened it. "I thought you would be long gone by now, Vic," she said quietly.

"I brought back your horse, saddle and rifle."

"You could have kept them. Dad still feels that he owes you something."

"Neither of you owe me anything."

She walked into the kitchen. "There's fresh coffee," she offered over her shoulder. She seemed to want to talk to someone.

He came into the kitchen. "It's pretty quiet around the Star Cross," he commented rather aimlessly.

"What else is there to do but wait for the end?" she asked bitterly.

"I thought you had the fighting blood of old Grandfather Eb Cross in your veins, Deborah." He wasn't being sarcastic.

She studied him. "You knew about him?"

"His name was legend in this country."

"I think I must have some of his fighting blood in my veins, as you suggested, but a wise person knows the odds against himself, or herself. What can *I* do alone? You've seen Dad. You've seen the type of men who take orders from Clayton Mostyn and that Texas killer Fresno who ramrods for him. No *vaquero* in his right mind would ride for us now. *Colonel* Mostyn has virtually cut us off from the outside world, Vic."

"You'd think he'd let some men work for you. If he plans to take over the Star Cross it would be wise of him to see that it is kept up."

She shrugged. "He can bide his time. You see, Vic, we've lost a good seventy-five percent of our stock in the past six months."

He acted startled. "Not just strays?"

She filled the coffee cups. She shook her head. "We've been practically rustled out of business. What's more, if Clayton Mostyn's claims are validated he may be able to hold us responsible for the missing stock. Can you see what that would mean?"

He nodded. "Are you suggesting that Mostyn's Scalp Knife outfit is behind this rustling?"

"Who knows? It has been a gradual whittling-away process, so gradual, that at first, I thought it was normal wastage until one day I realized with a shock that several hundred head were missing. After that our losses increased in leaps and bounds. We had no one to ride the range other than a man by the name of Bass Burnett who left us a short time ago. He was old and tired and seemed always to be preoccupied with something else. The work was beyond Dad and myself. One day, before the last of our *corrida* left us, I rode into the breaks of the Diablo foothills with three riders to round up strays. Vic, we didn't find a one! Old Ben Cox, who had ridden for us for years agreed to go into the Diablos to try and track down the missing steers. He never came back. After that, we couldn't get anyone to work for us until Bass Burnett drifted along into this country. I was up there looking for missing steers when I was caught by that flash flood." She smiled ruefully. "At first I thought you were one of the Scalp Knife men."

"I don't understand why the Scalp Knife would be involved in that much rustling. Surely, they don't have to rustle to survive. Yet you seem to think they are behind it."

"No one knows, or they won't talk about it, in any event. Some used to think it was the Mormons. They used to be pretty bold about rustling until an Arizona Ranger went up that way and did some purposeful talking to the Mormon bishops. After that, *their* rustling stopped, but it didn't stop the wholesale rustling we've been faced with the past year or so.

"Some say it's the Apaches," Deborah continued. "I don't believe that. Not *that* much stock at any rate. Dad used to allow them a beef or two now and then. He said we owed them *something* for taking over their land. I think it must be the Scalp Knife, and not for profit, but rather to drive the smaller ranches out of business so Mostyn can take them over. It follows a pattern. Heavy losses of cattle. Men killed or beaten who resist them. Men frightened away from riding for the smaller ranches. None of it can be proven.

"Our position here is almost hopeless. Mostyn has a claim on this ranch, and it is a substantial claim, despite his method of procuring it. A large part of our stock has vanished. We haven't any money to get more and even if we did, that stock too would vanish. We can't get men to work for us and even if they were willing, we would not be able to pay them."

She refilled his coffee cup and looked into his eyes. "What are your plans?" she asked, almost hopefully.

"I'm working for the Scalp Knife now," he replied.

It was very quiet in the sunlit kitchen. The ticking of a waggletail clock seemed inordinately loud. A horse whinnied from the corral. A soft footfall sounded in the hallway. Vic had suspected that someone had been standing just behind the half-ajar door into the hallway.

"I see," she said quietly. "But then, it doesn't really matter does it, Vic? We couldn't have really expected otherwise."

Vic stood up. There was nothing he could say. His duty must come first, and the way of an undercover agent is always difficult. Three good lawmen had died on this particular mission and one of them had vanished into the Rio Diablo Canyon and presumably was dead. "Goodbye, Deborah," Vic said.

She studied him for a moment. For a little while she had

dared to believe that the right man had come along at last. She turned on a heel and left the kitchen.

Vic walked to the front of the house to get his horse. As he untethered the chestnut the front door of the house banged open. "Jesus God," Vic breathed. Matt Cross swayed in his stride as he walked toward the end of the porch. A double-barreled shotgun was held in his left hand. "You sonofabitch," he said flatly. "I heard what you said in there. Scalp Knife, eh?" He rested the shotgun on the porch railing. "You got the guts to draw on me, Purcell?"

Vic's guts tightened up as he saw the twin muzzles staring at him. "I only came here to bring back your horse and gear, Matt," he explained. Cross was at least half drunk.

"Then you'll come crawling back some night to put a slug through my back!" Matt accused Vic.

"That's not my way. I've got no quarrel with you."

"It's your way now whether you like it or not!" Matt snapped. "You've got a quarrel with me when you ride on my land with a Scalp Knife brand on your flank!" The rancher smiled grimly. "Even a one-armed man has a chance now against a man-killing mercenary like yourself, Purcell! Go On! Draw, damn you! I'll give you that much of a break which is more than the Scalp Knife ever gave to me!"

Vic leaped to one side and clawed for his Colt as he saw Matt forecast his movement with his bloodshot eyes. Somewhere in the timber a rifle cracked flatly. The slug skinned the post inches from Matt's face driving a splinter into the left side of it. The rancher staggered back in shock and sudden pain. Vic vaulted the fence and ran to the porch. He gripped the barrels of the shotgun to force it upward. The Greener blasted both barrels upward into the roof of the porch. Dense smoke swirled about both men.

The door banged open, and Deborah ran to them. "For God's sake, Dad!" she cried. "You're beginning to act like one of *them!*" She turned toward Vic. "Get out of here! Now!" she commanded fiercely.

Vic wasted no time. He rode off and looked back from a rise. Deborah held the old man close to her while his body was racked with drunken sobs. Vic's heart went out to them but he stifled the impulse. There was no room for sentimentality or pity in his being now.

Vic approached a *bosque* near the Star Cross—Scalp Knife line. "You can come out of there now, Sorley!" he called out.

Jack Sorley led his horse from the *bosque*. "I thought that drunken old bastard had you cold back there. You should have seen your face through my field glasses when he threw down on you with that scattergun." He grinned. "You didn't look quite as cocky then as you usually do."

"How would you have felt?" Vic asked.

"I'd be scrapin' shit out of my Levi's with a bent stick about now," Jack admitted. He mounted his horse.

"Fresno sent you to tail me?" Vic asked.

Jack nodded. "Nothin' personal, of course. You're the new boy in town. Get it?" He hooked a leg about his pommel. "I think Fresno likes you," he added.

"That's something," Vic commented dryly.

"You'd better believe it. I'll be curious to see what happens when Cass Page gets back from Holbrook and finds you ridin' for. the Scalp Knife. Mostyn doesn't allow any personal feudin' in the *corrida*. On the other hand, Mostyn has been viewin' Cass Page with some suspicion these past months. He doesn't like the way he blunders about, bein' so damned obvious. Mostyn prefers the undercover type—like you and me, for example. Wouldn't surprise me none if he didn't hand him a month's pay and maybe a bonus and tell him the hell to go and get lost. You'd really have somethin' on your hands then if Cass leaves the Scalp Knife. He *never* forgets an enemy, amigo."

Vic nodded. "I'll have to remember that." He glanced toward the butt stock of Sorley's Winchester rifle where it protruded from the saddle scabbard. "You're damned good with the long gun, Jack. I know you didn't intend to hit Cross."

Sorley shrugged. "If I had, he'd be dead by now."

"Great shooting."

"It's my stock in trade. Mostyn likes specialists. You know what I mean—Buck Fresno can handle as tough a *corrida* as ours is such as few men could do. Buck is a leader! Sid Decker is as good a man with a six-gun as I've ever seen and I've seen some of the best. Cass Page is, or was, the bruiser. That is, until you came along and beat the crap out of him. Cass used to persuade ranchers to go along with Mostyn when Mostyn wanted somethin' from them, without havin' them shot up. Len Garret is the best rider in the *corrida*. I'll swear he was born on a horse."

Vic grinned. "Quite a trick for his mother, eh? What about the Kid? Gene Kelso? Somehow he doesn't quite seem to fit the pattern of the Scalp Knife *corrida*."

"He's got two things goin' for him, maybe three. He's Buck Fresno's favorite sister's only son, and he's the best man with a runnin' iron in the Diablo country. He was in business up in the Little Colorado country when he was only a kid until the Mormon bishops straightened out the errant members of their flock. Besides, Gene's dad is a pillar of the Mormon Church. He shipped him down to Buck Fresno to get him out of the way."

"What's the third reason?"

Sorley glanced quickly about as though someone might be listening. "Buck likes the bottle too much. He sort of used Gene as his conscience at times. He'll listen to the Kid when he won't listen to anyone else. Mostyn is sure death on hard drinkin'." Jack dropped his leg from around his saddle pommel and tucked his boot toe into the stirrup. "I suddenly remembered I got a little private business of my own in Tonto Springs. I think you can make it alone from now on. Just keep away from Matt Cross and that shotgun of his. *Vaya!*" He rode down the long gentle slopes to the west in the direction of Tonto Springs.

Vic shaped a quirly. He remembered now that Buck Fresno had sent Gene Kelso east into the Diablos. Why? Buck had said something about "them boys will be running short of grub". What boys? Vic glanced up at the sunlighted facade of the Diablos. He had some time on his hands. He wasn't due at the Scalp Knife until day after next. Still, he might yet be under surveillance. Sorley's cheerful and trusting departure might have been faked to lead Vic into believing he was not being watched.

Vic rode the chestnut into the timber, but hard to the right once he was under cover and then followed the stream to the east where great sheets of rock protruded through the thin soil. He crossed the rock until he reached hard ground at a higher elevation. Several times he dismounted and catfooted back to scan the terrain through the secondhand field glasses he had bought with part of the one hundred dollars Buck Fresno had advanced him. His own fine Vollmer glasses were now somewhere at the bottom of the Rio Diablo.

Vic reached the foothills and threaded his way through them toward the Canyon of the Rio Diablo. He seemed to be the only human being in many square miles.

CHAPTER SEVEN

Vic found the corpse of the Star Cross mare half buried in the mud and slime downstream from the natural rock bridge. He took the scabbarded rifle, the saddlebags and a pommel pack from the mare. The saddlebags were well filled with trail food. The pommel pack contained a blanket, a waterproof ground sheet that could be rigged as a shelter and a pair of powerful binoculars. Deborah Cross had evidently intended having quite a stay in the Diablos. She had been hunting down those elusive strays, if one might call them that. He loaded Deborah's gear and rifle on his horse and then continued up the twisted canyon.

The sun was slanting far to the west when Vic found a pile of stale manure. He raked through the drying mass with a stick. Traces of oats showed in the pile. It was likely the droppings of a white man's mount rather than a grass-fed 'Pache mount. He led the chestnut on up the canyon until he found a set of almost washed-out hoof tracks crossing some soft ground. A shod horse and a big one at that, likely ridden by a heavy man. There were more hoof tracks, small and dainty, of two loaded burros.

The shadows had filled the canyon when he found himself looking upward at what looked like an impenetrable wall of rock. Here the canyon probed deeply into the tangled, seemingly impassable reaches of the Upper Diablo. The shallow river leaped and frothed in its mad race to reach the lower levels of the country beyond the foothills. Vic looked up at the sides of the canyon. Here and there were grim reminders of the flash flood that had overtaken both Deborah Cross and himself. Shattered tree trunks were wedged into great cracks in the canyon wall. Brush hung from ledges and crannies like the hair of those drowned. The bloated body of a coyote half protruded from a pile of stinking branches and even as Vic eyed it the body moved as though it still had a semblance of life, emitting foul gases. It served to drive Vic back out of the area, that and the distant muttering of thunder high over the Diablos. It was no place for a person to get caught if another flash flood occurred.

He led the chestnut back out of the dangerous canyon, still wondering about the hoof marks he had seen. Prospector? That seemed the only possibility. Sam Nelson had played such a part and had vanished into the Diablos, never to be seen again.

Vic followed the course of the river until he found a break in the canyon wall to the east where he could lead the chestnut up the steep, broken slopes onto more level ground, a great expanse of barren rock strewn with great boulders and slabs of rock. The sun was gone when at last he stopped for the night.

There would be a gibbous moon that night, provided the muttering of the mountain thunder was only bombast and not the forecasting of a storm. It was chancy weather at that time of the year. Vic grinned wryly to himself as he prepared his simple camp for the night—thanks to Deborah Cross and her skillful preparations for the trail. The wry grinning came about as he thought of his position. To stay down in the canyon was to invite death by flash flooding; to stay on the naked heights was to chance death by lightning.

He stretched the ground cover between two boulders, resting against a sheer wall of rock that tilted forward. He satisfied himself with a cold supper—beans and bread, washed down with the contents of a can of peaches. A cigar and a drink of rye from his flask topped the meal. He picketed the chestnut in a small box canyon a quarter of a mile from his camp where rainwater had pooled itself in the hollows and where there was enough grass growing in shallow earth pockets on which the horse could feed.

When the moon arose in a cloudless sky, he took off across the high ground toward the estimated position of the head of the Upper Diablo Canyon. It was rough going. Sometime in the geological history of the area there had been a cataclysmic disturbance that had riven and shattered the solid rock, throwing it up into fantastic formations of gigantic size that loomed over the one puny mortal who plodded across the terrain, losing and finding his way toward the northeast, only to lose his way and then find it again. It was like wandering into a labyrinth or maze designed by some superhuman wizard, for the sole purpose of showing man how puny and insignificant he really was compared to the forces of nature.

The gibbous moon was fully up and casting a soft clear light over the great Diablos when Vic sensed, rather than saw, a great opening in the living rock of the mountains somewhere up ahead of himself. He worked his way through natural passages and tunnels until at last he reached a wide area of sloping rock riven with shallow fissures and dotted with water-filled hollows, which shone like silver in the reflected light from the moon.

He knew he had been climbing steadily but had had no

idea of how high he had ascended. He knew it was at least a third of the way up the great slopes to the ultimate height of the Diablos, which afforded a tin-cut silhouette like the irregular teeth of an immense saw blade against the clear moonlit sky.

Then he saw the immense canyon spreading out before him and he had almost a feeling of vertigo when at last he stood on the brink of the canyon. To his left the canyon seemed pinched off but he was sure there was an outlet there, for a shallow, swiftly running stream bisected the floor of the canyon. To his right, at the far, or eastern end of the canyon the great walls trended inward. The feathery streak of a waterfall was centered against the eastern wall. The water plunged downward at least one hundred and fifty feet from the rim to explode into a veil of spray in a great rocky pool at the base of the cliff. From there the water flowed into the stream that centered itself the full length of the canyon.

He found a sort of a trail that descended into the canyon. It was formed from a transverse fault. He gingerly worked his way down the trail until he reached the bottom of the canyon. There was an eerie feeling within him as he stood there alone in that immense bowl. It was very quiet. There was no wind. He could not hear the falling water at the far end of the canyon. He felt as though somehow everyone else on earth had vanished and had left old Vic Jamison alone on the globe to meditate on the futility of man's existence and the myriad sins he had committed in his colorful life.

"No women, booze or tobacco," he said aloud, "Not necessarily in the order named." With that trenchant thought he sipped a little of his rye and then shaped and lighted a cigarette of Ridgeway's Fine Cut.

The moon was slanting to the west. Already the western end of the canyon had been inked in by shadows. It was time for Vic to backtrail out of the lost canyon and get back to his camp or he'd be trapped in there until daylight.

He stopped again at the top of the trail and scanned the eastern end of the canyon with Deborah Cross' excellent field glasses. Nothing moved except the plunging water, which sent up undulating showers of mist from the great rocky pool at the base of the cliff. Not a sound could be heard. The place seemed as lifeless as a lunar landscape.

He turned his back on the great canyon but even as he walked away from it, he would quickly turn now and again with the feeling that someone or something was watching him or following him. He reached his camp just about the time the moon was gone.

Vic pulled off his boots and shaped a cigarette. He lay down on the blankets and rested his head in the big cup of his right hand. He began to remember all too well the fullness beneath the wet shirt of Deborah Cross when he had dragged her from the raging flash flood of the Upper Diablo. He thought of those full lips in that mouth of hers which was a little too wide to be considered beautiful, but the objection had not come from him. He recalled how she had looked up into his face when he had drawn her close to himself to protect her from the rain and the wind. At the time, he recalled, that had been his only purpose in doing so. It was the way she had looked up at him that had suggested perhaps that she might be thinking his purpose was twofold. "Sometimes I'm not too bright," he mused aloud.

He sipped a little of his rye. In his long years of following the bitter and dangerous trails of manhunting throughout the Southwest and Mexico he had met and "loved" many women. There were only a few of them he could recall completely to memory while most of them were but shadowed faces and forgotten voices.

He recalled only too well the invitation she had

extended to him to stay at the Star Cross and ramrod the practically nonexistent spread. He had been rough on her then, *not* because he had wanted to be but because he had his work to do and there was no place in that work for a woman.

Vic closed his eyes. He had almost dropped off to sleep when he noticed the ever so faint aroma of the blanket upon which he lay—that of woman, piquant, fragrant, enticing... Even in the lonely Diablo Mountains he could not seem to get Deborah Cross out of his head.

Several times during the night he awoke and rested his hand on the cold wood and metal of his rifle as it lay beside his bed. There was nothing; that is to say, there was nothing material menacing him in the post-moon darkness, but there was a feeling... He could not explain it.

He was up before daylight. He ate a cold meal. He broke camp and cached the gear nearby in an L-shaped cave. By the time the false dawn tinted the eastern sky beyond the saw-edged silhouette of the Diablos, he was leading the chestnut through the tangled maze between himself and the rim of the lost canyon.

The early morning sun was flooding the mountain slopes when Vic led the chestnut down the precarious trail he had found the night before. Now and again a stone or rock shard would tumble or be kicked out from the edge of the trail to fall clattering far below. The early-morning wind blew through the canyon and feathered out the waterfall. A lone red-tailed hawk hung high over the canyon on motionless wings riding the strong updraft.

He swam the chestnut across the river and on the northern side of it he found hoof marks. He squatted and studied them. They seemed to be much like those he had seen the day before much further down the canyon, but he wasn't too sure; they were too faint for anything like positive identification. The burro tracks didn't seem as deep as those he had seen before.

Vic followed the faint trace of the tracks toward the sheer northern wall of the canyon. He stopped midway between the wall and the stream. The faint trace of a transverse trail switchbacked up the almost sheer wall.

Vic led the chestnut to the foot of the trail and then looked up it. "Jesus God," he murmured.

He did not look downward as he led the horse up the trail to the rim. Now and then a rock would break loose and fall far, far below, with the faint echo of its clattering bouncing back from the opposite side of the canyon. Vic led the chestnut back from the rim and off the skyline. He lay belly-flat on the rim and studied the canyon through the field glasses. It was just as empty of life as the evening before. Not even the red-tailed hawk rode the wind with outstretched wings. The only way in or out of the canyon—with the exception of the switchback trail he had just ascended and the trail on the far side which looked as though it had not been used in many years, possibly because of the difficult country at the top of it—was by the slot-like river gorge, through which the river plunged out of the canyon and roared through the gorge on its hurried way down to the lower ground and a much more leisurely way of passage.

In all the time he had been scouting about on this rugged flank of the great Diablos he had not seen any trace of mining or prospecting; no "glory holes" and no indications of any types of workings, no matter how primitive. That left the true purpose of the big man mounted on the big horse and leading two loaded burros into the reaches of the Upper Diablo.

Vic shaped a cigarette. "Gene Kelso," he said to himself. Buck Fresno's phrase came back to Vic's photographic memory: "Now get moving! The boys working along the

Upper Diablo will be short of grub." Just what type of "work" were the "boys" doing along the Upper Diablo? Vic wasn't even sure if the river flowing swiftly through the canyon with the impetus of the waterfall and the steep rate of incline was the Upper Diablo at all.

"Beats me," Vic murmured.

A quarter of a mile from the canyon he found more hoof tracks that vanished into a vast clutter of tumbled, jumbled, broken rock that trended northeast. Nowhere, at any time, had Vic found the slightest trace of cattle since he had entered the broken ground on the great slopes of the Diablos.

He worked his way toward the lower slopes through the broken fields of rock. Some of the boulders and great slabs of rock were twice the height of his head as he was mounted on the chestnut. At times he threaded narrow passageways with just enough room for himself and the horse. He knew he was trending away from a direct route to Tonto Springs and toward the north and east.

Vic turned in the saddle and looked behind himself and upward. He could see the great spiked horn of Mount Diablo to the south and east. "Where the hell am I?" he asked himself. He half closed his eyes and began to color a picture in his memory. It was of the large-scale map hanging on the wall of Clayton Mostyn's office in Tonto Springs. The greatest blocks of property had been colored in sky blue, evidently the property of Mostyn Enterprises. To the south there had been an irregular patch of pale green which had been partially cross-hatched with sky blue lines— possibly the Star Cross range, with the hatchings indicating that part of the property which was under the legal guardianship, so to speak, of Clayton Mostyn, as Sid Decker had specified. To the north and east of the Tonto Springs area was a rather large and oddly shaped patch of property colored a vivid red. If Vic's calculations were right, he would be somewhere on the border of that patch of sinister-looking red-colored property. Vic recalled the words of Bass Burnett: *"Three good ranches have been rustled and hurrahed out of business. Another one will go any day now-the Star Cross. That leaves only one good-sized one beside the Scalp Knife-Jemson's Slash Bar J, as tough a bunch of boots in one family as I've ever seen, but no tougher than the Scalp Knife corrida and a helluva lot smaller."*

"Slash Bar J," Vic murmured. An uneasy feeling came over him. He withdrew his Winchester from the saddle scabbard and rested it on his thighs.

The natural rock passageway made a sharp turn to the left and widened out somewhat. The horseman was riding toward Vic, but he had turned his head to look behind himself. His rifle too was across his thighs.

"Hold it, friend!" Vic called out.

The horseman turned with the speed of a striking diamondback and raised his rifle.

"Friend," Vic said politely and dryly, "you try to shoot that rifle and I'll put a bullet through your arm to stop you."

The man slowly lowered his Winchester. He had the look of an angry eagle about him. His beaked nose was boldly outthrust in a seamed face the color of old saddle leather. A pair of icy green eyes held the eyes of Vic Jamison. A great dragoon mustache stained with tobacco juice hung down on each side of a thin seam of a mouth. "The name is Charley Jemson, mister," he said coldly in a voice seemingly corroded from too much drinking of strong whiskey.

"Purcell," Vic said. "Vic Purcell."

"My name mean anythin' to you?"

Vic shrugged. "I've heard of the Jemson Slash Bar J."

"You're on it right now, mister."

Hoofs clattered on the trail behind Jemson. "The boys got him cornered in a box canyon, Charley!" a man yelled.

"Shut up!" Jemson snapped. "We maybe got another one here, Beck."

The man behind Charley Jemson was the sort that seems to be solidly and roughly hewn rather than grown, like most humans. He was built like Cass Page and even solider. He must have outweighed Cass by at least thirty pounds. Vic thought of the big horse mounted by the heavy man whose tracks he had found in the reaches of the Upper Diablo. Beck rode up behind Charley Jemson and eyed Vic with a pair of blue eyes that didn't seem too unfriendly.

"Says his name is Purcell. Vic Purcell, Beck. You maybe ever hear of him?"

Beck shook his head.

Jemson spat tobacco juice to one side. "Where you from? What are you doin' here? Who do you work for?" He eyed the ready Winchester, the tied-down Colt and then the lean, scarred face with the glacial-looking gray eyes.

Vic smiled a little. "Come from New Mexico over the Diablos. Damned fool that I was. I ain't working for anyone right now. Just passing through, Jemson. Peaceable-like..."

"What do you think, Beck?" asked Jemson.

Beck shrugged. "We got nothing on him. Hell's fire! How the hell else could he get out of them damned mountains unless he came this way? Come on, Charley! Carl and Billy got him cornered. We been waiting for this to happen for months."

Jemson shifted his chew. "There's something about this jasper I don't like."

Vic grinned. "You don't exactly appeal to me either, Jemson. Be that as it may, I've got no hard feelings."

Jemson looked away from Vic. He shifted in his saddle. "Make room for the man, Beck. He wants to get by."

Vic shook his head. "After you, gentlemen."

Beck grinned. "He's got a point there, Charley."

Charley Jemson kneed his horse around. He looked back at Vic with those frosty green eyes of his. "You just keep on ridin', *Mister* Purcell. You just ride right off the Slash Bar J and *stay* off. The next time you might not be so lucky."

Vic watched the two of them ride back down the widening passageway. He followed them after a time and when he reached the more open terrain, he saw the two of them riding fast to the north and east. In the distance he saw several other horsemen. Vic wasted no time in getting to hell off the Slash Bar J Range. He looked back once or twice wondering who it was they had "cornered". Vic had the feeling that whoever *he* was was in for a bad time.

CHAPTER EIGHT

Vic Jamison Reached Tonto Springs and placed the tired chestnut in a livery stable. He crossed the street and bought a bottle of brandy, cigars and cigarette makings, then entered the Tonto Springs House and indulged in the luxury of a room with bath. He went to the room, stripped down to the buff and then soaked in the bathtub with a cigar cocked up out of the side of his mouth and the brandy bottle resting on the floor beside the tub within easy reach. He then trimmed his beard and lay down on the double bed. He reached over and withdrew his Colt from its holster. He placed the six-gun under his pillow and dropped off into a dreamless sleep.

The insistent tapping on the door awakened Vic. The room was dark. "Who is it?" he called out. He reached under his pillow and withdrew his Colt.

"Len Garrett, Purcell. One of Fresno's *segundos*. Buck Fresno wants to see you in about an hour."

"This is still Sunday. I ain't due to work until tomorrow."

Garrett laughed. "You ain't been with the Scalp Knife long enough to know that when you're wanted, you're *wanted*. I'm heading out to the ranch now to round up some more of the boys. Get over to the Springs when you're ready, prepared to ride. You got the message?"

"Keno!" Vic said cheerfully.

Buck Fresno sat at his usual table in The Springs. He looked up as Vic entered the saloon. "You sober?" he asked sourly.

Vic nodded.

The foreman studied him. "Where'd you go last night?"

"Went up into the Diablos looking for my horse and gear."

"That's loco!"

Vic shrugged. "Had a good Frazier saddle on him and a new Winchester."

"You find them?"

Vic shook his head.

"What happened at the Star Cross yesterday?"

Vic knew, of course, that Fresno had probably heard the story already from Jack Sorley. "Matt Cross threw down on me with a shotgun when he heard I was going to work for the Scalp Knife."

"Maybe you should'a killed the old drunken sonofabitch. That was your chance." The foreman's speech was slurred from too much drinking.

Vic shaped a cigarette. He shook his head.

"Why not?" Buck challenged. "He threw down on you first, didn't he?"

"I didn't have any orders from you to get rid of him." Vic lighted the cigarette and looked sideways at the foreman. "Besides, if I had orders, I wouldn't have done it."

The cold eyes narrowed. "What the hell do you mean? If I give you an order to kill anyone, you better do it..." The man's voice trailed off as he realized how neatly he had been trapped by this easygoing, smiling stranger.

"There are easier and less obvious ways," Vic continued. Vic looked at the bartender. "Beer," he ordered.

"Take it easy on the booze," Fresno said.

"I can hold it, Buck."

Fresno opened and then closed his mouth. He had been wondering all day long *why* he had taken this man up to see Mostyn. Mostyn had recently called him down several times in private for too much drinking and for not using more subtle and devious ways to carry out his orders. Besides, having Sid Decker and Len Garrett as *segundos* didn't help much. Both men were after his job, and they were both capable enough men. Now this Vic Purcell had shown up, rather mysteriously. He looked and acted all right but that wasn't the point. Buck's uneasy sixth sense warned him against this man. There was a bitterness in Buck Fresno. In the early days of the Scalp Knife, he had been like Mostyn's good right arm and Mostyn would never have progressed as far as he had without the backing up of Buck Fresno. Now that Mostyn was well on the way to his "empire"—as he sometimes referred to it in private, and *only* in private—he seemed more and more dissatisfied with Buck Fresno.

Sid Decker walked in. "Rye, Baldy," he said to the bartender.

"You know your limit, Decker?" Fresno asked.

Sid eyed him. "I always know *my* limit, Buck."

The inference was obvious. Buck would not look away from his *segundo*. His eyes were like chips of glacier ice, but he said nothing. He got up from the table. "I'll be out in the street when you gentlemen finish your social drinkin'. Butgawddammit!! Snap it up!" He pushed his way through the batwings.

Jack Sorley looked sideways at Vic. "Be careful of him, Vic. He's not as sober as he acts. He ain't supposed to drink at all, leastways on the job. If he isn't careful, he'll lose his job, at least as foreman. Watch him tonight. He can be damned dangerous to a friend or an enemy alike when he gets that way."

They rode from Tonto Springs. When the moon tinted the eastern sky beyond the Diablos, Buck Fresno forded a stream and drew rein on the far side. "Keep quiet. No smoking," he ordered the others as they crossed to his side of the stream.

"What's up, Buck?" Sorley asked as he dismounted.

"My nephew Gene ain't showed up all day. I sent Art Scott out hours ago to look for him and he ain't showed up either."

"You don't suppose the Kid went wanderin' on to Slash Bar J land like he done a few weeks past?" Sorley asked.

Buck didn't answer. He walked on into a thick stand of timber.

"Jesus," Jack Sorley breathed. "Gene was supposed to have gotten that grub into the boys in the Upper Diablo country and then come right out and stay off of Slash Bar J range."

"What happened a couple of weeks ago?" Vic asked.

"Damned fool had a runnin' iron with him. He can't seem to get over the bad habits that he got run out of the Little Colorado River country for. Couple of weeks ago, he almost got caught by the Jemsons when he was changin' a brand, against strict orders from Buck. He just made it back to Scalp Knife range ahead of a cupful of .44/.40 slugs. If those hardcase bastards had been able to catch him, they would have branded his fat ass with his own runnin' iron. Them Jemsons are *badddd* medicine!"

Hurried hoofbeats thudded on the ground beyond the stand of timber. Buck Fresno came catfooting back out of the timber. He fanned out his hands and the others spread out with ready rifles.

The horseman appeared in the dimness.

"Hold it right there!" Buck ordered.

"It's Art Scott, Buck!" the horseman called out nervously.

"Where the hell you been?"

Scott swung down from his mount. "Jesus! You gave me a start. I thought it was the Jemsons."

"You see the Kid?"

"Damned fool got caught this time," Art Scott explained. "I spent most of the day back in the *malpais* land figuring that's where the Kid would have ended up if he had come out of the canyons. I saw the Jemsons at a distance and they were sure as hell hunting something! Then I saw the Kid hotfooting it away from them and I thought he got away from them, but he didn't."

It was very quiet in the timber. Now and again a horse would stamp its hoof. Buck Fresno walked to the edge of the timber and looked toward the *malpais* land as though he could see through the darkness and find his errant nephew.

Vic remembered the exultant words of the man named Beck: "The boys got him cornered in a box canyon, Charley!"

"Maybe they turned him over to Sheriff Baggott, Buck," Sid Decker suggested slyly.

The foreman turned. His face was a set mask. "That ain't funny, Decker! Not by a damned sight! If he had, Baggott would have turned him loose long ago." He looked suspiciously at Scott. "How come you're just coming out of the *malpais* land now?" he demanded.

"First chance I had, Buck. Had to wait until darkness."

"Where'd they take him?" Buck asked.

Art Scott shrugged. "Ain't sure. I think I saw them taking him into Caballo Canyon. I didn't see them bring him out though."

"Goddamned idiot!" Sid snapped. "Ain't got the brains to pound sand down a rathole! Stupid sonofabitch!"

"Decker!" Fresno shouted.

"Well, it's true, isn't it?"

"Gene is my sister's boy!"

"I ought to know, Buck."

The foreman stalked stiff-legged toward Sid Decker.

"I ain't going to take no whipping from you, Buck," Sid warned.

Fresno stopped. "Who runs this *corrida?*" he demanded.

"You do, Buck."

Both of them had been doing some heavy drinking. Vic knew now that Buck was almost out of control from his drinking.

Buck tilted his head to one side. "You always did want my job, eh, Decker? Only you ain't man enough to come right out and say so. Ain't that the way of it?"

"You're doing the talking," Sid replied evenly.

There was a long pause as the two hardcases faced each other, neither one of them willing to back down and lose face.

"This ain't exactly the time and place for a showdown between you two," Jack Sorley suggested.

Horsemen rode through the timber on the far side of the stream. "It's Len Garrett and Jody Barnes!" Len Garrett called out. "We could hear you clear back to near the road."

"Call it quits, Buck," Sorley said.

"You keep out'a this!" Buck warned.

"You're letting the booze talk now, Buck," Decker said.

"Why, gawddamn you!"

"Sid is right, Buck," Vic put in.

Buck turned slowly and looked at Vic. Vic did not turn away. Buck nodded slowly. He swung up onto his horse and touched him with his spurs. He rode on into the timber.

"Close, that," Jack Sorley suggested to Vic.

"I've never seen one closer," Vic agreed.

In twenty minutes, Buck drew rein. A barbed-wire fence stretched in front of him. "Lenny," Buck said over his shoulder.

The tall Texan dismounted and cut the strands of wire so that the others might ride through. The foreman halted his horse and drew his Winchester from the saddle scabbard. He levered a round into the chamber and the rest of the men followed suit. The foreman rode on into the pre-moon darkness followed by the others. Half a mile beyond the fence Buck stopped.

"How far are we from the Slash Bar J?" Vic whispered to Jack Sorley.

"We've been on it ever since we come through that fence. I think Fresno has slipped a cog or somethin'."

"Purcell! Take a pasear on foot along that draw there," Fresno ordered.

The moon was now flooding down the western face of the Diablos. Vic handed the reins of his horse to Jack Sorley. He removed his spurs and placed them in a pocket. He walked toward the draw. Once he looked back and saw the Scalp Knife men silently sitting their horses with their loaded rifles resting across their thighs and their hard eyes watching one— Vic Jamison.

An uneasy feeling came over Vic. Maybe they hadn't come onto Slash Bar J land just to rescue Gene Kelso and roust the Jemsons. Maybe the story about Gene being caught with a running iron had been pure fabrication. No one could have been *that* stupid. Maybe they had found Vic out. Maybe this was the Vic Jamison's execution. *Ley del fuego!* Let a prisoner run and then shoot him down as he ran.

"Andale!" Buck snapped.

How much did Buck Fresno know? The thought was like a worm of fear in the back of Vic's mind. Forty yards from the waiting Scalp Knife riders he paused in his silent striding. Something had warned him, that honed sixth sense of the professional man-hunter.

There was a movement in the timber. Vic raised his rifle.

"Don't shoot! For God's sake don't shoot!" Gene Kelso called out in an agonized tone of voice.

"It's Vic Purcell, Kid!" Vic called out.

Vic looked closely at the big young man as he stumbled closer. There was something different about his face and his hands seemed to be gloved as he held them straight out in front of himself. Then Vic knew the truth. Gene's hands were black with thick dried blood and his face had been burned on the left side. Vic looked closer. A Slash Bar J brand had been burned cleanly into the cheek.

"They never turned me over to the sheriff!" Gene screamed. "They branded me with my own iron and they busted up my hands! *Lookit my hands!*"

Buck Fresno galloped up to them and reined in his mount to a sliding halt. He swung down from the saddle. His lean gray face worked as though there were moving wires beneath the taut skin. His eyes glittered like rime ice. "It's that bastard of a Charley Jemson!" he grated between his teeth. "Jack!" he yelled back over his shoulder. "Get this boy to a doctor right away! Likely he'll be scarred for life."

"There's his horse," Len Garrett said. He rode to the big gray and led it back to the Kid. Gene was hoisted up into the saddle. He sat there, hunchbacked, with his poor mutilated hands resting on the saddle horn. Bright tears coursed down his cheeks.

"Did you get them supplies into the boys, Gene?" Buck asked.

"No. I figured I'd take the Slash Bar J strays in with me. Them Jemsons took the burros and the supplies."

"They ask you where you was going with them?"

Gene nodded. "But I didn't tell them. I said I was goin' to supply some of our line shacks. They believed me. At least I *think* they believed me. Did I do all right, Uncle Buck?"

"You damned idiot! You can't do *nothing* right! Jack, you

get him to a doc and then get back to the ranch. Get two burro loads of supplies and get them into the boys."

"*Tonight?*" Sorley asked incredulously.

"Tonight! Gawddammit! Now git!"

Buck looked at his men. "Likely Jemson planted them strays so this young idiot could find them—like a bait. It would be like him to sucker the Kid in like that. He's smart! Oh, he's slick as goose grease all right."

"They was all there!" the Kid cried. "Old Man Jemson, young Billy Jemson, Jemson's nephew Carl and his son-in-law Beck Paulson. I tried hidin' in the *malpais* land and almost got away from them but then Billy and Carl trapped me and the old man and Beck Paulson came ridin' up. I just thought they was goin' to whup me and then run me into Sheriff Baggott, but they messed up my hands and branded me with my own runnin' iron!" His voice rose into a scream and then broke piteously. "What's more, they said to tell you and Colonel Mostyn that they'd do the same to any Scalp Knife rider they'd find on Slash Bar J land and they'd ear-notch him as well with a cornet-split like they do their own cows!"

"Get him out'a here, Jack!" Buck snapped. He looked about himself a little wildly. "We'll give them Jemsons a hurrahing tonight they won't expect. He won't expect us on a Sunday night."

"After what he did to the Kid?" Sid asked. "That's loco!"

Buck Fresno did not reply. He mounted and rode down into the draw. The others followed him.

"I don't trust that Texas sonofabitch," Sid Decker said privately to Vic.

"It's only a hurrahing," Vic said. He wasn't so sure about that.

"Sure! The hurrahing is fine. Jemson has been long overdue for one, but we've never been able to catch him flat-footed. Seems like nothing we can do will force him to sell out to Mostyn. Mostyn has tried everything, and it's been no go. Mostyn finally offered him a high price for the place, far more than it's worth, maybe triple the value, but that old catamount won't give in."

"So Mostyn seems to be fighting a losing battle against the Jemsons."

Decker looked sideways at Vic. "He finally *convinced* Mawson of the Rocking M and Keith of the Tumbling K. Jemson is a horse of another color. The trouble is that Jemson's Slash Bar J is right in the path of Mostyn's planned expansion to the northeast."

"So Jemson has to go."

Sid nodded. "Mostyn practically has the Star Cross in his back pocket. Once we whip Jemson and finish off Cross there won't be anyone standing in the way of the Scalp Knife. Some spread, eh? It's more than just a spread, Purcell. A man who sticks with Mostyn can make something out of himself. He's going a long ways."

The man was doing well despite the liquor he was carrying, but he was talking a little too much.

"A man like you, eh, Sid?"

"And you too, if you play the game right. I'll need a few good men to back me some day."

"When you take over Fresno's job?"

Sid shrugged. "It's bound to happen. Fresno's time is about over around here. Mostyn needed him when there was violence and shootings. Once Mostyn gets what he wants out of this valley he'll turn completely respectable overnight. Then he'll have to get rid of such men as Cass Page, Buck Fresno and that damned idiot Gene Kelso."

"You keep riling Fresno, and he'll get rid of you first," Vic warned Sid.

Decker shook his head. "I'm too smart for Fresno. Mostyn will need shrewder men around him in time. He's got big ideas for the future. *Big* ideas... He's thinking far, far ahead."

"To what?"

"He's got friends in Prescott and in Washington and he's gaining more influence with them every day. That man wants power! Mark my words. Someday he'll be governor, then perhaps senator, then after that, who knows? You get it? Now you know why I aim to stick around after Fresno is gone. Mostyn needs smart, slick men around him."

"Meaning you, of course."

"Exactly! Maybe even you, Purcell. You got rough edges and a chip on your shoulder, and you don't give a goddamn who you rile, but you play your cards right and stick with me, and you'll see."

Vic grinned. "Loyalty! That's the key word, eh, Decker?"

Sid Decker seemed to swell up a little bit. "You got the idea! That's all I ask out of a man."

Vic passed a big hand over his face to hide his expression. It seemed as though Mostyn, the big frog in the little puddle, and Decker, the little frog in the big puddle, had somewhat the same ideas. *"Gracias,"* Vic murmured.

"Por nada," Decker responded.

CHAPTER NINE

The Scalp Knife Riders drew rein on a tree-shrouded ridge overlooking the Slash Bar J spread. Buck Fresno studied the ranch buildings through his field glasses. "I want the shit shot out of that place," he said. It was almost as though he were talking to himself. "I don't want a window-busting, bullet-hole-shooting hurrahing. I want to put the fear of God into them Jemsons. There's likely only four men down there."

"Don't forget Stella Paulson," Len Garrett suggested. He grinned. "I used to play in the feathers with her before she married that jackass Beck Paulson. By God, I heard she told him she was a virgin and he believed it!"

"Shut up!" Fresno snapped.

Sid Decker lowered his field glasses. "I don't think we'll fool that old copperhead Jemson, Buck," he warned the foreman. "He isn't stupid. He knows the store you set on Gene. He likely rooked Gene into coming onto his range by setting out a few head of cattle playing like being strays. Maybe right now he's setting up a trap for the rest of us."

"He ain't that smart!" Buck rapped out.

"I say we call it off," Decker suggested.

"I told you before that I'm ramrodding this outfit. Now you get going! You and Lenny cross the road into that *bosque* over there. Get a clear line of fire on the house. In exactly twenty minutes, both of you open fire and give 'em a full magazine! Shoot the shit out'a them! Keep firing for about fifteen minutes and then haul your asses out of there and make damned sure you don't ride directly back to the Scalp Knife. Got it? *Bueno! Andale!*"

Len and Sid vanished into the shadows along the ridge. Sid Decker drew rein when out of sight and hearing of Buck Fresno. "This is loco, Len," he said in a low voice.

"Keno," Lenny agreed. "What's got into Buck anyways?"

"Booze mostly."

"By God! That's what I been thinking ever since we started out. You think Mostyn knows about this?"

Sid shook his head. "He'd have stopped Fresno right off. Maybe fired him."

Lenny nodded. "Jemson ain't stupid, like you said. He knows the store Buck sets on Gene. I wouldn't put it past that slick coyote Jemson to figure we might come in here like a lot of stupid sheep and walk right into a trap like you said."

"I think the both of us have enough sense not to open fire," Sid suggested. He slanted his eyes sideways at Lenny.

"Shit on Buck and his revenge," Lenny agreed.

"Let's get out of here. Pronto!" Sid urged.

"What happens when Buck comes back to the Scalp Knife? He'll be wild, amigo."

"What makes you think they're coming back?"

There was no answer from the tall Texan as the two men rode off into the shadows of the thick timberland heading for the Scalp Knife line.

Buck Fresno ground-reined his horse in a draw and catfooted through the shadows followed by Vic, Jody Barnes and Art Scott. They waded a shallow stream and stood in the shadow of an outbuilding. Fresno nodded. He climbed a sagging stake-and-rider fence and walked swiftly toward the big barn followed by Vic. Vic glanced back over his shoulder. Barnes and Scott were nowhere in sight. If Buck and Vic had to pull foot in a hurry, they'd have a hell of a time getting back to the horses. The thought of Gene Kelso's branded face and broken hands came into Vic's mind in chilling fashion.

Fresno eased open the rear door of the barn. Vic followed him inside. "Where's Art and Jody?" the foreman demanded.

Vic shrugged. "Pulled foot, I guess."

"Them yella sonsofbitches! They never did have any guts."

Fresno climbed a ladder into the loft. Vic ascended the ladder. The foreman was making it just that more difficult to get out of there in a hurry.

Buck eased open the hay door that had a clear view toward the big ranch house. He grinned wolfishly back at Vic. "They make a break from that house, and we can cut 'em down like scything ripe wheat."

"I thought this was just a hurrahing."

Fresno shrugged. "It was just a thought."

Minutes ticked past. Mice rustled in the hay. The wind hummed softly through the locked windmill blades. Now and again, Buck Fresno would glance toward the dark and silent *bosque* across the road. "What the hell is the matter with them?" he growled.

"Give them time," Vic whispered.

"They've had enough time!" Fresno snapped. He shifted and looked toward the house. Suddenly he stiffened. "By God," he whispered hoarsely. "I plumb forgot about them damned lion-hunting dogs of Charley Jemson's!"

Vic felt cold all over. He had been wondering about dogs

around the ranch. They should have been heard or scented by a good dog before now.

Fresno stood up. "Jemson has four or five of them. Big, ugly brutes that can tear a cougar apart with their teeth. I seen them do it once. Where are they now?" Some of the alcoholic fighting guts seemed to have run out of the man.

Cold sweat began to run down Vic's sides. Sweat greased his palms against his rifle.

"Where the hell are Sid and Lenny?" Buck husked. "Where are them damned dogs?" He quickly wiped the sweat from his face. "Let's get to hell out'a here!" He plunged back through the thick hay and scuttled down the ladder. He waited for Vic at the bottom of the ladder. "Take a pasear outside," he ordered. He turned and opened the rear door.

Vic eased through the doorway and peered around the side of the barn. "All clear," he whispered back over his shoulder.

"It's too goddamned quiet," Fresno whispered nervously.

There was the stabbing of rifle muzzle flame and the almost instantaneous flat crack of a rifle from the timber. The slug slapped into the barn wall between Vic and Buck.

"Run, you sonofabitch!" Vic barked as he fired high over the place where he had seen the rifle flash.

Fresno ran awkwardly toward the stake-and-rider fence. Vic fired another round and then raced after Fresno. "Not that way!" Vic yelled. "Get beyond the corral!"

The foreman ran toward the corral, crawled between two of the lower peeled poles and then ran clumsily through the mud and manure toward the far side of the enclosure. Vic fired again into the timber and then legged it after Buck. Buck scaled the far fence and fell from it into the muck on the other side of it. Fear and booze were making a tanglefoot out of the tough Texan.

Another sound came to join the cracking of the rifles. It

was the deep-throated baying of hounds—a sound that sent an icy chill up Vic's spine and into his guts. Five huge hounds had been released from the kitchen door of the house and were plunging toward the corral. There was a young and buxom woman standing behind the racing hounds and she was laughing uproariously. Vic fired, dropping the first of the hounds.

Fresno turned. "The bitch!" he yelled. He raised his rifle and fired.

The woman spun sideways, gripping her left arm. She went down on her knees and Buck Fresno's second round of flat-nosed .44/.40 smashed into her face and flung her backward into the mud. Fresno vanished into the timber.

Vic whirled and dropped another hound. He hurled himself over the corral fence. A bullet plucked his Stetson from his head. He plunged into the shadowed timber. A rifle flashed near the barn. Vic dropped into a draw and ran to where the horses had been tethered. Both horses were gone. The distant sound of hoofbeats came to Vic. He splashed across the stream and ran into the timber on the far side of it. The eerie howling of the pursuing hounds carried clearly.

Vic plowed across a rain-soft meadow into which his boots sank as though into glue. He reached a loop of the shallow stream and waded up it while casting anxious looks back across his shoulders. A man shouted in the timber on the far side of the stream. Hoofbeats sounded in the distance. The sound was drifting away from Vic.

He waded from the stream and struck off toward the east and the distant moonlighted foothills. Buck Fresno had killed the woman deliberately. *That had been no accident!* His first shot had put her out of action. There had been no need for the killing shot. To kill a woman made it far worse. It didn't matter who or what she was in life—whore, drunkard, slattern or anything else disreputable; it was sufficient that she was a woman, and in that time and that country it was an unspeakable crime for which there was no pardon.

Further, thought Vic, Buck Fresno had abandoned him, the very man who had saved him from the vengeful hands of the Jemsons. God would have been of little help to Buck Fresno back there if they had captured him. If they had mutilated Gene Kelso, as they had done, just for using a running iron on their stock, their vengeance on Buck Fresno would have been horror indeed.

The moon was on the wane when Vic reached the foothills, hopefully far from the Slash Bar J range. He looked up at the moonlighted Diablos as he worked his way toward the south. Somewhere up there in the rock mazes and tangled, almost impassable canyons and gorges was perhaps the secret of the lost Star Cross cattle. Gene Kelso had failed in his mission to bring supplies into the "boys", whoever *they* were, and by now perhaps Jack Sorley was likely riding into those canyons with supplies for them.

Somehow Vic had to get back up in there again to check out the "boys". He needed a horse, and he would have to get it back at the Scalp Knife. He had a little vague evidence against the Scalp Knife after the aborted hurrahing of the Jemsons, but none of it bearing on the missing cattle and the murdered lawmen. Too, the only evidence he had was against Buck Fresno and *not* against Clayton Mostyn. Mostyn was the big fish. It was Clayton Mostyn that Vic Jamison had to land.

CHAPTER TEN

The moon was gone when Vic walked down the road from the foothills toward the Scalp Knife spread. A dog barked somewhere in the darkness and an uneasy feeling came over Vic. His memory of the savage hounds at the Jemson's ranch was still too fresh. He neared one of the outbuildings. Something grated on the ground.

"Just drop that rifle, mister," the voice came out of the shadows.

"I'm Vic Purcell. I was hired by Buck Fresno to work for the Scalp Knife," Vic explained.

"I know all about that." A short, broad-shouldered man came out of the shadows. "Where you been, Purcell?"

"Who are you? What's it to you?" Vic asked.

"The name is Bert Hanna. Colonel Mostyn is waiting to see you at the house."

Vic started forward.

"Wait," Hanna ordered. "Drop that rifle. Let me have that six-gun."

"What the hell!" Vic cried.

"You got some talking to do up at the house. Now get along! Pronto!"

There were four saddled horses tethered to the fence rail in front of the house. A man lounged against one of the porch posts. "That Vic Purcell, Bert?" he asked.

"It's him all right, Taylor." Hanna laughed. "Walked right into my hands."

"Take him in then." Jim Taylor opened the front door. A dimmed lamp stood on a hall table and the odor of tobacco smoke drifted down the hallway to Vic. He was escorted into the large living room and then Bert Hanna closed the door behind Vic.

Clayton Mostyn stood near the fireplace. A heavyset, rather handsome man gone to big belly flesh on a well set-up frame stood in the center of the room with a cigar in his hand. He studied Vic. The lamplight reflected from the polished sheriff's star he wore on his coat lapel. Beyond the sheriff were Buck Fresno, Len Garrett and Sid Decker.

"This is Sheriff Baggott, Purcell," Mostyn said quietly. "He wants to ask you a few questions."

"Where have you been, Purcell?" the sheriff asked.

"Walking back to the Scalp Knife," Vic replied. He glanced at Buck Fresno. There was no expression on the Texan's hard-set face.

"Where were you?"

Fresno moved a little. His eyes held Vic's. He nodded a little as though to let Vic know that it was all right to tell the lawman where he had been. There was a dead woman lying in her blood on the Slash Bar J and Vic was likely the only witness that Buck Fresno had shot her down.

"Well?" Baggott asked.

"Answer him!" Mostyn demanded.

"You were on the Slash Bar J, weren't you?" Baggott asked.

"Yes," Vic agreed. He could hardly lie out of it.

"What were you doing there?"

There would be no help from Buck Fresno, Sid Decker and Len Garrett. They would cover each other about the murderous incident at the Jemson spread.

Baggott reached into a deep chair and brought up Vic's stained and battered Stetson. He poked a blunt finger through a black-rimmed hole in the crown. "This yours, Purcell?" he queried.

There was no use denying it. Vic's assumed initials were inked within the sweatband. "It's mine," he admitted.

Baggott shifted his cigar from one side of his mouth to the other while he ruminated. "There was a hurrahing over there early this evening," he said at last.

An ember snapped in the fireplace. A boot scuffled in the hallway. Buck Fresno coughed.

"You know anything about it?" Baggott asked softly.

"I didn't kill or wound anyone, if that's what you mean," Vic explained.

Baggott raised his eyebrows. "How did you know anyone was killed or wounded, Purcell?"

Vic looked at Buck Fresno. "Buck Fresno can tell you about it," he suggested.

"He's a damned liar!" Buck snapped. "I'll admit I got riled up because of what the Jemsons done to my nephew Gene. We rode over there, me, Sid Decker, Len Garrett, Jody Barnes, Art Scott and Purcell there. All we figured on doing was to shoot them up a little as a warning. Sid and Lenny didn't do any shooting. They got suspicious because of the quiet and took off. Art Scott and Jody Barnes done the same. Me and Purcell went into the barn. They turned their dogs loose and I took off, but Purcell stayed behind. I heard a lot of shooting. That's all I know."

Vic looked at the expressionless faces of Sid Decker and Len Garrett. They hadn't seen what had actually happened.

Buck Fresno was the only one of the Scalp Knife riders who had been in sight of Vic all the time. It was his word against Vic's, and Vic knew damned well how much weight his word would hold against Buck Fresno's around the Scalp Knife and before the sheriff, who, according to Matt Cross, was on Mostyn's payroll.

"Purcell?" Baggott asked.

Mostyn likely had too much control over Baggott for Vic to reveal himself even secretly to the sheriff as an Arizona Ranger.

"I didn't kill that woman," Vic insisted.

"How did you know it was a woman who was killed?"

Vic had neatly trapped himself. The odds were rising against him. They were neatly weaving a rope for his neck.

"He did it all right," Fresno insisted.

"But why, Purcell?" Baggott asked. "Did you know Stella Paulson?"

"Never saw her in my life."

"Maybe she just got in the way of a stray bullet, eh?"

"I suppose that was the way of it."

Baggott tossed the hat into the chair. "She was hit twice. Once in the arm and once through the face for a killing shot. Seems deliberate, doesn't it?"

There was no chance for Vic. They had neatly hung the murder on him. The Scalp Knife men could even deny he had been hired by them.

The sheriff relighted his cigar. He pointed it at Sid Decker and Len Garrett. "I'm deputizing you two men to take this man, Vic Purcell, into Tonto Springs jail until such time as he can be removed to the county seat."

Vic knew he'd never reach Tonto Springs alive.

Vic whirled, driving a left into Len Garrett's lean gut. He slammed a hooked right against Sid Decker's jaw to knock him sideways against the sheriff. Buck Fresno clawed for his

Colt, but Vic came up off the floor with a driving boot heel that caught the Texan in the privates. As Fresno's head came forward, Vic clasped his hands together and smashed them down on the nape of Fresno's neck while at the same time bringing a knee up into the foreman's face. Fresno fell to one side as limp as a rag doll.

Clayton Mostyn yelled in panic. He whipped out his stingy gun from the half-breed shoulder holster but the lean fighting man in the midst of the Scalp Knife gunslingers was just a little too fast. One hand knocked the hideout gun to one side and then a rocky fist drove against the side of Mostyn's jaw, driving him back and seating him on the embers of the fireplace. He screamed in pure agony as the glowing embers seared through his trousers seat.

Vic hurled a chair at Sid Decker. He upended a table between himself and Len Garrett. He hurled a lamp at Sheriff Baggott. The shattered cylinder splattered burning oil across the room and the flimsy curtains on a side window caught fire.

Vic crossed his arms in front of his face and charged full tilt against the front window. The big window glass crashed outside as Vic went through the opening. Vic rolled up onto his feet and ran toward the front of the house to where the horses were tethered. The man named Taylor rounded the corner with ready rifle. Vic gripped the barrel of the Winchester and forced it up and to the right as he raised a hard knee into Taylor's groin. The man went down groaning. A boot heel against the jaw kept him down for the long count.

Vic ran to a horse. He fired a slug through the front door of the house and then mounted the horse. He drew his sheath knife, cut loose the rest of the horses and then slapped wildly about with the butt of the rifle to stampede them. Vic hammered past the bunkhouse. Lights flicked on inside of it.

A bullet crashed through a window and the light went out. Vic turned in the saddle and fired five rounds rapidly in the general direction of the buildings, and then was on the road making time for the darkened foothills.

In an hour the lathered horse was blowing hard as Vic reached the mouth of a canyon. He slid from the saddle. He whacked the horse across the rump with the barrel of the Winchester and then loped up the canyon like a hunting lobo. He worked his way over steep and crumbling slopes with his breathing coming short and harsh in his dry throat. Somewhere far behind him a rifle cracked. He hoped to God they were chasing his riderless horse. He drove himself on and on, working his long legs like pistons, until he reached the high ground where he dropped flat on his face and heaved out his guts.

CHAPTER ELEVEN

THE STAR CROSS ranch buildings were dark and silent when Vic Jamison came through the misty timber an hour before the dawn. Low pools of wooly white mist hung in the meadows. Vic worked his way under cover until he could see the rear of the barn. The corral was empty. Perhaps Deborah and her father had finally abandoned the ranch. He placed an ear against the rear wall of the barn. He was rewarded by hearing shod hoofs striking the hard-packed earth of the barn floor. He softly slid back the rear door and entered the darkness of the interior. He catfooted to the front of the barn and peered through a wide crack in the wall. The house was still dark and quiet.

Vic swiftly saddled the clay bank he had once borrowed from the Crosses. He led it to the rear door of the barn and slid back the door to step out into the darkness.

"Stand where you are!" Deborah Cross commanded out of the darkness. There was the crisp metallic working of a rifle action.

"I only wanted to borrow the horse, Deborah," Vic explained. It didn't sound very convincing.

"You might have asked for it, Vic."

"Not after the reception I got from your father the last time I was here."

"You're working for the Scalp Knife."

"Was," Vic admitted dryly. "I had to leave there in a hurry."

"That's sort of the story of your life, isn't it?"

"Look! I only need the loan of this horse and not a damned sermon!"

"What happened over at the Scalp Knife?"

He grinned faintly. "Let's just say we didn't get along."

"Wasn't there something about a murder over at the Slash Bar J?"

He was startled. "How did you know that?"

"Deputized Scalp Knife riders were here not more than an hour ago looking for you. I had a feeling you'd show up here sometime. You don't seem to have anyone else left to turn to."

He moved so quickly she didn't have time to resist. He twisted the rifle from her hands and then pulled her inside the barn. He slid the door shut. She struggled in the strong crook of his left arm. "Dammit!" he snapped. "Stand still! I'm not going to hurt you! Those killers might still be out there!"

"Killers? *You* call *them* killers? What about yourself?"

"I did not kill that woman," he insisted firmly. "It was Buck Fresno that killed her."

"You're lying! Buck Fresno was one of the men who came here looking for you."

"That figures. He's got to make sure the murder is pinned on me and he's going to make damned sure my mouth is shut forever."

"You're on the run again! You're always on the run!"

Vic drew her close and kissed her hard. For a few seconds she resisted him and then she pressed against him and slid her arms about his neck. Then, just as quickly, she withdrew her arms and stepped back from him.

For a moment, he studied her in the dimness and then he clambered up the ladder to the loft. He cat-footed across the hay-littered floor to the hay door at the front of the loft. He peered through the partially opened door. He could see the meadow beyond the corral backed by the dark line of timber, with the soft wooly mist drifting tenuously about the trees. There seemed to be a deadly waiting quality in the darkness, almost as though some grim hunting animal was out there somewhere, watching and waiting to strike swiftly and kill without mercy.

He came down the ladder. "Nothing," he reported. "And yet..." He shook his head. "How many of them were there?"

"Five," she replied.

He tilted back her head and looked into her eyes. "I'm on the run all right," he admitted. "But not the way you think. Would you believe me if I told you I was an Arizona Ranger working undercover to get evidence against the Scalp Knife and other rustlers and killers here in the Rio Diablo country?"

"That's a whopper," she said dryly.

"It's true," he insisted.

"Then you've done a great job so far."

He grinned at the jibe. "I'm not done yet. The others who tried before me are dead or missing without trace. It's dangerous work and the price is high."

"Prove that you are a Ranger," she challenged him.

He shrugged. He slid his fingers down inside his left boot into the pocket within the lining and retrieved his commission. He thumb-snapped a lucifer into flame and held it over the commission so that she might read it.

She looked up into his eyes. "It could be a fake."

"You're a trusting soul," Vic murmured.

"If it *is* true, what do you plan to do now? You've got the Scalp Knife *corrida* hunting for you. Fresno said Sheriff Baggott was forming another posse to hunt for you. They said Charley Jemson has sworn to kill you on sight. My father has said the same thing."

He grinned. "Popularity, popularity..." he murmured. "The story of my life. It's this blasted irresistible charm of mine."

"Run! Isn't *that* your way of life?"

"You know I did not kill that woman and that my work here is not done."

"You haven't a chance, Vic! Run! Get out of this country! Have them send in another Ranger."

He shook his head. "Can I take the clay bank?"

"Of course."

He eased open the door and led the clay bank out of the barn. The wind was dying away fitfully, feeling about uncertainly, not quite sure of where and when to blow and preparing to shift with the coming of the dawn. Vic suddenly raised his head. A shift in the wind had brought a faint sound to him.

"Deborah," Vic called softly.

She came up behind him. "What is it?"

He pointed toward the darkness of the timber. Something was moving slowly through the mist and swirling it about in the process. The shadowy shape, of the upper body of a man appeared half out of the mist. A rifle was in his hands. Vic led the clay bank into the timber behind the barn. "Where's your father, Deborah?" he whispered.

"Asleep in the living room. Dreaming of the past. That room *is* his past."

"Stay here," he ordered. He drew her close. "Listen to me. If anything happens to your father and me ride out of here and keep going until you reach Globe. Report what has happened to the Rangers there."

"What's wrong, Vic?"

"I think the Scalp Knife *corrida* has returned."

Vic bellied out of the timber until he reached the front porch of the house. The wind brought the faint sound of metal striking metal somewhere near the corral. He crawled to the front door. It opened at the touch of his hand. He could see the red ember eyes on the broad fire hearth. The draft from the open door swirled the ashes and embers and brought forth flickers of flame that danced along a partially burned chunk of log to partially illuminate the big room.

"You looking for me, Purcell?" the cold voice asked.

Vic turned quickly. Matt Cross stood near a front window. He was gun belted with his holster at his left side and with his one hand resting on the pistol butt.

"Cross," Vic said. "I've come from Deborah. The Scalp Knife *corrida* is outside, closing in on this place."

"Looking for you?"

"Yes."

"Why don't you go out and face them?"

"They might be after more than just me, Cross."

"I can take care of my own, Purcell!"

"You're loco!" Vic snapped. "Come on! There isn't much time!"

"Get out of my sight! You make me sick to my guts!"

"We can settle our differences later, Matt," Vic pleaded.

"Get to hell away from me!" the rancher cried.

A rifle slammed outside. The slug smashed through a window not a foot from Matt Cross and struck the big, unlighted Argand lamp that stood on a marble-topped table in the center of the room. The oil reservoir was punctured as the impact of the heavy bullet drove the lamp from the table onto the rug. Oil spread quickly from the shattered reservoir. A spark leaped from the burning log in the fireplace onto the oil. The oil flared up and the fire spread quickly. The flames rose higher and higher to touch the fringe of the table runner and then swept across the table. Pieces of burning fringe scattered here and there on the rug to start little fires of their own.

"Come on, Cross! Damn you!" Vic yelled.

Another shot punctuated the quietness outside. The slug struck the heavy stone fireplace and ricocheted. The mutilated slug struck Matt Cross in the chest with the sound of a stick being whipped into heavy mud. Cross staggered sideways clawing for his Colt. Vic caught him as he fell. Another bullet slapped into Matt's back as he stood there in Vic's arms, starkly silhouetted by the rising flames. Sparks swirled about and settled on the big horsehair settee.

The flames ate swiftly into the taut dry fabric. Matt fell from Vic's arms. His Colt clattered to the floor.

Bullet after bullet struck the house, shattering through the windows and crashing into the interior walls. Matt's clothing began to burn. Vic slapped at the flames. Matt opened his eyes. "I'm done, Purcell," he said thickly. He coughed and a bright spate of crimson flooded from his slack mouth. "Get her out of here, Vic." A slug struck the old man in the side of his head as Vic tried to pull him to his feet. He was gone.

Vic snatched up Matt's Colt and ran to the hallway. Thick acrid smoke swirled about in the blazing living room. Slugs whined through the shattered windows. Vic darted left into a bedroom and crawled through a partially opened window. He crouched down in some shrubbery. A man fired at Vic from near the barn. The barn itself was alight with bright flames. It was a real hurrahing—Scalp Knife style.

Vic crawled through the shrubbery. A rifleman arose from the shrubbery near the fence and looked toward the house. Vic fired and dropped him back into the shrubbery. Vic ran for the fence and vaulted it, to land flat on the ground as bullets swept through the air where he had just cleared the fence. Vic crawled into the timber. He waved Deborah back into the shadows and then snatched the Winchester from the saddle scabbard of the clay bank. He rapid-fired into the timber beyond the house. A slug knocked a running man off his feet.

"Where's Dad?" Deborah cried.

Vic reloaded the hot Winchester.

"Vic?" she called out.

Vic turned a smoke-blackened face toward her. She saw the answer in his eyes. "The Star Cross is gone, Deborah," he said. "Lead the horse through the timber. Then ride toward the creek. I'll follow along." He bellied through the timber as she led off the horse. The firing had died away. The firelight glistened on the staring eyes of a dead Scalp Knife rider. The roof of the house collapsed into a roaring mass which drove a great gushing of gas and smoke upward. Smoke and fat sparks whirled out from the incandescent column and settled on the outbuildings. The first faint gray traces of dawn showed in the eastern sky above the serrated heights of the Diablos.

Vic catfooted through the timber. She stood beside the clay bank on the far side of the creek. He waded across to her. A searching wind swept through the timber and swayed the branches. He tilted up her face and gently kissed her. He gave her a leg up into the saddle and she rode along beside him as he loped through the woods. The smoke from the burning buildings had mingled with the drifting mist, and through this pall they were unseen by anyone back around the buildings.

She looked down at him once. "It's all right, Vic," she said. "He had stopped living long ago. I don't think he ever wanted to die in bed."

By the time the dawn light came down the western facade of the Diablos they had reached the line shack where they had spent the night together. They gathered the food, blankets, a tarp, a lantern, oil, matches, candles, a hand axe and anything else they thought they might be able to use. Vic shaped cantle and pommel packs. The sun was driving away the morning mist when Vic and the girl moved out across the meadowland toward the first breaks of the foothills.

Vic halted the clay bank on the highland west of the Little Diablo. He walked back and looked down the long sunlighted slopes toward the far distant meadow and the shack. The sun reflected from something bright near the shack. Something moved about on the meadow. They were mounted men.

Vic shaped a cigarette. The hand of every man in the Diablo country now seemed turned against him. There was no way to break out to the north, west or south. His only retreat could be into the Diablos. He also had the girl to think of now. He had plenty of evidence against the Scalp Knife now except for the unsolved murders of the lawmen and the rampant rustling.

Vic went back to Deborah. "We're trapped now," he told her. "If you like, you can go down the mountain and risk the chance that they won't harm you. Other than that, you'll have to risk going deeper into the Diablos with me, like hunted animals, until we can find an escape route. Right now, our main and only purpose is to stay alive."

She shook her head. "I'm not going down that mountain." She studied him closely. "There's something else, isn't there, other than just staying alive?"

He nodded. "Somewhere in these mountains may be your Star Cross cattle and the rustled cattle of other ranchers. That is, unless they've been driven from there into New Mexico, or possibly down south. I doubt that. The Rangers would have located any stolen cattle that came from here by now. By God, Deborah, if I can locate those cattle it would likely put a clincher on the evidence I already have against the Scalp Knife and Clayton Mostyn."

"We," she said simply.

He looked quickly at her. "What do you mean?"

"We'll find them together."

"It's too dangerous for you."

She shook her head. "You'll need someone to back you, Vic. I can do that. If you'll have me."

He kissed her. "I don't know of anyone else I'd rather have," he said quietly. He grinned. "You're really the granddaughter of old Eb Cross, aren't you?"

They climbed back into the broken hills until they reached the canyon country and heard the muted roaring of the Upper Diablo echoing back from the stark heights that seemed to have no way past them, trending on for many miles to the south, while to the north the cliffs died broken in a mammoth welter of shattered rock, stunted trees and thorned brush, mixed with twisted and box canyons.

As the day began to die Vic found a trace that allowed them to ascend a torturous way to higher ground that leveled off into a broken-edged mesa. Vic found the L-shaped cave where he had cached Deborah's gear. It was protected by a rampart of broken rock, while within twenty feet of the cave mouth was a shallow *tinaja,* or rock pan that was evidently kept filled from some underground source. Vic tasted the water and found it good. They dumped the packs and the saddlebags within the cave, and then Vic picketed the clay bank a quarter of a mile from the hideout in a box canyon that had some grazing and shallow pools of rainwater.

Vic came back to the cave in the gathering darkness. "Cold fodder tonight," he said. "No fire for heat or cooking."

She nodded. "And it will be a cold night up here on the heights."

He lighted a candle in the long arm of the L and shielded

it from outside viewing by hanging up the tarp. "Not bad quarters, at least for a drifter," he announced cheerfully.

"I thought you said you weren't a drifter, Vic."

He hunkered down and shaped a pair of cigarettes. "Not a saddle tramp, if that's what you mean, but a drifter just the same. My work makes it necessary."

"Being a Ranger?"

He lighted the cigarettes and placed one between her full lips. "That's only temporary, Deborah."

"What else do you do?"

He shrugged. "I've been a soldier, a rancher, an army scout, a Texas Ranger for a time. I've hunted for lost mines and treasures. I've fought in revolutions."

She watched him as he grew silent. "That's not what I meant," she said at last.

He looked up at her and into her great eyes.

"What is your real work?" she asked.

"Manhunting," he replied.

She saw the scarred face and the hard gray eyes that seemed able to probe into the very heart and soul of a person, and a faint shadow of fear seemed to drift through her mind.

"Have you ever thought of settling down?" she asked.

He shrugged. "At times. It never lasts very long."

She looked about the cave. "It's snug in here," she said to change the subject. "We can fix it up in the days to come."

"No. We'll have to keep on the move. I want no settled base. There's plenty of water available up here and we have enough food for a week at least, on short rations, of course." He looked up at her. "Do you think you could make it to Globe on your own?"

"I'm not leaving you."

"It will be hard and dangerous work, for a woman at least."

"My pregnant grandmother came into this country riding

on a broken-down buckboard with all her worldly possessions in one small rawhide trunk and a few potato sacks. She spent her first winter on what is now the Star Cross living in a tent, and my father was born in that tent and my grandfather did the delivering. Does that give you an idea of my background, Vic?"

He studied her with the soft candlelight limning the hollows and facets of his lean hawk-like face. "These mountains could be a death trap for us," he reminded her. "I don't want you to play the role of the heroic pioneer woman, Deborah."

"You don't know me very well," she chided him.

"I think I'm beginning to, a little, at least."

She began to open a can of beans. "It seems to me that you're the one playing the heroic role."

"It's not heroic, but it is my profession. I'm going to stay here until the job is done."

She nodded. "Agreed. Now how about digging out some more grub?"

When they had finished eating the cold fare, he draped a threadbare blanket about her shoulders and placed the Colt in her lap along with some extra cartridges. "There will be a moon," he told her. "I'm going to take a pasear outside. Sit tight. If anything happens, don't come running."

"Stay here," she pleaded.

He shook his head. "Don't be afraid. The time to look for an enemy is before he comes looking for you." He blew out the candle and then pulled aside the tarp. He vanished into the pre-moon darkness.

The Diablos were still shrouded in darkness, but there was a faint trace of the rising gibbous moon limned along the serrated rim of the mountains. Vic felt his way along the dangerous ground until he reached the canyon of the Upper Diablo. By the time he reached the natural bridge the moon was haloing the tips of the mountains with silvery light.

There was an unnatural stillness about the night. It was almost as though *someone,* or *something* was brooding in the shadows and watching one Vic Jamison, the manhunter. Suddenly he raised his head. A moment later, he vanished into the rock tangle beyond the natural bridge as silently as drifting smoke.

A hoof rang like a cracked bell against the rock. The dim shape of a horse and rider seemed to rise up into sight as though string-manipulated by a giant marionette master somewhere up in the sky. The horseman halted the horse and began to fashion a cigarette. A match flared and was cupped about the tip of the cigarette. The man wore a white bandage aslant over his left eye. There was no mistaking the broad and brutal-looking face of Cass Page.

Vic knew why Page was in the Diablos. He might still be working for the Scalp Knife, and then again he might not, but in either case he was hunting for the man who had cost the sight of an eye—Vic Jamison.

Cass Page rode slowly up the gorge of the Upper Diablo. Now and then he would look behind himself, as though suspicious that someone was there.

Vic swiftly scaled the high ground behind the gorge. He listened for the hoof falls and catfooted just back of the rim of the gorge following along after Page until the sound of the hoofs died away. Now and again, he would peer down into the gorge but there was no sign of Cass Page. He reached the broken northern rim of the mesa and looked down into the canyon wherein tumbled the feathery waterfall of the Little Diablo. A lone horseman sat his mount in the swiftly growing moonlight. He looked about the lonely and isolated canyon. Even as Vic watched Cass Page the man turned his head and looked directly up at the rim almost as though he knew Vic was up there watching him.

Vic slid back from the rim. He kept off the skyline and worked his way two hundred yards toward the east. He peered between two boulders. He narrowed his eyes. Cass Page was no longer in sight. Vic looked across the canyon toward the steep switchback trail. There was no one on it. Page would hardly have had time to return the way he had come but it might have been possible.

Vic returned to the gorge of the Upper Diablo. It was now flooded with moonlight. There was no one there.

CHAPTER TWELVE

The pattering of rain awoke Vic an hour before the dawn. Deborah was still asleep. He sheathed his Colt and left her own Winchester beside her. He took the tarp he had found on the body of her drowned mare and cut a slit in it for his head and then draped it over his shoulders poncho-style. He took her field glasses and left the cave.

The rain came down a little heavier as he neared the mesa rim. He could hear the muted roaring of the Upper Diablo as it surged over the canyon rim and plunged down into the great rock pool at the base of the cliff.

The canyon was empty of life. He worked his way toward the east where the falls plunged over the rim. Beyond the upper river was a sheer facade of rock rising high into the rain-veiled air. He followed the south bank of the rain-swollen Diablo for a mile until he saw where it emerged from the dark low mouth of a cave, at the bottom of a sheer two-hundred-foot cliff that towered up into the mingled mist and rain.

He turned back and walked to the rim. He descended the

mesa side into the gorge of the Upper Diablo and then followed it upstream into the empty canyon where the waterfall plunged from the rim. By late afternoon he was no wiser than he had been that morning.

Vic climbed the switchback trail to the north rim and found a place where two great tip-tilted slabs of rock formed a shelter from the steady drizzle of the cold rain. He shaped and lighted a quirly and sat there like a joss Buddha, draped in the wet tarp, his face immobile and with a faint wraith of tobacco smoke about his head. He was *na-tse-kes,* as the Chiricahuas would say—turning one thought at a time over and over again in his mind to the exclusion of all others. No parts of the puzzle he had found so far seemed to fit together. Somewhere, perhaps within a few miles of him, was the key to the damnable puzzle of where the rustled cattle had been driven and hidden.

The wind shifted. A horse whinnied in fright. Vic was up and out of the shelter, trailing his rifle, in a matter of seconds. He went to ground in a hollow, inches deep in cold rainwater not twenty yards from the top of the trail. Even as he lay down, he saw a wet hat rise as though by magic from the trail, followed by the head and shoulders of a slickered man. The man turned to drag on the reins of a horse. The head of the bay horse appeared, and he was led back from the rim, trembling with fright.

The man turned back toward the mesa rim, pausing to roll a cigarette. He was Jack Sorley. He lighted the cigarette and then disappeared down the trail. A burro brayed down on the trail and the sound was echoed by another burro. Sorley reappeared leading two burros whose small hoofs clattered on the rim-rock. Both burros were fitted with kyack packs but the packs were empty. Something came swiftly back to Vic. Buck Fresno had ordered Jack Sorley to take supplies in to the "boys" after Gene Kelso had failed in that mission. It was obvious that Jack *had* taken the supplies somewhere but now the kyacks were empty. Sorley was evidently on the way back to the Scalp Knife. He wouldn't likely know about the hurrahing at the Slash Bar J and the fact that Vic was now on the run from the Scalp Knife *corrida* and the sheriff's posse.

Vic took a chance. "Jack! Jack Sorley!" he called out.

Sorley whirled to reach for his scabbarded Winchester.

"It's Vic Purcell, Sorley! Take it easy!"

"Show yourself!"

Vic stood up and grinned friendly-like at the rifleman.

Sorley was suspicious. "What the hell are you doin' up here?" he demanded.

"Buck Fresno sent me up after you. Said I was to go in and give the boys a hand."

"So?"

"My horse fell and broke its leg."

Sorley eyed the ragged tarp. "Where's your hat?"

"Blew off in the gorge."

Sorley grinned. "You look like hell." He lowered the rifle. "How did the hurrahin' go?"

Vic shrugged. "All right."

"Fresno was pretty drunk," Jack reflected. "I was damned glad to get out of that one."

"How's Gene?"

"He'll be scarred for life. I don't know about his hands." Sorley glanced slantways toward Vic as he turned toward one of the burros. "You'll have to ride this burro. Maybe you'd better come out with me and get another horse and start out again in the mornin'. It'll be pitch-dark in there in an hour."

Vic shook his head. "I got my orders to go into the boys. I ain't about to go back to Fresno and tell him I let my horse break a leg up here."

"You've got a point there. Well, you can get a horse in there." Sorley took the kyacks from the back of the biggest burro and threw them over the empty kyacks on the back of the other burro.

"How's the trail in there?" Vic asked.

"All right. Wet as usual."

Vic hesitated. "Can you give me an idea on how to get in?" he asked.

"Didn't Buck tell you?" Sorley asked over a shoulder.

Vic grinned weakly. "I forgot."

Sorley nodded. "You look like you could stand a drink."

"You're on, Jack."

Sorley suddenly whirled and then worked the lever of his rifle. The first shot crashed out and the slug whipped through the air where Vic's head had been an instant earlier. The second slug ricocheted from the rocky ground right where Vic had dropped only to roll quickly away from it. Vic snapped out a shot to bother Sorley and then rolled into the hollow. Sorley darted behind his bay. When Vic peered out of the hollow there was no sign of Sorley.

Vic crayfished back toward the rim. A rifle crashed. The slug picked at the back of Vic's improvised poncho. A thin wraith of gun smoke drifted through the rain from a clump of brush fifty feet from the bay. Vic shrank down into a cleft right at the lip of the rim. Sorley had not been taken in by Vic's improvised story. He might have believed the first part of it, but when Vic had probed him about the way into the "boys" he must have known damned well that Vic didn't *know* the way, and that he had never been told the way by Buck Fresno.

Vic let himself down into the bottom of the cleft. Sorley fired a shot. The slug bounced from rock and hissed off across the canyon. The echo died away. Vic looked down into the canyon and his guts tightened. He stripped off the poncho and tore a strip from it which he used to improvise a rifle sling. He slung the Winchester across his back and then trusted his weight to a narrow, crumbling rock ledge. His powerful fingers felt along the cliff face for cracks, and he began to inch his way toward the switchback trail. Now and then bits of rock broke off and dropped far below. Vic reached the trail and dropped flat on it to get back his breath and regain his courage. If Sorley looked over the rim, he'd have Vic trapped cold. Vic bellied along the trail until he found a transverse fault. He wedged himself into it and worked his way up until he could crawl out onto the rim a good fifty yards from where he had gone to ground at Sorley's first shot. He crawled belly-flat into a thick clump of bear grass. He eased his Winchester forward.

There was no sight or sound of Jack Sorley. Finally, Vic's probing eyes settled on the tip-tilted slabs of rock beneath which he himself had earlier taken shelter. The shadow within the opening was darker than it should have been. Vic flipped a small rock over the rim. It rattled on the trail. Sorley's head and shoulders appeared within the rock shelter. He raised his Winchester and peered toward the canyon rim.

Vic fired. Sorley whirled, firing as he did so. The .44/.40 slug almost parted Vic's hair. Sorley went to earth. The gun smoke and echoes drifted off. It was very quiet.

Vic softly cursed himself. He had missed his chance and now Sorley knew where Vic lay hidden. Kill or be killed—that was the law now. *It's him or me now*, thought Vic, *and it won't be me*.

There was the faintest of movements within the rock shelter. Vic aimed at the slanted inner rear wall of the shelter, perhaps a yard above Sorley's prone body. Vic fired. The slug slapped into rock. Then it was quiet again except for the increased pattering of the rain. Minutes ticked past.

Vic wormed his way through the bear grass and into a hollow. He looked into the shelter. Sorley lay still on top of his rifle. Vic walked to the shelter. "Jesus," he breathed. The soft .44/.40 slug of two-hundred grains had caromed from the rock wall of the shelter right into the back of Sorley's skull, taking out a piece of it about the size of half a saucer.

Vic dragged Sorley into the open and rolled him over. He stripped the body of slicker, bloodstained and bullet-holed Stetson which lay to one side, gun belt and Colt, as well as Sorley's Durham Pride tobacco. He shrugged into the slicker and put the hat on his wet head. He dragged the body back into the shelter and then worked at one of the slabs until it fell inside on top of Sorley. He piled rocks on top of the improvised tomb.

Vic shaped a cigarette from Sorley's tobacco and lighted it. "The Tonto Springs whores will miss you, Jack," he murmured.

One of the burros had strayed. Vic lead-roped the remaining burro to the bay's saddle and then led both animals down the crumbling trail in a swift, blinding downpour of cold rain. He halted at the bottom and studied the canyon. The pounding rain had effectively washed out any tracks. Where had Jack Sorley come from? It wasn't likely that he had come from the canyon of the Little Diablo. There was no place south and west of the gorge where cattle could be hidden. There was no trace of any other human beings along the canyon route.

A rumbling sound came from behind Vic. He turned to see great shards of the cliff face above the switchback trail peeling off from the rim to fall crashing down on the trail. Vic sprinted out into the open leading the frightened animals away from the falling rock. Tons of rain-loosened rock fell heavily onto the trail and wiped it out completely. The burro broke loose from the lead rope and galloped off into the rain shroud, braying his lungs out.

Vic worked downstream toward the gorge mouth. Dusk was thick on the mountains. The rain slanted coldly against his face as he worked his way along the slippery rock banks of the Upper Diablo. He was fifty yards from the trace that led up to the top of the mesa when the bay whinnied sharply.

"Just stand right where you are, mister," the cold voice commanded from the other side of the stream.

Vic edged behind his bay and raised the rifle. Vision was difficult in the rain and the dusk.

"I got the bulge on you! Just throw down that rifle and come out into the open grabbin' air." The voice was vaguely familiar to Vic. "I ain't alone, mister," the unseen man warned Vic. "Just you throw that rifle into the clear!"

Jack Sorley's Winchester was in the saddle scabbard on the same side of the bay where Vic was standing. He tossed his Winchester out into the open.

"Go get him, Carl!" the hard voice ordered.

Carl? The name touched a memory chord in Vic's mind. Carl Jemson maybe? *Jesus God,* thought Vic. The unnerving thought of what the Jemsons had done to Gene Kelso rankled through Vic's mind. "Are you Charley Jemson?" Vic called.

"No, I'm Beck Paulson."

"Then you don't want me, Paulson."

"You're Vic Purcell, ain't you?"

"Yes."

"You're the sonofabitch who shot down my wife!"

"Who told you that?"

"Sheriff Baggot."

"You ought to know what a liar that bastard is. He'll do or say anything Clayton Mostyn tells him to."

"Keep talking," Paulson said dryly. "I almost believe you."

"It's Buck Fresno you want," Vic explained.

Boots thudded on rock to Vic's left. A man walked toward Vic. He was young. Maybe Carl Jemson, Charley Jemson's nephew.

Paulson whistled sharply. His rifle blasted once to awaken

the gorge echoes. Likely a signal for the rest of them, thought Vic. How many of them were there? Vic knew of the vicious old man himself, his nephew Carl, his son-in-law Beck Paulson and young Billy Jemson, Charley's son.

"I don't like this, Beck!" Carl called out.

"Get over there!" Beck shouted. "He ain't got his rifle now and his six-gun is likely under his slicker."

Slowly Vic eased Sorley's Winchester from the scabbard. He had no quarrel with these men, but he would be damned if he'd let them get their hands on him, at least after what they had done to Gene Kelso.

"Where's Uncle Charley?" Carl called out nervously. He seemed to be scared of Vic.

"Go on, boy," a chilling voice said from the shadows behind Carl Jemson. "I'm here, nephew." It was Charley Jemson.

Carl stumbled over Vic's Winchester. When he looked up, he stared right into the muzzle of another Winchester held in Vic's hands. The lever was snapped down and up again. "Get back!" Vic ordered.

Beck Paulson fired across the narrow river. Vic whirled, fired once over Paulson's head to keep him down, levered a fresh round into the chamber and swung back again to cover Carl, but the kid had lost his nerve and was running awkwardly in his spurred boots along the mud-slippery rock bank of the river. He lost his footing and plunged sideways into the stream. "Uncle Charley!" he shrieked just before he went under the water.

A tall, hook-nosed man came plunging out of the shadows. He raised a rifle to fire at Vic.

Carl's head bobbed up. "I can't swim!" he yelled.

Charley Jemson danced sideways to get a clean shot at Vic.

Vic darted forward. He reversed the Winchester and

brought the butt against the side of the old man's head. As Jemson went down, Vic hurdled his body and then ran alongside the river. He dropped the rifle and then dived cleanly into the water. He came up to the surface and swam with powerful strokes, aided by the rushing current, until he could reach out and grab Carl's thick hair with one hand and a rock spur on the bank with the other. He shoved the kid forward —toward the bank. "Grab a hold!" he yelled. Carl gripped the rock spur with both hands and Vic lost his hold. He was swept downstream. He caught hold of a log that lay half in and half out of the water and managed to pull himself out onto the rocky bank where he lay exhausted, his breathing coming harshly and erratically from his squared mouth.

Vic heard footfalls on the rocky ground. He slewed his eyes sideways and then upward to look into the cold bearded face of Charley Jemson. The old man reached down with a strong gnarled hand and pulled Vic up to his feet.

Beck Paulson ran downstream and crossed the river on the natural bridge. He ran along the bank toward Vic and Charley Jemson. "You ain't going to kill that man, Charley!" he yelled.

Jemson spat to one side and wiped his mouth with the back of a hand. "Sonofabitch raised a welt on the side of my head," he growled.

"He saved Carl's life, Charley. He could have got away instead," Beck argued.

Charley Jemson looked at Beck. "Don't you think I know that?" he demanded. He looked at Vic. "You all right?"

Vic shrugged. "A little damp, is all, Jemson."

"You've got guts," Jemson grudgingly admitted.

"What happens now?"

"I would have killed you back there but now I owe the kid's life to you. I'll take you back to Tonto Springs for a fair trial. That's the best I can do."

"You figure I'll get one there?"

Jemson shook his head.

"Wait," Vic said. He reached down inside his boot and withdrew his commission. He unwrapped the oil cloth covering. Beck Paulson lighted a match and Jemson and he read the commission in the hand-cupped light. The old man looked up from the commission and into Vic's gray eyes. "What's the truth behind the killin' of my daughter?" he asked.

"I was with the Scalp Knife men when they came to your spread. I was working undercover trying to find out who was doing all the rustling and killing in the Rio Diablo country. I had to go along with the hurrahing. I didn't kill your daughter, Jemson. She was murdered by Buck Fresno. He tried to pin the murder on me." God help Vic if Jemson and his Slash Bar J riders were behind the rustling and the killing.

The hard blue eyes of the old man held the hard gray eyes of Vic Jamison. "You've got guts, Jamison," he said at last. "I don't believe a man like you would have murdered a woman in cold blood."

"*Gracias,*" Vic breathed.

The old man waved a hand. "Por *nada.* I'm going to risk letting you go. But, before God, if you're lying to me, and you did kill Stella, I'll track you down and kill you if it takes me the rest of my natural life. You understand?"

"Fair enough," Vic agreed.

They walked back to the horses. Vic thrust Jack Sorley's Winchester into the saddle scabbard. He picked up the other Winchester. He looked sideways at Charley Jemson. "Where to?" he asked.

"To find Buck Fresno and kill him."

"You may have to wait in line. Listen, Jemson, all you'll do is start a war between yourselves and the Scalp Knife and they'll be bound to win one way or another. Besides, they're backed by Sheriff Baggott and his deputies. Even if you beat the Scalp Knife in battle, you'll lose in court."

"What the hell do you want me to do?" Jemson demanded.

"Sit tight. Spread the word through the valley that you killed me here in the Diablos. If and when I finish my work in here, I'll need some affidavits from you and your family to back me up."

"It ain't my way!"

Vic turned slowly. He held the old fighting man eye to eye. "It *is* your way, Jemson."

"*Who* says?"

Vic held up one long first finger. "I say!"

Jemson stood there for a moment. "All right! All right!" he snapped. "Come on, you two!"

The Jemsons walked into the darkness to get their horses.

Beck Paulson looked back over a shoulder. "First time I ever seen anyone tell *you* what to do, Charley."

Jemson looked back toward Vic. "He's a fighting man," he said quietly. "I think law and order is on the way to the Rio Diablo country."

Vic wearily led the bay to the top of the mesa. He picketed the horse in the box canyon with the clay bank and then walked back through the chilling rain to the hideout. He whistled softly. She came to him through the rain and gripped him tightly while she pressed her face against his chest. He picked her up and carried her into the hideout. They would risk a fire that cold night.

He stripped to the skin while the fire gathered heat in the cave. She eyed him in the firelight, noting the puckered bullet holes in his skin. "Where did you get the horse and the rifle?" she asked.

He wrapped a blanket about himself. He shaped a

cigarette and placed it between her lips. "Courtesy of Jack Sorley," he replied at last.

"Where is he?"

He lighted her cigarette. "He'll never bother us again." He grinned as he shaped a cigarette for himself. "Neither will the Jemsons." He told her of what had happened.

She shuddered a little. "Maybe we can leave these mountains now, Vic." She saw the look on his scarred face. "All right," she said quietly. "I should have known better. But I'm not going either."

She cooked their meal. The fire light died down. The rain was slamming down on the rocky ground outside the cave and tapping impetuously on the tarpaulin.

She came to him in the dimness.

CHAPTER THIRTEEN

Vic was up in the cold darkness before the dawn. He made fire and while he was making up the packs Deborah brewed the coffee. "We'll move north," he told her. "I've lowered the odds, a little at least. Jack Sorley and the Jemsons are no longer against us. All that leaves are the Scalp Knife *corrida,* Baggott's posse and Cass Page. I..." Immediately he sensed that something was wrong. He turned slowly to see her staring at him.

"Cass Page?" she said. "You didn't tell me about him."

"Forget it," he said quickly.

"No, Vic! Is that man in these mountains looking for you?"

"Yes," he admitted. "I lost sight of him in the canyon north of us. I don't know whether he is still with the Scalp Knife or if he's working alone. Likely he's left, in any case."

She pulled on her boots. "No! He's still around. I know that man. He'll never rest until he can get at you. He means to maim and kill you."

He filled their coffee cups. "I can do a little maiming and

killing myself if I have to." It was no use. He could see the lurking fear in her eyes.

Vic loaded the cantle and pommel packs on the two horses in the faint light of the dawn. Together he and Deborah led the horses toward the canyon rim. The feathery white falls had a ghostly quality in the darkness of the canyon. As the light grew, Vic studied the canyon bottom through the field glasses. He could see the burro that had broken loose grazing near the great *tinaja* at the foot of the falls. He studied the far rim for a time and the collapsed switchback trail. He looked again toward the *tinaja*. The burro had vanished.

"Loco," Vic murmured.

"What is?" she asked.

"There was a stray burro near the *tinaja*. He broke loose in the canyon yesterday. Now he's gone."

"I saw him too. He must still be down there."

He handed her the glasses. "See for yourself."

She shook her head after a time. "This doesn't make sense. He couldn't have reached the canyon entrance in that short period of time. We would have seen him if he had tried for the entrance."

"He'd never be able to make it up that trail, if he's still hidden somewhere down there."

They rode the horses back toward the gorge of the Upper Diablo and then descended to the gorge. They led the horses upstream to the canyon entrance. Vic led the way to a stand of stunted timber close under the south wall. "Stay here," he ordered her. "Keep under cover." He took the field glasses and his rifle and walked along the base of the southern wall toward the falls.

He skirted a wild tangle of fallen timber and shattered rock. The growing sunlight reflected from something white. Vic worked his way through the interlocked branches of the

trees. A skull grinned up at him from a litter of animal-scat-
tered bones. Moldy clothing and leather gear lay about the
bones. A broken Winchester thickly scaled with rust lay to
one side. The sun shone on a tarnished brass belt buckle. Vic
picked it up. The initials B.C. had been embossed on the
buckle. "B.C.," Vic mused. "Couldn't mean Before Christ."
Something tripped the sear of his memory. "Old Ben Cox,
who had ridden for us for years, agreed to go into the Diablos
to try and track down the missing steers. He never came
back," Deborah Cross had once told him.

Vic picked up the skull. He turned it over. The back of
the skull revealed a ragged hole big enough for Vic to thrust a
fist through. "Big bore soft-nose probably at short range," Vic
mused. "Maybe a .50/.95 Express. He likely never knew what
hit him."

Vic kept on to the east until the roaring of the falls
drowned out the wind song. He found the little sharp tracks
of the grazing burro and a pile of fresh droppings. He looked
about. "Where in hell are you, jughead?" he asked. All other
tracks had likely been pounded out by the recent heavy rains.

Vic paused on the rim of the rock *tinaja*. It wasn't very
deep. The falling water boiled up from within the curved
bottom of the rock pan and flowed over the edges of it. A
mist of cold spray blew about Vic. He looked about at the
ground. There was a soft patch of spray-wet ground. Sharply
incised in it were the dainty hoof prints of a burro—facing
the *tinaja*.

Vic shoved back his hat and eyed the falls. He walked to a
cleft and placed his weapons and gun belt within it. He
stripped to the buff and then picked up his Colt. He waded
into the *tinaja* shivering in the cold blast of the falls. The icy
water rose about his privates. "Jeeeeesus!" he gasped.

Suddenly he was under the falls and then beyond them
with a great dark void ahead of him, but he seemed to

imagine a vague lightness deep within the darkness. The water shallowed to knee-deep and the distant light grew, and then he realized he was wading in a rock tunnel perhaps thirty to forty feet wide and fifteen to twenty feet high, with an arched roof. Then on each side of the tunnel he saw rock embankments perhaps eight to ten feet wide. He stepped up on the right-hand side and walked toward the light. His left foot skidded in something mushy, and he nearly toppled back into the water. He raised his foot and saw that it was covered with a brownish material and the odor of manure came to his big nose. "I might have known it," he said dryly. "Even in *here*. Steer manure!"

He catfooted on until he reached the end of the tunnel. Sunlight revealed grass and trees which screened the mouth of the tunnel. He worked his way through the timber to look out on a fair and immense canyon bright in the sunlight. Running water over toward the east reflected the sunlight. Dotted here and there were the humped shapes of many grazing cattle. A sudden braying startled him. He whirled with outstretched pistol and saw the burro he had loosed back in the other canyon. The Scalp Knife brand was sharp on its flank.

Vic returned to the tunnel, waded through it and passed again under the chilling falls. He dressed quickly. He walked back to where he had left Deborah and the horses. He whistled softly and she whistled in return.

She looked at him in surprise as he entered the timber. "You look blue with the cold, Vic," she said.

He nodded. "I just spent twenty minutes underneath that waterfall."

She stared at him. "Are you all right?" she asked.

Vic quickly told her of his discovery of the passageway behind the waterfall. "There were hundreds of steers in there," he added. "I couldn't see the brands on them from that distance. Is there, by any chance, some spread whose range extends into that canyon?"

She shook her head. "No wonder those rustled cattle were never found."

"It's a perfect setup. Shelter, grazing, water and timber and likely those cattle can't get out of there by themselves. It isn't likely they'd ever enter that tunnel on their own. They'd have to be driven into it. The burro evidently had been in there a number of times and naturally wanted to return when he found himself alone in this outer canyon."

"Did you see anyone?"

He was almost about to tell her about poor Ben Cox and then he thought better of it. No good purpose would be served by him telling her about the killing. "No," he replied.

"What will you do now?"

He shaped cigarettes as he looked toward the distant waterfall. "I'm going back in there."

"Alone? That doesn't make sense!"

He placed a cigarette between her lips and lighted it. "That is why I came to the Diablo country," he reminded her.

"Good! You've found your proof. Now let's get out of here and get help."

He shook his head. "You've forgotten we were driven in here and the chances of getting out aren't too good."

"So you'll get yourself in deeper than ever by going back in there!"

He shrugged as he lighted his cigarette. "Those cattle could well be driven from there by the time we got back with help, *if we* got out of here at all. No, Deborah, I'm here *now* and those cattle are in there *now* and I'm going back in there *now!* There may be another outlet for those cattle to be driven out of that canyon without coming back through the tunnel and under the waterfall. There's no way they can spirit those cattle out of that canyon and bring them out on this side of the Diablos without being seen."

"All right," she agreed. "Do we go in now or do we wait until darkness?"

"You're not going."

"I'm not sitting here!" she snapped. "Not when you might need help."

He began to strip the bay of its saddle and packs. "Strip the clay bank," he said over his shoulder.

"Why?" she asked.

"We can't take them in there with us."

They cached the saddles and some of the gear. They rolled light packs of one blanket each and some food. Vic took the reins of the clay bank. He drew his honed sheath knife.

"What are you going to do?" she demanded.

He looked sideways at her. "We can't leave them here."

"No!"

He seemed to be a different man when he turned and looked at her. "If these horses are found in here, they'll know we're around somewhere. We can't afford to take that risk. It's our lives or those of the horses. Take your choice."

She turned quickly away as he led the clay bank out from the timber and to the edge of the river. Vic ran a hand down the neck of the horse and then suddenly gripped the reins, turning the clay bank's head hard to one side and up to tighten the neck and throat muscles. One hard clean drag of the knife across the throat did the trick, at the same time Vic threw his weight against the side of the horse so that he fell sideways into the flood. The horse went down without a sound. For a little while the waters were tinged red and then the Upper Diablo ran clearly again. Vic went back for the bay. Deborah was somewhere in the timber. He disposed of the bay as he had disposed of the clay bank. He erased all tracks between the river and the timber.

Vic slung his pack over one shoulder. He checked his rifle and pistol. "Come on," he said roughly as she appeared white-faced from the shelter of the timber. She said not a word as she picked up her rifle and pack and followed him into the shadows of the timber.

Vic waited for her at the edge of the *tinaja*. "Strip," he ordered her.

"Here?"

He shrugged. "Unless you want to spend the rest of the day and a damned cold night in wet clothing. I'll go ahead. The water isn't deep, and it takes only seconds to get under the waterfall. The longer we stay out here the better the chances for our being seen. Look the other way, please."

Vic stripped and then wrapped his clothing within part of the tarp that covered his pack. He waded into the icy pool and then passed beneath the falls. He stepped out on the right-hand bank of the tunnel and quickly dressed himself. He saw a slim white shape under the tenuous curtain of the falls, and he looked the other way.

"Hove these dates you take me on," she chattered from just behind him. "You could easily turn a girl's head that way, Jamison."

He grinned. "You wanted to come along and play a man's game. Old Eb Cross's granddaughter. Remember?"

Together they walked along the rock bank until they could vanish into the quiet serenity of the sun-dappled timber. "Stay here," he ordered. He vanished into the timber. He worked his way to the south until he found a timbered knoll that afforded a clear view of the canyon. A thread of smoke rose lazily from the chimney of a log structure near the far end of the canyon. The ground sloped upward beyond the log cabin and clumps of grazing cattle were scattered here and there along the stream bank. Vic whistled softly. There were hundreds of steers and they all looked like prime beef. The sun glinted on something. A man had come out of the log cabin to fill a shiny new tin bucket at the stream.

Nowhere in the canyon could Vic see riders watching the cattle. "Pretty sure of themselves," he mused. "It's obvious the cattle can't stray out of here. They have to be driven out." He studied the peeled-pole corral behind the log structure. There were at least six horses in it. Beyond the corral in a fenced pasture were five or six more horses. Vic carefully scanned the nearer terrain. There wasn't a sign of human life anywhere near the western end of this hidden canyon.

Vic went back for Deborah. He led her to the knoll and beyond it, then along the southern wall base of the canyon to a place where the eastern end of the canyon could be easily surveyed, while at the same time there was excellent cover, easily defensible. There were pools of clear fresh rainwater in many rock hollows.

"How can they get the cattle out of here?" Deborah asked. "Other than through the passageway under the falls?"

He pointed toward the eastern end of the canyon. "Likely up that way. I'll know tonight. There will be a full moon."

"What do we do now?"

He grinned. "Take it easy. We can't move around for fear of being seen. We can take turns keeping an eye on them through the field glasses."

There was a movement in the timber north of the cabin and in a little while two horsemen appeared driving about twenty head of cattle toward the stream. Smoke began to rise from a fire near the stream. Vic's glasses picked out a small, fenced enclosure within which several men moved about. The powerful binoculars picked out the lean face of Lenny Garrett as one of the two men driving the cattle. Vic didn't recognize the other man, but he had the Scalp Knife stamp all over him.

"They're branding cattle, Deborah," Vic said over his shoulder. "Changing brands, most likely. That might mean that they're getting ready to move them out. But to where?"

"Perhaps up north to the Little Colorado country," she suggested.

He shook his head. "That's Mormon country. They won't buy such cattle. They learned their lesson earlier this year."

While Deborah relieved Vic at the glasses he stripped down the weapons each in turn to clean and dry them. He oiled them and reloaded them with fresh cartridges.

"Vic," she said. "I just saw Buck Fresno down there."

"Great," he said dryly.

"There's Sid Decker too!"

"Salt, pepper and gravel in the grease."

"There are at least six men working down there." She was silent for a time as she studied the men and the area. "I don't see Cass Page," she said at last.

Perhaps Cass Page no longer rode with the Scalp Knife. It would have been better for Vic if Page had been working for the ranch. At least Vic would have had an idea of where he was. The thought of that deadly one-eyed mankiller wandering around in the Diablos looking for Vic Jamison might have unnerved a less strong man than himself. As it was, it still gave him an uneasy feeling.

Vic dozed off in the warming sun.

"Vic!" she called back. "There are two men riding from the west, probably from the passageway!"

Vic focused the glasses on the two horsemen. The boss is here, Deborah," he said quietly. "Clayton Mostyn himself. I don't know the other hombre, but he looks to be as tough a boot as any of the other Scalp Knife riders."

"How many does that make down there now?"

"Eight, at least. Maybe more."

"Almost too many for us to take on," she commented dryly.

He shrugged. "Who's going to take them on?"

"How else do you plan to stop them? Seems to me it's rather obvious that they plan to move out those cattle very soon."

He nodded. "That's probably why Mostyn is here. They might have found out who I am. Mostyn maybe doesn't trust Fresno anymore and wants to see that the job is done right. It'll probably be their last drive out of here." He grinned wryly. "Who else has any cattle left worth rustling?"

"That leaves only the Jemsons to take care of," she added bitterly.

He shook his head. "They won't bother us anymore."

"You'd be loco if you tried to stop the Scalp Knife alone."

Vic smiled. "Like they say, you don't have to be crazy to be an Arizona Ranger, but it sure does help."

The long warm day drifted past. All that time the faint bawling of cattle came to the two watchers below the cliffside, as the Scalp Knife riders drove the cattle to the corral for the brand changing. Then they were turned loose to be herded east of the log cabin and the corrals.

When dusk came Deborah and Vic shared cold fare. There was an uneasiness in the thick darkness before the rising of the moon. It was the season for quick changes in the weather and those usually for the worse.

CHAPTER FOURTEEN

Vic led the way down the dark and treacherous slope to the floor of the great canyon. The wind was shifting. It now blew from the east and carried the faint sound of the cattle to Vic and Deborah. They were restless, perhaps sensing something unknown to human perception.

"How did they ever get them through the canyon of the Diablo and into here?" Deborah whispered.

"It took cattlemen to do it. Likely they drove them along the Upper Diablo when the water was low and then into the outer canyon. They could have used a belled steer to get them under the waterfall—sort of a Judas. I suppose you could call him. It proves one thing for certain—the Scalp Knife *corrida* are cowmen as well as gunmen."

They followed the base of the canyon's southern wall until they could see the dimly lighted windows of the log cabin. There was a growing uneasiness in the night air. A faint flickering of lightning like a spider's web touched the northern sky, and yet the moon was scheduled to rise later. The wind shifted uneasily back and forth. Sheet lightning suddenly blinked eerily against the northern sky and then vanished as swiftly as it had appeared. Then the air became hushed, and the wind died away.

Vic led the way along the south side of the herd until he could turn east beyond the herd. He led the way up a broken slope. He studied the eastern canyon wall. The great canyon was a box canyon—it *had* to be a box canyon. Suddenly he ran full tilt into a barbed-wire fence and reeled back with a torn hand and a ripped chest. "Christ's blood!" he cursed in border Spanish.

She wrapped her bandanna about his torn hand. Vic walked along the fence until he reached a strong Texas gate. Beyond the gate to the east was upward-sloping ground. A sharp flash of lightning revealed that the fence ran the full width of the canyon north to south.

"Come on," Vic whispered. He elbow-worked his way on his back beneath the lower strand of the fence and then held it up for her to crawl under. Together they legged it up the slope to hit the dirt when the lightning silently exploded, followed by a distant muttering of thunder. They now could see over the fence and across the herd to the log cabin. The lightning died, plunging the canyon into darkness.

"Vic," Deborah whispered. "There's a track beyond us heading to the east."

They lay quietly until the lightning flashed again. Plainly to be seen was a wide-worn track and, in the quick luminescence of the lightning, a great dark split in the eastern facade of the canyon wall.

When the darkness covered the land, they ran up the slope and leaped over a fallen log a second before the next flash of lightning. Ahead of them the track continued on to enter a great fault in the canyon wall between tangles of fallen timber and shattered rock. They catfooted into the fault.

Vic looked about. "We found the entrance and now we

have the exit," he said quietly. He walked on, with his passage illuminated by the flashing sky, to find that the fault widened into a pass of fairly level ground. He waited for her.

"Clever. This pass must eventually trend north. They can bring out the herd miles from here, unseen by anyone in the valley of the Rio Diablo. Then they can easily scatter the herd into small groups to run them into New Mexico where they have a quick, unquestioning market. Serves two purposes. Makes a neat profit on cattle that didn't cost a cent and puts the local competitors out of business," Vic explained.

"Like the Star Cross."

"We could hang an anvil of evidence around Mostyn's neck with all this."

"If we get out of it, Vic."

He looked down at her. "What makes you think we won't?"

"I haven't got your confidence," she replied.

He grinned in a lightning flash. "Think big, girl. Think *BIG!*"

Thunder rolled its uneasy drums in the hidden northern canyons. The tenseness grew in the darkness as the air became warmer. Vic and Deborah returned through the pass to the canyon and took cover behind a fallen tree.

"Beautiful," Vic murmured. "They run the rustled steers in here through the old underground watercourse and the steers wouldn't try to get back through there, at least without a lead steer. The cattle can't drift east of the fence. Plenty of water and grazing. They had it made until we showed up."

They worked their way down toward the fence.

"Listen," Deborah whispered.

An eerie wailing came to them, a high, rising tremulous sound with long and trembling notes.

Vic whispered in Deborah's ear, "They've got night

herders out because of the lightning. They're singing the 'Texas Lullaby'. Hasn't any words and likely no composer could ever put it down in notes. I've never heard of anyone but Texans using it. I suppose it came about because Texans have done so much of their cattle working alone in deep thickets and in darkness. They use it when it is dark and when a herd is restless like this one is now."

They crawled along the fence line and then under it and then took cover in a ghostly-looking motte of aspens on a knoll where they could see the log cabin. The door was opened, emitting a flood of pale, yellow light on the trampled ground. Vic uncased the binoculars and focused them on the doorway. A brilliant display of staghorn lightning revealed a man roping horses in a corral. Three saddled horses fitted with cantle and pommel packs were tethered at the front of the cabin. A man came from the cabin and slung a pack over the cantle.

"By Christ!" Vic whispered. "They're getting ready to pull out."

"Tonight?" she asked incredulously.

He nodded. "Something is spooking them. Maybe they had figured on bright moonlight for the drive through the eastern pass, and now they'll have to use the lightning for illumination. That herd will be spooky."

Vic studied the terrain east of the log cabin through the glasses during the intermittent flashing of the lightning. Some of the herd were slowly milling about there while others were bedded. The ground upon which they had been bedded sloped down toward a shallow stream. Beyond was the cabin, backed almost into a thick stand of timber which in turn thrust against the northern wall of the canyon.

"They'll likely wait until dawn light," Vic said at last.

A thin wraith of smoke arose from the chimney of the cabin. The odor of cooking food drifted to Deborah and Vic.

The horses were still saddled and tethered to the hitching rail in front of the cabin.

"Likely cooking rations for the drive," Vic said. "They won't have much time to stop for cooking on the way."

Staghorn suddenly struck wildly across the sky and thunder rumbled in the gorges to the north and east. In the brilliant flash of the lightning a steer slowly lifted his head and then rose to his knees. He looked about himself as he did so. Darkness again filled the canyon. In the next faint flickering of light, the same steer was now on his feet and raising his nose to scent as he looked toward the approaching storm. The herders began to sing again. Another steer stood up and then several more did so.

A man came quickly from the log cabin. He mounted his horse and rode toward the restless herd.

"They're maybe getting ready to move out or perhaps only changing the night guards," Vic explained to Deborah. "If they are planning to move out, we've got to stop them."

"How, Vic?"

"I'm going to try to stampede the herd. If I can, it will take hours, perhaps days, for them to round them up again."

"What must I do?"

"Go back to the east pass. Take a position to cover it with rifle fire. If they do manage to get the herd or part of it at least started up the slope toward the pass, it'll be up to you to stop them one way or another. Stay well back. Drop some of the leaders. Don't let any of the riders get near you."

She nodded as she picked up her rifle. He stood up and tilted back her head to kiss her. He looked into her eyes. "I'll be all right," he promised her. He wasn't too sure about that himself.

She slipped toward the edge of the motte.

"Deborah!" he called out.

She turned.

"Have you ever killed a man?" he asked.

Her great eyes studied him. "No. Why?"

He shrugged. "I just wanted to know," he replied lamely. "Sometimes, Deborah, that's the only way a man *can* be stopped."

There was no answer from her. She was gone in the darkness.

Vic worked his way toward the fence during the dark periods, freezing absolutely still during the flashes. Once he thought he saw Deborah near the fence but when the next flash came, she was gone.

Vic squatted near the fence not fifty yards from the nearest steers. He picked up two flat pieces of brittle rock. At least a dozen steers were now on their feet, noses toward the approaching storm, their eyes lighted incessantly like swamp fire by the reflection of the flickering lightning.

The Texas Lullaby rose stronger now. Three herders worked their way along the outside of the herd at intervals trying to quiet the steers. Thunder rumbled. There was a particularly loud, splitting crash of lightning and the whole canyon was lighted up like a theatre stage, while the kettle drums of the Thunder Gods played the overture to the rapidly approaching storm. The thunder died away.

Vic smashed his two flat pieces of rock together and hurled them toward the herd. Lightning flickered. Steers were on their feet and moving at a slow walk. Other steers lurched uncertainly to their feet. A shaft of lightning lanced right across the canyon with a ripping, splitting sound that was deafening. The steers were now walking a little faster in the direction of the stream. One steer after another joined those who were moving. The herd was gathering momentum and new recruits every fifty feet of the way. The next cannon crack of lightning tripped the sear of their panic.

Hooves began pounding on the ground. Horns clacked

against horns. Great moist eyes stared wildly. A man yelled hoarsely from downwind of the herd. Vic snatched up piece after piece of rock and hurled them with all his strength among the steers.

The night herders tried to swing the leaders in toward the trail of the moving herd to form it into a mill, until the whole mass of steers would wind itself into a self-stopping ball and the momentum of the herd would die down like a spent top. It was no use. The herd was now moving, lashed on by insensate fear and sheer momentum toward the stream, and the riders on the downwind side knew they had to get to hell out of the way and as Vic ran along the fence line, hitting the ground when the lightning flashed, only to jump to his feet and make a few yards in the darkness. By the time he could cut west and was even with the log cabin the herd was already pouring across the shallow stream, scattering great gouts of water upon which the lightning reflected like masses of quicksilver.

One rider went down in front of the herd. An arm shot up above the herd with the hand still gripping the quirt as though seeking mercy from an unseeing God, and then the arm was gone. A second rider lost his nerve. He swung along in front of the herd and tried to reach beyond the left horn of the stampeding herd, riding directly toward where Vic Jamison lay hidden in the motte of aspens.

Vic could not help himself. He had been a cowman once himself. *"Jesus Christ no!"* he shrieked. His voice was drowned out by the uproar of the bawling cattle and the crackling of the lightning.

The rider's horse went down on his knees. The rider kicked loose from the stirrups and landed spraddle-legged on the ground. He tried to outrun the herd. The herd was on him in an instant, pounding his unresisting body down into the mud, macerating him into nothing that resembled a human.

Vic looked away. An odd thought crept into his mind. The flowers would grow beautifully there come springtime and for many years to come.

The wind began to blow across the herd and the body heat of the massed steers carried to Vic as though someone had opened a furnace door. The herd pounded through the stream and out onto the flats beyond it.

The men at the log cabin tried to quiet their rearing, terrified mounts, then abandoned them when the right horn of the stampeding herd diverged around the branding corral and hammered toward the cabin. The door was slammed shut just as the lead steers crashed against the terrified horses and either trampled them down or carried them along with the stampede.

The wrangler went over the far side of the horse corral and legged it awkwardly toward the timber, just ahead of the herd that crashed through the peeled-pole corral as though it had been made of twigs and carried the frightened remuda with them like chips on a dark tide.

The flood of sweating beef parted to spread around the log cabin and then joined the main part of the herd beyond it, to charge down the center of the canyon. The wind lashed them onward with an eerie falsetto of malicious crackling and inhuman laughter, aided by the incessant thunder that pealed constantly through the gorges to the north and east.

Ghostly balls of phosphorescent fire suddenly appeared on the tips of the tossing horns of the steers as though an invisible magician had ignited each of them with his magic wand. When the lightning winked out letting the sudden darkness flood in, the eerie balls of fire remained atop the horn tips, as though a torchlight parade of the insane was being held down the canyon.

A gigantic thunderbolt leaped across the sky and loosed the sluice gates of the heavens. Rain poured down in wall-like leaden-colored sheets that seemed to smoke, and blotted out the sight except for a few yards.

Vic ran into the cover of a huge overhanging rock slab that thrust itself up out of the ground like an ancient megalith. He pressed his back against the rock and felt for the makings. No fear of his being seen now. Those sweating waddies in the log cabin would be too busy cinching up their weak guts to keep from filling up the seats of their long Johns. Vic grinned evilly at the thought.

"Two down, anyway," he murmured around his cigarette as he lighted up. He grinned again. "Scalp Knife, you ain't so gawddamned tough!"

Two men were already dead under the sharp pounding hoofs of the herd. That left six, as close as Vic could figure. Probably one herder had escaped being run down and the wrangler had made it into the timber, as far as Vic knew. That should leave four men in the cabin. The herd was safe enough for quite some time. They'd run out of steam somewhere in the western part of the canyon and, in any case, they'd hardly attempt the tunnel entrance.

If the herd drifted back the next day, the fence would keep them from leaving the canyon by the east pass. It wasn't the herd that concerned him now. It was the Scalp Knife *corrida.* "Let well enough alone, Jamison," a mind voice seemed to whisper. Vic shook his head. They would be short of horses, and in any case, six Scalp Knife men were hardly the type to be stampeded by a lone Arizona Ranger and a girl.

The rain died away. It stopped as suddenly as it had begun. The canyon was now pitch-black and the low thunder of the still running herd came on the wind from the west. Faint chain lightning fingered its way across the dark sky. It illuminated the churned-up wet earth that marked the wide path of the herd. The muddy stream was now overflowing its smashed and leveled banks.

The thunder rumbled off to the north. The lightning flickered soundlessly. The rumbling of the herd died away. An eerie quietness now had replaced the hellish uproar of the past forty-five minutes.

Vic swiftly worked his way across the clinging mud and threw himself belly-flat behind a hummock two hundred yards from the darkened log cabin. A light flared up slowly behind one of the windows. Any minute now, they'd open the door to get their horses. One man outside against the four in the cabin and at least two others somewhere out in the darkness.

"A Ranger has to charge hell with a bucket of water sometimes, Vic," a dry voice seemed to whisper into Vic's left ear. It sounded like the voice of Cal Hayden. Vic looked about quickly. There was no one there.

Vic slid the heavy Winchester forward and levered a round of .44/.40 into the chamber. He rested his finger on the trigger, taking up the slight slack. He sighted on the door.

The door swung open flooding the wet ground with a rectangle of smoky yellow light. A man was silhouetted. Vic picked up the silvered blade front sight with the curved tips of the rear buckhorn sight. Slowly and inexorably his right hand closed on the small of the stock and at the same time he squeezed the trigger. The Winchester bucked back hard against his shoulder as it spat flame and smoke. A man yelled. The door was slammed shut. The gun report echo rumbled down the canyon and died away. It was very quiet again.

Vic was up and running before the death of the shot echo. He levered a fresh round into the chamber as he ran and then he hit the dirt fifty yards north of this original firing position. He fired at the single west window of the cabin and was rewarded with the sound of shattering glass. The light went out.

He moved again. He crossed the muddy herd track to the edge of the timber. He fired at one of the two rear windows and then moved swiftly eastward to just within the shelter of the timber, hoping to God he would not run full tilt into the wrangler.

He went to ground in a hollow, feeling the cold water soak through his Levi's and belly clothing. A cool touch of wind drifted through the canyon and dried the sweat on his forehead. His breathing was short and harsh, and he stayed quiet until it ran full and even once again.

He wormed his way across the wet grass to the north of the cabin until he was twenty yards from the rear of it. A flicker of lightning revealed that there was no rear doorway. A window slid quietly up. Some acoustical quirk brought the sound of voices to Vic.

"How many of them do you think, Buck?" someone asked hoarsely.

"Shut up, Len!" Buck Fresno snapped.

There was a long and pregnant pause.

"Apaches, you think, Buck?" Len asked.

"Gawddammit, how'd I know? Yuh never know what them thievin' bastards will do."

Vic fingered his rifle. *That* trenchant thought had never entered his mind. He grinned. Even a tough Texan gunfighter usually walked quietly and thought twice when Apaches were about.

A horse whinnied from the darkness to Vic's left. Vic ran at a crouch until he could see the animal drifting toward the smashed corral with his saddle hanging under his belly. Vic stepped back behind a tree. Something had moved at the edge of the timber. In the faint illumination of spiderweb lightning he saw a man running toward the horse. He looked back over his shoulder as he did so. It was Jim Taylor.

Vic hated the thought of what he had to do but there was no alternative. None of these criminal men must be allowed to escape from the canyon. Vic fired. The horse crashed down with a slug in its head. Taylor leaped to one side, dropped flat on the ground and then fired at Vic. The slug slapped into a tree a foot away from Vic. Damned good shooting in the dark. Vic hit the mud. *Too* damned good!

It was quiet again.

In the next flash of lightning Vic saw Taylor running for the log cabin. A rifle flamed from a window and the man went down on his knees. "For Christ's sake!" he screamed hoarsely. "It's me! Jim Taylor!" The next slug stopped his voice forever.

Quietness overcame the great canyon broken only by the dry whispering of the wind and the soughing of the pines.

Vic raised his head and gave vent to a ululating cry that echoed from the canyon wall. He fed fresh rounds into his rifle magazine. He had given the Chiricahua women's cry— one given to welcome home to the *rancheria* triumphant warriors laden with much loot and driving many stolen horses. The men in the log cabin of course, wouldn't know exactly *what* it was but they'd sure as hell know it was *Apache*.

Vic padded through the timber. The lightning had died out. The thunder was long gone. There was the faintest suggestion of pale pearl-gray light in the eastern sky. The full moon was trying to force its way through the overcast.

Vic turned to look toward the distant fence line, hoping that Deborah was all right. He fell over a log in a clattering of snapping dry branches. A fusillade of slugs poured from the two rear windows of the cabin. Bits of bark and sheared-off leaves and twigs floated down about Vic. If he had been standing...

Vic worked his way through the timber. He dropped flat behind a log and opened fire at the log cabin. He poured round after round of 200-grain slugs at the cabin. Glass shattered. The rifle grew hot and ran dry.

Vic sprinted for cover fifty yards away and dropped behind a log to reload the smoking rifle while round after round poured toward his last position.

The moon was rising. First it tinted the tips of the Diablos, and then it flooded silvery light down the naked upper slopes to the timberline, then through and over the timber to touch the canyon rim. In a little while, it almost seemed to *flow* over the rim into the great canyon itself.

Vic eyed the trampled battlefield, for so he now considered it. Three of the Scalp Knife men were dead; two from the stampeding herd and the third man killed by his *own corrida* mates. That left at least five, as far as Vic knew. Four of the five were still in the besieged cabin which left one more somewhere in the canyon. He was the one that bothered Vic.

Vic crossed the canyon beyond rifle range from the cabin, which was partially hidden by a swale in the ground. He took cover in the motte where he had sheltered from the downpour. He saw a saddled horse trotting up the center of the canyon toward the cabin. The horse was a black with two white fore-stockings. That horse would be one helluva temptation to those four men trapped in the cabin. Maybe by now they were sure the rimrock and the canyon were infested with bloodthirsty bronco Apaches.

The black drifted closer to the cabin. In the stillness Vic could hear the hoarse entreating voices of the men trapped within the log cabin as they tried to lure the black to them. The horse moved closer to the cabin. He stopped fifty feet from it. Vic rested his rifle on a low tree branch and sighted on the cabin.

The black tossed his head and trotted closer to the cabin. A man broke from the darkness of the cabin and legged it toward the horse. He gripped the mane and swung himself up into the saddle. He sank his spurs into the flanks of the black. The black buck-jumped toward the stream with the rider clinging leechlike to the saddle and the mane.

"Come back, Lennie, yuh damned fool!" Fresno yelled from the cabin.

The black ran for the stream.

Vic moved. He stepped into the open for a clean shot. A rifle flashed from the cabin. The slug slapped into a tree trunk inches from the side of Vic's head, driving fine, needle-like splinters into the left side of his face. His rifle cracked. The black panicked. He reared and turned at the same time throwing Len Garrett clear from the saddle. The horse galloped toward the timber.

Vic hit the dirt. Garrett did not get up. He lay flat in the shallow water of the stream. Vic bellied through the motte softly cursing as the blood ran down his punctured face and dripped on the ground.

Vic uncased his field glasses. The moonlight was strong enough to reveal that Len Garrett would never ride again. His neck was bent at an awkward angle and his eyes stared unseeingly at the moonlit sky. He floated a short distance, turned over slowly and sank out of sight in a deep pool. He did not rise.

Vic trotted to the west and then across the canyon toward the timber. He went through it as silently as a wraith of wind-driven mist, until he saw the black grazing at the edge of the timber just below the north wall of the canyon.

Vic looked up at the moon. There would be moonlight for some hours yet and when darkness came, the three men left in the cabin would likely make their break. When they did make that break, Vic intended to be mounted.

Vic called to the black. He walked quietly toward it, talking gently. The black was spooky, but he was lonely too, and the sound of Vic's voice soothed him. He trotted to Vic. Vic led him through the timber to where the cabin could be clearly seen.

Something snapped in the timber behind Vic. Vic drifted into cover and raised his rifle. A shadow seemed to grow in size and then to move as a man catfooted through the shadows while looking constantly back over his shoulders. The wrangler or the last of the night herders—probably the last man of the Scalp Knife *corrida* in the canyon outside of the three men in the cabin.

Vic stayed behind a thick-boled tree as the man came toward the black. He reached for the reins, talking gently as Vic had done. The black tossed his handsome head a little.

"Stand right where you are, mister," Vic warned.

The man whirled, clawing for a draw. He *was* fast! His Colt was out and up, thrusting forward as the big spur hammer was thumbed back to full cock. The 200-grain slug from the Winchester fired from hip level caught him low in the guts. His Colt exploded flame and smoke as he went down. The black reared back but could not run. His reins were held in a dead man's stiffening hand.

The canyon became almost intensely quiet after the shot echoes died away. The moon was on the wane.

The cabin was dark. Three desperate men in the dark would be more than a double handful for Vic Jamison. Vic eyed the black. Len Garrett had taken his chance on riding free from the cabin, lured by the tempting black. If it worked once it might just work again. Vic slapped the horse on the rump with the flat of his butt stock and then vanished noiselessly into the timber to get upwind from the black. The horse moved about uncertainly and then drifted toward the rear of the darkened cabin.

Vic lay low, biding his time as the moon drifted further and further to the west, and the thick shadows drifted down the southern side of the canyon and inked in the depressions.

The horse was now within twenty feet of the cabin's east side. A door slammed. Boots thudded on the wet ground. A man rounded the front of the cabin and ran toward the horse.

Another man leaped from a window. "Damn yuh, Sid!" he yelled.

Sid Decker whirled to face Buck Fresno. "Keep out of this, Fresno," he warned.

"The black ain't for you!"

Decker jerked his head toward the cabin. "Is it for *him,* or maybe you?" he asked.

"Colonel Mostyn is boss of the Scalp Knife."

"That's not an answer, Fresno."

Vic raised his rifle.

"Let that black be," warned the foreman.

"You damned fool!" Decker snapped. "You want the Apaches to hear you? Let me take the black out of here and go for help."

"That'll be the day!" the Texan jeered. "Once you get out of this canyon, we won't never see you again. You thought I was asleep in there. Was that it? You were pulling foot. You always wanted my job, Decker. Well, there's one thing you forgot—you got to *take* the job away from me!"

Decker slapped leather. He was fast. Buck Fresno's six-gun seemed to clear the leather by itself. It cracked once. Decker staggered backward with the impact of the heavy slug. He dropped his Colt. "For God's sake, Buck!" he pleaded. "Don't shoot again! I'm hit bad!"

Sid Decker might just as well have tried reasoning with the devil himself. Fresno grinned. He was enjoying this triumph. He took his time, slowly raising his smoking pistol as though he were on a dueling field. The Colt flamed. The slug struck Decker in the guts and as he toppled forward screaming to his death, the next slug hit him on the top of his head.

The black stampeded. Fresno cursed. He started after the horse. Vic fired right over the Texan's head. Fresno wasted no time in running awkwardly back to the cabin to plunge through a rear window.

Shadows crept across the canyon. They lapped across the stream and reached for the timber. Vic sat with his back against a tree. Six gone for sure and two to go, he thought, and the worst of them were still in the cabin—Clayton Mostyn and his good right arm, Buck Fresno.

CHAPTER FIFTEEN

The Moonlight Was almost gone. The deepening shadows gave Vic good cover, but it did the same for the two men who were still within the cabin. They were hard enough to risk leaving the cabin if they knew there was only one man waiting outside for them. The Apaches were another matter. No white man could ever out-stalk an Apache in the darkness.

Vic worked his way through the darkness to the barbed-wire fence. Somewhere up on the shadowed slope was Deborah with a Winchester in her hands. She knew how to use it. She would be nervous, tense and concerned over all the shooting she had heard from the canyon.

Vic stopped short. The wind had died. Sound carried well in the quietness. Something clicked not far from Vic. Vic went down on his knees and then onto his belly in an attempt to skyline anyone who might be out there. Something moved. It might be Deborah and if it was, she might shoot toward anything she heard or saw.

Vic bellied under the wire and wormed his way up the slope, cradling his Winchester in his elbow-hollows and using elbows and knees to work along the wet ground. He could just make out the dark slash of the pass mouth. He felt, rather than saw or heard something move in the darkness. He went to ground in a litter of broken rock, where he could look down the slope against the last vestiges of moonlight to pattern anything moving against the dimness.

A dark figure moving slowly. It was a horse with dragging reins. Vic was about to move toward it when he stopped short. How had the horse gotten through the fence? The Texas gate had not been opened.

"Stay where you are! Grab your ears, mister!" The voice came out of the shadows behind Vic.

Vic stood up slowly.

"Drop the rifle and the Colt!"

Vic did as he was told.

"Turn around!"

Vic turned.

"For Christ's sakes! It's Purcell!"

Vic smiled easily. *"Como esta,* Bert?"

"Don't give me that spic talk," Bert Hanna ordered. "What the hell are *you* doing here?"

Vic waggled his upheld hands and tilted his head to one side, friendly-like. "I came in to give the boys a hand," he replied lamely.

"Bullshit! They're looking all over for you for killing that Jemson woman."

Vic knew damned well he had miscounted the Scalp Knife riders in the valley. It could be a fatal mistake... A rifle cracked out of the darkness. Hanna whirled and raised his rifle. Vic ripped his stingy gun from out of his left wrist spring clip and cocked it. Hanna whirled back toward Vic. The derringer cracked. The soft .41 caliber slug struck Hanna in the chest at point-blank range and slammed him backward just as he fired. The rifle bullet plucked at Vic's shirt collar as it passed him.

Hanna was down on one knee but he was dead game. He levered a fresh round into the chamber of the Winchester. Vic dropped belly-flat and rolled over twice, to rise onto his feet and fire his last cartridge. The bullet slapped into the side of the Scalp Knife rider's head and slammed him sideways. He rolled over onto his belly and then spasmodically tried to push his hands down against the ground to rise but it was no use. He dropped flat and lay still. The echoes died away. The gun smoke drifted off.

Bert Hanna was gone, taking his Colt and Winchester with him.

Vic raised his head from behind a log. Nothing moved.

A soft whistle came through the darkness.

Vic chanced it. "Deborah?" he called out. He dropped flat on the instant.

She came swiftly and silently through the darkness to him and dropped beside him and into the shelter of his arms. She covered her eyes with a hand and her body shook as though with fever chills. "Is he dead?" she whispered.

Vic drew her closer. "Yes," he replied.

"I fired to distract him."

"You sure did."

"Then I'm just as responsible as you are, Vic."

"It was him or me, Deborah."

"And those are the rules?"

He nodded. "Those are the rules."

"Are you all right?"

"Not a scratch."

"And the rest of them?" Her voice faltered. "I heard all that shooting."

"As far as I know there are only two of them left down there, possibly still in the cabin. Clayton Mostyn and Buck

Fresno. Mostyn could be dead or wounded. I *know* Buck Fresno's still alive and is there."

"And you did all this alone?"

He shrugged, slightly modest. "Not really. Some of them were killed off by their own stupidity. Besides, they think there are Apaches out here."

"There isn't an Apache within thirty miles of here," she said. "They avoid this place. To them it is haunted."

"They didn't know that, Deborah."

She drew back her head and eyed his lean scarred face. "Maybe there *was* an Apache here after all..."

"Perhaps in spirit if not in the flesh."

She was silent for a time. She rested her head on his chest. "Let's get out of here," she pleaded softly.

He shook his head. "I want them all."

"You've prevented them from taking the herd from here. You've broken up the Scalp Knife *corrida*. Mostyn and Fresno won't dare show their faces in the valley of the Diablo now."

"My job is to bring them in—dead or alive, if it comes to a choice, but I mean to bring them in."

"I don't want you going down there again."

He gently disengaged her and stood up. He picked up her Winchester and handed it to her as she got to her feet.

"Go back to your post," he told her.

"No, Vic! I won't go without you!"

He was gone into the darkness, moving like a night-hunting cat.

Vic reached the broken-banked stream. There was no sign of life about the cabin. He waded the stream and approached the destroyed corral. His hunting senses were alert and coupled with that sixth sense gifted to few men, which had been whetted and honed by years of facing danger and swift death. It was this sixth sense that led him on toward the cabin.

He rested his rifle in a fence corner and drew his Colt. Swiftly he closed the gap between the fence and the cabin until he flattened his back against the east wall and the one window therein. The shattered glass lay about his feet. There was no sound from within the structure.

Vic eased along the wall to the front corner. He rounded it to stand just beside the front door. A draft came through the doorway. The door was ajar. Not a sound came from within the cabin. He picked up a stone and heaved it back-hand up and over the cabin. He heard it thud into the wet ground beyond the cabin. No sound or movement came from within.

Vic went down on his knees and worked his way noise-lessly into the cabin. He waited until his eyes grew accus-tomed to the darkness. The place was empty of life. He stood up. One of his boot soles rolled on a spent cartridge case.

He thumb-snapped a lucifer into flame and cupped it within a hand, taking care to stand back behind any of the windows and out of view from anyone on the outside of the cabin. The place was a shambles. Broken glass and empty cartridge cases littered the floor. A bullet-punctured table had been upended in front of one of the windows. Blankets were strewn about on the floor and some of them hung from several double-tiered bunks beside the walls. Soot had come from the bullet-shattered stovepipe to coat some of the inte-rior. The acrid odor of burned gunpowder mingled with the sharp odor of urine. He eased through a rear window. They might have tried for the route under the waterfall but that was much farther than the east pass. On the other hand, if they had planned to return to the Rio Diablo Valley the waterfall route was the shortest by far. Did they still believe that it had been Apaches who had besieged them? If that were so, they would have no fear of returning to the Rio Diablo Valley. On the other hand, if they suspected or knew it had been Vic who had been hurrahing them, they would try for the east pass.

The rifle cracked on the slopes of the east pass and made up Vic's mind for him. He was on his way before the second shot. The two shots were followed by a fusillade. The shot echoes slam-banged back and forth between the sheer walls of the pass to die away angrily in the distance.

Vic neared the barbed-wire fence. Another shot crashed out. This time he saw the flash of the rifle up on the slope about where Deborah should have posted herself.

Boots thudded on the wet ground. The Texas gate had been opened. Two men came running, the lead man with a pistol in his hand and the taller man who followed carrying a rifle. The first man got through the gateway. He ran toward the west and Vic Jamison. He was making heavy going of it on the wet ground and Vic could hear his harsh and erratic breathing. The man was Clayton Mostyn.

Buck Fresno turned and looked back up the slope. The rifle flamed from the higher ground. Vic ran between the fleeing Mostyn and the barbed-wire fence. He slammed a shoulder against the Texas gate and closed it just as Buck Fresno ran full tilt into it. The Texan cursed as the rusty barbs tore at his flesh. He threw himself sideways as Deborah fired again.

Vic poked his rifle barrel between the strands and rammed the muzzle against the foreman's ribs. "Drop the rifle, Fresno," he ordered.

Buck dropped the rifle from his left hand and then drew and cocked his Colt to thrust it between the strands. The Colt blasted flame and smoke close to Vic's side. He felt the burning passage of the bullet across his flesh and involuntarily dropped his rifle. He gripped Fresno's right with his left-hand wrist and forced the arm upward as the Colt cracked again. Fresno backhanded Vic across the top of the fence.

Vic hooked a right toward Fresno's jaw. The Texan gripped Vic by the neck scarf with his left hand and dragged his head down and across the wire. The barbs tore at Vic's throat skin. Vic gagged as Fresno twisted the scarf in a powerful hand. Vic swung Fresno's right arm hard down on the top strand, broke free from the neck hold and then dragged down hard on the Texan's right arm to hook the armpit atop the wire. Fresno screamed hoarsely as the rusty inch-long barbs stabbed into his armpit.

The Texan spat full into Vic's face and tried to drag him across the wire. He thrust a leg through the lower strands and tried to boot Vic. The top strand of wire loosened and sagged with the weight of the two big men struggling across it. The wire sagged toward Fresno's side and then snapped. The foreman lay flat on his back. He placed a foot against Vic's lean gut and lifted him up into the air to drive him back. Vic lost his hold on Fresno's right wrist. The Texan got up on his feet with the blood running down his lean face. He snatched up his Colt and thrust it toward Vic. Vic gripped the loose strand of wire and the loop of it settled about Fresno's neck. Vic jerked hard just as Fresno fired. The bullet whined off into space.

Vic dragged back on the wire to upset Fresno. Fresno gagged thickly and tried to get the choking wire from about his neck. A gun flamed from somewhere behind Vic. He let go of the wire and dropped flat on the ground. Mostyn came running through the darkness, firing wildly.

"For Christ's sake, Mostyn! It's me! Fresno!" the Texan yelled thickly.

A bullet struck Fresno's left arm. He went down in a tangle of rusty barbed wire and rolled over to get out of the line of fire. The loose wire about his throat snubbed itself about a post. He screamed hoarsely as the wires tightened inexorably because of his frenzied thrashing.

Vic couldn't help him. He'd get a bullet in his back if he tried. He crayfished back from the fence trying to locate Mostyn by a gun flash if he fired again.

For a little while the only sounds to be heard were Fresno's silent struggle with the deadly wire that entangled him and then it was fully quiet except for the soft, dry whispering of the faint wind.

Water splashed. Vic raised his head. Mostyn was retreating, fording the shallow stream.

He went softly up the slopes. "Deborah?" he called.

She came to him through the darkness trailing her rifle.

"You did well," he told her.

"Who was it?"

"Mostyn and Fresno."

"Where are they now?"

"Fresno is dead. Mostyn is running scared."

"Can he escape?"

Vic shook his head. "Not now, or ever. We can probably pick him up by dawn light."

"What do we do now?"

He took her rifle from her hands. "Follow me," he said. They returned to the simple camp they had on the slope below the south wall of the canyon.

"Sleep?" he asked.

She shook her head. "I can't."

"Then you can have first watch, ma'am."

"How can you sleep after all that killing?"

"Simple," he replied. "Just watch me."

She watched him for a little while, and sure enough, he was right.

CHAPTER SIXTEEN

Vic was up before the coming of the false dawn. He found a saddled dun and a sorrel in the thick timber behind the cabin. Deborah joined him as the sky lightened.

Vic went ahead on foot followed by Deborah leading the horses. From cover he saw a man walking hastily toward the southern wall of the canyon. The field glasses picked out Clayton Mostyn.

Vic waited for her. "I saw him," he said. "I'll cross the stream and flush him. You ride on the northern side of the stream and keep him from crossing. He hasn't got a rifle, so you don't have to worry about keeping out of range. If we can keep him on the move, we can trap him at the west end of the canyon."

Vic rode the dun across the stream and then dismounted. He led the horse on until he saw a furtive movement in the thick brush at the base of the canyon wall. He sighted on the wall fifty feet above Mostyn's head and fired. Bits of decomposing rock pattered down into the brush. Mostyn moved quickly, revealing his passage by the movement of the brush.

Vic lost Mostyn for half an hour and then he saw him crawling through the brush toward the stream. Vic put the glasses on him. The growing light revealed his pale, drawn face. Vic could almost sense the sick underlying fear within the man.

Vic let him crawl into the open toward the stream. The first bullet pocked the wet ground a foot off his face. The second bullet fanned over his head as he galloped frantically back toward the brush.

Vic hooked a leg around the saddle horn of the dun and slowly shaped a quirly while watching Mostyn's frantic passage through the brush.

Vic smoked as he rode slowly across the stream and toward the brush. He snubbed out the cigarette and then spurred the dun forward, crashing through the crackling brush and giving vent to wild yells that echoed back and forth in the canyon. He punctuated the yelling with rifle shots.

Mostyn broke from the brush and wearily legged it across the soft wet ground. Occasionally, his pale frightened face would be turned to look back at the brush but he never saw anything, except now and again the pale bluish wraith of gun smoke hovering over the brush, and always the sibilant hissing of the bullet past his face when he tried to turn toward the east and the safety of the east pass.

There was a great talus slide that flowed from a broken part of the canyon wall. At the foot of it were large tip-tilted boulders. As Vic passed around and among them, he lost sight of the rancher.

The sun was now up high, and the canyon grew warm with its heat. When next Vic saw Mostyn he had made it across the stream and was plowing toward the safety of the timber. A rifle cracked from within the shelter of the timber. Mostyn stopped short, looked back over his shoulder with a puzzled look, and then ran for the stream.

He almost dived into the water to get under the shelter of the bank. He raised his head to look north toward the timber. A bullet ricocheted from the surface of the water. This time Mostyn looked to the south with fear etched on his sweating face.

Mostyn at last stood up, knee-deep in the cold water. He looked neither to the right nor the left as he slogged along in the water, crouching under the dubious shelter of the low stream banks. Once he stood up and looked back to see a woman riding slowly along the edge of the timber. The sun shone on the rifle she carried across her thighs. Mostyn looked to the left. A lean man sat on a rock with a faint wisp of cigarette smoke about his face. A horse cropped the grass behind him. The sun reflected from his rifle barrel.

He reached close to the underground passage and churned his legs in a desperate attempt to get into the shelter of the passageway. Slug after slug struck the top and sides of the opening. Shards of lead and bits of decomposed rock flew back in a shower about the rancher. Some of them struck his face and hands. Tiny trickles of blood ran down his bared flesh.

"Mostyn!" Vic yelled. "The game is up!"

"Mostyn! Mostyn! Mostyn! The game is up! The game is up! The game is up!" dutifully echoed the canyon.

Then it was quiet again.

Mostyn stopped in his stride. He turned and passed a shaking hand across his mouth. Then he fell forward in a dead faint into the stream.

Vic galloped to the stream. He dismounted and dragged Mostyn from the stream and dumped him face downward on the ground. Vic hooked a boot toe under the man and heaved him over on his back so that his arms were outflung. His mouth was agape revealing his small and even white teeth, like those of some rodent.

Deborah looked away in revulsion. "Is he dead?" she asked.

"No," Vic replied.

"It would have been better for him to have died," she said quietly.

Vic looked east along the great canyon. It was now filled with bright sunlight that reflected from the dancing ripples of the swift stream. The grass shivered in the searching wind and the trees swayed in a slow and pleasing rhythm with the wind, soughing softly. It was a pleasant place, indeed a beautiful place, but the shadow of sudden and violent death still overhung it. It would be a long time before that shadow was gone and perhaps it would never leave. Some places have long memories, even into eternity.

"It's a fine day," Vic observed quietly.

He thrust a stick through the inner parts of Mostyn's elbows and across his back. He tied the wrists across the paunch of the man. "Keep an eye on the little Napoleon, Deborah," Vic said. "I'll check out the valley for strays."

"The cattle are all at this end of the valley."

"I was thinking of human strays," he said.

Vic rode east along the stream bank. He found wire cutters, a coil of barbed wire and a hammer and staples within the cabin. He took them and a spade with him. He checked the barbed-wire fence from one end to the other for breaks. He had to cut Buck Fresno loose from the barbed wire that had strangled him. He dumped the body over the saddle of the dun and led the horse to where Bert Hanna had died. Vic placed both bodies in a rock cleft and filled it in with loose rock and earth. He marked the improvised grave with a crude cross of branches wired together. "Our loss is heaven's gain," he murmured.

There was no use in looking for the bodies of the two men who had died under the trampling hoofs of the herd. A clump of greener grass or a bouquet of bright spring flowers would eventually mark their graves. He found the other bodies and buried them as he had buried Fresno and Hanna. If the Apaches had feared the canyon with superstitious dread before this time, they would surely never come there now.

"Deborah!" Vic called.

"Deborah! Deborah! Deborah!" the canyon echoes mimicked.

There was no answer.

He looked at the mouth of the passageway. The two of them must have gone through it to the outer canyon. Why? Clayton Mostyn could not have possibly gotten loose and overpowered her. Why had she gone back through the passageway?

Vic picketed the dun and then withdrew his Winchester from the saddle scabbard. He walked toward the passageway. Once more he looked toward the east and the glory of the quiet canyon in the bright sunlight, and then he entered the wet and darkness of the passageway.

He could hear the muted roaring of the falls at the other end of the passageway. Vic paused ten feet back from the inner side of the falls with the cold spray of it drifting back against him. He could see the brightness of the sunlight through the falling water but nothing else. He knew better than to walk out into that sunlight.

Vic pulled off his boots. He left them with his hat and Winchester as he waded into the icy water of the pool beneath the falls with his cocked Colt held under his left armpit. He tried to eye-pierce the roaring, opaque veil of water but it was no use. He kept back against the rock wall beyond the mouth of the passageway and worked his way to his right with the water rising icily up his thighs and then to his waist. He slid a little and it became armpit deep. His breath was expelled from his lungs by the paralyzing action of

the icy water. He waded on until the water reached his neck
and then he was under the icy, insensate pounding of the
pouring water that threatened to completely numb his senses.

He was close to the edge of the falls now where a froth of
spume and water swirled up from the pool surface. He went
under the water and thrust his Colt under his belt, then swam
to his right until his questing hands touched rock. He turned
his head and looked upward to see the bright sunlight shining
on the water of the rock pool beyond the edge of the falls.

Carefully and slowly, he raised his head from the water.
His breath was gone. He opened his mouth to inhale, fighting
against the cold paralysis of his torso. He blinked his eyes
free of the clinging water.

A man sat on the edge of the pool across from where Vic
had broken water. He was steadfastly watching the falling veil
of water. He wore a dirty bandage across his left eye. A
Winchester rifle rested across his thick thighs.

There was no sign of Deborah and Clayton Mostyn.

Vic kept back as far as he could, trying to make sure he
was in the blind spot of Cass Page's left eye. He slid from the
pool and behind some rocks and as he did so his Colt was
dragged from his belt, and it slid into the pool.

Vic lay still, trying to fight off the enervating chill of the
icy water. Cass Page had not moved. His one eye was fixed
steadfastly on those falls, waiting for Vic Jamison to come
through into the bright sunlight and dark death.

Vic worked his way back under cover. He slid his right
hand behind his back and withdrew his sheath knife. It was a
good one of Sonoran make, tempered with blood and
balanced like a watch wheel.

Vic stood up beyond the arc of vision of Cass Page's one
eye. The man was a good fifty feet away. The sound of Vic's
approach was muffled by the roaring falls.

Thirty feet and no sign of recognition from Page.

Twenty feet. A man yelled hoarsely from somewhere up the canyon. Cass Page jumped to his feet and whirled, raising his rifle as he did so. The balanced Sonoran blade flashed in the sunlight and struck deep into Page's throat. He dropped the rifle. It exploded and the bullet hissed over Vic's head. Page gripped the haft of the knife in both hands. He fell sideways into the pool like a felled pine.

Vic picked up the rifle. He ejected the spent cartridge case. He turned it over to read the base of it—U.M.C. .50/.95. He ejected the fresh round that was now in the chamber. The tip of the bullet had been drilled out to take a .22 blank cartridge.

Vic faded into the brush at the south side of the falls. Some man had yelled about the time Vic had been stalking Page. He narrowed his eyes and scanned the canyon.

"Vic! Vic!" she called.

"Deborah!"

She ran to meet him.

Clayton Mostyn lay unconscious in a rock hollow. Vic eyed him, then looked at Deborah. "Well?" he asked.

She grinned. "They didn't tie me up, Vic. That was where they made their mistake. I wasn't fast enough to stop Mostyn from yelling at Cass Page, but I made damned sure he wouldn't yell again."

THEY HAD RIDDEN TOGETHER from Tonto Springs. A faint and misty rain was falling as they neared the charred ruins of the Star Cross buildings. They drew rein. Vic took out the makings. He shaped two cigarettes and placed one between her full lips. He lighted her cigarette and then his. They smoked quietly for a time.

He looked sideways at her. "What is it to be?" he asked.

She would not look at him. "I can't rebuild, Vic. Not now. There are too many memories here."

"They'll fade someday."

"I hope so."

"I can collect almost fifteen thousand in reward money, Deborah. Part of it was donated by Clayton Mostyn." He grinned.

"You've earned it, Vic."

He shrugged. "I thought of giving most of it to the widows and children of the Rangers who died in the Rio Diablo Valley."

"Or?"

He looked at her. "Half of it could go to buy part of the Star Cross."

The wind soughed through the rain-dripping pines.

"Is that what you really want?" she asked.

"I think so. With you, of course."

She bowed her head and passed a gloved hand across her eyes. "I had thought of returning to Denver, Vic. I can teach there. I might come back someday."

"Someday..."

She looked at him. "And you," she said quietly. "You're not ready to settle down nor will you come to Denver with me."

It was the truth. There could be no denying that.

He flipped his cigarette away. He kneed his horse away from hers. It was a long way to Stray Horse Canyon and Vic's first stop on his way to Globe. The day was shortening.

Impulsively she leaned toward him to kiss him. He shook his head. "I might just change my mind if you did that," he said.

She watched him ride off.

He turned in the saddle. That fine grin of his broke the hard lines of his scarred face. "*Vaya!*" he called back. Then he was gone in the drifting mist and rain.

THE PROUD GUN

CHAPTER ONE

The Standard whistled for the crossing just outside of Sundown and the echo of the locomotive whistle died away in the low New Mexican hills just to the west of the mining town. Bright morning sun shone through the dirty windows of the coach. Les Gunnell opened his eyes as the train ground to a bone-shaking halt at the station. He rubbed his stiffened right shoulder, then stood up, gathered his warbag, saddle, and Winchester, and carried them out onto the platform. He looked across Railroad Avenue down Front Street. Sundown hadn't changed too much in the years he had been ranching in the remote Soledad country. It was still the curious amalgamation of thick-walled adobe buildings of the Mexican Colonial period interspersed with the warped and ugly false-fronted structures of the American period.

Above the town, to the west, on the scrub-tree stippled slopes of the hills, were the rusting structures of the old Silver Nugget mines, sagging in decay. Below the dark skeletons of the abandoned buildings were the blackened slag and weathered tailings dumps. The mounds had always reminded

Les of graves. In a sense, they were graves for the mines had been dead for a good many years.

The Silver Nugget. That was where the Mexican kid who had known too much about the death of Marshal Will Ripley had been found with a broken neck. Will Ripley, the name itself was a stab into Les' heart. Rumor had it that Will Ripley had not only inherited Les' star and the woman he loved, but Les Gunnell's enemies as well.

He descended to the street. Front Street was practically deserted. Not a horse was tethered to the railings in front of the saloons. Here and there an industrious shopkeeper was sweeping out his store, scattering clouds of thin dust through which the morning sun shone on the dancing dust motes.

A swamper was flushing the boardwalk in front of the Miner's Friend. A dog lay asleep on the walk edge and next to him, on the street, lay a sleeping drunk. Les grinned a little. He could have sworn he had seen that same drunk and that same dog lying there when he left Sundown years ago.

He walked down the center of the street to avoid the dust and the water. There was no use in trying to appear inconspicuous. In less than an hour the whole town would know that Les Gunnell had returned to Sundown. At Willow and Front he stopped and looked down the street toward Cottonwood. The *Sundown News* office was midway between Willow and Cottonwood on the south side of the street. He wondered if Ruth Ripley was there that early.

There were two hotels at Willow and Front, on diagonal corners. The Sundown House and the Silver Nugget. He crossed over to the Silver Nugget, the massive hotel that had been built from proceeds of the mine that had given it its name. The lobby was deserted. To his right was the wide doorway into the barroom, and for the first time in his life he decided he needed a morning drink.

He placed his gear on the floor just outside the doorway

and walked into the long barroom. A swamper was busy cleaning out the back of the long mahogany. "Ain't open yet!" snapped the swamper sourly.

"Hello, Foss," said Les easily.

The old man's head came up like that of an angry turkey buzzard and his washed-out blue eyes stared at Les. He hastily wiped a hand on his dirty apron and thrust out the hand. "Fergodsakes! Les! Les Gunnell!" he said with pleasure.

Les gripped the damp hand. "Do I get my drink?"

"Sure, Les! Sure!" The old man bustled for a bottle and a glass. "Rye, ain't it?"

"It'll do. Get one for yourself, Foss."

"Now that's right kind of you, Les!" Foss filled the glasses and glanced sharply at Les. "Been a long time," he said.

Les sipped the liquor. "Surprised to see you still swamping, Foss. What happened to that little business you were going to buy?"

The washed-out eyes blinked. "Oh...that? Well, it was like this, Les. I..."

"Forget it, Foss."

The old man had been around Sundown from the days when it had been a sleepy New Mexican *placita* in the hills. That had been before silver had been discovered. Some people claimed Old Foss had first found silver in the hills and had been gypped out of his claim. The old man's life was a continual battle between absolute sobriety and complete drunkenness, and no one seemed to know when he was due for a high lonesome or a stretch on the wagon. They didn't really care, for that matter. Les had always used Foss for the one valuable asset the old man had. He knew everybody in Sundown and the county, too. There was very little he didn't know about the events, past and present, in the history of Sundown. He might not remember where he had been the night before, but he could remember names, faces and personal descriptions of every outlaw, high-binder, tinhorn and madam in that county.

Foss raised his glass. *"Salud!"*

"Salud!"

Foss drank and then wiped his mouth. He squinted at Les. "Come back for your old job?"

"No. Besides, I understand Tracy Gant is marshal now."

Foss snorted. *"Him!* Three top men in a row and then we get Tracy Gant."

"Tracy is a good man," said Les. He raised his glass and eyed the clear liquor.

"Sure! Sure! But there ain't no man like Gant can keep peace in this damned country. Used to be Matt Horan ran Sundown and the county, too. That was before Ted Varney run him out'a Sundown."

"And got killed by the Chacon Boys for his trouble."

Foss swallowed and his Adam's apple seemed to run up and down his throat like a tin monkey on a string. "Fer-chrisakes, Les!" He glanced toward the outer door. "Well, anyways, they wasn't no hanky-panky when you was marshal here. Never could figger out why you left Sundown until one day I was coming out of a three-day drunk and I thought to myself, I would'a done the same thing if I was in your boots."

"Why, Foss?"

Foss refilled his glass. "With the Chacon Boys, Matt Horan and half a dozen other hombres thirsting for your blood? I would'a dusted out'a here long before you did."

Foss tossed down his drink and refilled his glass. "Now Will Ripley was a good man. Trouble is that he and Ruth tried to clean up the county as well as the town."

"Ruth Varney is what they call a 'crusading newspaper-woman', Foss."

"Yes, but it ain't *Varney,* Les. You forget she married Will Ripley after Ted Varney was killed."

The gray eyes clouded a little. "No...I didn't forget."

"Now things go from bad to worse. That colt of Ted Varney's shows up in town carrying two guns in tied down holsters, looking for trouble because of the death of his steppa. Heath Sabin wings the boy. Lucky for the kid he ain't wearing a pine suit with brass handles trimming it."

"How bad is it, Foss?"

Foss leaned closer. *"Real* bad, Les Worse than I ever seen, and you know there ain't no one knows more about Sundown than Old Foss here. There'll be more killings, Les. You get out'a here on the afternoon train and don't come back. Go on back to wherever you was hiding these past years. You played it smart when you left here. Git, and don't come back no more, amigo!"

The front door opened. Foss glanced quickly toward it. He paled a little. "Chihuahua!" he said softly.

Les did not turn as he heard the steady striking of boot heels on the floor.

"Bourbon, Foss," said a pleasant-sounding voice. "How are you, Mister Gunnell?"

Les turned. A tall man stood a few feet behind him, right arm resting lightly on the bar. There was a smile on the lean handsome face. The blue eyes seemed to dance with friendliness, but Les had been in that country too long to make any mistake about a man's character from his outward appearance. "Hello, Sabin," he said.

"I heard you were in town, Gunnell."

"Morning train."

"I saw you from my room in the Sundown House. Staying long?"

Les sipped at his rye. For a moment a strange feeling of fear crept over him. In the old days a man like Heath Sabin would have been tough enough to handle, but now, with Les long away from his old profession and with a stiff shoulder to boot, he had a feeling that Heath Sabin would be too fast for him.

"You didn't answer me, sir," said Sabin. His southern accent was soft, but there was steel beneath it.

"I'll be here a while."

"You've been gone a long time. Changed some, too, haven't you?"

"How so?"

The careless blue eyes flicked up and down. "Touch of gray at the temples. Very distinguished, though. A few lines here and there."

"It comes to us all, Sabin."

Foss placed a bourbon bottle and a glass in front of the gunman. Sabin poured a drink. His hand was as steady as an anvil. "I don't suppose you've come about the shooting we had here last week?"

"Why I came is my own business."

Sabin smiled. "Sure!" He downed his shot quickly. "I thought what with Will Ripley hardly cold in his grave after getting shot down and his step-kid looking for trouble so that I had to wing *him*, you might have some idea of coming back here to be the big auger in Sundown, as you used to be."

Foss swallowed hard.

Les was tired and his right shoulder ached like an abscessed tooth. "I don't know who murdered Will," he said quietly. "From what I heard about you winging the kid, you made damned sure he couldn't shoot back. Why, Sabin? Did you think he was too fast for even you?"

In the sudden silence they could hear the steady ticking of the big clock in the lobby. Sabin's eyes were like pools of blue ice. "You heard a lot," he said softly. "I can take him easy, Les Gunnell."

"So? Why didn't you? Or were you paid only to warn him?"

"Oh my God," said Foss weakly.

There was a flickering of fire beneath the ice in the blue eyes. The southern hotspur blood was heating. Sabin swung up an arm to slap Les across the face but Les blocked the blow with his left forearm and drove in a hard jolting right that caught Sabin flush on the button and sprawled him flat on his back with a dazed look in his eyes. An upset cuspidor's contents flowed under the gunman, soaking his coat and trousers.

"Good Christ!" said Foss. He snatched the rye bottle from the bar and disappeared behind the mahogany.

Hot liquid pain seemed to be running through Les' right shoulder. "Get up, Sabin! Make your play!"

Heath Sabin got to his feet. His eyes were still dazed.

Les smiled. "Get out of here, Sabin. Go back and tell Matt Horan your bluff didn't work."

The gunman turned and walked toward the door. The filth from the cuspidor made an irregular stain across the back of his coat and trousers. Les waited for the catlike turn and the fast draw but it never came. Instead, the swinging doors closed behind the tall southerner.

Les spoke out of the side of his mouth. "Where's that bottle, Foss? Don't hog it all!"

The swamper stood up and filled their glasses and the bottle danced a rigadoon against the shot glasses. "My God, Les! That was Heath Sabin! *Nobody* does things like that to him!"

"I did. I'm not so sure it was the right thing to do, though."

"Yeh," said Foss dryly. "Not the *right* thing to do."

Les felt a consuming weariness. In an hour the story would be all over Sundown like wildfire. A fast rider would ride a lathered mount into Matt Horan's Box H spread to tell the political sachem that Les Gunnell was back in town and had knocked Heath Sabin down in the barroom of the Silver Nugget. Old Foss would be hard at work, with bottle and with tongue. It really didn't matter.

Les downed his last drink and placed the money on the bar. "When you sober up, Foss," he said. "I might have work for you to do."

"Sober up? Me? Why I ain't hardly dampened my whistle, Les."

"I guess not. See you later, Foss."

A sleepy desk clerk eyed Les, turned the register and reached for a key. He yawned as he turned the register again and saw the name. His sleepiness vanished and his head snapped up. "Les Gunnell! I'm sorry, Mister Gunnell! I'll give you a better room. Second floor, corner, overlooking Front and Willow."

"Fair enough."

He walked up the carpeted stairs followed by a yawning bellboy carrying his gear. It seemed a long way to the room, but he made it without seeing anyone else. He was sick of people, particularly of people in Sundown, and he hadn't been there more than forty-five minutes.

The door closed behind the bellboy. Les pulled off boots, coat and hat and stood at the window letting the morning breeze play with his damp hair. He looked up and down Front Street. A street of blood in the old days. He could almost hear some of the ghostly voices of the past murmuring to him on the breeze. He dropped on the bed and closed his eyes. He had come home. For better or for worse he had come back to Sundown, almost like one of the ghosts he thought he had heard in the voice of the breeze.

CHAPTER TWO

The knuckles struck the door again in a steady tattoo. Les Gunnell sat up and yawned. "Yes?" he called out.

"Les?" The voice was familiar. "It's Tracy Gant."

Les rolled from the bed and opened the door. "Howdy, Tracy," he said.

The big marshal nodded as he walked into the room followed by a bellboy carrying a coffee pot, cups and rolls on a tray. He eyed Les half fearfully and half in admiration as he placed the tray on a marble-topped table.

Gant paid the boy. "Beat it, Esteban," he said.

Les smiled at the kid. "I know an Esteban," he said. "Esteban Rios. We rode the rio together some years ago. He used to be deputized for me at times."

The kid's face brightened. "Tio Esteban!" he said. "It was for him I was named!"

Les flipped him four bits. "*Dukes* for the brothers and sisters, Esteban the Second."

"*Gracias,* Señor Gunnell!" The boy closed the door.

Gant took out a silver cigar case and offered it to Les. Les selected a short six and bit off the end. Gant snapped a match on his thumbnail and lighted the cigar. "Welcome back to Sundown, Les," he said dryly.

Les sat down and eyed the big marshal. He was going into soft flesh. He had been a powerful man in his day, winning many a bet in catch-as-catch-can wrestling and in weight lifting. He was a good-natured man, hated conflict, and had always managed to play one side of the law against the other, acting more in the role of peacemaker than law enforcer. Yet he was no coward.

"How's Amy?" asked Les.

Gant's round face seemed to light up. "Fine, Les, just fine! She talks about you once in a while."

"A fine woman, Tracy."

"Yes, Les. Too bad you never got married. Does a man good."

"How did you know I wasn't married?"

"The kid told me."

"Holt Varney?"

"Yes." Gant sat down and poured coffee. "But then you always had a soft spot in your head for Ruth, didn't you?"

"You didn't come here to talk about that, Tracy."

The amiable face clouded. "No, I didn't."

"Get on with it then."

"You haven't changed much, Les."

If the man knew, if only all of them knew!

"Gracias," said Les.

"No offense. You always did take the bull by the horns."

"Like this morning, eh?"

The brown eyes were half lidded. "Well, yes, now that you mention it."

"I didn't come back to Sundown to get faced down by Heath Sabin."

Tracy moved a little and the morning sun streaming

through the window glinted from the silver and bronze marshal's star, one of the prides of the City Council of Sundown. It was the same star Ted Varney had passed on to Les Gunnell, who in turn had passed it on to Will Ripley, and...

"Why *did* you come back, Les?"

"*Quién sabe,* Tracy?"

The marshal lighted a cigar and puffed a cloud of smoke toward the window. "I could hazard a few guesses."

"Do," said Les politely. He refilled his coffee cup. Thoughtful of Tracy to bring coffee and rolls, but then that was Tracy Gant's way.

"Like I said, and no offense to you or to a fine upstanding woman, but it might be because you still have a soft spot in your head for Ruth Ripley."

"Go on."

"Her kid got shot down, right in front of her, Les. The kid had been thirsting to avenge Will Ripley. Maybe you figured he couldn't handle the job and came here after all these years to do it yourself."

Les shook his head. "Holt Varney stopped by my *estancia* at Soledad on his way from Colorado to here. I thought, by God, I was looking at Ted Varney come to life again."

Tracy nodded. "Same looks. Same ways."

Les' eyes were troubled.

Gant shook his massive head. "A young rooster with spurs so damned long he'll trip on them, and they'll lay him out in a neat black suit and all the cute little whores on Oak Street will cry their eyes out for him. Some dirty, ornery fighting man with cowcrap on his heels will cut him down to size."

Les sipped at his coffee. It was almost pleasant sitting there talking to a man he had really liked in the old days. "The kid said they were looking for me when they killed Will Ripley," he said quietly.

"That's the story, Les." Tracy sighed. "He never would give an inch and they killed him for it."

"*They?*"

The brown eyes studied Les. "Yeh...they. Shot in the back he was."

Les raised a hand. "Holt told me the story. Will was bowling with Frank Hendries. Seems as though Frank was nervous and asked Will to step back. Lot of money on the series they were playing. The shotgun was rammed through the glass upper half of the rear door. Will whirled and caught the blast in his face. Ten-gauge gun. Split wads. Jesus, couldn't they have used a six-gun?"

Gant refilled his coffee cup. "I guess there ain't much I can tell you about the murder then."

"No. Except who did it."

The curtains fluttered and the tobacco smoke drifted and flowed through the open window. "If I knew, Les, I would have picked them up long ago."

"I'm sure of that." Les leaned forward. "The kid wanted me to come back here with him and clean up Sundown, as he put it. I refused. He didn't exactly like that."

"No?"

Dark blood was beneath Les' skin. "I took more crap from him before he left than I ever took from any man."

"He's feisty, I'll admit."

Les eyed the big marshal. "But there was one witness at least."

"In a way. A Mex kid said he had seen two men run out of the alleyway behind the bowling alley. A third man was holding three horses. The three men rode toward the Estancia Road."

"And they found the kid a few days later at the bottom of a shaft in the Silver Nugget with a broken neck."

"Yes."

"Neatly done."

Tracy waved a hand to clear the tobacco smoke. "So you came back to clear up the mess, eh?"

"I didn't say that."

"There isn't any other reason. You and your damnable pride. You were the big auger around here. Five years ago, you ran Sundown. It wasn't our beloved mayor and his stupid council. It wasn't the people, and it wasn't Matt Horan. It was Les Gunnell."

The town was coming to life. Wagons rattled by in the streets. Horses whinnied. Whips popped. The ringing of steel against metal came from a blacksmith's shop on Willow.

"Who actually killed Will, Tracy?"

Gant looked out of the window. "I don't know."

"You sure?"

"Dammit! Yes!"

"I had heard Will and Ruth were doing a good job around here cleaning up things."

"It wasn't the time or the place."

"Why did you deputize Holt Varney?"

Gant turned quickly. "Everyone asks me that!"

"Well?"

The big marshal flushed. "Well, he's fast with a gun and has the guts to back it. Besides, I owed it to Will Ripley."

Les relighted his cigar. "Why?"

Gant tilted his head to one side. "What the hell is riling you, Les?"

Les looked through the wreathing smoke. "Seems to me you didn't do much of anything after the mines closed down, Tracy. You were an armed guard up there. You look flush. Certainly, Sundown hasn't increased a marshal's pay that much?"

Gant wet his lips. "What are you driving at?"

Les walked to the bed and reached for his boots. "Amy

still running the boarding house on Sage Street near the Mexican quarters?"

"Dammit! No!"

It was an old wound with Tracy Gant. He had never been much of a provider and Amy Gant had helped out by running a shabby, but *genteel,* boarding house.

Les pulled on his boots and then took a clean shirt from his warbag. He slowly tied his string tie.

Gant shifted his feet. "Well, if you have to know, I own the Sundown House now."

Les glanced through the window. It was the second-best hostelry in the town and worth quite a sum. It had a good bar and an excellent dining room, rated the best in Sundown. "Quite a pile," said Les over his shoulder. "The best I could afford with my marshal's pay was a down payment on a rundown range in the Soledad country."

"So *that's* where you were hiding!"

Les shrugged into his coat. "Who said that?" he asked mildly.

Gant flushed. "It wasn't me!"

"Then who was it? Matt Horan? The Chacon Boys? Heath Sabin? Who, Tracy? Who?"

"It's all over town is all."

Les slid a hand into his left coat pocket to feel the cold metal of the double-barreled derringer in there. Odd how the habits of years returned to a man when the chips were down. Or were the chips down? He could pull out of Sundown as quietly as he had reappeared. "You'd like to see me leave, wouldn't you, Tracy?"

"Now, Les!"

Les took his hat and put it on. "Where did you get the money to buy the Sundown House?"

"None of your damned business!"

"I've heard tell that Sundown is getting to be the way it

used to be before Ted Varney took the marshal's star and cleaned up the town."

"You're talking too much now, Les. I warn you…"

Les walked to the door and turned and it seemed to Tracy Gant that the years had fallen away and he was facing the marshal of Sundown instead of being the marshal himself. "Don't warn *me*, Gant," Les said quietly. "Find out who killed Will Ripley. *If you don't, I will.*"

Gant stood up. "You're not the law here anymore, Gunnell. You can't bully people like you used to."

"No? Then who is the law here? Did Matt Horan give you the money to buy the Sundown House? What did you tell Amy when she asked you where you got all that money? That must have been a masterpiece of lying. You never could gamble worth a damn and if you had won the money gambling, she would have made you give it back. I know Amy, Tracy."

Gant was fish-belly white beneath his ruddy complexion. "Damn you! I hope to God Heath Sabin gives you a comeuppance today, Gunnell!"

"Maybe he will, Tracy, maybe he will," said Les thoughtfully. He opened the door. Tracy Gant put on his hat and walked ponderously into the hallway. They walked downstairs together and as they crossed the lobby people looked up at them.

"Where's the kid?" asked Les.

"At my place."

"Home?"

"No…the hotel. Amy insisted on taking care of him. You know how she is, Les."

Les nodded. They walked out to the street and a stranger, looking at them, would have said Gant was the real *man* of the two. They stopped on the boardwalk, beneath the overhang of the second story of the hotel. Those who passed may have remembered Les Gunnell from the old days. The Les Gunnell of the Tascosa fight. When the gun smoke had cleared two of the Danvers *corrida* had been dead on the floor at Les Gunnell's feet. Then there had been the fight at the Horsehead Crossing of the Pecos between Gunnell and the Seven Rivers crowd. Les still carried a chunk of lead in his shoulder from that hassle. Some of them may have remembered him as the man who had cleaned up Sundown and had made it a good place for a man to raise a family. There may have been others who hated his guts, knowing that if he became marshal again there would be hell to pay in Sundown.

"Where to?" asked Gant.

"To the Sundown House. I want to see the kid."

"I'll be in my office, Les."

Les waved a hand and crossed the street. Tracy Gant caught the eye of a bench-legged cowpoke. "Lee!" he called.

"Yes, marshal?"

Gant looked up and down the street. "Ride out to the Box H," he said in a low voice. "Tell Matt Horan that Les Gunnell is back in Sundown."

"That all?"

Gant flushed. "Ain't that *enough!* Get moving!"

Tracy relighted his cigar as Lee left. He moved his coat a little so that the marshal's badge would get the full benefit of the bright sunlight, then he walked with a heavy stride along Front Street, nodding seriously to the men who spoke to him, tipping his hat to the ladies, eying suspicious-looking characters coldly. The very picture of law and order was Tracy Gant.

CHAPTER THREE

H olt Varney was propped up in bed reading the latest issue of his mother's newspaper when Les walked into the room. "Howdy, kid," said Les pleasantly.

Holt lowered the paper. His handsome face was pale, and a bandage covered his right upper arm. "Gunnell," he said. There wasn't much of a welcome in his tone.

Les picked up a chair, twirled it, thrust it between his legs and sat down, resting his arms on the back of the chair. "How's the arm?"

"It was just a flesh wound." The kid flushed. "I never had a chance. I had a drunk by the arm when Sabin drew on me."

"That figures."

"I'm not afraid of Heath Sabin, Gunnell!"

"No."

"I'm as fast as he is. Maybe faster."

"It's possible."

"I didn't see you anxious to match draws back in Soledad!"

Les took out the makings and rolled a cigarette. "Smoke?" he asked.

"Thanks."

Les placed the cigarette between the kid's lips and lighted it for him, then he slowly fashioned one for himself. "I suppose you're wondering why I came back to Sundown alone after refusing to come back with you?"

"I really don't give a damn anymore, Gunnell."

"You're lucky you're not dead."

The eyes hardened. "I can take care of myself!"

"Did it ever occur to you that the wound you got was intended to be just a warning?"

"No."

"It was."

"Just what do you mean?"

"They could have dry-gulched you. Put a drunken gun-toting fool up to bracing you. Slipped a knife between your shoulder blades in some dark alley. One way or another they could have put you out of the way."

"You think you know all the dodges, don't you?"

Les grinned. "No, but I know a good many of them."

"All right! Why didn't they kill me then?"

"Your father died because he fought them. Your stepfather was murdered for the same reason. The townspeople here stomached a lot because of the death of two good marshals."

"Then why didn't they do something about it?"

"They will, kid."

Varney spat into the cuspidor. "Sheep!" he said.

"Don't delude yourself. These people have as much guts as any gunslick or outlaw. Takes a long time to really rile them, but when they're riled..."

"That'll be the day."

"If Sabin had killed you this town would have risen like a volcano and blown hell out of Sundown."

"You really believe that?"

"I *know* it."

"Then why wasn't anything done when I was wounded?"

"Maybe all they need is a leader, kid."

"Like you?"

"I didn't say so."

"No." The kid flipped the cigarette into the cuspidor. "There's a helluva lot you don't say." His eyes narrowed. *"Les! Get down! Hit the floor!"* he yelled.

Les rolled from the chair, carrying it along with him, at the same time a gun flatted off across the street. The slug smashed through the upper part of the window and struck the wall just over where Les had been sitting, showering the kid with plaster.

Les drew his Colt and bellied off to one side. "Get off that bed," he said.

The kid rolled over onto the floor.

"Where did it come from?" asked Les.

"Second floor corner room of the Silver Nugget."

"Jesus Christ!"

"What's wrong?"

"That's *my* room!"

"I saw the rifle barrel poke between the curtains. That shot a warning, or they mean to get you?"

Les stood up, out of line with the window. "They won't shoot again. Whoever it was is long gone now. They cover up well."

"You said *they.*"

Les smiled. "Did I?"

They walked into the hallway together in time to see plain-faced Amy Gant hurrying toward them. Her hands worked. "Les Gunnell! I might have known there'd be trouble when you came back to Sundown!"

"Now, Amy!" said Les with a smile.

"I've been trying to give this *establishment* a good name, Les Gunnell!"

Les grinned. "With Heath Sabin as one of your *guests?*"

She glanced nervously over her shoulder. "I can't pick and choose, Les. Besides, he's always smiling, and he always pays his bill on time."

"That surely covers a multitude of sins."

She peered past them into the room. "My, my! What happened in there?"

"Bird flew through the window, Mrs. Gant," said Holt. "It was so clean he didn't see the glass. I'll pay for it."

"Well, now, that's right nice of you!"

"No bother, Mrs. Gant."

She scurried down the long hall.

"I'll see you later, kid," said Les. "Your mother at the office?"

"I imagine so."

Les walked toward the stairs.

"Gunnell!"

Les turned and eyed the kid.

"She hasn't forgotten Will Ripley," he said.

Les nodded, then walked down the stairs. As he crossed the lobby people turned to look at him. "That's Les Gunnell!" a woman said breathlessly.

"Yore loco, Ruby," said her husband, rudely.

"It's him, I tell you, Sid! I'd know him anywhere."

Les stopped on the boardwalk and looked up and down the crowded street. He looked up at his hotel window. The curtains blew innocently in and out. People jostled past him. With a start he suddenly realized it was Saturday.

He crossed Willow and walked toward the newspaper office. The saloons were open and doing a good business. Many of them had been established since his time there. At least three of them looked brand new. Probably opened since

Will Ripley had been murdered. There had been a time when the number of such establishments had been limited. The whirring of roulette wheels came to him, and the noise of chuck-a-luck cages being twirled. Sundown was wide open again.

Ranch wagons and buckboards rolled along the dusty street, with poke-bonneted ranch women seated beside their husbands, while kids stuck mopheads over the tailgates. Saturday was always a big day for the kids.

A drunk staggered right down the center of the street, narrowly avoiding teams and wagons. He stopped in front of a saloon, drew out a Colt and fired three times in the air. The reports echoed back and forth, and the smoke drifted up the street. "I got bobcat bristles on my belly!" he yelled. "And I aim to drink Sundown dry by sundown! Hawww!" He emptied the pistol, staggered to the boardwalk, then fell flat on his face through the swinging doors.

Les looked at a gray-haired man beside him. "This happen often?" he asked.

The man nodded. "This is nothing, stranger. Wait until tonight. Front Street becomes a suburb of Hell itself about midnight!"

"I can hardly wait," said Les dryly. He glanced up at his hotel window. No wonder the shot had probably gone unnoticed. In the noise of traffic, it would have been ignored. Whoever had fired that rifle had known his business.

He walked into the *News* office. A young woman stood behind the long counter, clipping items from a newspaper. Les found himself looking into the biggest and darkest blue eyes he had ever seen. Coupled with jet-black hair and a creamy skin, the girl was enough to make a man lose all interest in anything else in sight. "Good morning," she said with a dazzling smile. "May I help you?"

"The teeth match the rest," said Les, absent-mindedly.

"Sir?"

He took off his hat and smiled. "Nothing, ma'am! I was looking for Mrs. Ripley."

"She isn't here right now, Mister Gunnell."

He narrowed his eyes. "You know me, ma'am? You have the advantage on me there."

She smiled and glanced back at the room which was the morgue of the *Sundown News*. "I've seen pictures drawn of you," she said. "I'm Rae Weston."

"Pleased to meet you, Miss Weston. When will Mrs. Ripley be back?"

"She went to the Silver Nugget to get a story about a shot being fired from the second floor into the second floor of the Sundown House."

"I might have expected that."

"What do you mean, Mister Gunnell?"

He smiled. "The shot was fired at me."

She paled a little. "They said you were in Holt Varney's room."

"News travels fast," he said dryly.

She tilted her lovely head to one side. "About you in any case, Mister Gunnell."

"I wish you'd call me Les."

"I will if you call me Rae."

"It's a deal then."

"Keno!" she said with a flashing smile. Then the smile vanished. "You seem all right. How is Holt?"

"Better than I am."

She shook her head. "I wish he'd turn in his star. This town is no place for him. He's too wild. Too sure of his guns. Next time they'll kill him."

"You believe that, too?"

"That's what his mother said."

Les placed his hat on the counter. "He'll be all right if he does turn in that star or gets into some other field. Something solid and respectable. The newspaper business for example."

"Do you think he would?"

"If he doesn't he's a fool. Imagine working in the same office with Ruth Ripley and Rae Weston!"

She flashed that glorious smile again and it seemed to light up the rather drab office. "I had a quite different picture of you, Les. The cold, hard-bitten man of law. Yet it doesn't quite seem to fit you. There seem to be some softer qualities about you."

"Thanks," he said.

"But those stories are all true."

"It was a long time ago, Rae."

"Why did you come back?"

"*¿Quien sabe?*"

"You do know!" She leaned closer to him. "Your presence here in Sundown will start gunplay and killing all over again."

"It certainly will," a quiet voice said behind Les.

He turned and saw Ruth Ripley and the old pain stabbed at his heart. The same calm gray eyes, so like those of Holt, studied him. "Hello, Ruth," he said quietly.

She held out a hand, man-fashion, and he took it. The touch seemed to warm his whole body. "I wish I had known you had planned to return," she said.

"Why?"

"I would have written, pleading with you to stay away. I would have made the trip to Soledad to stop you if it was necessary."

"I'm beginning to feel like a pariah in Sundown."

A fleeting shadow crossed her lovely face and eyes. "It isn't that, Les. Holt told me all about his visit with you at Soledad before he came here. It was obvious to me that he had wanted you to come with him to avenge Will's death. I gave you great credit then for refusing to come. Why did you change your mind?"

"I heard that Holt had been wounded."

"It was nothing."

"It was a warning, Ruth. The whole town must know that. The next time they will kill him. Just as they killed Will and Ted."

She paled a little. "You were never one for tact, Les."

"Aces are aces, Ruth."

"Don't you see? They'll know why you came back. They'll know you will ally yourself with Holt. There will be more killings, and two of those killings will be of you and my son."

He studied her. "You don't sound like the crusading news-paperwoman now," he said quietly.

"I know this, Les: You'll never settle the problem here in Sundown by using guns."

Les bowed his head a little. "I had hoped you would have dinner with me tonight, Ruth."

"I'm sorry, Les."

He nodded and picked up his hat.

"It isn't you, Les. But people will talk. I can't be seen with people who create violence in this town."

"I'm glad to know where I stand."

Her face clouded. "Can't you see? It isn't you alone, Les. Oh, why did you have to come back?"

He walked to the door and then turned. "It's been said that I was afraid to come back."

"Is that the only reason?"

He studied her. "Isn't that reason enough? Good morning, ladies." He closed the door behind himself.

Ruth Ripley walked into her little office and shut the door. Rae Weston walked into the morgue and took out the file of clippings about Marshal Lester Gunnell. There was a pen drawing of him looking confidently at her from the center of a page. The headline read: MARSHAL LES GUNNELL DELIVERS THE GOODS. The subline was: Gunnell Brings in Charlie Bowdrey as Expected.

She was still poring through the file when she heard a quiet voice behind her. "Everything you read there is the truth." It was Ruth Ripley. "Les Gunnell was a legend here, Rae."

"*Was?*"

She shrugged and walked to the front of the main office to look through the window. "He *has* changed. You should have known him in the old days. Perhaps he is just the shell of the man he was. They say men sometimes try to return to their past, to recreate it. They never do."

"He doesn't look like a shell to me."

"I don't mean physically. He is just as hard as he ever was, and few men would dare to challenge him on these streets. But it's something in his eyes that I don't understand."

"Perhaps it's you, Ruth."

She turned slowly. "He told me he loved me. I married Ted Varney although everyone in town assumed it would be Les. I don't know why I did it. Ted was handsome, and a good man, but quite different from Les. Ted was killed in the line of duty."

She nodded and shuddered a little. The story of Ted Varney's death was a gruesome one. The Chacon Boys had caught him in the river bottom willows twenty miles from Sundown, helpless with a bullet-smashed thigh. What had been found after the Chacons had gone to work with their *saca tripas* would have been the envy of Apache squaws. They had never been apprehended or brought to trial for the hideous crime.

Ruth paced back and forth. "Then Les Gunnell took over the marshal's star. He had been a sheriff's deputy before then and a good one. His gunfight with the Danvers brothers at

Tascosa and his fight at the Horsehead Crossing of the Pecos are classics of their type, Rae. But after the fight on the Pecos, he was never quite the same. He was wounded in the shoulder, and they could not cut out the bullet. It's still in his body, a constant reminder of his way of life."

Rae studied the older woman. "But after Ted died there was always Les."

Ruth Ripley stopped pacing. "I had a young son. For his own reasons Les did not come to see me. I began going with Will Ripley. Will and Les were like brothers. There never was a finer man than Will Ripley. He was quiet and generous, but a brave man and a fine law officer." She looked away. "It wasn't until I was married to Will for some time that I learned from him that Les had encouraged Will to court me. Will had always liked me but would have kept away from me if he had known Les wanted me. Can you imagine Les Gunnell wanting *anyone?*"

The younger woman carefully folded the papers on the counter and brushed them flat with her fine hands. "Yes, Ruth, I can," she said softly.

Ruth walked toward her office and then stopped. "Do you think he'll leave Sundown before trouble starts?"

"No, I don't."

They looked at each other and both of them knew he'd never leave Sundown until he was ready, or until he was taken from there to Boot Hill.

CHAPTER FOUR

L es worked the lever of his Winchester and the empty brass hull tinkled on the marble-topped table. "Nice," he said quietly. "Used my own saddle-gun to shoot at me."

Little Esteban paled. "I heard the shot, Señor Gunnell. Then I heard a man running in the upper hallway. I ran up the stairs and saw him leave by the door at the end of the hall which leads to the stairway down to the alleyway."

"Who was it, Esteban?"

"I saw nothing but his back, señor. He was a big man. That is all I know. But there are many big men in Sundown."

Les looked from the window. He could still see the splintered shards of glass in Holt Varney's window frame. The light had changed, but at the time the shot had been fired it would have been possible to see into the room. Les raised the rifle and sighted it. It would have been easy to kill him.

"You have the enemies, no señor?"

Les smiled. "I have the enemies, yes, *chico.*"

"It is said you are afraid of no man."

"That is not so, *muchacho.*"

"The señor Foss has been talking."

"He usually is."

"He tells of the fight you had at Tascosa and how you killed five of the Danvers *corrida.*"

"Two, *chico!*"

"Of the fight at the Horsehead Crossing of the Pecos when you downed seven men of the Three Rivers *corrida.*"

"My God," breathed Les. "It was *three* men of the Seven Rivers *corrida.*"

"What does it matter? You have come back to clean up Sundown and that is as it should be."

"Who told you that?"

The boy smiled. "My people know," he said wisely. "Tio Esteban knows. He has the second sight."

"When I get hold of Tio Esteban I'll boot his skinny rump for him."

"That would not bother Tio Esteban! He says you are the *lobo!* A fierce wolf who takes no insults from anyone."

"God in Heaven!"

"My father says you are to come for dinner tonight. There is much to talk about."

Les nodded absent-mindedly.

"The Street of the Burritos at seven o'clock, señor."

"Yes, *chico.*"

The boy silently left the room.

Les sat down on the bed and placed his derringer, Colt and Winchester on newspapers. The tools of his trade. It had seemed to him, when he had left Sundown in the care of Will Ripley, that Will could have kept the peace. There always had been a struggle in Sundown for control of the bordellos and the gambling halls. It had seemed as though the failure of the mines would force Sundown to die at last, but better producing mines had cropped up deeper in the hills to feed payrolls into Sundown, the biggest town within miles. Then too, there were the ranchers and farmers in the more open country who needed the shops and services of Sundown.

Sundown was a rich sugar plum for gamblers, saloon keepers and madams. It was a bonanza for the politicos of the county and none of them was more powerful than Matt Horan. It had been a long battle between Matt Horan and the city fathers of Sundown for control of the town.

Matt Horan had all the money he could ever use in his lifetime. He owned ranches, mines, real estate and business blocks in Sundown and other towns, and he had no need to run for political office to feather his nest. But there was a greed for power within the big man, and the office of sheriff had been practically his by seignioral rights as far back as most people could remember.

It had been Ted Varney who had first challenged Matt Horan's power, aided and abetted by Old Man Hollis and the struggling *Sundown News*. No one had ever connected Matt Horan with the brutal slaying of Ted Varney, but most people had considered it score one for Horan.

Les Gunnell had taken up the challenge and had driven Horan's gun-slicks, crooked gamblers and madams from Sundown. But Les' troublesome shoulder wound and a premonition of the violent death he would suffer if he stayed behind the star in Sundown had eventually driven him away. Perhaps, in effect, Matt Horan had scored twice.

Will Ripley had been next in line, aided by Ruth, who fought as hard in the newspaper columns as he did on the streets. But there must have been an uneasy truce for a long time. It had snapped when Will Ripley had been murdered by a person, or persons unknown. Score three for Matt Horan. It was almost a certainty that the Chacon Boys had done the job and there was a curious relationship between them and Matt Horan.

Les methodically cleaned his weapons, thinking of the

mysterious sharpshooter who had fired at him. Suddenly he stood up. The Mexican kid who had seen Will Ripley murdered had been found at the bottom of a mine shaft with a broken neck. Esteban Rios had seen the man who had fired at Les! *Had that man seen Esteban?*

Les pulled on his coat, then took Colt and derringer. He left the room and hurried downstairs to ask the desk clerk where Esteban was.

The clerk glanced at the clock. "Gone home to eat," he said. "Usually does. Anything wrong, Mister Gunnell?"

"No. I just wanted him to do an errand for me."

"Smart kid. Hard worker, too."

Les hurried out to the street. The boy lived in the Street of the Burritos, one of the nondescript, wandering alleyways in the Mexican quarter near the river.

He walked west, along the north side of Front Street, past the well-remembered saloons and gambling halls. The "run" of the town was from Railroad Street, down Front Street to Oak Street, three blocks, then back up Silver Nugget Street, which was south of Front Street, to Railroad Street. Silver Nugget had been strictly red light in the days before Les had taken over as marshal. Mostly cribs, with the raddled prostitutes who couldn't work out of the fancy houses on Oak Street.

He stopped on the corner of Oak and looked south. The houses were neat and trim, with little yards and picket fences. The houses themselves, despite white-painted gingerbread along eaves and porch roofs, had a secretive look about them.

"Looking for a girl, mister?" a man asked Les.

He was a dowdy-looking character wearing a bowler hat and a checked suit. He winked suggestively and dipped two fingers into a vest pocket to take out an engraved card which he flourished and presented to Les. "At your service, sir!"

"Oak Street?"

"All the girls you want, friend. Redheads, blondes and brunettes. All young. All gay. All experienced, but not too old for the trade. Get me?" He winked.

"The houses look pretty nice for their business, friend."

The man grinned. "Wait until you get inside, mister! You'll see the elephant! Ask for Sylvia DeVine. Tell her Cully sent you."

Les fingered the card. "I didn't know they allowed pimping in Sundown," he said quietly.

Cully laughed. "You're a stranger here. The old marshal didn't allow it, but Tracy Gant is a good man. Far be it from me to say anything, but he tries the girls himself once in awhile." He winked. "Can't blame him. You should see his wife!"

Les crossed the street. So Oak Street was back to its old ways, like a well-dressed woman with a dirty petticoat showing beneath her finery. He wondered if Meg Merrivale, born plain Maggie Murphy, was running her plush call house again.

It was a little early for the high-class girls to be up and about. A colored woman was sweeping the porch of the largest house. "Meg Merrivale in business along here?" called Les.

"Yes, sah! This is the place!"

Les nodded. He might have known. In the old days Meg had left Sundown for other pastures, but she had always had a soft spot in her head for Les. That hadn't stopped her from coming back, for as she liked to say, "The air and water of Sundown is best for my girls."

"Madam Merrivale am asleep right now, sah. Who shall I say called?"

"Les Gunnell."

He walked to Silver Nugget and looked east toward the railroad tracks. It was as it had been years ago. The long adobe walls of the little houses built right against each other. The narrow brick sidewalk and the doors at twenty-foot intervals. Inside each of those doors was one windowless room, containing a big brass bed, a garish counterpane, a chair, a rickety wardrobe, a washstand and a charcoal brazier. Even this early in the day he could see girls, some of them barely in their teens, standing outside their individual rooms, draped with gaudy shawls, looking up and down the street for customers, while a cigarette was pasted in the corner of each overpainted mouth.

He shook his head as he walked west along Silver Nugget toward the river. He passed the same little taco shops, Chinese groceries, cantinas and one-room dwellings.

The Street of the Burritos had been well named, for the side of it next to the river was one long corral crowded with the shaggy little beasts. He found the house of Esteban Rios and rapped on the door. It was opened by a pretty woman who bore a startling resemblance to Esteban. She smiled. "It is Señor Gunnell!" she said in delight. "You are early for supper, but there is lunch. Come in! Come in!"

He smiled as he took off his hat and entered the humble little house. She turned and took his hat. "It is good to know that you have come back to Sundown to make it as it once was."

The legend had started and was being embellished. He had heard it before, even in the remote Soledad country, told to him by wandering peddlers and saddle tramps. The story was told about the fireplaces of Sundown, and also in the cantinas. Señor Les Gunnell would come back some day. It was written, they thought.

"I am no longer marshal, señora," he said quietly.

"I hope you will become marshal once more. There is always trouble in the streets. The young girls are no longer safe. The Mexican boys fight with the gringo boys. There is too much gambling and shooting. And the *putas! Ay de mi!* There are more whores in Sundown than there are in El Paso Del Norte!"

"I have come to see Esteban," he said.

"But he has not yet come home for the lunch. He is late. He has never been late before. Such a good boy. My oldest and my best."

He looked about the shabby little room. She flushed. "It is not much, *señor*. But times are hard here in Sundown. My husband Orlando used to work for the Sundown Freighting and Warehousing Company, but since the death of Señor Ripley he has not done so."

"Why, señora?"

Her face grew troubled. "It was my husband who found the body of the little Melgosa boy in the mine shaft after the murder of Señor Ripley."

"So?"

"Orlando is not a tactful man, Señor Gunnell. He talked too much about what he had found."

"What do you mean?"

She looked about her as though someone might be listening. "He has said that the Melgosa boy did *not* die from the fall. He had seen footprints of men at the top of the shaft in the damp earth. Orlando is a great hunter. That was why he was near the mines. There is water up there and the deer come there instead of to the *rio*. As I told you, he saw footprints of men up there. He did *not* see the footprints of a boy!"

Les slowly rolled a cigarette. "Does Matt Horan still own the Sundown Freighting and Warehousing Company?"

"That is so."

Les lighted his cigarette. Little by little pieces were beginning to fit into the puzzle.

She passed a hand across for forehead. "Why is Esteban late? He has never been this late before."

"I'll look for him, Senora."

Les left the house. There was a sprout of fear within him. Not for himself but for Esteban. Yet it was foolish to think that anyone would try to do away with the boy in broad daylight. He walked to Front Street and looked across the sluggish river toward the Silver Nugget mines. The sun was beating down on the hills and a hazy shimmering was in the hot air. There was no sign of life at the old works other than a lone hawk circling high overhead.

He turned up Front Street and walked back toward the hotel. Perhaps the boy had returned there. A horseman kneed his roan close to the edge of the walk and looked down at Les. "You Les Gunnell?" he asked.

"Yes."

"Matt Horan wants to see you."

"Where is he?"

"At his ranch."

"Tell him if he wants to see me, he can come into town."

There was the ghost of a smile on the man's lean face. "If I was you, I'd come along to the ranch," he said.

"You're *not* me, friend. What does he want?"

The man shrugged. "He said that before you got any ideas on what you were going to do in Sundown, he'd like to talk it over with you."

"Nice of him, I'm sure."

"Come on then."

"I'm busy," said Les.

The man spat leisurely. He turned his hind a little. Another man stood at the head of a rangy sorrel. He eyed Les steadily. Les turned. Another man leaned against the front of Dancey's Livery Stable. He jerked a thumb toward the open door. "They've got a clay bank ready for you, *Mister* Gunnell," he said softly.

It was the Matt Horan touch, sure enough. "You think of everything, don't you?" asked Les of the mounted man.

He smiled quickly. "Not me, *Mister* Gunnell. Matt Horan does the thinking."

Les walked into the stable and got the clay bank. He led it out into the street. The first man rode up beside him. The other two fell in behind. Neat as sin. They clattered across the bridge. A crowd of people were grouped on the riverbank. Two men were thigh deep in the water and they held the slim body of a boy in their arms.

"It is the oldest son of Orlando Rios!" cried a woman. She threw her shawl over her head.

A cold feeling crept over Les. He remembered the soft smile of the boy; the look of admiration he had flashed at Les. What was it he had said? *"You have come back to clean up Sundown and that is as it should be."*

"What's wrong, Gunnell?" asked the man beside him. "You look pale. Seeing a drowned Mex kid bother you? They pull one of them out'a that *rio* about once a month. Good thing, too. Them Mexes have too many kids anyways. Don't let it bother you."

Les looked at the man and the hardness of the scythe of death was in his eyes. "Maybe a drowned Mexican boy wouldn't bother me too much as a rule, hombre. But *that* one does."

He looked back as they reached the river road. The crowd was following the two men who carried the limp body of Esteban Rios up the Street of the Burritos. His people *knew*, he had said, *that Les Gunnell had come back to clean up Sundown.*

CHAPTER FIVE

The Box H ranch buildings showed out clearly from the dun-colored hills to the west of the river. They had been whitewashed and the shutters and doors had been painted a bright green. Vines and plants had been planted in profusion. A *madre acequia* ran from the river between rows of weeping willows and great cottonwoods and the sun sparkled on the clear water in the irrigation ditch.

The ranch buildings took up quite an area and there were many of them. Blooded horses galloped about in a fine three-bordered meadow behind the stables.

The place reeked of opulence, and Les was willing to bet there was hardly a more imposing ranch in that part of New Mexico.

Les' nameless companion swung down in front of the big house. "I'll take your horse," he said.

"I might riot be here long."

The man smiled. "Depends on Mister Horan, doesn't it?"

"I get your point, hombre."

Les walked toward the casa. Matt Horan had done well for a man who had come into that country shortly after the war, with no seat to his pants, one spur, and a battered cap-and-ball Remington with a rocking cylinder as his sole possession. At least that had been the legend spread about him. He had fought for various shady interests until he had risen to the rank of subordinate leader, then he had branched out on his own, some saying that he had done it by the judicious use of blackmail against his old bosses. Not too much, you understand, for Matt Horan liked to be liked. The result was that many of his victims laughed it off, praised Matt as a man with his ear to the ground, and saw that a few political plums came his way. Not too many, you understand, don't let the late saddle tramp get too biggety. They had misjudged their man again. Matt Horan got biggety on his own.

Les slapped the dust from his clothing and walked to the great door set into a wall almost three feet thick. The casa had been the pride and joy of the old Chacon family whom some people had said had come to New Mexico before the devil. The Chacons had gone broke and the old *estancia,* a granted one, had fallen into evil days. Matt Horan had come along in time to marry Consuelo Chacon, fifteen years younger than himself, and, in time, had taken over the management of the Chacon *estancia,* buying out the interests of the three Chacon brothers. It seemed as though he had bought out their loyalty, too, for they had become outlaws, in a country where a *ladron* was sometimes thought of as a shabby Robin Hood, robbing the *ricos* and helping the peons.

In time the Chacon brothers had become known as the leaders of a band of *ladrones* known as the Chacon Boys and if ever there was a band of men whose name brought fear and terror to that part of New Mexico it was the Chacon Boys.

Les lifted the knocker and let it drop. The noise echoed through the hallway behind the thick door. In a few minutes the door swung open, and a maid ushered Les in and led him down a long, tiled hallway toward a door which opened into a patio.

A fountain played in the patio. Flowers bloomed in profusion. There were patches of shade from thick-foliaged trees which rose from the patio to protect parts of the roof of the house from the sun. The patio had been paved with old brick, rose and yellowish in color, and the effect, with the dappled shade upon it, was beautiful.

A broad-shouldered man stood with his back to Les, and he did not have to turn to show his face as identification of Matt Horan. His mellow voice seemed to fill the patio as he talked to a middle-aged man who stood in front of him. The man's shoes were broken, and his trousers were patched at the knee. His huck shirt seemed to hang on his bones. He turned a battered and sweat-stained hat in his gnarled hands and his eyes were upon Matt Horan as though God himself was speaking on the Mount of Olives.

"Now, Prather," said Horan in a sympathetic voice, "you go right home and forget the whole thing. I'll tell my foreman you've got every right in the world to use water from my tanks. Mind you, Prather," he said loudly, holding up an admonishing finger, "I don't agree with your principles, but you need water and as long as Matt Horan has water, a fellow man is welcome to it!"

"My God," breathed Les.

Prather nodded. "I'll fix the fence, Mister Horan. It was my boys done it. They get a little hotheaded. My wife has been poorly, and the baby died last night, sir."

Horan placed a well-manicured hand on the man's shoulder. "Deepest sympathies, Prather," he said solemnly. "Here, my friend." He handed the broken man a bill. "For the baby's funeral. Take the poor little tike into town and tell Mister Dineheart the expense of the coffin is on Matt Horan."

The man was too broken to speak. He walked toward the

door with the bill in his hand and his washed-out eyes were wet with tears. He looked at Les as he passed. "That man has a heart of gold, mister, pure gold!"

Matt Horan turned as Prather left. He smiled. "Les Gunnell! By the powers! It's good to see you, Les."

"You made sure of that, didn't you, Horan?" asked Les dryly.

The great laugh boomed out. "I wanted to talk with you, Les, before it was too late. Set, partner!"

The big man bustled over to a table and fiddled with some bottles. "Rye, isn't it, Les?"

"Always was."

"Odd how I can remember, isn't it?"

"Yes."

"I like brandy. Not the local slop, but Napoleon brandy, the real thing."

Les sat down and watched Horan. He had put on weight but there was still power in the wide shoulders. His face had filled out, but his good looks had remained. The slightly ruddy complexion, the dark hair tinged with gray, the fine hazel eyes.

Horan placed the glasses on a table and leaned back in his seat. "Let me look at you, Les!"

Les sipped at his rye. It was damned good, the best he had tasted in years.

Horan handed a silver cigar case to Les. Les took a cigar and lighted it. Nothing but the very best for Matt Horan.

"I have them sent directly from Cuba," said Matt.

"Figures," said Les quietly.

Horan lighted a cigar and blew out a smoke ring. "Why did you come back, Les?" he asked abruptly.

"I'm not sure myself."

The hazel eyes studied him. "Was it because of what happened to Will Ripley?"

"It was part of the game, Matt."

"Yes." The eyes half closed. "Maybe it was because of Ruth then?"

"You're talking too much, Matt."

Horan laughed. "I always do."

Les drew in on the cigar. Horan had everything, and no matter how he gained it, it was *his*. Why *did* he go on, wearing the star, reaching out for more and more? Perhaps, with all the money in his possession that he could ever use, there was some underlying drive within him which required him to seek power. Yet he had always been satisfied with being sheriff even though there had been talk that Matt Horan could go on, to governor, perhaps; to the Senate; perhaps—*¿quién sabe?* —the presidency itself.

Horan leaned back in his chair. "It didn't take you long to get back into your harness," he said. "By God, Les, why did you knock Heath Sabin down?"

Les closed a big right hand into a fist and looked at it. "Sabin thought he was going to slap my face. To provoke me into a gunfight."

Horan shook his head. "From what I heard you practically threw him out of the Silver Nugget barroom."

Les looked at him quizzically. "You hear everything, don't you, Matt? That was only this morning. Did you hear about the rest of it? How some bastard tried to kill me by firing across Front Street into Holt Varney's room? With *my* rifle, Matt!"

Horan reddened.

"Why did you let Tracy Gant take on Holt Varney as his deputy, Matt?"

"Me? I'm sheriff, Les, not the mayor of Sundown. Gant can hire any man he pleases. It pleased him to hire Varney."

"Anyway, the kid was hot to solve his father's murder."

"That may be."

"You knew damned well what would happen. Sabin warned him, the only way he knew, with the mailed fist. A bullet in the arm."

"You're building castles in the air, Les."

"It would have looked bad to kill Holt Varney, particularly because his stepfather had hardly stiffened in his grave after being murdered in Sundown."

"Will made some enemies here, Les."

"Who? *You* perhaps?"

There was a cold yellowish tinge in the hazel eyes now. "You haven't learned much in the past five years, Les. I don't have anything to do with running Sundown."

Les looked about him. "I know your *estancia* pays well. Does it really pay for all this?"

"Well, certainly I have business interests in Sundown, Les."

"The whorehouses, saloons and gambling hells?"

There was a white tinge beneath Horan's ruddy complexion. Then a startling change came over him. His laugh boomed out. "Always the same, eh, Les? How's the ranching business?"

"All right."

"Hardly making a go of it though, Les."

"How would you know?"

There was no answer and then Les knew that Matt Horan had known all along where Les had been the past five years. Keeping tabs on him, so to speak, and a cold feeling came over Les. It would have been easy for Matt Horan to hire a gun-slick or a dry-gulcher to take care of Les, and no one would have been the wiser.

Horan was watching Les closely. "You see?" he asked.

Les nodded.

"I knew you'd come back. One way or another, you would come back."

"So you waited for me to make the move. Why?"

"You stand aces high with a great many people around here, Les. To most of the Mexes you're a sort of hero. Certainly, they like me. I spend enough money on them. But I never really rated with them the way you do."

"So?"

Horan relighted his cigar and his eyes were intent on Les through the smoke. "What do you want, Les?"

It was quiet in the patio, beyond the splashing of the fountain and the murmuring of the wind through the trees. It was a lovely place and had been until Matt Horan had formed and aimed his question. Now there was a feeling of filth in the sunlit place.

Horan leaned back in his chair. "I need a good deputy, Les. A man I can *trust*."

A whimsical smile passed across Les' tanned face. "Me? After the war we fought years ago? You were either a Horan man or a Gunnell man in those days. There wasn't anything else. Do you think the people would stomach an association between the two of us?"

"These people are fools. Tell them a big lie and they believe it. Tell them a little one and they don't believe it. Come, let's pass the word we've become friends. I can set you up on a nice ranch not far from here, Les. Your duties as deputy wouldn't interfere too much with your other activities."

"Such as?"

A faint smile passed across Horan's face. "That would be up to you."

Les stood up. "That's what I thought."

Horan waved his cigar. "Take your time, Les."

"Is that how you bought Tracy Gant?"

Horan slowly took the cigar from his mouth. His face seemed frozen and when he spoke his voice had a metallic sound. "I might have known, Gunnell," he said. "It was useless to try and talk sense into you."

Les dropped the expensive cigar into a flower bed. It had suddenly become tasteless to him.

Horan stood up and it seemed as though some of the ruddy vitality had evaporated from his body. "I know better than to ask you what you intend to do here in Sundown," he said quietly.

There seemed to be a faint shadow of worry on Matt Horan's face.

"I don't know myself, Matt."

Horan looked up, beyond Les, toward the dun-colored hills to the west of the *estancia*. "You'll do what you think is right," he said. He sounded as though he knew Les Gunnell a great deal better than he had years before that time. "Tracy Gant is a good man," he said, almost as an afterthought.

"Maybe he was, Matt."

Horan waved a hand. "Go back home, Les. Ask Ruth Ripley to marry you. Go back to Soledad. Forget Sundown. Forget Will Ripley. Forget that you ever wore the star."

"Have *you* been able to forget, Matt? The way you fought and bullied your way up the ladder? Can you see the shades of some of the men who stood in your way and died for it?"

"I've never killed a man, Les," said Horan quietly.

Les looked down. "Not with those well-manicured hands, Matt. But with other weapons. Fear, hate, blackmail and any other weapon you chose. The one that fitted best. Every man has a weakness. Every man has a price. One way or another you drive them off, kill them or master them."

"Now you're talking too much, Les."

"Do you sleep well nights, Matt?"

Matt Horan hurled his cigar into the flowerbed. He picked up his glass, drained it, and turned to refill it. Les walked toward the doorway which led into the long hall.

"Gunnell!"

Les turned.

Horan leveled a long finger at Les. "Go back to Sundown," he said. "Do whatever you have to do. You won't be bothered, providing you're out of here within the next two days."

"And if I'm not?"

The faint ghost of a cold smile drifted across the handsome face. "Every man has a price. Every man has a weakness. You said that yourself."

"So?"

"What's *your* weakness, Gunnell? What's *your* price?"

"You'll never know."

"Don't be too sure!"

Les walked into the hallway. He glanced back. Horan downed his drink, jammed his hat on his head and walked to a door which led out through the back of the house. A moment later, Les heard the tattoo of hoofs on the ground behind the house.

"Señor Gunnell?"

Les turned. It was the maid. "Yes?"

"Señora Horan wants to see you."

Les followed the maid through a hallway and was ushered into a large room. The door closed behind him.

Consuelo Horan sat in a chair near a large window looking across the sparkling *madre acequia* and with a fine vista of the hazy hills to the north and west of the ranch.

Consuelo Chacon had been the belle of that country when she had married Matt Horan. Now, when she turned to look at Les, he was startled. Her dark beauty was still there—the oval of her white-skinned face, the great dark eyes, the thick glossy hair, drawn smoothly back on her well-shaped head—but it had a doomed and tragic look about it.

"*Buenos días,* Señor Gunnell," she said quietly.

"*Buenos días,* Señora Horan."

The room seemed full of the scent of her perfume and the cut flowers in their vases, a soft feminine odor, and underlying it all was the subtle scent of liquor. Les suddenly realized the woman was drunk.

She gestured toward a chair. "Sit down please."

He shook his head. "I'm sorry, señora. I was about to leave."

She smiled faintly. "My husband is gone. I saw him ride toward the hills. Sit down please. I want to talk with you."

Les sat down. She gestured toward an array of bottles on a sideboard, but Les shook his head. He wasn't off the Box H as yet, and he didn't want alcohol to slow down his reflexes.

She studied him. "You are still handsome, Les," she said at last.

He smiled and bowed his head. *"Gracias,* señora," he said.

She made an impatient gesture. "You used to call me Consuelo, Les. Amongst other things. *Mi vida. Mi corazon. Mi chula. Mi princesa...*" She refilled her glass. "Have you forgotten, Les?"

"No. But that was a long time ago, Consuelo. Before you married Matt."

She emptied her glass in one gulp and eyed him unsteadily. "Perhaps it would have been better had I married a common *vaquero.* Or a man such as you, Les."

"Why? You have everything."

She smiled faintly. "Everything? This was my casa. Now it is *his.* This was the *estancia* of my brothers and myself. Now it is *his. I* am *his.* My brothers are *his.* Everything is *his!* Do you understand that?"

There was great bitterness in her rising voice.

Les looked away from her. A drunken woman was an outright mess, and he had never been able to stand the sight of one.

"Look away," she said harshly. "There was a time when you could not keep your eyes from me, hombre!"

"I'd rather not talk about it, Consuelo."

"No! *I would!* I want to leave this place forever."

"Then go."

"I cannot leave my brothers, Les."

Jesus God, he thought. *Her brothers...* Santiago, Fedro *and* Aurelio, *three of the toughest ladrones in New Mexico, descendants of one of the conquistadores. Three men whose family name had once meant that which was good and noble in New Mexico.*

She was one of them, too, he realized. Beautiful and warm, with a sharp cruelty in her which rose in moments of stress and shadowed her beauty.

Les stood up. "Your trouble is Matt Horan," he said.

"Yes. But what can I do? I cannot get a divorce because of the church. I cannot leave him."

"It's up to you to decide, Consuelo."

"My brothers are fools! They worship that devil in human form! They turn against me for him!"

Les walked to the door.

"Les! Look at me!"

He turned.

She stood up and he could see that time hadn't ruined her figure as it had many of the lithe young girls of her race he had known in years past. She was still beautiful. She held out a hand toward him. "Don't leave me," she pleaded.

"This is no place for me," he said.

"Look at me! Am I not still beautiful?"

"Yes."

"Then stay!"

He opened the door.

"Les," she cried. "Have you come back for me?"

God she was drunk.

"Or have you come back to kill my husband?"

He turned and stared at her.

She laughed. "My people believe in you. They say it is pre-ordained, that you will kill him. That you will right the wrongs in this country."

"Fairytales," he said.

She shook her head in profound drunken seriousness. "I know, *mi vida*. I *know* you will kill him."

"Let the bottle alone, Consuelo. You're talking nonsense."

He stepped swiftly into the hallway and closed the door. As he walked away, he heard a bottle smash against the back of the door.

The house seemed deserted as he made his way to the great front door. He opened it, and as he did so he loosened his Colt in its leather-lined pocket.

He stopped on the wide porch and peered through the thick vines which hung down from the roof of the porch. His horse was still there, tethered to a post. There was no sign of any men around the place.

He walked toward the horse, half-expecting to be hailed and stopped, but there was no voice to stop him as he mounted the clay bank and rode toward the bridge which spanned the river.

He turned and rested a hand on the saddle cantle as he reached the east side of the river. The Box H was a scene of peace and plenty, but there was something undermining it.

Les rode swiftly on the Sundown road. But he could not erase the tragic face of Consuelo Horan from his mind no matter how hard he tried, and the bitter-sweet memories of years past came back to haunt him.

CHAPTER SIX

He turned the clay bank toward the house of Orlando Rios. The Street of the Burritos was crowded with the people of the quarters, standing silently, watching the house. Les tethered his horse to a railing of the burro corral and began to work his way through the crowd.

"It is the Señor Gunnell," said a man. "Let him pass."

Les was acutely conscious of the glances he got from these people. It was as though everything would be all right again in Sundown now that he was back.

He was let into the quiet house and a tall hawk-faced man met him. "I am Orlando Rios, Señor Gunnell," he said quietly. "My brother Esteban Rios rode with you many times."

"He was my *companero*, Orlando." Les looked down. "I am sorry to hear about the boy."

"Esteban had been so proud of him," Orlando said brokenly. "We named him after Esteban."

"What happened to the boy, amigo?"

"They said he had been swimming in the deep pool above

the bridge, where the river turns from the east and goes south. It is a lonely place."

Les could hear a woman weeping softly in another room.

Orlando struck his hands together. "There is something wrong about this thing," he said fiercely.

"How so?"

The dark tragic eyes held Les' eyes. "Esteban could not swim, señor. Never has he been known to go into the river. Then, too, always he came home on Saturday noons to give his mother the money he had earned at the hotel. He was so proud of that. Never, never, do you understand, was he ever late for his lunch. He was a good boy."

Les rubbed his jaw. He felt for the makings, then let them alone.

"It is all right to smoke, señor."

Les handed him the makings, then took them and rolled a cigarette for himself. They lighted up. "You said something was wrong about this thing," said Les.

Orlando nodded. He looked behind him. "The boy did not drown, señor. *There was no water in his lungs.*"

Les took the cigarette from his lips. "Perhaps I might have had something to do with his death," he said in a low voice.

"What is this you say?"

Les quietly told him of the unknown sharpshooter who had fired at Les from the room in the Silver Nugget and of how young Esteban had seen a man hurry from the hotel by a rear exit.

"But you said Esteban did not know who it was," said Orlando.

"Yes. But this man did not know that. Perhaps he had seen Esteban and was afraid that Esteban might have recognized him. There was only one thing for him to do. Get rid of Esteban."

"But why?"

Les looked away. "Because of me, Orlando. He didn't want me to know who it was."

"Perhaps it was Heath Sabin. It is said you disgraced him in the barroom of the Silver Nugget early this morning."

"Perhaps."

"Matt Horan did not know you were in town so it could not have been by his orders."

"I'm not so sure of that, amigo."

"But no one knew you were coming back."

"Perhaps."

Orlando stared at him. "You mean they *knew* you would come back?"

"Matt Horan knew where I had been these past years. I was foolish enough to think no one here in Sundown knew where I was. True, Esteban Rios did, and he perhaps told you, but I know you would not tell anyone."

Orlando quickly crossed himself. "That is so!"

Les walked into the next room where the boy was laid out. Weeping women knelt on the floor beside the bed. Les looked at the calm face of the boy, now so cold and still, and remembered all too acutely how the boy could smile. He looked at the boy's throat. There were faint dark marks on it. Les turned and walked outside. Orlando sat at a table with his face covered by his hands. "Who was the doctor that examined him?" Les asked.

"Doctor Reinhardt. His office is at the corner of this street and Front Street."

Les placed a hand on Orlando's shoulder, then walked outside and through the silent crowd. He knew they watched him surreptitiously as he led the clay bank toward Front Street, to tether it beside the doctor's office.

Doctor Reinhardt was seated at a huge rolltop desk when Les entered. He stood up and smiled. "Les Gunnell," he said in his thickly accented voice. "Goodt to see you, sir!"

Les took his hand. "I want to talk with you about the Rios boy, Doctor."

The doctor shoved a box of cigars toward Les. Les selected one and lighted it. "What is idt you want to know, Les?" asked Reinhardt.

"That boy did not drown, Doc."

"No."

Les drew in on the cigar. "And the marks on his neck?"

The keen blue eyes studied Les. "Why do you ask, Les? You are no longer a lawman."

"He was my friend, Doc."

"Yes, undt mine, too." Reinhardt learned back in his chair. "I was making oudt a report for the coroner, Les. That boy was strangled before he was thrown into the water."

Les took the cigar from his mouth and he seemed to taste green bile deep in his throat.

"By a powerful person," said Reinhardt quietly. "A man, of course. A man with huge powerful hands. Bigger than yours undt mine put togedder."

Les stood up. "When do you turn in that report?"

"The coroner is oudt of town. I will not be able to give idt to him until Monday."

Les leaned forward. "Another thing, Doc: As far as you are concerned the boy drowned. Until Monday at least, that's what you'll tell anyone who asks you."

"There is a madder of ethics and professional repudashun."

"Doc, that boy was murdered. Give me two days to try to find out who did it. If the murderer thinks he is safe he might get a little careless. If you spread it around that he was strangled, rather than drowned, the murderer might get clear away. You wouldn't want that to happen, would you?"

"He was a fine boy."

"How about it, Doc?"

"Yes. I will do it."

"If we get the killer, we can clear up your ethics and professional reputation."

Reinhardt waved a hand. "Idt is more impordandt that the killer be found." There was a suspicious wetness in his blue eyes. "That poor little lad."

Les walked out of the office and led the clay bank down to Dancey's Livery Stable. The hostler took the horse. "What do I owe you?" asked Les.

"Matt Horan paid for the horse."

"Thanks."

Les walked to the door and then turned. "Say," he said, "do you know Frank Hendries?"

The man grinned. "Who don't?"

"Where can I find him?"

"In a bar. Where else?"

"Thanks."

"Try the barroom at the Silver Nugget Hotel. Frank goes there now that he made a killing."

"What do you mean by a killing?"

"Frank used to hang out in the Miner's Friend and in the Sundowner when he was broke. Now he hangs out in the plushy places when he ain't in a hurdy-gurdy house."

"Where'd he get the money?"

The man shrugged. "One story is that an old-maid aunt died and left him money. Another is that he made a killing at cards."

"What do you think?"

The man winked. "What old-maid aunt would leave a bum like him money? Besides, if you ever played poker with Frank, you'd know he never took in a worthwhile pot in his whole life."

Les waved a hand and walked out into the street. Frank Hendries had been bowling with Will Ripley the night Will was murdered. What puzzled Les was the fact that Will Ripley rarely talked about anyone behind his back, and if he didn't have a good thing to say about a man, he usually didn't say anything. But he had detested Frank Hendries. Perhaps because of the fact that Frank Hendries considered himself quite a stud and thought no woman could resist him.

Les relighted his cigar as he stood on the corner of Oak and Front. One of Will's weaknesses was that he considered himself quite a bowler, and, in fact, he had been about the best man in Sundown in the game. But then Les remembered that Frank Hendries, who rarely worked and spent most of his time chasing whores, playing poker and drinking, also had added the useful skills of billiards and bowling to his repertoire so as not to spend any boring afternoons while building up his strength for the usual evening's entertainment along Oak Street.

It would have been logical enough for Will and Frank to tangle horns in the bowling alleys. What was it Holt had said? *"He was bowling. It was about midnight. Frank Hendries was bowling with him. Well, Dad finished and stepped back. Frank took his time. I guess the game was pretty close. Frank turned and told Will he was making him nervous standing behind him like he was. So Dad moved. Right in line with the back door. It was a door with a window in the top half. Someone poked a shotgun through the glass. Dad whirled; you know how fast his reactions were... The blast, both barrels, caught Dad full in the face."*

Les walked toward his hotel and into the lobby. He looked into the barroom. The long mahogany was lined with men with hardly a place for a newcomer. The tables were all taken. The steady hum of voices, the tinkling of glass and an occasional laugh came to Les.

He looked up and down the bar until he saw Frank

Hendries leaning against the end of the bar nearest the side door. The man was rather tall and lean, and he wore what he considered a true Western outfit. Tight-fitting trousers calculated to let any wandering female know what hidden charms Frank possessed, a ruffled shirt and string tie, a tailored black coat and a neat black hat, a real Stetson, hung on the back of his head, exposing his mass of dark curls, slightly shot with gray.

Les walked into the bar and a hush fell over the talking men. Eyes followed him as he walked to the end of the bar and moved in beside Frank. "Rye," said Les. He looked into the rear mirror and found himself staring right into the slightly bloodshot eyes of Frank Hendries. "Hello, Frank," he said. He turned to look at him.

Frank paled a little. His slim hand tightened about the sangaree glass he held. He glanced at Les. "Hello, Les. I heard you were in town."

"Have a drink, Frank," Les invited.

The dark eyes studied Les suspiciously. "Don't mind if I do."

They stood there drinking and then Frank looked at Les. "It's been a long time," he said.

"Five years."

"I figured you might have come back for Will's funeral."

"I didn't know about it until a few days ago."

"So you came back, eh?"

"I'm here," said Les dryly.

"It was a terrible thing. I guess you know I was with him when it happened?"

"Yes."

Frank emptied his glass. "Well, thanks, Les. I've got to get going."

"Where to, Frank?" asked Les quietly. *"You working now?"*

Hendries flushed. "Well, no, but..."

"Come on up to my room. I want to talk with you."

"I'm in a bit of a hurry, Les. I..." He looked into Les' eyes and faltered in his speech.

"Come on, Frank."

Hendries nodded.

Les beckoned to the bartender. "Give me a bottle of rye."

They walked out of the barroom together, followed by the eyes of most of the men in there. Frank was a little white beneath his tan, but he walked steadily up the stairs with Les.

A man lighted a cigar and looked up the stairs after the two tall men. He blew out a cloud of smoke. "Odd," he said. "I never heard of Les Gunnell and Frank Hendries hitting it off."

The clerk nodded. "Yes," he said quietly, "but then a lot of odd things have been happening since Les Gunnell came back to Sundown."

CHAPTER SEVEN

Les Gunnell stood at the window looking down into Front Street as Frank Hendries rambled on behind him, while the level of the rye bottle dropped steadily. Frank did not notice that he was doing all the drinking himself.

"Like I told everybody," said Frank a little thickly, "I was sure surprised when old Will got it, right behind me, so to speak. Some of the blood flew onto me. There was glass and blood all over the place. Old Will never had a chance. I was lucky I didn't get cut down along with him, don't you think, Les?"

"Yes."

Les rolled a cigarette and lighted it.

Frank refilled his glass. "Nice of you to have me up, Les. I meant to look you up anyway and let you know how I felt about poor old Will. He was a good bowler. Not as good as me. Wasn't quite as steady, but then I bowl a lot."

"Yes."

"Well, I had old Will a little nervous I guess because I was taking him. I was as cool as a cucumber."

What was it Holt Varney had said? *"Frank turned and told Will he was making him nervous standing behind him like he was."*

Les turned. "You didn't see who did the job, eh, Frank?"

Frank vigorously shook his head. His face was flushed, and his eyes glistened.

"But the Melgosa kid saw them, didn't he?"

"He said he did."

"Odd that he should suddenly fall into the mine shaft, wasn't it?"

"You know how kids are. Always fooling around those places."

Frank emptied his glass and refilled it. Les walked toward the door and while he rattled a chair about on the floor, he turned the key in the lock and placed the key in his pocket. He placed the chair not far from Frank. "You seem to be pretty prosperous, Frank," he said with a smile.

The drunken man waved a hand. "I get by. Long's I got enough for clothes, women and liquor I do all right." He hiccupped. "I would have done all right if Will had finished the game with me. We had quite a bet on. Best of a series, for five hundred dollars."

Les inspected his cigarette. "A lot of money. More than a marshal could afford to pay."

Frank grinned crookedly. "His wife makes plenty on that damned rag she runs."

There was an instant impulse in Les to smash the grinning face in front of him.

Frank sipped at his drink. "Yes, sir," he said with a grimace. "There was blood all over the place. Doc Reinhardt said they used heavy shot and probably split the wads. Jesus, you couldn't have told *who* Will was. His head was just blood and torn flesh and bone. Like I said: There was blood all over the place."

The word *blood* seemed to have a morbid attraction for

Frank Hendries and yet Les remembered that the man had been known to faint at the sight of it when it was his own.

"Who do you think did it?" asked Les.

"I don't know."

"You're sure you didn't get a look at any of them?"

Frank seemed to sober up a little. "No," he said emphatically.

"Seems odd that Will should be bowling with you. You and Will never got along."

"This was business."

"*What kind of business,* Frank?"

The dark eyes tried to focus on Les. "We had a big bet."

"Supposing you had lost, where would you have gotten the money?"

"I...that is..."

"You never intended to pay off that bet if you lost."

"I ain't no welsher!"

"I didn't mean that, Frank."

Their eyes clashed. Frank got unsteadily to his feet. "I'm getting out of here. A man can't sit and drink like a gentleman with such as you, Gunnell."

Les let him get almost to the door. "Where do you think you're going?" he asked.

Frank stopped with his hand extended for the doorknob.

"Turn around, Frank."

He turned and dropped one hand to a side pocket, but he lost his nerve when he saw the look on Les' face. The color seemed to drain from his own face. "What the hell is riling you, Gunnell?"

"Who killed Will Ripley, Frank?"

The man passed a hand across his sweating forehead.

"Who did you set him up for, Frank?"

Frank swallowed hard and reached behind him for the

doorknob. He tried it and then a sickly smile passed across his handsome face as he realized the door was locked.

"Who took the Melgosa kid to the shaft and dropped him into it, Frank?"

"You talk like you're loco. A lot of people around here think you are a little off, Gunnell."

"Maybe I am."

Les stood up and smacked his right fist into his left palm and the noise made Frank jump a little. Les kept on and every time he hit his fist into his palm, he did it a little harder and moved a little closer to Frank Hendries.

Frank suddenly jumped to one side and rammed a hand into his right coat pocket, which was a mistake, because before he could withdraw the hand, Les had hit him with a right cross which drove him back against the wall. Then a hand clamped about Frank's left wrist and a hard palm began steadily to slap Frank's head from side to side in painful rhythm.

There was deep-seated fear beneath the pained look in Frank Hendries' eyes. "For God's sake, Gunnell!" he pleaded.

Les stopped slapping the shaken man. He took him by the lapels of his coat and turned him, with his back toward the bed. "Who killed Will?" he asked harshly.

"I don't know!"

This time Les' right hand cracked like a pistol shot against the side of Hendries' head and he fell back on the bed. Les walked to the window and shut it. He knew there was no one in the room next to his and the room across the hall was unoccupied.

Frank sat up and reached for the bottle but Les snatched it from the table, corked it, and placed it on the dresser. Hendries wiped his mouth. "Jesus, Gunnell," he said. "You've no right to bully me this way."

Les thrust a finger under Hendries' nose. "Talk, damn you," he grated.

"All right! But give me a drink first."

Les reached for the bottle and as he did so Hendries butted him in the gut. As Les' head came down Hendries kicked out with both feet striking Les atop the head and driving him back across a chair.

Frank Hendries laughed deep in his throat as he got up. He kicked Les alongside the head. "You sonofabitch," he said wildly. Spittle flew from his mouth.

Les rolled over and got kicked in the kidneys. In his excitement Frank fell over Les. Les got to his knees and pulled himself up to his feet by holding onto the brass rail at the foot of the bed. Hendries was too fast for Les. The man was up on his feet and battering at Les' face with both fists until Les went down again.

Hendries reeled around the room. "You bastard," he said. He laughed. "Tricked you, didn't I? Well, I'm going to work you over, Gunnell."

Les staggered away from the bed, wiping blood from his mouth.

Hendries launched his attack. He struck at Les with both fists and feet until Les staggered into a corner and covered up. Then Hendries stepped back and picked up the Argand lamp from the table. He struck Les with it and the glass globe shattered. Blood spattered from Les' cut scalp, but he stood there, and a metamorphosis seemed to come over him. He walked toward Hendries with blood streaming down his face. His eyes looked like the windows of Hell.

"Get back!" shrieked Hendries.

Les walked steadily on.

"Get back, damn you!"

Les neared the frightened man.

Hendries battered at Les with both fists, but the power

was gone from them. Then he dropped his arms and stared at Les until the left fist measured him and the right fist smashed lips and teeth together in a bloody hash. He went down and got up in time to get a left into the pit of the gut and a right uppercut which caught his chin, skidded over his bloody mouth and smashed his nose. He went down flat on his back, dabbled a shaking hand at his nose, saw his *own* blood and fainted dead away.

Les walked toward the bed. He took the bottle and drank a deep slug, then fell face downward on the bed while the room seemed to whirl and dance in a wild rigadoon.

He touched his head and felt the lacerations. He had never expected Hendries to put up such a fight, and another thing, he realized his years away from wearing the star had made him a little careless. Only the grace of God had kept him from being knocked loco twice in Hendries' savage attack. Les walked to the dresser and poured water into a bowl. He bathed his cuts. They were mostly superficial. There was a salty taste in his mouth. He washed out his mouth and took another stiff drink.

He glanced out the window as he passed it, then turned and looked between the curtain parting once more. Two men stood on the street across from the hotel, looking up toward his window. There was no mistaking them. Fedro and Aurelio Chacon, the two youngest of the Chacon Boys, and where Fedro and Aurelio happened to be, it was a surety that Santiago wouldn't be far away. Santiago was the oldest, the biggest and the strongest, but it was Fedro, the second of the three brothers who was the brains, while Aurelio was the wildcat, fancying himself quite a man with gun, knife, bottle and the ladies, particularly the last item.

All three of them were top men with knife and gun, while Santiago was a veritable ox of a man, huge for his race, and had the vitality of a grizzly and the cruelty of an Apache.

Frank Hendries groaned. Les poured water on him. The man opened his eyes. Les sat down on a chair and shoved the beaten man with a foot. "Talk," he said.

Hendries sat up and wiped the blood from his smashed face. "Give me a drink, Gunnell," he pleaded.

"After you talk."

Hendries was shaking in pain and fear. "I didn't want to do it," he said slowly. Then he spoke more quickly. "But they forced me to. They got me in one of the hurdy-gurdy houses, Gunnell. They paid the girl to stall and keep me there. They paid the madam to get out with the rest of the girls. I was in bed when they came in and I was helpless. They ran the girl out of there and sat there looking at me until I agreed to do what they said.

"But just to make sure, they worked me over a little bit." He shivered and placed a hand near his crotch. "They cut me up a little here, just enough to make me pass out."

"Go on."

"I was scared, Gunnell. I agreed to get Will into a bowling game and spot him for them. It worked, but I was sick for days afterwards."

"Who are *they*, Hendries?"

He swallowed and looked despairingly at the bottle. "The Chacon Boys," he said in a low, shaken voice.

"The Chacon Boys? You're sure?"

Frank nodded. "Aurelio held the horses. Fedro and Santiago came to the back door. I didn't want to go through with it, but when I looked through that window and saw the look on Santiago's face, I knew damned well he'd kill me along with Will. You understand?"

Les spat into the garboon. There was a sickness within him. "What makes you think you're a man?" he asked.

Frank walked to the basin and washed his face. He turned. "What are you going to do now?"

"I'm not interested in you any longer, Frank."

"But you'll tell the authorities!"

Les shook his head. "You can turn state's evidence, when and if the Chacon Boys are brought to trial, which I doubt very much."

Frank looked down into the street and his breath caught in his throat. "Jesus!" he said. "There's Fedro and Aurelio down there!"

Les nodded.

Frank's face was fish-belly white. "What can I do? They probably know I'm up here. They know me. They know I'll talk to you. What can I do, Gunnell?"

Les slid a hand into Hendries' side pocket and drew out a short-barreled, double-action Colt. "You were ready to use this on me, Frank. Why not use it on them?"

"Three of them? Three Chacons?"

Les shrugged. "Then get out of town, Frank. Get out of town and keep moving, because if they don't kill you someone else will."

"Who?"

Les rolled a cigarette and looked down into the street. The two of them were still there.

"Who, Gunnell?"

Les lighted the cigarette. "Holt Varney, maybe. You set up his stepfather for the kill. You have no idea how much Holt thought of Will Ripley."

Frank dabbed at the blood on his face.

Les drew in on the cigarette. "Get out of here," he said.

Frank touched his smashed face. "Give me a break, Gunnell. Go out of here with me. They won't jump *you* in the street."

"Get out!"

"Let me stay here then."

"Get out!"

Frank picked up his hat. He slid his hand into his coat pocket and then withdrew it. "They'll kill me," he said softly.

Les walked to the door and unlocked it. Frank Hendries walked out into the hall, looked up and down, then walked quickly toward the rear stairs. Les stood there, with one eye squinted as the smoke curled up from his cigarette, listening to the rapid tattoo of Frank's bootheels on the stairs.

Les walked to the end of the hall and stood by the open window, rolling another cigarette. He heard the first-floor door creak open. He lighted the cigarette and waited.

"For God's sake, Santiago!" yelled Frank.

Les looked down into the alleyway. Santiago Chacon stood there, his thick legs like the twin trunks of a great oak. His bullet head was bent slightly forward, and his ham-like hands were reaching out for Frank.

Frank darted to one side, drew out his pistol and fired it wildly. It caught the huge man by surprise. Frank darted down the alleyway running like an antelope. The next street was Cottonwood. Les leaned from the window and watched the frightened man dash across Cottonwood and into the next alleyway.

Santiago slowly lowered his big hands and stood there. He shrugged as if to say that Frank Hendries would be found soon enough. There was no place for him to go. No place for him to avoid the Chacon Boys, for those people who were not mortally afraid of them were their allies. Hendries could ride for two days in any direction and still not get out of the territory ruled by the Chacons and their *ladrones*.

Santiago looked up and his dark eyes met those of Les Gunnell. The big man grinned, revealing two rows of massive teeth as white as snow. He beckoned to Les as though inviting him to come down. Les eyed the huge man. "Go home, Santiago," he said. "Go get your brains; your brother Fedro. You can't do much without your brains, *hombre*."

"I'll come up there, *cobarde,* and break you in half like a dry reed."

"With a bullet in your fat belly, *bazofia?*"

Santiago started for the door, but a man had entered the alleyway from Willow Street. "Where is he, *hermano?*" he asked. It was Fedro, the shrewd, the brains of the Chacon *corrida.*

Santiago gestured toward Cottonwood Street. "He ran," he said.

"*Pobrecito!* Poor little thing! You let that *canalla* escape?"

"He was too fast, *hermano!*"

Fedro took his cigarette from his mouth. "No matter. I think I know where he has gone."

Santiago jerked a thumb upward in a clumsy gesture meant to be secretive. Fedro flipped away his cigarette and glanced up at Les and their eyes met like clashing tempered steel. The man smiled, but there was no mirth in his eyes. He looked at his huge brother. "There will be good hunting in Sundown, *hermano,*" he said.

"There is no hunting in Sundown, Fedro," the big man said. "Let us go to the hills for deer."

Fedro shook his head. "I do not mean deer, *hermano.* You will see, Santiago."

They walked toward Willow Street.

Les walked back to his room and began to tidy it up. A big tip would keep the mouth of the chambermaid shut.

Les took a short drink. Things were falling into place, but his position was too dangerous to suit him. After all, he had no official status. Then, too, he had many enemies in town. It wouldn't be long before the Chacon Boys found Frank Hendries. They would make him talk as Les had made him talk. Then there would be no other course for the Chacon Boys but to kill Les as quickly as possible.

CHAPTER EIGHT

The sun had died above the hills west of Sundown and the sky was still painted rose and gold. Farmers and ranchers were pulling out of town for the long and dark ride home. The town seemed to drop off into a doze after the hurry and excitement of the afternoon.

Les Gunnell had bathed and dressed himself in fresh clothing. His scalp had stopped bleeding and there were only a few bruises on his face. He buckled on his gun belt and closed the door behind him. Young Esteban Rios had invited him for dinner but now Esteban was dead and there was sorrow in the Rios house and on the Street of the Burritos.

Les wondered what Tracy Gant had been doing. Certainly by now he should have been told that Esteban had not drowned. There were many native New Mexicans in Sundown and in the neighboring areas and they were a hot-blooded people. They could be easily aroused if they knew Esteban had been strangled to death rather than accidentally drowned. Orlando Rios had said the boy could not swim, nor had he ever been known to go into the river. The people of the Street of the Burritos would have known that, too.

Les reached the quiet lobby. The clerk eyed him curiously. The muted hum of voices and the tinkling of glasses and ice came from the barroom. Les walked outside and stood on the corner. Lights showed in the shop windows. The sky was just tinged with color. and a cool wind swept down from the hills scattering dust and paper along the street.

Les lighted a cigar and strolled west toward the marshal's office. Tracy Gant was a huge plaster facade, with very little to back it up, but he was the law in Sundown, and Les meant to sound him out about the death of the Rios boy. He reached the corner of Oak and Front. A hearse had stopped in front of Meg Merrivale's place. People crowded against the neat picket fence. Les saw his pimp acquaintance of the afternoon staring up at the second floor of the house. "What's up, amigo?" asked Les.

The man turned and showed his pale face. "A man's been murdered up there. He was with one of the girls, name of Ruby, a nice bit of goods. I used to pimp for her in Albuquerque."

Les took his cigar from his mouth and looked up at the second floor of the house. A curiously cold feeling crept over him. "Who was the man, Cully?"

"Fella by the name of Frank Hendries."

Les felt his mouth go dry. They hadn't wasted much time.

"Worst part of it is they got the gal, too."

"What do you mean?"

Cully turned and swallowed hard. "He was up there with Ruby. Ruby was Frank's gal. She kept him in drinking money when he was broke. Well, now maybe she's buying him drinks in hell."

Les pushed through the crowd and walked up the steps. A huge man with a battered face stopped him. "Keep out, hombre," he said.

"Meg in?"

"Yes."

"Tell her Les Gunnell is here."

The man was back in a few minutes. "She's in the back drawing room," he said. "Says for you to come on back."

Les walked along the heavily carpeted hallway, past the potted ferns and the baroque pictures on the walls. A familiar odor hung in the place. No matter how many flowers there were, or how much perfume was sprayed around, these places always had an aroma of their stock in trade, feminine flesh.

Meg Merrivale was seated in a velvet-covered platform rocker and her face was streaked with tears. She was still a helluva fine-looking woman, thought Les. "Hello, Meg," he said.

She held out her beringed fingers and pressed his hand. "Good to see you, Les. I heard you were in town."

"What happened?"

She dabbed at her big eyes with a lacy fluff of a handkerchief. "Frank Hendries came in here some hours ago, Les. The man seemed scared to death. He wanted to see Ruby, but I told him she needed her sleep. We've been rather busy of late. But Frank insisted on seeing her and he stayed up there with her. I think she loved him, Les. I really do."

"So?"

"A fight started out in the street about forty-five minutes ago and the girls all ran out to the porch to see what was going on. I went to tell them to go back into the house and act like ladies. It was just then I heard Ruby scream. Just once. I ran upstairs..."

"Go on, Meg."

The woman looked away. "God, but it was awful! They had been in bed together when the killer came in. He used a knife." Meg suddenly stood up, clapped her handkerchief to her mouth and fled from the room.

Les walked into the hall and up the rear stairs. Two men were carrying out one of the bodies. It was the woman.

Les let them pass and then looked into the room. It was a rear room papered with white paper covered with roses and leaves, but with the red of the roses there was another darker and fresher red, and it wasn't in a pattern. It looked as though a drunk had been splashing red ink in every direction. The bed sheets were soaked in it and beyond the bed something lay on the floor, entangled in part of the sheets. A clawed hand was twisted in the sheets at the edge of the bed.

Les walked to the end of the ornate brass bed. Frank Hendries lay on the floor and now Les knew why Meg Merrivale had become sick at the thought of what she had seen.

Les glanced from the rear window. There was a shed roof close beneath the window. A man could pull himself up on that roof and walk up the slope, step into the room and be there before any of the occupants could do anything about it.

Les wondered how Frank Hendries had felt when he saw his nemesis step into the room with naked blade in hand.

Les walked to the door and closed it behind him. He went downstairs and into the drawing room. Meg stood at the rear window. She had repaired her face and in the soft light of the lamps she looked damned attractive. She turned. "Well?" she asked.

"You were right," he said quietly. "It *was* awful."

She twisted her handkerchief in her lovely hands. "But why, Les? Frank had enemies, but I don't think anyone would have wanted to kill him."

"You never can be sure of that, Meg."

She nodded. "I didn't like Frank. I only tolerated him because of Ruby. After he got here, she came downstairs and got some liquor and she seemed happy as a lark because Frank was going to take her from here and marry her."

"Yeh," said Les dryly.

"She was a fool, but she was a nice kid."

"I imagine."

Meg paced back and forth and then stopped to look at Les. "Well, they're gone," she said. "Let the dead bury the dead. Now, about you, I don't know for sure why you came back but it wasn't for a social visit, was it, Les?"

"*Quién sabe?*" He held out his hands, palms upward.

"Don't joke with me, Les! You're in danger in Sundown. Damned *sure* danger! Get out of town. Now! If you need money, I'll let you have all you want."

"I'm OK, Meg."

She came close to him and held him by the arms, and he seemed to see beyond her painted face and into the big heart the woman had. "Please leave, Les," she said in her husky voice.

"I'll stay awhile, Meg."

"You damned stubborn fool! Matt Horan hates you. Heath Sabin will never forgive you for what you did to him this morning. The Chacon Boys have been openly boasting in town that they'll take care of you!"

"Maybe I'll do a little taking care of someone myself."

She rested her head on his chest. "Jesus God, Les," she said, "I've always thought that fate played a hell of a trick on me by letting me meet you long after I should have."

"You're aces with me, Meg."

She looked up into his face. "Yeh...*aces*...some deal, amigo."

Les felt, rather than heard, someone behind them. He turned his head and looked into the calm gray eyes of Ruth Ripley. Her face was set as she coolly eyed him and Meg. Meg looked at her. "Hello, Missus Ripley," she said.

Ruth nodded. "I came to cover the story," she said.

"Please don't go up there!" said Meg.

"I don't intend to."

Meg moved away from Les, touching her hair here and there, and it seemed to Les that there was a little sly triumph on her face. She never had had much use for Ruth Ripley.

"I'll be on my way, Meg," said Les.

"Drop in again, Les."

"I will."

Ruth stood aside to let him pass. He stopped in the hallway and looked back at Meg. "You never did tell me what the fight was about, Meg."

"It was between Fedro Chacon and his younger brother Aurelio. It seemed as though Aurelio was pretty drunk and Fedro wanted to take him home. It was quite a fight while it lasted."

"I'll bet it was," said Les dryly.

Meg turned up the lamp a little. "It quite surprised me not to see Santiago. When Aurelio gets drunk it's usually Santiago who takes him home."

"It doesn't surprise me," said Les.

She stared at him, then her face seemed to whiten beneath powder and rouge. "You mean.,.?"

"I mean nothing," said Les. "Good evening, ladies."

He walked to the street. They were loading Frank Hendries into the hearse.

Les walked toward Front Street. There was no sign of Tracy Gant. Tracy seemed slightly remiss in his duties that day.

The light was still on in the combination marshal's office and jail. Les stopped outside of it and rolled a cigarette. The office hadn't changed much. The paint was more faded, the boards were more warped, and the place seemed to have settled down on its tired haunches a little as though weary of the whole damned business.

Les opened the door. Tracy Gant was seated at his desk, with his hands clasped in front of him, a cigar jutting from his mouth while tobacco smoke lifted over his head in the sudden draft from the door. He looked up at Les. "I wish to God you had this damned job back again, Les," he said.

"Getting rough, Tracy?"

Tracy nodded. "I don't mind a decent killing. God knows I've seen enough of them. But a killing in a whorehouse always sickens me."

"You haven't been up there yet?"

The big marshal shook his head. "I've been told about it. You know, Les, I figured on making early evening rounds, then having a good dinner with Amy. I had a fancy for pork and cabbage tonight. Then I thought I'd make night rounds and get a good night's sleep. Now I get a killing in a *whorehouse!*"

Les dropped into a chair and flipped his cigarette into a garboon. Gant shoved a box of cigars toward Les but Les shook his head.

"You got any ideas who did it?" asked the marshal.

"I might."

Gant eyed Les. "I might have known you would. I heard you and Frank Hendries were drinking up in your room this afternoon and later on Frank was seen coming out of an alley heading for Meg's place like a bat out of hell. They say his face was all smashed up."

Les leaned back in his chair, letting the back hit the wall. "So?"

"You look a little bruised yourself. I didn't think Frank could lay a knuckle on a man like you, Les."

Les touched one of the bruises. "I'm slipping, Tracy," he said a little ruefully.

"What did Frank tell you?"

"Meaning?"

Tracy leaned forward and worked his cigar from one side of his mouth to the other. "Frank Hendries was with Will

Ripley the night Will got shot down. Now you and I know Will couldn't stand the sight of Frank. Then all of a sudden, they were playing a bowling series against each other for five hundred bucks. Seems to me if I wanted to know who killed Will, I'd have asked Frank a few leading questions."

"Keep talking, Tracy."

"So you asked Frank a few leading questions. He's seen running like hell from your hotel, with his face all smashed up, then sometime later he and his lady friend get all carved up like a Christmas goose. Where do you fit in, Les?"

"You don't think I killed them, do you?"

"Jesus Christ, no! Not with a knife, Les. And maybe you wouldn't have killed Frank at all, not actually that is."

"You're making riddles, Tracy."

Tracy shook his head. He pointed a big finger at Les. "Whoever killed him knew he had talked to you. They knew you had beaten hell out of him to make him talk. His killing was to pay him off for what he said. That leaves another killing they have to do. A more important killing than that of a man like Hendries."

"Like who?"

"Like you, dammit! You think they're going to let you walk out of this town alive? Maybe they're watching us right now! Maybe they think you're telling me who killed Will Ripley!"

"Maybe that's why I came here."

There was a curious expression on Tracy's face. *"Did you, Les?"*

"I'll have one of those cigars now, Tracy."

Gant shoved the box toward Les. Les lighted a long nine and leaned back in his chair. He drew in the smoke and blew it toward the light.

"Well, Les?"

"It was the Chacon Boys."

"You're sure?"

"Positive."

Tracy moved quickly and raised a short-barreled Colt from his lap. "That's just what I thought you were going to say."

Les did not move. "You knew it all the time then, didn't you?"

"Yes."

"They killed him at Matt's orders."

"I didn't say that."

"You might as well."

A bead of sweat broke out on Tracy's broad forehead and ran down the side of his face. He seemed nervous but his gun hand did not waver. "Why the hell did you have to come back?" he said, and it was almost as though he had forgotten Les was there, as though he was doing some right wishful thinking.

Les was in a bad position. If he reached for a gun he'd be too slow at it from his awkward situation. He was sure now that Gant was in with Horan. At least, he was on Horan's payroll. But the man seemed to be on the horns of a dilemma.

"You're something out of the past," said Tracy Gant quietly. "A bad smell reminding you of something you had thought forgotten."

"Gracias," said Les dryly.

"Did you ever stop to think about what your return has done to Sundown? What it has done to a lot of people?"

"I never thought too much about it, Tracy. I haven't been here over twelve hours."

"Yes, and in that damned twelve hours, a lot of things have happened: Heath Sabin has sworn to kill you. You practically accused me of being on Matt Horan's payroll. Someone shoots across a busy street at you with your own rifle. Little

Esteban Rios was strangled because someone thought the boy had seen who shot at you."

Les relighted his cigar. *How had Tracy Gant known that the Rios boy had been strangled,* unless perhaps, Doc Reinhardt had told him, and it wasn't like the doctor to betray Les.

The marshal went on talking in a slow, low voice. "You beat the truth out of Frank Hendries and the Chacon Boys kill him because of it. And they also kill an innocent whore because she had the misfortune to love a man like Frank."

There was no chance to draw on Tracy. The gun hand was too steady, and the muzzle of the gun wasn't more than five feet from Les.

"You seem to *wade* in blood," said Tracy softly. "Amy said that about you."

"Amy always did have a sharp eye," said Les.

"I could kill you, Les. Then maybe things would go back to the way they had been. It wasn't so bad. They look up to me here in Sundown. I have money and a prosperous business. Now you come along, like a skeleton out of the past and the whole damned house of cards crumbles."

Les narrowed his eyes. Tracy Gant had changed. He had always wanted prestige. In earlier years his great strength had made him well known and had given him the prestige he needed so badly. But now he was aging, and the man had a good many years ahead of him to live with his neighbors and townsmen when he would have to show more than strength and athletic ability to keep his prestige. Les began to feel almost sorry for Gant.

"Amy and I figured we'd keep the Sundown House a few more years, then sell it and get out of here. Figured on a little place in California maybe, to grow old in."

"I'm sorry, Tracy."

"Forget it! You couldn't help doing what you had to do. The whole loco business had to crumble some day, but I thought I'd get out of here before it did. It was wishful thinking, Les."

There was a tapping at the door and Tracy Gant lowered the gun beneath the desk. He smiled thinly at Les. "I can shoot right through the wood, Les," he said quietly. "The slug would be mutilated. If it didn't kill you, it would put a helluva big hole in you."

Les nodded.

"Come in!" called out Tracy.

A Mexican came in and took off his hat. "Good day to you of God, Señor Gant."

Tracy nodded. "What do you want, hombre?"

The man hesitated. "It is said that the people of the Street of the Burritos are angry about the death of the boy Esteban Rios."

"Yes."

The man turned his battered hat in his hands. "Orlando Rios has hinted that the boy did not drown. It is said there is a reward for anyone who could say that he saw Esteban shortly before he died, so that one would know who was last with him."

"So?"

The man smiled. "*I* know," he said.

"Tell me then, hombre!"

"It was *you,* Señor Gant. It was by the *rio.* You were talking to the boy and later walked through the willows with him. In a little while you came back, and you were alone. After that the boy was found in the water."

Les' eyes met those of Tracy Gant like crossing knives.

"There is a reward?" the man asked.

Gant nodded. He reached for a piece of paper, anchored it with his left elbow and began to write on it, and Les knew the Colt was in his left hand. The marshal handed the paper to the man, and smiled as he said, "Take this to the *estancia* of Sheriff Horan. You know where it is?"

"*Sí.*"

"They will take care of you there, amigo."

"*Gracias!*"

"It is nothing. *Vaya con Dios,* amigo."

The door closed behind the man.

"Neat," said Les. "He'll go with God all right, Tracy."

"The man is a fool."

"He must have been to come here and tell you that. Then it was you who fired at me?"

"Yes."

Tracy Gant raised his left hand and transferred the pistol from it to his right hand. Those hands were huge and thick and full of power. Les remembered the marks on Esteban's throat.

"I was only trying to warn you to get out of town, Les." Gant wet his lips. "I might have known it wouldn't work. If the kid had told you, you might have killed me, or the people here might have turned against me for it."

"*The kid didn't see who it was,* Tracy."

In the silence that followed, Les could hear the ticking of the big wall clock in the hallway which led to the cells.

Tracy Gant was white beneath his tan. "You're lying," he said.

"No, Tracy."

"For the love of God!"

"You've come a long way down the ladder, Tracy."

The hand tightened on the pistol. "They say the second murder is always easier, Les."

"Yes."

Les knew the man was going to shoot and it wasn't in Les to sit there and take it. Better to die on one's feet in a last cast of the dice than to die like a dog waiting for the smash of the bullet.

Les jumped from the chair and dived across the desk to grip the thick wrist of Tracy Gant. He swung a wild hook which crashed against the broad jaw of the marshal. Gant went backward in his swivel chair and the springs snapped beneath the heavy weight of the two big men, dropping Les atop Tracy. The man's breath went out of him. Les twisted the Colt free and as he did so the big hand closed on his and he felt the bones starting to give. The Colt crashed and the bullet sang from the cast-iron stove at the rear of the room.

Gant threw Les to one side. Les chopped at him with the barrel of the Colt but the man was like a mad bull as he closed in on Les. He hurled the table to one side and the lamp fell to the floor and went out. The stink of kerosene rose to mingle with the powder smoke.

Les dropped the Colt as Gant gripped him in a bear hug and drove him back against the wall so hard that pictures fell from it and Les lost half of his breath. The man was like a damned grizzly.

Les forced a hand up under Gant's jaw and applied all the pressure he could bring to bear and then he raised a knee hard into the man's groin. Tracy grunted in savage pain and released his grip. Les swung up a chair and brought it down on Tracy, but he might as well have used a chair of straws for all the good it did.

They circled in the darkness and their breathing was harsh. Tracy closed in and met a savage right jab which shook him and stopped him long enough for Les to get home with a left to the meaty belly. Gant staggered back.

Les sensed rather than saw or heard someone in the cell corridor. He turned and stared into the darkness and as he did so he heard the hammer of a gun click back. He dropped to the floor. The weapon crashed and the leaping, stabbing tongue of flame was right over Les' head. He heard Tracy Gant grunt with the shock of the heavy bullet.

Gant fell heavily against his desk and rolled over. Boots thudded in the hall. Les was half-blinded by the flash of the gun. He heard the rear door open and close as he ran toward it, then he heard the rapid tattoo of boots on the hard earth of the alleyway.

The front door crashed open. Les turned. He walked back toward the office as someone lit a match. "Jesus God," a man said. "It's Tracy Gant! Dead as sin!"

More matches were snapped into life in other hands. Then the eyes lifted from Gant to look at Les. "It didn't take you long to make your first killing in Sundown did it, Gunnell?" one of the men asked.

Les felt blood running from the side of his mouth.

"Get a lamp," one of the men said. "This one is smashed. Go get Holt Varney. He's deputy now. He ain't hurt so bad he can't take over for poor Tracy."

Les stood there looking at them as one of the men frisked him and took his Colt and derringer. "I didn't do it," he said quietly.

A man had been standing near the door and now he came forward. He lighted a match. "No?" he asked with a smile. "You'll have a helluva time explaining that to a jury, Gunnell, unless you get tried by Judge Lynch before you get to trial." It was Heath Sabin.

CHAPTER NINE

He could hear the angry humming of voices in the street from where he lay on the cot in a cell. Like bees when a hive is overturned, thought Les Gunnell. He sure *had* overturned a hive all right. A bumbling, stumbling bear looking for honey in Sundown. That was Les Gunnell.

He had heard the mob sound more than once in his life behind the star. Twice in his lawman career he had stood off mobs. Once with Ted Varney, back in the days when Ted had been marshal of Sundown, and once when Les himself had been marshal. That time he had been alone in the streets, trying to save a degenerate killer from the mob, although Les himself detested the sight of the man. Then it had been calm, smiling Will Ripley who had stood beside Les, and the threat of the two of them had been too much for the angry mob. They had been a good team.

The killing of Tracy Gant had come at a bad time. Men had been drifting into the saloons ready for a night's drinking, and some of them had a head start. There were men in that town who had little use for Les Gunnell. There were other men who might have liked Les but who would be afraid to show their like now that Matt Horan controlled Sundown.

Somewhere, above the noise of the crowd in the street, Les thought he heard a pistol flat off.

The door at the end of the cell corridor swung open and boots sounded on the warped flooring. Les looked up into the pale face of Holt Varney. Varney gripped the bars with his slim hands. "I had a feeling you should have stayed at Soledad," he said quietly.

"I didn't kill him, Holt."

"You were fighting. It's obvious enough. But why kill him, Les? The man was harmless. All he wanted to do was get out of the job and get out of Sundown. What were you fighting about?"

Les swung his long legs over the side of the cot and stood up. "Give me a smoke, kid."

Holt passed the makings in between the bars. Les grinned as he took them.

"What's so damned funny?" snapped Holt.

"If you plan a lawman's career don't ever do *that*. I could have smashed your hand down on the cross bar and held it there while I reached through and took your six-shooter."

The kid flushed. "You say you're innocent!"

"I am. But listening to that mob can make a man nervous."

Holt nodded. "They've been stirred up. The Chacon Boys are out there doing a lot of talking. They even say you killed Frank Hendries and that girl. They don't give a damn about Frank, those people out there, but you know well enough how a mob can feel about the death of a woman. Even a woman like that."

"Keno," said Les as he rolled a smoke. "What are *you* going to do about it?"

Holt wet his lips. "I've sent a man out to get some deputies."

"You think you'll get them?"

"Why not?"

Les lighted the cigarette and blew a puff of smoke toward the barred window. "You're kidding yourself, kid."

Varney took the makings from Les and fashioned a smoke. "I'll stand them off alone," he said at last.

"Don't bet on it."

The kid lighted a cigarette and then dropped both hands to his sides. The twin Colts came out like greased pigs from a sack. "No?" asked Holt Varney.

Les shook his head. "Keep them where they belong. In those fancy carved sheaths. There are sawed-off shotguns in the office. Load both barrels with Blue Whistlers after you split the wads. Let that mob know what's in those barrels. Pick out the closest man and keep the scatter gun at belly level while you talk to him. No man in his right mind wants to be the first to die in a mob. They might face down a pair of Colts, but they won't face down a pair of twelve-gauge gun barrels."

"And if they do rush me?"

Les took the cigarette from his lips. "You just pray to God, kid, that they don't rush you."

"Listen to them!"

Les nodded. "Now you know how your real father felt at times. How Will Ripley felt. How *I* felt when I wore the star and faced a mob alone. It's part of the job, kid. You have to measure up to it."

The kid had guts. He was fast and accurate with his twin six-guns. He came of fighting stock on both sides. But he was still a kid, and afraid. Perhaps not so much about being wounded or being killed as about making a fool out of himself or doing the wrong thing.

The door opened and a man walked up to them. It was Heath Sabin. "Heard you were looking for deputies," he said.

Varney eyed the gunman. The temptation was strong to take him. They wouldn't bluff Heath Sabin.

"Well?"

"I can get by without you, Sabin."

"They want this killer, Varney."

"They won't get him. Besides, he claims he didn't kill Gant."

"No?" The gunman smiled thinly.

Les eyed the man. "You're a witness, maybe?"

"No."

"Then keep your mouth shut."

Sabin grinned. "Me? Why should I? I know something that doesn't tally in your story, Gunnell."

"Such as?"

"You said that Tracy Gant had the drop on you and that you jumped him when you thought he was going to kill you. Then you said his gun went off in the struggle and that the slug hit the stove. That right?"

Les nodded.

Sabin rubbed his jaw and grinned again as though secretly enjoying his knowledge. "Then you say you heard someone in this corridor. You dropped to the floor when you heard a hammer being cocked. The gun goes off and Gant gets the slug. *Somebody* beats it out of the corridor and runs down the alleyway. Right?"

"Right."

"You said you didn't use either of your guns. The Colt or the derringer. Right?"

"Yes, damn you! Get on with it!"

Sabin reached inside his coat and drew out a six-shooter. "This yours?"

"*Was,* I guess," said Les dryly.

Sabin handed it to Holt Varney. "Check it," he said.

Varney opened the loading gate and turned the cylinder. He looked up at Les. "You keep five rounds in it?"

"Yes. Empty chamber under the hammer."

"You say you didn't fire this?"

"Yes."

"There are five rounds in here all right. Four live loads and a fired cartridge case."

Les stared at him. "That's impossible! I cleaned that Colt just before noon today! I reloaded with five live cartridges! That gun hadn't been out of my hands since then, until it was taken from me after the fight."

"After the fight?" sneered Sabin. "*What fight?* You shot poor Gant in the belly. He never had a chance!"

Holt Varney placed the muzzle of the gun under his nose and sniffed at it. His eyes were on Les. "This was fired just a short time ago, Gunnell."

"Get the man who took it from me."

"Who was it?"

"How should I know?"

"Dumb as a fox," said Sabin.

"I'll keep this as evidence," said Holt.

Les gripped the bars. "For God's sake, kid! That gun wasn't fired by me! Who knows who had it after it was taken from me!"

Varney shrugged. "I don't know. You were alone with Gant in his office. There was bad blood between you. You had a fight. You admitted that. Tracy Gant is dead with a bullet in his guts. Your six-shooter has a round fired from it. All I know is what I've just told you. The rest is up to the jury."

"Maybe up to Judge Lynch," said Sabin with a grin. "A walk up Ladder Lane and down Noose Street."

"Get out of here, Sabin," said Holt Varney.

The gunman's grin vanished. "Don't give me orders, Varney."

The kid turned slowly to face him. "You pulled a fast one on me when you plugged my arm, Sabin. This time I'm not holding up a drunk. I'm marshal here in Sundown and what I say goes. *Now get to hell out of here or make your play!*"

Varney had him cold. Maybe his hurt arm might slow him down matching draws with Heath Sabin, but the kid had Les' Colt in his hand, just inches from Sabin.

Sabin looked down at the Colt. "Sure," he said with a cold grin. "Sure." He walked to the door at the end of the corridor and then turned. "You may be marshal in Sundown, kid, but you won't have much to say very long. Sheriff Horan is due in town any minute now. I'll be outside waiting to see who runs Sundown. Ought'a be interesting." The door closed behind him.

Varney looked at Les. Les leaned against the wall. "Let's have a smoke, kid."

They rolled their cigarettes and lighted them. The smoke drifted through the bars and out of the little window. The kid inspected his cigarette. "Did you shoot this Colt, Les?"

"No."

"You wouldn't lie about it, would you?"

"No."

The kid nodded. He walked to the rear door and checked the lock and the heavy bar which crossed the door, then he walked toward the other door. He looked back at Les. "I believe you," he said quietly.

"Thanks."

"It makes a difference to me, Les."

"How so, kid?"

"I might not fight very hard to save your neck from a lynching if they tried to get you. That is, if I thought you were guilty."

"And now?"

The gray eyes studied Les. "They'll kill me first, Les."

Les sat down on his bunk. The odds were stacking up against him. They hadn't done an autopsy on Tracy Gant as yet. The slug that had killed him could have been any of half a dozen different calibers. Les' Colt was a .44/40, about the most common caliber in that country. If the slug extracted from the death wound was anything but a .44/40 there was hardly a chance they'd think he had killed Tracy Gant, although Les knew well enough whoever had engineered the job would do everything else in his power to have Les convicted. If the extracted slug was a .44/40...

Les drew in on his cigarette and blew a smoke ring. There was one thing he didn't know. *Had the killer been after Les or after Tracy Gant?*

He looked at the cracked plaster of the ceiling. He had heard a shot just before Holt Varney had come into the cell corridor, and not long after that Heath Sabin had showed up with the so-called "death weapon" in his hand.

He could hear the noise of the crowd more plainly now. Then it died away and was followed by a ragged cheer. Minutes later the corridor door opened. Les sat up. Matt Horan stood there, impeccably dressed as usual, with his expensive Stetson square across his wide forehead. Holt Varney stood behind the sheriff. The lamplight glistened on the star pinned to Horan's coat.

Horan had slipped from the role of the expensive rancher into that of the implacable officer of the law. The county officer especially charged to execute the laws and preserve the peace. God himself in the county and in Sundown.

Horan walked toward the cell. "It didn't take you long, Les," he said quietly.

He had Les right where he wanted him. In the *juzgado,* charged with murder. There was no need for him to offer Les money now; no need to offer him a deputy's badge; no need to threaten him.

"I'm sorry to see you in here, Les," said the sheriff.

"Thanks," said Les dryly.

"Is there anything I can do for you?"

"Leave the door open, Matt."

Horan shook his head. "You always did have a joke when you were in trouble, Les."

"Gay, lovable Les Gunnell."

Their eyes clashed and it was Horan who looked away. "Have a cigar, Les?"

"Sure."

The silver case came out and the lid came open exposing the plump rolls of weed. "I have them..." said Horan and then his voice died away as he saw the smile on Les' face.

"Sent directly from Cuba," finished Les. He selected a cigar, bit off the end and lighted the cigar.

"It has been rather quiet in this county for a long time," said Horan softly. "Now, I don't know..."

"Quiet?" asked Les. He blew a smoke ring. "Will Ripley gets shot in the back. The little Melgosa boy sees who killed Will Ripley and ends up at the bottom of a mine shaft for being too observant. Orlando Rios finds the boy and gets the heave-ho from his job at the Sundown Freighting and Warehousing Company."

Horan selected a cigar and lighted it. "Go on," he said softly.

"Holt Varney gets a lead warning from Heath Sabin. I get a warning from the same gun-slick when I get to Sundown. Someone shoots at me across Front Street on a busy Saturday morning. Young Esteban Rios suddenly drowns in the *rio* because he may have seen the man who shot at me. You want me to go on?"

Horan relighted his cigar and his eyes were on Les

through the flare of the match. "The point is, Gunnell, that you're sitting here in the *juzgado,* with a sure charge of murder against you and all the flapping of that big mouth of yours won't talk you out of that one!"

"Neat as sin, eh, Matt?"

"Take it easy, Les," said Holt Varney. "I might not be able to hold that mob back, but Sheriff Horan can do it."

"Sure he will! Providing he can make the murder charge stick on me. He can play a wonderful role, lining Les Gunnell up for the trial! But if, by any chance, the charge is disproved, there are other ways of getting rid of me."

The cold yellowish tint crept into the hazel eyes. "You two-bit, four-flushing tin-star wonder," sneered Matt Horan. "Talk all you want to. Blow wind blow! Sit in that damned cell until we're ready for you and then let's see how much talking you can do in court!" He turned on a heel and walked out of the corridor, slamming the door behind him.

Holt shook his head. "I gave you credit for more brains than you just showed, Les."

Les dropped onto the bunk and blew a smoke ring. He grinned. "I was just checking my insurance," he said in a low voice. "Matt Horan wouldn't miss the chance of getting me into court for a real field day. Now he's so damned mad he'll make sure I'll be safe until that big day."

"You said you were innocent."

"I am."

"Supposing we can prove that *before* the trial?"

Les looked up at him and the grin was gone. "Then the odds of my living very long after that are high against me, kid, with a stacked deck."

"You play close to the belly, Les."

"Why not? I've got a big bet on—my life." Les took the cigar from his mouth and hurled it into a corner. "For God's sake give me the makings! Him and his damned Cuban weeds!

They stink just as much as he does no matter how he tries to perfume the stench away!"

Holt passed the sack and papers to Les.

Les rolled a smoke. "'Go back to Sundown,' he told me. 'Do whatever you have to do. You won't be bothered, providing you're out of here within the next two days.'"

"You've done a hell of a lot of traveling in your one day here, Les."

"Never even had a chance to use that hotel room for much," agreed Les.

Holt Varney smacked a fist into his left palm and winced as his wounded arm felt the strain. "What can I do?" he demanded.

Les eyed him. "You know well enough that Matt Horan runs Sundown just as he used to in the old days. Tracy Gant was on his payroll."

Varney stared at him. "You gone loco?"

"No."

"That's a helluva way to talk about a dead man."

"The fact is that he *was* on Horan's payroll. Tracy Gant owned the Sundown House, didn't he?"

"Yes."

"Just ask a few questions around town. Ask anyone about Gant. He was a ne'er-do-well. A big friendly man who had gained a reputation because of his size and his muscles, but he never had the ability or brains to make more than a two-bit living all his life."

Holt studied Les. "You're holding something back," he said quietly.

Les grinned. "You're learning, kid. Make a lawman out of you yet, or better still, maybe a crusading editor. Gant *was* on Horan's payroll. Horan began to operate in the open again after he got rid of Will Ripley."

"You think Matt Horan killed my stepfather?"

"No! But listen to this: Tracy Gant killed the little Rios boy, Esteban.".

"The kid drowned!"

"No. You keep all this under your hat. It was Tracy Gant who fired at me while I was in your room. Not to kill but to warn. Esteban Rios saw a man leave after the shot was fired. Gant was afraid the kid would talk. He took him to the *rio*, strangled him and threw him into the water."

"You sure of all this?"

Les nodded. He told Varney about Gant's admission, about the fight and the shot that killed the big marshal.

Holt Varney listened, then stared thoughtfully at the cell bars. Finally, he said, "Tomorrow is Sunday."

"You think that means anything in Sundown?"

"No one will be working. The saloons are open again on Sundays. Plenty of time to drink and talk about you, Les. Plenty of time for Horan's men to slink around and buy drinks and spread lies."

"Where's Andy Dover?"

There was a sarcastic look on the kid's face. "Our esteemed mayor?" He laughed dryly. "He was seen pulling out of town in his buckboard, heading for his ranch on the Ocotillo, and he had three of his councilmen with him. Someone said Mayor Dover planned a barbecue at his *estancia* and wouldn't be back until about the middle of next week."

Les nodded. "The old struggle resolves itself again. Horan against the marshal of Sundown."

"The native New Mexicans think a lot of you, Les."

"Horan has the Chacon Boys."

"I can call for deputies again."

"Not a chance."

"I can release you on your word you will turn yourself over to a law officer elsewhere. A man who would take you under his safe custody."

Les shook his head. "Horan will have the train watched. Every road will be watched. If Horan wanted to catch the last mouse in Sundown the poor little bastard couldn't get out of here."

In the silence that followed Les' words they could hear the ticking of the big clock. It was quiet in the street. Horan had probably seen to that. But there was a brooding quality about the silence.

The kid cleared his throat. "Then it's up to me, Les."

"Yes."

"What can I do?"

"Walk out of here and leave the front door open. No one would blame you. Not me, anyway."

The kid looked at him. "Someone would blame me."

"So? Who?"

"My mother."

"She wouldn't want to see you die, kid. Remember she lost two husbands in this business. She's suffered too much already."

The kid nodded. "Maybe my father and stepfather would blame me."

"They're not here, kid."

Holt walked toward the office. "Coffee?" he asked.

"Keno!"

He was back in a few minutes with a pot and a cup. He opened the cell door and placed them on the little table. As Les reached for the pot the kid drew a short-barreled Colt from his coat pocket and placed it and a box of cartridges on the cot. He looked at Les, and they both knew what was in his mind. If anything happened to Holt Varney, Les Gunnell could at least die like a man, with a hot empty gun in his hand.

CHAPTER TEN

The sweet-toned bell of the Catholic church began to ring, and, in a little while, the sound died away in the hills, to be followed by the heavier tones of the Baptist church bell, like an echo out of tune.

Les Gunnell opened his eyes and looked at the shaft of light streaming into his cell from the little window. Dust motes danced in the golden slant of light. He sat up and rolled a cigarette and lighted it. Surprisingly enough he had slept through the night after lying awake until well after midnight listening to the pulsing life-beat of the town. But no one had bothered the jail.

Les stood up and walked to the window. He craned his neck to look toward Front Street. The sun glinted from an empty whiskey bottle lying in the middle of the thoroughfare.

The door at the end of the corridor swung open and Holt Varney came to the cell door. "Morning, Les," he said. "Want to wash up?"

"Sure thing, kid."

Varney smiled. "I was going to order you to do it anyway. You see, my mother wants to see you a little later on."

Les looked quickly at the kid. "I'd rather not," he said.

The kid was tired. There were circles under his gray eyes. Probably had spent the night sitting in a chair, with a shotgun across his lap, watching the front door of the office. "Why?" he asked.

Les shrugged. "She told me she wished I had stayed away from Sundown."

"Yes."

What had been her words? "'They'll know you came here for that purpose. They'll know you'll ally yourself with Holt. It will end with more killings, and two of those killings will be you and my son. Certainly, I know you'll both give a good account of yourselves, but they'll get you one way or another.'"

"She might be right at that," said Holt.

It wasn't until the kid had spoken that Les realized he had repeated Ruth Ripley's words aloud.

Holt unlocked the cell door. "I've often wondered why my mother married men like my father and stepfather. She hates violence and bloodshed."

Les picked up his Colt and slid it into a pants pocket. "She was allying herself against violence and bloodshed by doing that," he said quietly.

"She has a great deal of courage, Les."

He nodded. "More than many a man I've known."

After he had washed up, Les stood at the little window of the small front cell which looked out on Front Street, drinking his morning coffee. The kid leaned against the wall, idly breaking open the breech of his shotgun and snapping it shut again. He looked at Les. "This town is as quiet as a church, Les, and yet there are more people in it right now than I've ever seen before."

Les put down his coffee cup and felt for the makings. "So?" he asked quietly.

The kid nodded. "Matt Horan is staying in his suite at the Sundown House. The Chacon Boys held court on Silver Nugget Street last night and are tapering off over at the Miner's Friend. There are at least half a dozen of Horan's hired gun-slicks lolling about in the lobby of the Sundown House, much to Amy Gant's disgust."

"I thought she'd be all broken up about Tracy."

The kid shrugged. "Heath Sabin is in the bar at the Silver Nugget Hotel. The Mex *cantinas* are packed to the doors. The churches haven't done much business this morning."

"Where did you learn all this?"

"Orlando Rios told me. He's been scouting the town ever since dawn."

"A good man."

"He says the Mexican people are with me, but that they are afraid. They aren't gunfighters and they aren't organized. They're brave enough, Orlando says, but they haven't got the skill with weapons we Anglos have. Seems odd that these people come from families that have lived in New Mexico for a couple of hundred years and yet *we* think of *them* as foreigners."

"The all-conquering Anglo-Saxon," said Les dryly.

"They like you, Les."

Les turned. "In this state, those people can be your friends or your enemies. I found it easy to make and keep them as friends. I've never regretted it."

Holt nodded. "Orlando says there will be trouble. His people are fingering their knives. There was a meeting of some of the more prominent businessmen in the Silver Nugget Hotel banquet room late last night."

Les smiled faintly. "I'll bet they were fingering their knives, too."

He saw her coming across the wide street. A man lounged in a doorway and Les recognized Aurelio Chacon. There were other men on the boardwalks watching Ruth Ripley. It was hard to realize she had a grown son, and that son a man wearing the marshal's star of Sundown, the toughest town in that part of New Mexico.

A rockaway appeared in the street from the west, drawn by a pair of slim, matched blacks, and the sun shone on the polished wood and leather of the sumptuous vehicle.

Ruth Ripley walked in front of the vehicle, and the driver drew in the horses a little. One of the windows of the rockaway slid down and Les saw the dark brooding face of Consuelo Horan watching Ruth.

"I had a feeling she'd be in town," said Holt Varney from behind Les.

Les turned and studied the kid's face. How much did he know about Consuelo Horan?

"They say she takes a suite at the Silver Nugget when Matt Horan is in town. Sits up there drinking steadily until they take her back to the *estancia*," said Holt quietly.

"Maybe she has reason to."

Their eyes held steadily for a fraction of a moment, then Holt walked to the front door to admit his mother.

Les straightened his string tie. He glanced across the street. Aurelio Chacon had been joined by his brother Fedro, and where Aurelio and Fedro were, it was sure that big Santiago was not far away. The glistening vehicle had stopped in front of the Silver Nugget and Les saw the coachman get down to open the door for Consuelo Horan, *nee* Chacon. She was still a beautiful woman. *"You used to call me, Consuelo, Les. Amongst other things. Mi vida. Mi corazon. Mi chula. Mi princesa..."*

He could hear Holt talking to his mother in the next room. Consuelo Horan had entered the hotel. *"They say it is preordained you will kill my husband,"* she had said. Perhaps she had come to Sundown that day to see it done.

Ruth stood in the doorway. Les smiled. "I had thought I'd see you again under different circumstances," he said.

"I only wanted one thing, Les. That was for you to leave Sundown. I knew something like this would happen."

"I didn't kill Tracy Gant, Ruth."

"I know that," she said simply.

He studied her, and he wondered deep in his heart why he had ever let her go, not once, but twice, to other men.

She sat down in the one chair. "I sent a wire to the governor this morning, Les."

"Yes?"

"I told him of the situation here."

"*Gracias.*"

"You don't think it will do any good?"

"*Quién sabe?* Matt Horan has a lot of political influence."

"Not that much, Les."

He smiled. "The pen is mightier than the six-gun. Is that it, Ruth?"

"Don't be so bitter."

He leaned against the wall. "Perhaps you were right. I should have stayed at Soledad."

"I don't know. I'm selfish enough to think that your coming here might possibly have saved Holt's life."

"Roundabout, isn't it?"

The front door of the office opened and Les heard the soft voice of Rae Weston speaking to Holt, asking for Ruth. Then the girl stood in the doorway. Her face was flushed. "Ruth," she cried, "I waited at the telegraph office for the answer to your wire. Then the clerk told me the wires are down and your message didn't get through."

Ruth paled. A hand crept to the smooth column of her throat in a well-remembered gesture.

Les looked over Ruth's head into the eyes of Holt Varney and both of them knew how those wires had come down.

Matt Horan was effectively cutting off Sundown from the rest of the territory. Whatever happened in Sundown that day, and perhaps the next day, would be settled by those actors who were already on the stage or in the wings, without benefit of audience or interference.

Rae placed an arm about Ruth's shoulders, but the older woman shook it off and raised her head. She was a fighter who carried the fight. "What can we do now, Les?" she asked.

"So far as I can see there are only two of us against them," said Les. "Holt and myself. I think he could get out of town without any trouble. They don't want him."

"He's the marshal, Les."

He cut a hand sideways in an impatient gesture. "He'd be a fool to stay here."

"I'm sticking," said the kid. "Besides, Les, you said that Matt Horan would want to save your skin for a trial."

"If he's sure I'll be proven guilty," said Les dryly.

"And if that can't be done?" asked Rae Weston.

There was no answer from the other three. They had known beforehand, and now she knew, as well as if they had spoken to her and explained what would happen.

"Can't you escape, Les?" asked the girl.

He shook his head. He'd be shot to doll rags before he got to the nearest corner.

"This can't be possible!" she cried. "This is a civilized country! They have to give you a fair trial!"

Les looked out of the window. Doc Reinhardt was walking on the far side of the street. Fedro Chacon eyed him, then spoke to him.

"The autopsy been made yet?" asked Les of Holt.

"No."

"You'd better talk to Doc Reinhardt about it."

"I will."

The doctor passed on down the street. A good man,

skilled in his profession, but with a slight weakness for the bottle, and at such times he talked too much.

"What will the autopsy prove, Les?" asked Ruth.

He smiled. "All or nothing."

"What does that mean?"

He looked at her. "If they take a .44/40 from the death wound, it just about seals my fate."

"And if it isn't a .44/40?"

"Then they'll kill me either here or in the streets. Either way I lose. By a trial and a hanging or by no trial and a bullet in the back."

Her face was set and white. "I'll ride to Quatros Jacales," she said quickly. "There is a telegraph office there." She turned on a heel and left the room, followed by Rae Weston. Les watched them hurry down the street toward the newspaper office.

"What do you think?" asked Holt.

Les turned. "Not a chance," he said.

"They won't hurt her?"

He shook his head. "If they hurt a newspaperman, it would be bad enough. But to hurt a newspaperwoman would be like opening the gates of hell in this territory."

"It won't do you any good, Les."

"No."

The kid leaned against the side of the doorway. "Well," he said calmly, "I'm damned hungry. I'm having breakfast sent in and I don't intend to eat solitary. I'd admire your company for same, *Mister* Gunnell."

Les smiled. He bowed a little from the waist.

"A pleasure, I assure you, *Mister* Varney!"

The kid grinned. "We won't have soft lights and music but we'll both have damned good company. I'll hurry up the process." He walked to the outer door.

Les rolled a cigarette. There were times when Ruth Ripley

showed up in the kid with startling clarity, but this time it had been Ted Varney speaking. It had been his way. Then there were times when the touch of Will Ripley's influence could be seen in the kid. He lighted the cigarette and looked out into the street, toward the Chacons. All three of them were there now, watching Holt Varney as he spoke to a kid in the street. The kid scurried off toward the nearest restaurant.

What would Les Gunnell's influence be on Holt Varney? Perhaps the kiss of death.

The long afternoon was dragging to a close. From down the street came the curiously intermingled and jangling tunes of the mechanical pianos and hurdy-gurdies. Horses and buckboards lined Front Street, but oddly enough, on both sides of the street, for a good distance on either side of the marshal's combined office and jail, the hitching racks were empty. The sun was low over the hills, and the town seemed to throb with a nervous life which was quite different from the usual Sunday evening.

Les Gunnell threw down his cards and stood up. Holt Varney looked at him. "What's wrong, Les?"

"It's the damned waiting, kid."

"I'd like to leave and look around town."

"Go ahead. I'll lock myself in."

"I was wondering about Doc Reinhardt."

"Probably on a high lonesome by now."

A cold wind blew down Front Street, scattering papers and rolling tin cans. Signs banged back and forth in front of the stores. There was a feeling of rain in the air.

The kid shuffled the deck and began to deal a hand of solitaire. "Take it easy, Les," he said.

"It isn't myself I'm worried about. It's your mother. Why haven't we heard from her?"

"She can take care of herself."

"Don't be so damned cool about it!"

Holt Varney put down the cards and studied Les. "I'm not," he said quietly. "They won't hurt mother. It's you I'm thinking about."

"I've been in jams before."

"But nothing like this, Les."

Les looked at the kid. "Yes," he said in a low voice.

The wind was whispering now. Moaning softly along the street and whispering through the windows and along the eaves. It gave a feeling of uneasiness and tension.

Sundown was as restless as a cat when darkness comes. All over town people were coming to life; an alert awareness; a feeling that something was going to happen, soon.

The kid stood up. "I can't wait much longer," he said.

"Go and see about her, Holt."

"What about you?"

"Lock me in."

"What about *them?*"

"They still think they have me neatly framed. They won't bother me. Besides, I have a little insurance policy here." Les tapped his coat pocket where the Colt was hidden.

The kid took his hat, settled his gun belt about his lean hips, rolled a cigarette and lighted it. He waited until Les walked into the cell at the front of the building, then he locked the door. He hesitated a moment and then he passed the key through to Les. They both grinned. Holt fingered the peak of his hat, passed slim fingers along the brim, then walked to the front door. "I won't be long," he said over his shoulder.

It was quiet in the place after Holt left. The stub of a cigarette lay in an ash tray and the tendril of smoke rose toward the harp lamp which hung from the center of the office ceiling. Now and then a loud burst of tinny music came to Les as he sat in a chair tilted back against the wall, behind a locked door with the key in his pocket.

He heard the low whistle above the moaning of the wind. Les stood up and walked to the window, flattening himself against the wall. "Who is it?" he asked quietly.

"Orlando Rios."

"What do you want, amigo?"

"There is something I must tell you."

"Speak then."

There was a moment's hesitation and then the man spoke. "Señor Gunnell, I..." the voice trailed off.

"What is it?" demanded Les.

There was no answer. Then a man laughed softly.

Les looked from the window. Orlando stood staring at three men who stood in the street at the edge of the boardwalk, eying him. They were the three Chacon Boys.

Fedro took his cigarette from his mouth. "What do you do here, hombre?"

Aurelio grinned. "Perhaps he thinks his whore of a wife is in there?"

Orlando stepped forward, feeling for his knife, but big Santiago was in between him and the two brothers. He clamped a big hand down on Orlando's knife wrist, twisted it, forcing the man to drop the blade. Then Santiago picked up the knife and held it in his huge hands. Suddenly he snapped the blade like a twig and threw the pieces at Orlando's feet.

There was a flickering of deer-horn lightning over the darkening hills, and the face of Orlando Rios had the stamp of hate on it.

Fedro began to roll another cigarette. "Go home, *cabron*," he said quietly.

Aurelio leaned forward and made a gesture as though blowing his nose and flipping the contents towards Orlando's face.

"Someday," said Orlando. "Someday, I..."

Santiago gripped Orlando by the collar of his jacket and

lifted him easily from the boardwalk. His right hand cracked against the side of the man's head and when he placed Orlando back on his feet the man staggered back against the wall of the marshal's office. Then Santiago hit him again, just once, but hard enough to drop him unconscious. Santiago lifted a huge foot.

"That's enough," a quiet voice said.

The three men turned, as though amused that someone should try to stop them. Their faces changed as they saw Holt Varney standing in the street with his arms hanging loosely by his sides.

The lightning etched an eerie pattern over the low hills.

"It is the cockerel," said Fedro.

"The *bravo,*" said Aurelio.

Santiago grinned loosely. He cracked his knuckles and looked at Fedro for his usual orders.

Les eased his Colt from his coat pocket. Varney looked at him. Fedro moved a little, glancing at Les as he did so. "There is nothing more to do here," he said to his brothers.

"Why not?" asked Aurelio. He spat at Holt's feet.

Santiago grunted.

"There will be time for him later," said Fedro.

"I'll be around," said Holt quietly.

"*Sí,*" said Fedro. "He'll be around, eh, *hermanos?*"

Aurelio laughed.

Santiago looked stupidly at Fedro.

"The *saca tripas,* eh, Santiago?" said Fedro.

The broad face broke into a vacuous grin. "*Sí! Sí!*" he said delightedly. "The *saca tripas!*"

They weren't afraid. There had never been a time when the Chacon Boys could have been accused of being afraid. They combined a cold cruelty with hot courage. They turned and walked across the street, looking back to grin at Holt Varney.

The young marshal came into the office. "Give me a hand with Orlando, Les," he called out.

Les unlocked the cell door and joined the kid. They walked into the street and picked up the man. They carried him into the office and Holt bathed his face with water. The dark eyes opened.

"How are you, amigo?" asked Les.

Orlando shook his head. He pulled himself up and eyed the two men who watched him.

"You were going to tell me something," said Les.

He touched the bruise on his face and there was shame in his eyes. "What can one man do against three men such as them?" he asked.

"You are a brave man, Orlando Rios," said Les.

The man cut a hand sideways as though to dismiss such a thought. "That is neither here nor there," he said quickly. He looked at Holt. "It is about your *madre.*"

"Yes?"

"She had a fall from her horse."

"Where is she?"

"She is well enough, amigo. Some of my people found her walking on the road. They took her in. A messenger was sent to me. I am sorry you could not have learned of this sooner."

Holt looked at Les.

Orlando passed a hand across his forehead. "She did not get her message through," he said. "She asked someone to ride to Quatros Jacales and send the message. No one would go. They are afraid. You understand?"

"Yes," said Holt.

"They will bring her home," said Orlando.

"Go home yourself, Orlando," said Holt.

"Yes. There is something else..."

"Go on," said Les.

Orlando stood up, "No," he said quietly. "I would not raise

your hopes." He walked to the door and opened it. Then he was gone.

"Now what?" asked Holt.

"The same as before."

"I had a feeling she'd never get that message through. You don't suppose Horan had anything to do with stopping her?"

"What difference does it make?"

"Yes," said the kid quietly.

The wind had shifted. The windows rattled in their loose frames. A feeling of foreboding settled down over Sundown like an old familiar coat.

CHAPTER ELEVEN

Sundown was quieter that night than it had been for any night in years. But it was an unhealthy, brooding quiet. There was life in the town. Stealthy movements on the dark side streets. Low conversation in the saloons. Not a shop was open on Front Street and all of the restaurants had closed early. The night train, northbound, had come into the station and had left with not one passenger getting on or off the cars. No message had been passed to any of the train crew either, for the three Chacon Boys had made it a point to lounge on the luggage wagon, smoking and idly eying the train.

Doc Reinhardt had seemingly vanished, but it was said he was still in town, nourishing the father and mother of all drunks, while Consuelo Horan drank just as steadily in her suite at the Silver Nugget and was no drunker than she had been since that morning when she had arrived in Sundown.

Ruth Ripley had been brought back into town, a little shaken up from her fall, but otherwise physically unharmed. The lights were on in the office of the *Sundown News* as she prepared for the morning paper.

Matt Horan sat in the lobby of the Sundown House, behind a screen of potted palms, with Heath Sabin coming in now and then with messages for the sheriff.

One thing was most noticeable in Sundown; when Mayor Andrew Sumpter Dover had left for his *estancia* with three of his councilmen and cronies, there had been a general exodus of influential citizens from the town, and those that hadn't left had retired to their homes, behind drawn shades, sitting in their parlors, belting rye and bourbon and listening with cocked ears for the first bursts of gunfire on the streets.

Everything and everybody seemed to be waiting, but as yet, the spark which would start the first glow of fire and death in the streets had not been struck, nor did anyone know who would strike it. There was one sure thing: *Someone would strike it.*

Holt Varney sat in the marshal's office, behind Tracy Gant's desk, and filtered the reports which came to him, mostly whispered hoarsely through the partly open rear doorway, in the unmistakable accents of the native New Mexican, for there was unrest in the Mexican quarter along the *rio.* Unrest and a burning hatred. And this growing thing was what these people had wanted. They had made a legend of Les Gunnell, and the old ones had spoken wisely, with many noddings of their heads, that all this had been preordained, that this was fate, and that there would be no going back for any of them.

The young men waited, fingering their knives, rolling and smoking innumerable corn-husk cigarettes, and thinking of the glory which might descend upon them, particularly in the eyes of the slim brown girls of the quarter, should the young men be fortunate enough to fight beside Les Gunnell for the liberty of Sundown.

There would be no going back now; no reconciliation between the forces of Matt Horan and those of Les Gunnell.

But it was Matt Horan who held the aces. Those men who did not follow him had either left town or were doing their drinking in out-of-the-way saloons or in their kitchens. The streets of Sundown belonged to Matt Horan.

There was one place, an islet in Sundown, where the rule of Matt Horan did not hold sway. In the marshal's office, beneath a pool of yellow lamp light, a young man sat waiting like the rest of the Sundowners. Les Gunnell thought, as he stood at the door of his cell watching the kid, that if they came for Les, the kid wouldn't have a chance.

Les rolled a cigarette, wishing he could do something, or say something to make the kid's task a little easier, but there was nothing he could do except die beside the kid with a hot gun in his hand, and that way of dying, for both of them, was the most useless way of all.

The clock ticked on. It was almost midnight. The kid yawned. He looked at Les. "You want first watch?" he asked.

"What difference does it make? They won't bother us tonight."

"I haven't been able to find Doc Reinhardt."

"That figures. Besides, Horan should be looking for the doc."

The gray eyes held Les' eyes. "There are other doctors."

"Reinhardt is paid to do autopsies."

The clock ticked on. The kid yawned again. He got up and locked the front door. "I'll get some sleep on my cot," he said. He walked to the cot, which was in a smaller, little-used office behind the front office. Les heard him lie down on the creaking cot.

Les placed a hand on his Colt and then walked to the cell window. The wind was soughing down Front Street. The streetlamps guttered in the draft. Across the street a dim figure stood in a doorway watching the marshal's office, cracking huge knuckles. Santiago Chacon.

. . .

THE RAPPING CAME AGAIN. Les Gunnell stood up from his chair and walked to the front door. He didn't want to speak because he didn't want anyone to know that Holt Varney had given him the run of the *juzgado*.

"Holt!" The voice came clearly to Les. It was Ruth.

He unlocked the door and opened it, stepping back out of the way to make sure no one in the street would see him. It was almost three o'clock in the morning, yet there was a man standing across from the building watching it. This time it was Aurelio Chacon.

She looked up at him in the darkness as he closed the door and locked it. "Where's Holt?"

"Asleep, Ruth."

"Why don't you make a break for it, Les?"

He shook his head.

"I've one last chance," she said. "I've had the whole story printed. The southbound train picks up copies in the morning."

"It might work." There was no conviction in his low voice.

"Maybe some of the train crew will read about it."

"Maybe."

She leaned back against the wall. "I'm frightened," she said.

He placed his hands on her shoulders. "It will all work out."

She shook her head. "Matt Horan knows this is a trial of strength. Do they think they can stop you with a trumped-up murder charge?"

"Maybe they will. Either way, Ruth, they mean to get me."

"Not so much for yourself, but rather because you are a symbol to the people of Sundown."

He laughed shortly.

She studied his face in the darkness. "I never meant to tell you this, Les, but I wanted to see you so badly after Will was killed."

She looked away. "I never loved Will. He was so good and so patient and he loved Holt. It was the same way when Ted was killed. I wanted one man. Les Gunnell." She laughed dryly. "The man who didn't want me."

He tightened his hands on her shoulders and the old hunger came over him. "That isn't so."

"*Now* you tell me."

"You knew it all along, Ruth."

"This is madness."

"The times are mad. Sundown is mad. The whole world is mad."

She rested her head against his chest, and it seemed as though the long, lonely years fell away, and they were as they had been before he had practically given her to Ted Varney.

"I've always loved you, Les. Maybe there's something wrong with me, but I've never stopped loving you."

"What of Ted and Will?"

"I loved them in a way. But nothing like this, Les."

He placed a hand under her chin and raised her face so that his lips touched hers. There was no hot passion in the kiss, it was too late for that, but there was a deeper understanding between the two of them than there ever had been.

They heard Holt move on his cot. She drew back and touched her hair. "What happens now?" she asked in a low voice.

"*Quién sabe?*"

"You always say that. Are you really that fatalistic, Les?"

"Perhaps. I've seen too much violence and death to think optimistically of the future."

"Where will you go if you get out of this trouble?"

He smiled. "I don't know."

"I'm going to try and find help for Holt."

"Don't waste your time."

"You just can't sit here like this."

"There is nothing else to do."

"And if they come?"

He cupped a hand beneath her chin and kissed her again. "Why, I'll be waiting," he said softly.

SHE WAS GONE ONLY ten minutes when the kid came to Les' cell and looked in. "Get some sleep," he said.

"Can't, kid."

"You might need it."

"No."

"Everything quiet while I was asleep?"

"Yes."

"Anyone come?"

Les hesitated. "No."

"I see." Holt lighted a cigarette and over the flare of the match Les could see the kid's eyes boring straight at him and Les knew Holt Varney had heard every word spoken between Ruth Ripley and Les.

The match went out and the kid walked back through the cell corridor. He tested the back door.

Holt Varney had been proud of his father, Ted Varney. He had seemed to be prouder still of his stepfather, Will Ripley. But most of all he had been proud of the beautiful and capable woman who was his mother. Now he had heard her tell another man that she had never really loved either of her husbands; that she had always loved Les Gunnell.

It was gall and wormwood to the kid. Les felt for the makings and rolled a smoke. He heard the kid's measured tread as he came back to the office. Les lighted up. He sat there, chair tilted back against the wall, waiting for the kid to speak.

Holt did not light the lamp. After a while he spoke in a low voice. "No matter what," he said, "you're still my prisoner and under my care. No matter how I feel about you, Gunnell, you can make damned sure I'll defend you until the end."

There was no use in talking. Nothing Les could say would ever mend the savage break in the kid's mind.

The fire bell began to clang an hour before dawn and Sundown awoke to see flames leaping up from the wooden building which housed the *Sundown News.* There was little the volunteer fire department could do to stop the roaring conflagration fanned by the wind. After the building on both sides of the newspaper office had burst into flames, there was a sudden downpour of rain which effectively checked the fire so that the volunteers of fire company, Confidence Number One, could finish the job. The newspaper office had been gutted.

Holt Varney stood in the street in front of the marshal's office with the rain slashing down on him while he watched the fire company dragging their engine back to the shed next to Dancey's Livery Stable. Most of the people of Sundown stood under the dripping wooden awnings which ran along the north side of Front Street, watching the firemen. There was a great unfamiliar gap in the south side of the street where the newspaper office had been.

Here and there along the street the lights went on in the saloons as sleepy bartenders served their wet customers. There was little conversation among the customers. There wasn't a man on the streets that night who wasn't sure who had burned out the *News,* but none of them was stupid enough to voice his opinion. At least not while Matt Horan, Heath Sabin and the Chacon Boys stood at the bars and drank to fight off the night's chill.

· · ·

A COLD WET dawn broke over Sundown. The rain had died out shortly before the false dawn. A searching wind swept the muddy streets. The smell of wet, burned wood and paper hung along Front Street.

"Reign of terror," said Les to Holt Varney.

The kid nodded. He stoked up the fire in the stove. The coffee smell filled the jail.

"Doc Reinhardt been found yet?" asked Les.

"No."

Les rolled a cigarette. The body of Tracy Gant lay stiff and cold in the mortuary down the street waiting for the ministrations of Doc Reinhardt.

The kid straightened up. "I wouldn't put it past whoever killed Gant to sneak into the mortuary and dig out the slug," he said quietly. "Just to make sure it was a forty-four."

Les lighted the cigarette. "Why do they bother? One way or another they aim to get me. To show Sundown who rules it."

"You giving up, Gunnell?"

"No, kid. Maybe I'm a fatalist."

"Then keep your fatalism to yourself! It will take more than Matt Horan and his hired gun-slicks to make *me* crawfish!"

"Spoken like a man," said Les dryly. "Let's have that coffee."

The locomotive whistle broke the early morning quiet as Les and the kid finished the coffee left in the pot. Les glanced at the clock. "Right on time. Morning southbound. Nobody gets on; nobody gets off. Sundown is like a ghost town, kid."

Half an hour after the train pulled out there was a sharp rapping at the rear door of the jail. Holt picked up his pistol and walked to the door. "Who is it?"

"A man to see Señor Gunnell."

"Who are you?"

The voice was familiar to Les. "Open the door, kid," he said. "It's all right."

Holt opened the door and it seemed as though the space was instantly filled by a huge Mexican hat ornamented heavily with coin silver. Beneath the hat brim was the lean, hard face of Esteban Rios, who had ridden the *rio* with Les in the old days.

"*Hola,* Les," said Esteban quietly.

"Come in," said Les. "There will be coffee, amigo."

Esteban hurried to Les and gave him the *abrazo,* holding him close and pounding on Les' back until he almost coughed. "I don't know where the devil you came from, Esteban, but it is good to see you!" he gasped.

Esteban let go of Les and began to roll a cigarette. "My brother Orlando got word to me," he said quickly. "I came in on the train. I saw Horan's men on the platform, so I stayed hidden in the baggage car, then dropped from the train at Paloverde Draw and came back here."

"Why?"

The dark eyes stared uncomprehendingly at Les. "You are my amigo! Did they not kill my nephew who was named for his Tio Esteban! Why do you ask me *why* I came back?"

Les watched Holt prepare more coffee. "Matt Horan, the Chacon Boys, Heath Sabin and Horan's hardcases from the Box H are all over town."

"So?"

"Blood for blood!"

Les shook his head. "Tracy Gant killed your nephew. Gant is dead. This is not your fight, Esteban."

"This is madness! Gant was only a tool of that pig Horan! It was Horan who caused the death of the boy!"

Les walked to the window. He needed help. God how he needed help, and Esteban Rios was no mean ally to have on one's side. But the fight might develop into an internecine war between Anglo and Mexican, the feud that boiled up now and then with little effort on anyone's part. Esteban Rios had always been a champion of his people, and a good one, although the more stable, law-abiding New Mexicans shuddered a little when the tough Esteban Rios walked the streets with his hand on gun or knife. They would scream for him when they needed him, otherwise he was never welcome.

"I can deputize him," said Holt quietly.

"Sí!" said Esteban.

"No," said Les.

The two other men looked at each other. Esteban shoved back his heavy hat. "I can get the horses," he said thoughtfully. "We can make a break for it, Les."

"No! They'd shoot us down. *Ley del fuego!* Trial by fire. We run and they shoot. Horan would win hands down."

"True," said Esteban.

Les leaned against the wall and rolled a cigarette. "Your people always listen to you in times of trouble, Esteban. You'd be of more use working with them than standing beside me in the streets to get shot down. Go to them and work with them. Your brother will tell you what to do."

"It is not my way, amigo."

"It is *mine,* Esteban."

In the quietness that followed, Esteban shrugged. "Matt Horan and his *corrida* are but men as we are. It has been said that you would return to change things here in Sundown."

Holt silently served them coffee. The Mexican drank his quickly. "I waste time here." He gripped their hands. "I will be close, amigos! I will be there when needed!"

When the door closed behind Esteban, Holt looked at Les. "We might have been able to use him," he said.

"You don't know Esteban. He'd walk up to the Chacon Boys and spit in their faces. He might get one of them, or even two of them, but he'd be dead when the fighting was over. In a hot battle you'd find no better man to have by your side. But when things are tight, as they are now, he'd cause nothing but trouble. Orlando will calm him down."

"Maybe that's exactly what we don't want."

Les filled his coffee cup. "The deaths of the Melgosa boy and of Esteban Rios have been festering in the minds of their people. If they did stand up against Horan and his *corrida,* it would take guts, and even Matt Horan isn't loco enough to fight them in the streets. Even he wouldn't get away with that."

"How so?"

"Sundown is the center of wealth and power in this county, and no matter who runs for any office in this county, they must carry Sundown to win. So far it has always been Matt Horan who has managed to carry Sundown's vote, through bribery, fear and buttering up of the local merchants and politicians. These native New Mexicans are a volatile people. They can be easily swayed, and they always remember a kindness, but they have a strong sense of honor and decency, too.

"Certainly, Matt Horan has a strong weapon in the Chacon Boys, and they rule under him by fear and bloodshed, but if these people once turn against Matt Horan, not a battalion of Chacon Boys could stop them. But you can see what would happen if they did. It would end up in a massacre in the streets."

The kid nodded. "I'd rather die alone in these streets than to see innocent people shot down in cold blood because I had failed to do my job as marshal."

Les eyed the kid. "Well spoken, Holt. But this thing will resolve itself into a showdown between Matt Horan and me. He knows it as well as I do. No matter what happens now, this matter will be settled when we face each other for the last time for one, or perhaps even both of us. Once he thought he had gotten rid of me, and he almost did, until Will Ripley was murdered by the Chacon Boys. The Mexican people here think it has been predestined that I come back and free Sundown from Matt Horan and his *corrida*. Maybe they are right."

The wind banged the marshal's sign against its post.

Holt picked up his hat. "I'm going to find Doc Reinhardt, Les. The autopsy may prove nothing, but it's his duty to perform it, and my duty to see that it's done. I don't think Horan will bother much with you until we know what the autopsy proves."

When the kid had left, Les stood there a long time with the empty coffee cup in his hand. The loneliness of the office and his position would give him time to think. He finally placed the cup on the desk and began to knead the stiff muscles of his right shoulder. A coldness had gradually crept over him despite the heat of the potbellied stove. Matt Horan had given him two days. This was the second day. Les Gunnell knew that Horan had measured and meant every word he had said and that the final analysis of the matter would be tested and proven in the muddy streets of Sundown some time that very day.

CHAPTER TWELVE

A watery sun shone down on the muddy streets of Sundown. It was high noon and the quietness which had been hanging over the town since late Saturday night had not yet dissipated. The streets were hardly peopled. Only a few mounts stood hipshot at the racks in front of the saloons. The merchants stood behind their front windows, smoking and looking up and down the streets.

Les heard the noise as he lay on his cot, smoking and idly watching the smoke drift and waver in the drafty cell. It was a sound he had heard before. The noise of many people walking and talking, coming closer and closer.

He stood up and touched the butt of the Colt. He walked to the cell door. It was unlocked but whoever came into the office wouldn't know that.

He heard the crowd stop outside of the office. The door was unlocked and opened. Holt Varney walked in and there was a smile on his drawn face. He left the outer open and walked to the cell door. "You're free, Les," he said.

Les stared at him. "What do you mean?"

Holt held out his hand. A mutilated slug was in it. "Forty-five caliber," he said.

Les looked at the chunk of lead, then he looked at Holt. "My Colt is a forty-four," he said.

"So was Tracy Gant's, Les."

"Reinhardt finally came through, eh?"

Holt flipped the slug up into the air and caught it with a hard downward sweep of his left hand. "No," he said with a grin. "Doc Carter did the job. Reinhardt was just sober enough after half a dozen cups of black coffee to sign the report."

Les opened the door of the cell and walked to the stove. He filled two coffee cups.

"If they meant to frame you, Les, they should at least have used the same caliber pistol you use."

Les nodded. Then he turned slowly. "By God," he said.

"What's wrong?"

"Nothing with *me*. But I used to carry a forty-five caliber Colt in the days when I was marshal here. The Colt I brought with me this time was one I used as a spare. Whoever killed Gant thought I was still carrying a forty-five."

The murmuring of voices came to them through the open doorway. "Let us see Señor Gunnell!" a man called out.

Les walked to the door. The people of the Mexican quarter filled the street. In front of the crowd was Orlando Rios and his brother Esteban. *"Inocente!"* the brothers yelled.

"Inocente! Inocente! Inocente!" echoed the crowd.

Les looked over the heads of the smiling men and saw the trio of unsmiling faces on the other side of the street. Fedro, Aurelio and Santiago Chacon.

Holt spoke out of the side of his mouth. "You'd better get out of town while you have the chance, Les."

"This thing isn't done yet."

"Don't be a fool! Esteban and Orlando Rios will see that

the crowd goes with you to the station and stays there with you until you are safely on the train."

"No!"

"You damned stubborn fool!"

Les waved to the crowd, then walked back into the office. Holt closed the door. "I told you this would end up in a show-down between Horan and me. I'd leave too many rumors behind me if I left now. They'd never let anyone get the whip-hand on them again. The iron is hot now, kid."

Holt shrugged. He opened the door and looked at the crowd. "Les Gunnell is free!" he called out. "Go home now!"

"No!" yelled Orlando Rios. "We will stay here to see that he is safe!"

"No one will harm him."

Esteban Rios laughed harshly. "Listen to the young cock-erel," he jeered. "No one will *harm* him, indeed!"

Les walked to the door. "There is no need for a mob," he said. "We had no need for mobs in the old days and we need none now. Your new marshal will keep Sundown peaceable. Go home now. Thanks for your interest in my safety."

The crowd slowly began to break up.

"That was your only chance to get out of town, Les," said Holt.

"I knew that."

"I'll stick it out with you, but I don't think we can make it."

Les turned. "It really isn't your fight, kid."

"No? What about my father? What about Will Ripley?"

"You once said I was responsible for Will's death. That he had inherited my star and my enemies. That they really wanted me and not him. You also said I didn't know a hell of a lot about duty. Well, kid, maybe I *don't* know a hell of about duty, but I do know this: I came back here because you had the impression that I had a big obligation here, from which I had run away."

"I was just talking big, Les. I feel differently now."

Les shook his head. "It was the truth. I stayed away from Sundown for five years, thinking that time would wipe out all memories of Sundown and the people I had known here. The people I had fought for and the people I had fought against. It just didn't work out that way."

"Maybe Horan has learned his lesson."

"No. Times are changing in New Mexico. In the whole West for that matter. Maybe Matt Horan and myself belong in the past. Maybe we're just shadows in the present."

"Substantial shadows, Les."

Les buckled on his gun belt and put on his hat and coat. Holt handed Les the worn Colt that had been taken from Les when Tracy Gant had been shot down. "Where to?" asked the kid.

Les loaded the pistol and slid it into its sheath. "To my room. I want to get cleaned up."

"And then?"

Les smiled faintly. *"Quién sabe,* amigo? *Quién sabe?"*

Les walked out into the street. The sun had disappeared behind gray clouds. Puddles dotted the wide street. A cold wind swept down from the hills. He walked along the south side of Front Street, passing the blackened site of the *Sundown News.* He crossed the street at the corner and entered the lobby of the Silver Nugget. The clerk paled a little as he saw Les.

Les ascended the stairway and walked down the long hall toward his room. The hotel seemed strangely quiet. He opened his door, stepped in quickly and closed it behind him. He knew immediately that he was not alone. He turned quickly. Consuelo Chacon lay on the bed with her great eyes studying Les, and the woman was stark naked. It

gave Les a shock to see her there and it wasn't her naked-
ness which shocked him, but rather the look in her tragic
eyes.

Her expensive clothing was scattered on the floor or
draped over chairs and the mingled odors of her perfume and
the liquor she had been drinking hung heavy in the air. Her
head moved a little back and forth as she watched him and
waited for him to make a move or speak. There was an
instant's hunger in him for her, for her body was as tempting
as it had always been, and she knew only too well the arts of
lovemaking.

She held out a hand toward him and he knew if he
touched it his control might certainly leave him. She was
there for some reason other than just to slake her heat for
him. There was a subtle warning in the back of his mind.

"Les," she said a little thickly.

Her heavy-budded breasts were dewed with her sweat and
she passed her slim hands over them and looked at him. Then
he was reminded of something. Of the ornate, thickly daubed
nude which hung just over the bar in the Miner's Friend, like
a great cow ready for milking or for servicing. A thin smile
came to his face. She smiled for an instant, too, until she realized he was not smiling in anticipation but rather in ridicule.
"Canalla!" she said shortly.

"Get out," he said.

"Bazofia!"

"Go back to your husband," he said.

She sat up and spat at him. Then she jumped to her feet
and reached out with clawing hands for his eyes, but he
gripped her slippery wrists and held her close to him. "You
think I don't know why you are here?" he demanded harshly.
"I know those brothers of yours. I know what happened to
Frank Hendries on Oak Street when he was in bed with Ruby.
You thought you'd work the same dodge on me, didn't you?

What a setup for the three fearless Chacon Boys, the romantic *ladrones* of New Mexico!"

"That is not so!" she hissed, but the lie was in her face.

She struggled silently for a minute and then suddenly she slumped to the floor. Les wiped the sweat from his face and quickly locked the door. There might not be much time. He knew all too well how skilled Santiago and Aurelio Chacon were with the *saca tripas*.

It was one hell of a job getting the woman dressed. As he worked, with his lower lip between his teeth, he thought he'd never complain about a woman being late for a date again if this was what they had to go through every night. The wonder of it to him was how they managed to look so neat and cool after going through such a routine.

But he made it, and there was a touch of simple pride in him that he had done so, although some of the articles were askew, and not buttoned evenly. He eased open the door and looked up and down the hallway. There was no one in sight. He carried her down the hall to her suite and opened the door. The suite looked out on Front Street, but the windows were heavily curtained. The place was thick with perfume and liquor fumes. Expensive clothing was scattered about, and a jewel case was on the dresser with the lid open and some of the contents lying on the dresser top mingled with broken cigarettes.

She opened her eyes and looked at him as he placed her on the bed. *"Mi vida,"* she said thickly. "I knew you would make love to your Consuelo."

"Sí! Sí!" he said quickly. "But first let us drink together." He picked up a brandy bottle and filled a glass which he held to her full lips. She drank thirstily. He raised his head as he thought he heard footsteps in the hall. If they caught him in this room ...

He pressed the glass to her mouth again and although she

struggled a little bit he held it there until she had emptied it. She tried to focus her eyes upon him, then held up her mouth to be kissed. He shrank from the breath of the woman, but he kissed her and allowed her to press one of his hands against her breasts. *"Mi vida ..."* she said. Then she slumped in his arms, and he knew she was out cold.

He walked to the door and listened. There was no sound. He eased open the door and walked quickly to his room, closing the door quietly and turning the key in the lock. He drew his Colt, and a moment later he heard soft steps in the hallway. Someone was breathing heavily on the other side of the door. Then the doorknob turned a little. Les was tempted to shoot through the door at the height of a man's belly.

Then the footsteps receded down the hallway toward Consuelo's room, and he heard the door open and close.

Les wiped the sweat from his face as he walked to the window. He looked down to the muddy street. Fedro Chacon was standing in a doorway, and it seemed to Les as though the man was looking directly at him.

Les sat down on the bed. He poured himself a stiff drink. The odor of the woman still seemed to cling to him and to the bed. They would use any weapon now, anything to kill him, for this time they would never let him get out of Sundown alive. He walked to the door and slid the heavy dresser in front of it.

It would be a struggle to the death this time. He had thrown the gauntlet down in front of them when he had not allowed the mob to escort him to the station. Now it was back the way it had been five years ago. You were either a Horan man or a Gunnell man. Horan had tried to meet Les halfway and make him a Horan man, and there wasn't any doubt in Les' mind that Matt had meant what he had said. He had a feudal way of granting boons and keeping promises to his subordinates, providing, of course, that they gave him their utmost loyalty.

He heard the jingling of spurs in the hall and then hard knuckles struck the door. *"Patron?"* It was Esteban Rios.

Les slid back the dresser and opened the door. Esteban glanced down the hallway and then came in. He picked up the bottle, poured a drink and downed it quickly. He eyed Les. "You are still determined to face down Horan?"

"Yes."

"Alone?"

"Yes."

Esteban nodded. "We wanted to stand by your side."

Les shook his head.

"But you are facing the Chacon Boys, too!"

The gray eyes were like agate. "I want them, amigo, each one of them. For Will Ripley."

Esteban crossed himself. "And Heath Sabin?"

"I either get him or he gets me."

"Matt Horan is no coward, *patron.*"

Les rolled a cigarette. He lighted it and looked out the window. The streets were strangely empty.

"Five men, *patron.* Strong men. Brave men."

Les turned. "I will stay alone, Esteban."

Esteban shook his head. "But the ranch!"

"No matter how it works out I can't go back there anyway."

There was a long silence and then the Mexican spoke. "You have made up your mind. Perhaps it *is* your fight alone. The people say it was predestined that you must come back to Sundown as it used to be. So be it."

"You sound like a priest, amigo."

Esteban poured another drink. "I have been doing much talking. Orlando has been doing much talking. Perhaps the men of our people are no match for Horan's *corrida* in these streets. Heath Sabin and the Chacon Boys might be too much. But there is something we can do, and before the sun sets it will be done."

"So?"

Esteban smiled thinly. "There are many men in Sundown who would not face the five men you must face before this day is done. Matt Horan is across the street in the Sundown House with Heath Sabin. The Chacon Boys are along Front Street."

Les eyed the Mexican. "So what do you want to do?"

Esteban cut a hand sideways. "There will be no other Box H men coming in to Sundown to join them if you must do as you say you will do."

Les took the cigarette from his lips. "Straighten me."

Esteban glanced at the door and then came closer to Les. "We have men on the road between here and the Box H. Good men who can shoot straight. No Box H man come into Sundown from the ranch unless we let him."

"Goon."

"The Box H men who are in town have been taken care of."

"How?"

Esteban grinned. "They drank in the *cantinas*. Perhaps they drank too much. *Quién sabe?* Perhaps there was something they drank along with their whiskey which made them sleepy. *Comprende?*"

Les nodded.

Esteban took another drink. "So, I leave you. Do not fear the shot in the back unless it is from those you know you must fight this day."

Les smiled wryly.

"There is still time for us to back you in the streets."

"No, amigo."

Esteban shrugged. He opened the door, then turned and held out his hand. *"Vaya con Dios, patron."*

"Vaya con Dios."

As the sun dropped westward above the clouds, Sundown became quieter and quieter. Here and there a lamp was lighted in a store, but for the most part, usually busy Front Street was almost deserted. A hush seemed to fall over the tense town.

Les Gunnell stood at the window in his darkening room. He had seen no sign of the Chacon Boys since Esteban had left the hotel, but there wasn't any doubt in Les' mind that one or more of them was watching for him.

A tall slim man came along Front Street, across from the Silver Nugget Hotel, looked up and down the deserted street, then crossed it. It was Holt Varney.

A few minutes later, Varney tapped on the door. Les opened. "Get out of here," he said quietly.

The kid pushed his way in. "I'm staying with you."

"Your mother has had two murders in her family. She doesn't want another."

"I'm staying."

"This isn't your fight, Holt."

"I'm marshal now, Les, or have you forgotten that?"

"Turn in your badge."

The kid grinned in the dimness. "To who?"

"This isn't your kind of fight. You won't have a chance with those bastards."

"Maybe you are as good as they say you are, Les, but not against five of them."

Les walked to the window. How could he tell the kid that he never expected to leave Sundown alive? That it was better for Les Gunnell to die in the streets of Sundown with a hot gun in his hand rather than to run away to the ranch where he spent sleepless night after sleepless night believing he had run away not only from Sundown but also from himself? That no matter how far a man runs he knows that someday he'll have to face the truth no matter how painful it is.

Holt Varney was a composite of three people Les Gunnell had known, and two of those people he had loved. But there was still something missing in the young man. There was only one person who could fill in the gap. Les Gunnell. It would be something Les could leave behind. Perhaps no other person would know what he had given the boy, but Les Gunnell would know wherever he ended up...or down.

"What do we do first, Les?" asked the kid.

The street was dark now, lighted here and there by dim yellow lamps. A cold wind whispered along Front Street, banging signs and blowing papers, bringing with it the smell of wet, burned wood and ashes from the blackened husk of the *Sundown News* building.

"Les?"

Les turned. He picked up his hat. "Let's go and see how your mother is."

The kid stared at him in the dimness.

"You heard me, kid," said Les.

They walked into the hallway and along the thickly carpeted floor, turning to the left to walk along the rear hallway where the stairs leading to the first-floor lobby were located.

There was a chance that Ruth or else Rae could talk Holt into staying out of the forthcoming fracas. Maybe it would take both of them. If not...

"Quiet, isn't it?" said the kid.

Les nodded. The hall lamps guttered in the draft along the hallway. He wondered if Consuelo Horan was still out cold.

They reached the head of the stairs. The lobby was empty, and the clerk was not behind his counter. Les stopped short with one foot extended toward the first step. Something was missing. Something his honed senses warned him about. Then he knew what it was. The hotel was quiet, the kid had noted that in passing, but it was *too* quiet. There was no sound from the bar; no musical tinkling of ice in glasses, no irregular hum of masculine voices.

There was a mirror on the south wall, between two of the big front windows, and Les saw a movement in it. Les whirled and drove a shoulder hard against the kid, driving him back across the hallway and up against the wall. "What the hell!" said Holt Varney, just as the gun exploded near the foot of the stairs and a slug smashed one of the vases which stood on a pedestal in the hallway, showering Les and Holt with pottery and dirt.

Les jerked his head toward the other end of the hallway and he followed the kid until they were away from the stairwell. The stench of burnt powder drifted up the stairs and the big hotel was as quiet as it had been before the shot had been fired.

The kid rubbed his shoulder. "You hit like a piledriver," he said with a wry grin. "Nothing wrong with *your* reactions."

Les wiped the cold sweat from his face. "They've done the one thing I hadn't figured on," he said as he got to his feet. "Moved everyone out of the hotel and set up an ambush."

Holt stood up. "Easy enough," he said quietly. "Matt Horan owns this place."

Les bent his head forward. "Get out the back way," he said. Then he turned. "Wait! If they figured this deal out, they'd also figure on us making a break out the back way."

"So?"

Les turned with an odd, cold smile on his lean face. "This is what I wanted. They've given it to me."

"Us!"

Les rubbed his jaw with his left hand and eyed the kid.

"Yeh...*us.*" His right fist shot out and caught Holt on the button. He caught the kid before he hit the floor and dragged him along the hallway until he reached his room. He opened the door and dragged the kid inside the room. Les took his reata from his saddle and tied the kid's wrists and ankles in such a way that he could free himself with a little struggling. Les took one of the kid's fancy engraved Colts, then stepped out into the hallway, eying the end of the hall. It seemed to him that he saw the faint flick of a shadow against the far wall.

Les stepped back into his room and locked the door. He blocked the door with the dresser, then walked to the window and looked down into the deserted street. There was no sign of men there. Les stepped out onto the narrow, ornate wooden ledge which ran along the front of the big hotel and worked his way to the hallway window. He peered through it. The hallway was still empty, but he kept working his way along the ledge half-expecting to feel the crash of a slug between his shoulder blades.

He reached a half-open window and drew his Colt. Thrusting in a leg, he pulled the heavy drapes aside with his left hand. A familiar odor came to him. That of expensive liquor and more expensive perfume.

Consuelo Horan lay on her bed with wide-open eyes staring at the ceiling. She moved her head a little as he crossed the room. *"Mi vida,"* she said vaguely.

Les closed the door softly behind himself.

CHAPTER THIRTEEN

Les Gunnell knew the big Silver Nugget Hotel as well as any man. He had lived in it a number of times. It was built of the best available wood, was two-stories high and covered half of the block facing Front Street between Willow and Cottonwood Streets. The second floor was composed of suites, rooms and service rooms. The ground floor had the lobby, the dining room and adjacent banquet room, the barroom, kitchen and storage rooms. It was a vast pile of a building which had been built with no expense spared five years after the Civil War.

He walked to the western side of the building. There was a narrow service passageway which ran to the northern side of the building. There were doors at the end, one of which opened into a room where linen and cleaning implements and materials were kept. The other door opened into the north hallway, almost at the head of the wide staircase which led down to the lobby.

Les padded down the service passage and opened the door into the service room. The room was empty. He slowly turned the knob of the other door and eased it open. The hallway was empty, the carpeted floor littered with the pottery and dirt of the bullet-shattered vase. The hall lamps guttered in the draft.

Les looked to his right. He could see part of the upper staircase, but nothing more. The place was quiet with a brooding quietness. Les reached down and picked up a large piece of pottery. He threw it quickly down the hallway and almost instantaneously a gun rapped out in the lobby, and he heard the shattering of glass as he closed the door. There was no way to get across the upper part of the stairway to the hall beyond, and even if he did, he was sure at least one of his enemies would be waiting for him there, probably expecting him to come down the eastern hall from his room.

He entered the service room and walked to the rear of it to look out the window. The alleyway was dark, but he thought he detected a movement near the rear entrance of the hotel which opened into the west end of the big barroom.

There was a laundry chute in the room, and it was only a matter of minutes to fashion a rope from ripped sheets. He opened the chute cover, tied the end of the rope and let himself down in the darkness until his feet touched the piled laundry at the bottom of the chute. Sweat broke out on his lean body as he crouched there listening. Softly he slid up the door into the chute and stepped into the empty laundry room. He crossed it and looked into the kitchen. A lamp wavered in the draft and the room was empty of life. A chain lock had been fastened across the door which opened into the alley.

He crossed the kitchen and gently opened the swinging door which gave access to the big dining room. Lamplight showed on the white tablecloths and reflected from the silver service placed in settings on the tables. Across the wide room was the door into the banquet room. Les studied the mirrors which hung on the walls of the dining room and could see no man in the room. He got down on his hands and knees and crawled behind the tables until he reached the open door of the banquet room, glancing toward the lobby entrance to the dining room as he did so. He could see the outer doors which opened into Front Street but there was no sign of anyone.

Les crawled into the banquet room and found it empty. He knew he had to face five men before too long, and each of them was deadly enough in his own way. Les could not afford to gamble with them.

He stood up and gently moved the swinging door which opened into the barroom right beside a small service bar. A man stood with his back to Les, at the far end of the bar, pouring himself a drink.

The swinging door creaked a little. The man whirled, dropping the bottle, and stared incredulously at Les. It was Aurelio Chacon, the youngest of the Chacon Boys; the drunken wildcat and ladykiller. His hand darted down toward his pistol but Les jumped to the open end of the bar and fired twice from hip level. Aurelio grunted as the heavy slugs slammed him back against the curved edge of the bar. His eyes were wide in his head.

Incredibly the dying man began to walk toward Les. The thick powder smoke lifted before him. *"Cobarde,"* he said in a low voice. Then his extended right arm swept bottles and glasses from the back of the bar, and he fell heavily into the litter.

"Hermano!" a man yelled from the lobby. It was the voice of Fedro Chacon, the wily brains of the Chacon Boys.

Les darted into the banquet room with raised pistol, facing the barroom door.

"Hermano!" cried Fedro from the barroom. "Jesus Christ, Santiago! He has killed Aurelio!"

Les walked into something and the thick arms of Santiago

Chacon wrapped themselves about him. He looked up into the stupid but terrible face of the giant.

"Santiago!" yelled Fedro.

"Here, *hermano!* I have him, Fedro!"

The door swung up and Fedro screamed in rage. Les rammed a knee up into Santiago's crotch. The big man grunted and loosened his hold and as he did so Les threw all his supple strength into swinging the man to one side. The giant grunted again in savage pain. The thick arms dropped to the sides and Santiago staggered to one side, and as he did so Les saw Fedro still holding onto the knife which had been aimed for Les' back and instead had been driven deep into Santiago.

Les raised his Colt and fired once. Fedro released the knife and staggered back against the table. He drew his Colt and fired twice. A slug smashed into Les' upper right arm and the shock drove him back against the wall. He fired twice from his left hand and Fedro Chacon fell over the body of his huge brother.

The smoke was thick in the room. Les staggered a little as he headed for the lobby. He was whipped and he knew it. Shock and loss of blood would make him easy prey for Heath Sabin and Matt Horan before he could get out of the hotel.

There was a stench of burning material as he reached the arched doorway into the lobby. Lamplight glittered in the many mirrors. A man stood there, near the staircase, with a Colt in his hand. Then he raised the six-gun and fired twice, but he fired not at Les but rather toward the front of the lobby near the wide front doors, shattering a big mirror. Les fell against the side of the dining-room doorway and raised his pistol. He fired the last cartridge and Heath Sabin jerked with the impact of the bullet, then turned as he fell to stare wide-eyed at Les.

Les shook his head. The man had had him cold. Then he

looked toward the front of the lobby and knew why Sabin had fired in that direction, for the big mirror hanging there had given the gunman the illusion that Les stood at the front of the lobby rather than at the back of it.

Smoke drifted down the staircase and Les heard the crackling of flames. Then he remembered the shattering of glass he had heard when he had stood at the head of the stairway and someone had fired from the lobby. Les swayed as he walked toward the staircase past the sprawled body of Heath Sabin. He looked up toward the head of the stairs. Flames ran along the paneled walls in runnels and licked at the ceiling and the floor.

Les gripped the newel post and started up the stairs. Matt Horan was still alive and probably looking for Les. Trust him to be the last of the five. But Holt Varney was upstairs, and if he was still unconscious or had been unable to free himself, he would die horribly.

Les thrust the empty pistol beneath his belt. Somewhere he had lost Holt Varney's fancy Colt. Flames beat at him as he reached the head of the stairs. The fire had gained incredible headway and already had covered the door which led into the service passageway.

Les bent his head, covered his face with his left arm and ran through the smoke and licking flames into the far end of the long hallway. He turned into the eastern hallway and ran toward the front of the huge building. Flames were licking along the varnished wood of the hallway and the stench sickened him.

Blood ran down his right arm and dripped from his numbed fingers. His throat was dry with a terrible thirst. He reached the end of the hallway and tried the door to his room. It was still locked and barricaded by the dresser. Les hammered on the door with his left fist but there was no answer.

He heard a crashing noise and turned to see that gas had blown open the service-passageway door at the western end of the front hallway. Almost immediately the end of the hallway began to fill with smoke, and he could hear the intense crackling of the flames as they traveled along the passageway.

There was an ax hanging above a fire bucket on a stand in the hallway. He took the ax and held it in his left hand. He swung it high and struck the door to his room. Again and again, he hit it while sweat from the heat and his exertion ran down his face. Then a panel split completely, enough for him to reach inside and unlock the door. He shoved back the dresser and entered the room. "Kid!" he yelled.

Holt Varney still lay on the bed, and he was still unconscious. Les cursed as he freed the kid, then hoisted him up onto his left shoulder, grunting with pain and exhaustion. He staggered out into the hallway. It was a hell's tunnel of flame and smoke, but it was the only way he could go. He trotted down the hallway and turned into the northern hall. The far end of the hall, at the staircase, was a blazing mass of flames, but there was a slim chance of making it.

Les staggered wearily as he reached the head of the staircase. Fire had run down the side of the stairs and was licking at the carpeting at the foot of the stairs.

Les gripped the railings and went down slowly because of his weakness, while every nerve and fiber in his body seemed to cry out for more haste.

Heath Sabin's clothing was afire, and his eyes seemed to stare at Les as Les staggered past him into the lobby. Then Les stopped short. A man blocked the doorway. A big man, dressed in fine clothing, with a drawn Colt in his hand and a set look on his handsome face. It was Matt Horan.

Les tripped and fell heavily. The kid rolled away from him. Les looked up at Horan.

"You got Sabin," said Horan slowly.

Les nodded.

"Where are the Chacons?"

"Dead," said Les quietly.

"All of them?"

"All."

There was a curious yellow look in the hazel eyes of the big man. He cocked the Colt.

Les started to reach for his Colt and then remembered that it was empty.

"Get up and draw," said Horan quietly.

Smoke rifted about the two men as Les got up. Horan looked at Les' shattered arm, then shifted his Colt to his own left hand.

"Your wife is still upstairs," said Les.

Horan shook his head. "That won't save you, Gunnell."

"I tell you she's up there!"

Flames roared down the stairway and the carpeting flared up. No man could traverse it now.

Then above the crackling of the flames came the thin screaming of a woman. Matt Horan's face went white. He started for the stairs, then stopped as he saw the holocaust. He whirled.

Les picked up the kid and walked toward the door.

"Stay where you are!" cried Horan.

"Shoot and be damned to you, Horan," said Les.

There was no explosion of gunpowder, no slamming of lead into Les' back. He could hear people yelling in the street. He walked down the few steps and looked at Ruth Ripley running toward him, then pitched forward on his face as men took the kid from him. They dragged Les away from the fire and across the street. He looked up at the façade of the hotel. It was a leaping, roaring mass of flames.

Matt Horan came down the steps, then slowly turned to

look up at the second story. He stood there alone, and the crowd grew quiet. They all knew she was still up there on the second floor in the suite she used to drink in when her important husband was too busy to pay attention to her.

Doc Carter shook his head as he examined Les' arm.

"Tell me," said Les quietly.

"Well, Les..."

"Tell me!"

"It will have to come off, Les."

"No!"

The doctor wiped the sweat from his face. "It might cost you your life if I leave it on."

Holt Varney was sitting on the edge of the sidewalk while Esteban Rios told him of what Les had done. The kid stood up. "Let him do it, Les," he said quietly. "You know it will have to come off."

Les eyed the kid, then smiled wanly. "All right, kid," he said.

Ruth knelt by Les. "I need a man to help me at the paper," she said.

Les shook his head. "No, Ruth. I'm going back to where I belong. For a time at least."

They looked at each other and both of them knew he would be back someday.

The wind had started up and flames leaped and danced across the roof of the hotel. No one could enter or leave it now. The crowd was silent as they watched the fire and the motionless figure of Matt Horan.

There was a crackling snapping noise and then the roof collapsed sending up a tower of sparks and smoke. Matt Horan turned and walked west along Front Street. The crowd parted to let him through and watched him as he entered the livery stable. In a short time, he reappeared on his horse. He

rode slowly toward the bridge across the river and then disappeared from sight.

"No man can run away from his destiny," said Esteban
Rios.

Les held tightly to Ruth's hand and felt her hand tighten
against his as he did so. Esteban Rios was right. He had
always said he had the second sight.

TAKE A LOOK AT JACK OF SPADES AND AMBUSH ON THE MESA:

Two Full Length Western Novels

A blazing shoot-out waited for them South of Sonora...

In this classic western double, Hugh Kinzie and Holt Deaver have one thing in common: they've both found themselves in tough circumstances that may turn fatal.

A regiment was needed but they sent only one man, Hugh Kinzie – he saddled his dun and rode west. He found the party of men and women ambushed by Red Sleeves, the maniacal chief who hated the white man more than he feared death itself. Hugh counted on one thing to get them out—his old, battered, still-deadly rifle.

Holt Deaver, a young man who has drifted onto the wrong side of the law on occasion is running from trouble. After the men he was riding with robbed and murdered an army paymaster they agreed they would need to kill Holt to keep him quiet.

"If you're a fan of tough-minded Westerns, I highly recommend it and just about anything else by Gordon D. Shirreffs." –James Reasoner, author of Rattler's Law

AVAILABLE NOW

ABOUT THE AUTHOR

Gordon D. Shirreffs published more than 80 western novels, 20 of them juvenile books, and John Wayne bought his book title, Rio Bravo, during the 1950s for a motion picture, which Shirreffs said constituted *"the most money I ever earned for two words."* Four of his novels were adapted to motion pictures, and he wrote a Playhouse 90 and the Boots and Saddles TV series pilot in 1957.

A former pulp magazine writer, he survived the transition to western novels without undue trauma, earning the admiration of his peers along the way. The novelist saw life a bit cynically from the edge of his funny bone and described himself as looking like a slightly parboiled owl. Despite his multifarious quips, he was dead serious about the writing profession.

Gordon D. Shirreffs was the 1995 recipient of the Owen Wister Award, given by the Western Writers of America for "a living individual who has made an outstanding contribution to the American West."

He passed in 1996.

Manufactured by Amazon.ca
Bolton, ON